P9-DNL-223

SPRINGDALE PUBLIC LIBRARY
405 South Pleasant
Springdale, Arkansas  72764

# LUSH LIFE

**Also by Richard Price**

*The Wanderers*

*Bloodbrothers*

*Ladies' Man*

*The Breaks*

*Clockers*

*Freedomland*

*Samaritan*

# LUSH LIFE

### RICHARD PRICE

Farrar, Straus and Giroux

New York

SPRINGDALE PUBLIC LIBRARY
405 South Pleasant
Springdale, Arkansas 72764

Farrar, Straus and Giroux
18 West 18th Street, New York 10011

Copyright © 2008 by Richard Price
All rights reserved
Distributed in Canada by Douglas & McIntyre Ltd.
Printed in the United States of America
First edition, 2008

A portion of this work was originally published, in slightly different form, in *The Paris Review*.

Library of Congress Cataloging-in-Publication Data
Price, Richard, 1949–
    Lush Life / Richard Price. — 1st ed.
      p.  cm.
    ISBN-13: 978-0-374-29925-5 (hardcover : alk. paper)
    ISBN-10: 0-374-29925-0 (hardcover : alk. paper)
    1. Police—Fiction.   2. Lower East Side (New York, N.Y.)—Fiction.    I. Title.

  PS3566.R544J89 2008
  813'.54—dc22

                                        2007017280

Designed by Michelle McMillian

www.fsgbooks.com

10  9  8  7  6  5  4  3  2  1

As always, with love for
Judy, Annie, and Gen

# NIGHT FISHING ON
# THE DELANCEY

# QUALITY OF LIFE
## 11:00 P.M.

**The Quality of Life** Task Force: four sweatshirts in a bogus taxi set up on the corner of Clinton Street alongside the Williamsburg Bridge off-ramp to profile the incoming salmon run; their mantra: Dope, guns, overtime; their motto: Everyone's got something to lose.

"Is dead tonight."

The four car-stops so far this evening have been washouts: three municipals—a postal inspector, a transit clerk, and a garbageman, all city employees off-limits—and one guy who did have a six-inch blade under his seat, but no spring-release.

A station wagon coming off the bridge pulls abreast of them at the Delancey Street light, the driver a tall, gray, long-nosed man sporting a tweed jacket and Cuffney cap.

"The Quiet Man," Geohagan murmurs.

"That'll do, pig," Scharf adds.

Lugo, Daley, Geohagan, Scharf; Bayside, New Dorp, Freeport, Pelham Bay, all in their thirties, which, at this late hour, made them some of the oldest white men on the Lower East Side.

Forty minutes without a nibble . . .

Restless, they finally pull out to honeycomb the narrow streets for an hour of endless tight right turns: falafel joint, jazz joint, gyro joint, corner. Schoolyard, crêperie, realtor, corner. Tenement, tenement, tenement museum, corner. Pink Pony, Blind Tiger, muffin boutique, corner. Sex shop, tea shop, synagogue, corner. Boulangerie, bar, hat boutique, corner. Iglesia, gelateria, matzo shop, corner. Bollywood, Buddha, botanica, corner. Leather outlet, leather outlet, leather outlet, corner. Bar, school, bar, school, People's Park, corner. Tyson mural, Celia Cruz mural, Lady Di mural, corner. Bling shop, barbershop, car service, corner. And then finally, on a sooty stretch of Eldridge, something with potential: a weary-faced Fujianese in a thin Members Only windbreaker, cigarette hanging, plastic bags dangling from crooked fingers like full waterbuckets, trudging up the dark, narrow street followed by a limping black kid half a block behind.

"What do you think?" Lugo taking a poll via the rearview. "Hunting for his Chinaman?"

"That's who I'd do," Scharf says.

"Guy looks beat. Probably just finished up his week."

"That'd be a nice score too. Payday Friday, pulled your eighty-four hours, walking home with what, four? Four fifty?"

"Could be his whole roll on him if he doesn't use banks."

"C'mon, kid"—the taxi lagging behind its prey, all three parties in a half-block stagger—"it doesn't get better than this."

"Actually, Benny Yee in Community Outreach? He says the Fooks finally know not to do that anymore, keep it all on them."

"Yeah, OK, they don't do that anymore."

"Should we tell the kid? He probably hasn't even heard of Benny Yee."

"I don't want to come between a young man and his dreams," Lugo says.

"There he goes, there he goes . . ."

"Forget it, he just made us," Daley says as the kid abruptly loses his limp and turns east, back towards the projects, or the subways, or, like them, to simply take five, then get back in the game.


Right turn after right turn after right, so many that when they finally pull someone over, and they will, it'll take a minute to get their legs under them, to stop leaning into their steps; so many right turns that at three in the morning, six beers deep at Grouchie's, everybody silently, angrily watching the one lucky bastard getting a lap ride in a banquette by the bathrooms, they'll be canting to the right at the bar, then, later in bed, twitching to the right in their dreams.

At the corner of Houston and Chrystie, a cherry-red Denali pulls up alongside them, three overdressed women in the backseat, the driver alone up front and wearing sunglasses.

The passenger-side window glides down. "Officers, where the Howard Johnson hotel at around here . . ."

"Straight ahead three blocks on the far corner," Lugo offers.

"Thank you."

"What's with the midnight shades?" Daley asks from the shotgun seat, leaning forward past Lugo to make eye contact.

"I got photosensitivity," the guy answers, tapping his frames.

The window glides back up and he shoots east on Houston.

"Did he call us officers?"

"It's that stupid flattop of yours."

"It's that fuckin' tractor hat of yours."

"I gots photosensitivity . . ."

A moment later they're rolling past the Howard Johnson's themselves, watching as the guy from the Denali makes like a coachman, holding the door for all the ladies filing out from the backseat.

"Huggy Bear," Lugo mumbles.

"Who the fuck puts a Howard Johnson's down here?" Scharf gestures to the seedy-looking chain hotel, its neighbors an ancient knishery and a Seventh-Day Adventist church whose aluminum cross is superimposed over a stone-carved Star of David. "What was the thinking behind that."

"Twenty-eight flavors," Lugo says. "My dad used to take me every Sunday after my game."

"You're talking the ice cream parlor," Scharf says, "that's different."

"I never had a dad," says Geohagan.

"You want one of mine?" Daley turns in his seat. "I had three."

"I can only dream of a dad who'd take me to a Howard Johnson's after my game."

"Hey, Sonny." Lugo catches Geohagan's eye in the rearview. "Later tonight, you want to have a catch with me?"

"Sure, mister."

"Pokey as fuck out here, huh?" says Daley.

"That's because it's your turn to collar," Lugo says, waving off some drunk who thinks he's just flagged down a taxi.

"Somebody up there hates me."

"Hang on . . ." Scharf abruptly perks up, his head on a swivel. "That there looks good. High beams going west, four bodies."

"Going west?" Lugo floors it in heavy traffic. "Think thin, girls," as he takes the driver-side wheels up onto the concrete divider to get past a real cab waiting for the light, then whips into a U-turn to get abreast of the target car, peering in. "Females, two mommies, two kids," passing them, hungrier now, all of them, then Scharf ahoying once again: "Green Honda, going east."

"Now east, he says." Lugo does another 180 and pulls behind the Honda.

"What do we got . . ."

"Two males in the front."

"What do we got . . ."

"Neon trim on the plate."

"Tinted windows."

"Right rear taillight."

"Front passenger just stuffed something under the seat."

"Thank you." Lugo hits the misery lights, climbs up the Honda's back, the driver taking half a block to pull over.

Daley and Lugo slowly walk up on either side of the car, cross-beam the front seats.

The driver, a young green-eyed Latino, rolls down his window. "Officer, what I do?"

Lugo rests his crossed arms on the open window as if it's a backyard fence. "License and registration, please?"

"For real, what I do?"

"You always drive like that?" His voice almost gentle.

"Like what?"

"Signaling lane changes, all road-courteous and shit."

"Excuse me?"

"C'mon, nobody does that unless they're nervous about something."

"Well I was."

"Nervous?"

"You was following me."

"A cab was following you?"

"Yeah, OK, a cab." Passing over his papers. "All serious, Officer, and no disrespect intended, maybe I can learn something here, but what did I do?"

"Primary, you have neon trim on your plates."

"Hey, I didn't put it there. This my sister's whip."

"Secondary, your windows are too dark."

"I *told* her about that."

"Tertiary, you crossed a solid yellow."

"To get around a double-parked car."

"Quadrary, you're sitting by a hydrant."

"That's 'cause you just pulled me over."

Lugo takes a moment to assess the level of mouth he's getting.

As a rule he is soft-spoken, leaning in to the driver's window to conversate, to explain, his expression baggy with patience, going eye to eye as if to make sure what he's explicating here is being digested, seemingly deaf to the obligatory sputtering, the misdemeanors of verbal abuse, but . . . if the driver says that one thing, goes one word over some invisible line, then without any change of expression, without any warning signs except maybe a slow straightening up, a sad/disgusted looking off, he steps back, reaches for the door handle, and the world as they knew it, is no more.

But this kid isn't too bad.

"This is for your own benefit. Get out of the car, please?"

As Lugo escorts the driver to the rear bumpers, Daley leans into the shotgun-seat window and tilts his chin at the passenger, this second kid sitting there affecting comatosity, heavy-lidded under a too big baseball cap and staring straight ahead as if they were still driving somewhere.

"So what's your story?" Daley says, opening the passenger door, offering this one some sidewalk too, as Geohagan, all tatted out in Celtic braids, knots, and crosses leans in to search the glove compartment, the cup caddy, the tape storage bin, Scharf taking the rear seats.

Back at the rear bumpers, the driver stands in a scarecrow T looking

off soul-eyed as Lugo, squinting through his own cigarette smoke, fin-
gerwalks his pockets, coming up with a fat roll of twenties.

"This a lot of cheddar, cuz," counting it, then stuffing it in the kid's
shirt pocket before continuing the patdown.

"Yeah, well, that's my college tuition money."

"What the fuck college takes cash?" Lugo laughs, then finished,
gestures to the bumper. "Have a seat."

"Burke Technical in the Bronx? It's new."

"And they take cash?"

"Money's money."

"True dat." Lugo shrugs, just waiting out the car search. "So what's
your major?"

"Furniture management?"

"You ever been locked up before?"

"C'mon, man, my uncle's like a detective in the Bronx."

"*Like* a detective?"

"No. *A* detective. He just retired."

"Oh yeah? What precinct?"

"I don't know per se. The Sixty-ninth?"

"The fighting Sixty-ninth," Geohagan calls out, feeling under the
passenger seat now.

"There is no Sixty-ninth," Lugo says, flicking his butt into the gutter.

"Sixty-something. I said I wasn't sure."

"What's his name."

"Rodriguez?"

"Rodriguez in the Bronx? That narrows it down. What's his first
name?"

"Narcisso?"

"Don't know him."

"Had a big retirement party?"

"Sorry."

"I been thinking of trying out for the Police Academy myself."

"Oh yeah? That's great."

"Donnie." Geohagan backs out of the passenger door, holds up a Zip-
loc of weed.

"Because we need more fuckin' smokehounds."

The kid closes his eyes, tilts his chin to the stars, to the moon over Delancey.

"His or yours." Lugo gestures to the other kid on the sidewalk, face still blank as a mask, his pockets strewn over the car hood. "Somebody needs to say or you both go."

"Mine," the driver finally mutters.

"Turn around, please?"

"Oh man, you gonna lock me up for that?"

"Hey, two seconds ago you stepped up like a man. Stay with that."

Lugo cuffs him then turns him forward again, holding him at arm's length as if to assess his outfit for the evening. "Anything else in there? Tell us now or we'll rip that shitbox to shreds."

"Damn, man, I barely had that."

"All right then, just relax," guiding him back down to the bumper as the search continues nonetheless.

The kid looks off, shakes his head, mutters, "Sorry ass."

"Excuse me?"

"Nah, I'm just saying"—pursing his mouth in self-disgust—"not about you. "

Geohagan comes back with the baggie, hands it over.

"OK, look." Lugo lights another cigarette, takes a long first drag. "This? We could give a fuck. We're out here on a higher calling." He nods at a passing patrol car, something the driver said making him laugh. "You know what I'm saying?"

"More serious shit?"

"There you go."

"That's all I got."

"I'm not taking about what you got. I'm talking about what you know."

"What I *know*?"

"You know what I'm saying."

They both turn and look off in the direction of the East River, two guys having a moment, one with his hands behind his back.

Finally, the kid exhales heavily. "Well, I can tell you where a weed spot is."

"You're kidding me, right?" Lugo rears back. "I'll tell *you* where a weed spot is. I'll tell you where fifty is. I can get you better shit than this for half what you paid seven days a week with blindfolds on."

The kid sighs, tries not to look at the barely curious locals coming out of the Banco de Ponce ATM center and the Dunkin' Donuts, the college kids hopping in and out of taxis.

"C'mon. Do right by me, I'll do right by you." Lugo absently tosses the baggie from hand to hand, drops it, picks it up.

"Do right like how?"

"I want a gun."

"A *what*? I don't *know* a gun."

"You don't have to know a gun. But you know someone who knows someone, right?"

"Aw, man . . . "

"For starters, you know who you bought this shit from, right?"

"I don't *know* any guns, man. You got forty dollars a weed there. I paid for it with my own money, 'cause it helps me relax, helps me party. Everybody I know is like, go to work, go to school, get high. That's it."

"Huh . . . so like, there's no one you could call, say, 'Yo, I just got jacked in the PJs. I need me a onetime whistle, can I meet you at such and such?' "

"A whistle?"

Lugo makes a finger gun.

"You mean a hammer?"

"A hammer, a whistle . . . " Lugo turns away and tightens his pony-tail.

"Pfff . . ." The kid looks off, then, "I know a knife."

Lugo laughs. "My mother has a knife."

"This one's used."

"Forget it." Then, chin-tilting to the other kid: "What about your sidekick there."

"My cousin? He's like half-retarded."

"How about the other half?"

"Aw, c'mon." The driver lolls his head like a cow.

Another patrol car rolls up, this one to pick up the prisoner.

"All right, just think about it, OK?" Lugo says. "I'll see you back in holding in a few hours."

"What about my car?"

"Gilbert Grape there, he's got a license?"

"His brother does."

"Well then tell him to call his brother and get his ass down here before you wind up towed."

"Damn." Then calling out: "Raymond! You hear that?"

The cousin nods but makes no move to retrieve his cell phone from the car hood.

"So you never answered my question," Lugo says, skull-steering him into the rear of the cruiser. "You ever been locked up before?"

The kid turns his head away, murmurs something.

"It's OK, you can tell me."

"I said, 'Yes.' "

"For?"

The kid shrugs, embarrassed, says, "This."

"Yeah? Around here?"

"Uh-huh."

"How long back?"

"On Christmas Eve."

"On Christmas Eve for *this*?" Lugo winces. "That is cold. Who the hell would . . . You remember who collared you?"

"Uh-huh," the kid mutters, then looks Lugo in the face. "You."


An hour later, with the kid on ice back at the Eighth, good for another hour or two's worth of gun-wrangling, which would probably go nowhere, and a few more hours' worth of processing for Daley, the arresting officer, Daley good and taken care of, they were out again looking to get one for Scharf, a last-call drive-around before settling on one of the local parks for an if-all-else-fails post-midnight curfew rip.

Turning south off Houston onto Ludlow for the fiftieth time that night, Daley sensed something in the chain-link shadows below Katz's Deli, nothing he could put his finger on, but . . . "Donnie, go around."

Lugo whipped the taxi in a four-block square: Ludlow to Stanton, to Essex, to Houston, creeping left onto Ludlow again, just past Katz's, only to come abreast of a parked car full of slouched-down plainclothes from Borough Narcotics, the driver eyeballing them out of there: This is our fishing hole.

# ONE

# WHISTLE

**At ten in the morning,** Eric Cash, thirty-five, stepped out of his Stanton Street walk-up, lit a cigarette, and headed off to work.

When he had first moved down here eight years ago, he was seized with the notion of the Lower East Side as haunted, and on rare days like today, a simple walk like this could still bring back his fascination, traces of the nineteenth-century Yiddish boomtown everywhere: in the claustrophobic gauge of the canyonlike streets with their hanging garden of ancient fire escapes, in the eroded stone satyr heads leering down between pitted window frames above the Erotic Boutique, in the faded Hebrew lettering above the old socialist cafeteria turned Asian massage parlor turned kiddie-club hot spot; all of it and more lying along Eric's daily four-block commute. But after nearly a decade in the neighborhood, even on a sun-splashed October morning like this, all of this ethnohistorical mix 'n' match was, much like himself, getting old.

He was an upstate Jew five generations removed from here, but he knew where he was, he got the joke; the laboratorio del gelati, the Tibetan hat boutiques, 88 Forsyth House with its historically restored cold-water flats not all that much different from the unrestored tenements that surrounded it, and in his capacity as manager of Café Berkmann, the flagship of come-on-down, on the rare days when the Beast would take one of its catnaps, he enjoyed being part of the punch line.

But what really drew him to the area wasn't its full-circle irony but its nowness, its right here and nowness, which spoke to the true engine of his being, a craving for making it made many times worse by a complete ignorance as to how this "it" would manifest itself.

He had no particular talent or skill, or what was worse, he had a little talent, some skill: playing the lead in a basement-theater production of *The Dybbuk* sponsored by 88 Forsyth House two years ago, his third small role since college, having a short story published in a now-defunct Alphabet City literary rag last year, his fourth in a decade, neither accomplishment leading to anything; and this unsatisfied yearning for validation was starting to make it near impossible for him to sit through a movie or read a book or even case out a new restaurant, all pulled off increasingly by those his age or younger, without wanting to run face-first into a wall.

Still two blocks from work, he stopped short as he came up on the rear of a barely creeping procession that extended west on Rivington to a point farther than he could see.

Whatever this was, it had nothing to do with him; the people were overwhelmingly Latino, most likely from the unrehabbed walk-ups below Delancey and the half-dozen immortal housing projects that cradled this, the creamy golden center of the Lower East Side, like a jai alai paddle. Everyone seemed to be dressed up as if for church or some kind of religious holiday, including a large number of kids.

He couldn't imagine this having anything to do with Berkmann's either, and in fact the line not only went directly past the café, but solidly and obliviously blocked the entrance; Eric watching as two separate parties gingerly tried to break through then quickly gave up, stopping off to eat somewhere else.

Peering through one of the large side windows, he saw that the room was uncharacteristically near empty, the midmorning skeleton staff outnumbering the customers. But what really got his gut jumping was the sight of the owner, his boss, Harry Steele, sitting alone in the back at a deuce, his perennial sad man's face shrunken by agitation to the size of an apple.

At least from where Eric stood now he could finally see where the line was headed: the Sana'a 24/7, a mini-mart run by two Yemeni brothers, three blocks west of Berkmann's at the corner of Rivington and Eldridge.

His first thought was that they must have had a huge Powerball winner the day before, or maybe the state lottery had climbed into the hundreds of millions again, but, no, this was something else.

He followed the line west past the fresh ruins of the most recently collapsed synagogue, past the adjoining People's Park, until he got to the corner directly across the street from the Sana'a, the shadows cast by its tattered two-year-old GRAND OPENING pennants playing across his face.

"Hey, Eric . . ." A young Chinese uniform, Fenton Ma, working the intersection, nodded his way. "Nuts, right?"

"What is it?"

"Mary's in there," Ma said, getting bumped by the ripple effect of the crowd he was holding back.

"Mary who."

"Mary the Virgin. She showed up in the condensation on one of the freezer doors last night. Word travels fast around here, no?" Taking another bump from behind.

Then Eric saw a second crowd shaping up across the street from the one at the side windows: a crowd watching the crowd, this crew mostly young, white, and bemused.

"She's he-ere," one of them called out.

Eric was always good at weaseling his way through a mob, had plenty of practice just trying to get to the reservations pulpit at Berkmann's dozens of times a day, so he was able to pop into the narrow deli without anyone behind him calling him out. Directly inside, one of the Yemeni brothers, Nazir, tall and bony with an Adam's apple like a tomahawk, was playing cashier-doorman, standing with a fat stack of singles in one hand, the other palm-up, fingertips flexing towards the incoming pilgrims.

"Say hello to Mary," his voice singsong and brisk, "she loves you very much."

The Virgin was a sixteen-inch-high gourd-shaped outline molded in frost on the glass doors fronting the beer and soda shelves, its smoothly tapered top slightly inclined to one side above its broader lower mass, reminding him vaguely of all the art-history Marys tilting their covered heads to regard the baby in their arms, but really, it was kind of a stretch.

The people kneeling around Eric held up photo phones and camcorders, left offerings of grocery-store bouquets, candles, balloons— one saying YOU'RE SO SPECIAL—handwritten notes, and other tokens, but mainly they just stared expressionless, some with clasped hands, until the second Yemeni brother, Tariq, stepped up, said, "Mary says bye now," and ushered everyone out through the rear delivery door to clear space for the next group.

By the time Eric made it around to the front of the store again, Fenton Ma had been spelled by an older cop, his shield reading LO PRESTO.

"Can I ask you something?" Eric said lightly, not knowing this guy. "Have you seen her in there?"

"Who, the Virgin?" Lo Presto looked at him neutrally. "Depends what you mean by 'seen.'"

"You know. Seen."

"Well, I'll tell you." He looked off, palming his chest pocket for a cigarette. "About eight this morning? A couple of guys from the Ninth Squad went in there, you know, curious? And kneeling right in front of that thing is Servisio Tucker, had killed his wife up on Avenue D maybe six months ago. Now, these guys had been turning that neighborhood upside down looking for him ever since, right? And this morning alls they did was waltz on in and there he was, on his knees. He looks right up at them, tears in his eyes, puts out his hands for cuffs, and says, 'OK. Good. I'm ready.'"

"Huh." Eric entranced, experiencing a fleeting rush of optimism.

"So . . ." Lo Presto finally fired up, exhaled luxuriously. "Did I *see* her? Who's to say. But if what I just told you isn't a fucking miracle, I don't know what is."

On bright quiet mornings like this, when Berkmann's was empty, delivered from the previous night's overpacked boozy freneticness, the place was an air palace, and there was nowhere better to be in this neighborhood than sitting in a lacquered wicker chair immersed in the serene luxury of a café au lait and *The New York Times*, sunlight splashing off the glazed ecru tiles, the racks of cryptically stencil-numbered wine bottles, the industrial-grade chicken-wired glass and partially desilvered mirrors, all found in various warehouses in New Jersey by the owner, Harry Steele: restaurant dressed as theater dressed as nostalgia. For Eric personally, the first few moments of coming in here every day were like the first few moments inside a major-league ballpark: getting that whooshy rush of space and geometric perfection, commuting as he did from a three-room dumbbell flat with one of its two windows overlooking the building's interior airshaft, which was supposed to provide cross ventilation but in fact had served, since the year of the McKinley assassination, as a glorified garbage chute.

But with nothing to do this morning but rerack the newspapers on their faux-aged wooden dowels or lean against his pulpit, shaking like a flake from drinking coffee after coffee served up by the two probationary bartenders, even that momentary pleasure was denied him. In his jumpy boredom he took a moment to study the new hires behind the stick: a green-eyed black kid with dreadlocks named Cleveland and a white kid—Spike? Mike?—who was leaning on the zinc bartop and talking to a chubby friend who had successfully breached the procession. This friend, Eric could tell, was even more hungover than he was.

People said that after fourteen years of on-and-off working for Harry Steele, Eric had come to look like him; both had those dour baggy eyes like Serge Gainsbourg or Lou Reed, the same indifferent physique; the difference being that with Harry Steele, this lack of physical allure just added to the mystique of his golden touch.

A waitress from Grouchie's who had all seven dwarfs tattooed in miniature tramping up the inside of her thigh had once told Eric that people were either cats or dogs, and that he was most definitely a dog, compulsively trying to anticipate everyone's needs, a shitty thing to say to someone you just slept with, but fair enough he guessed, because right now, despite his constant "I am more than this" mantra, his boss's helpless exasperation had him humming with the desire to act.

At least Steele was no longer alone, sharing his small table now with his dealer, Paulie Shaw, a sharp-faced ratter whose alert eyes, spit-fire delivery, and generally tense aura reminded Eric of too many shadow players from back in the shame days. Passing on a fifth cup of coffee, he watched as Paulie opened an aluminum attaché case and from its velvet, molded interior removed a number of rectangular glass photo negatives, each in its own protective sheath.

"'Ludlow Street Sweatshop,'" holding it up by its edges. "'Blind Beggar, 1888.' 'Passing the Growler.' 'Bandits Roost'—that one right there, as I told you on the phone, worth all the rest combined. And last but not least, 'Mott Street Barracks.'"

"Fantastic," Steele murmured, eyes once again straying to the *milagro* line, to his empty café.

"Each one personally hand-tinted by Riis himself for his lectures," Paulie said. "The man was light-years ahead of his time, total multimedia, had sixty to a hundred of these fading in and out of each other on a huge screen accompanied by music? Those uptown dowagers had to be crying their balls off."

"OK," Steele said, half listening.

"OK?" Paulie ducked down to find his eyes. "For the, for what we, for the number we discussed?"

"Yeah, yeah." Steele's knees pumping under the table.

The hungover kid sitting at the bar abruptly laughed at something his friend said, the rude sound of it bouncing off the tiled walls.

"Mike, right?" Eric tilted his chin at the probationary bartender.

"Ike," he said easily, still leaning forward on the zinc like he owned the place.

He had a shaved head and a menagerie of retro tattoos inside both forearms—hula girls, mermaids, devil heads, panthers—but his smile was as clean as a cornfield; the kid, Eric thought, like a poster boy for the neighborhood.

"Ike, go see if they want anything."

"You got it, boss."

"Chop-chop," said his friend.

As Ike came from behind the bar and headed for the back deuce, Paulie pulled up the velvet interior of his booty case to reveal a second layer of goods, from which he took out a large burnt-orange paperback.

"You're an Orwell man, right?" he said to Steele. "*Road to Wigan Pier*, Victor Gollancz Left Wing Book Club galleys, 1937. What you're looking at right now doesn't even exist."

"Just the Riis plates." Steele's eyes yet again straying to that barely moving line. "I cannot fucking *believe* this," he blurted to the room at large.

"How about Henry Miller," Paulie said quickly, burrowing into his case. "You into Henry Miller?"

Ike's shadow fell across the table, Paulie half twisting around and rearing back to eyeball him. "Can I help you with something?"

"You guys want anything?" Ike asked.

"We're done," Steele said.

"Henry Miller." Paulie pulled out a hardback. "First-edition *Air-Conditioned Nightmare*, pristine wrappers, and get this, inscribed to Nelson, A, Rockefeller."

Out on Rivington, an argument broke out in Spanish, someone being bumped into the window of the café with a muffled thud.

"This neighborhood," Steele said brightly, looking directly at Eric for the first time this deader-than-dead morning. "A little too much mix, not quite enough match, yeah?" Then he turned to his dealer: "How are you fixed for splinters of the True Cross?"

"For what?"

And with that, Eric, the boy-faced dog, was out the door.

A block from the restaurant, his heart thundering as he wondered exactly how he'd go about doing what had to be done, someone called, "Yo, hold up," and he turned to see Ike walking towards him, lighting a cigarette.

"You going to see the Virgin?"

"Sort of," Eric said.

"I'm on break, can I come with you?"

Eric hesitated, wondering if a witness would make it harder or easier, but then Ike just fell in step.

"Eric, right?"

"Right."

"Ike Marcus," offering his hand. "So, Eric, what do you do?"

"What do you mean, what do I do?" Eric knowing exactly what he meant.

"I mean other than . . ." The kid at least quick-witted enough to cut himself off.

"I write," Eric said, hating to tell people, but just wanting to get them both off the hook.

"Oh yeah?" Ike said gratefully. "Me too."

"Good," Eric said briskly, thinking, Who asked.

His only viable project right now was a screenplay, five thousand down, twenty more on completion, anything about the Lower East Side in its heyday, Aka Jewday, commissioned by a customer from Berkmann's, a former Alphabet City squatter turned real estate gorilla, who now wanted to be an auteur; everybody wanting to be an auteur . . .

"Are you from here originally?" Ike asked.

"Everybody's from here originally," Eric said, then, coming off it: "Upstate."

"No kidding. Me too."

"Whereabouts?"

"Riverdale?" Then, grabbing Eric's arm as he put on the brakes: "Oh, check this out."


The roof of the massive synagogue had caved in just two nights before, leaving only the three-story back wall with its lightly damaged twin Stars of David, shafts of sunlight streaming through the chinks. In the lee of that wall, the cantor's table, Torah ark, a menorah with the spread of a bull elk, and four silver candleholders still stood like props on a stage, an intact row of six pews further enhancing the suggestion of an open-air theater. All else was reduced to an undulating field of rubble, Eric and Ike pausing on their way to the mini-mart to stand on the roped-off sidewalk with a gaggle of kufied deli men, off-duty sweatshop workers, and kids of various nations all cutting school.

"Check this out," Ike said again, nodding to a large Orthodox in a sweaty suit and fedora, his ear glued to his cell phone as he picked his way through the hilly debris to rescue the tattered remains of prayer books, piling loose and torn pages beneath bricks and chunks of plaster to keep them from blowing away. Two teenagers, one light-skinned, the other Latino, were following him and stuffing the salvaged sheets into pillowcases.

"Looks like one of those modern stage sets for Shakespeare, you know?" Ike said. "Brutus and Pompey running around in full camo with Tec-9s."

"More like Godot."

"How much you think he's paying those two kids?"

"As little as he can get away with."

A tall young guy wearing a kelly green yarmulke emblazoned with the New York Jets logo stood next to them writing furiously in a steno pad. Eric had the uncomfortable impression that he was taking down their conversation.

"Who are you writing for?" Ike asked without edge.

"The *Post*," he said.

"For real?"

"Yup."

"Excellent." Ike grinned and actually shook his hand.

This kid, Eric thought, was a trip.

"So what happened here, man?" Ike said.

"Fell the fuck down." The reporter shrugged, closing his pad. When he walked away, they noticed that he had a clubfoot.

"That's got to suck," Ike said under his breath.

"Excuse me, sir!" a bespectacled black man, his clothes nearly in rags but carrying an attaché case, called out to the Orthodox, still on his cell. "Are you rebuilding?"

"Of course."

"Very good," the raggedy man said, and left.

"We should go too," Ike said, slapping Eric on the arm and heading out for the Virgin.


As they came up on the Sana'a, Eric turned to Ike, ready to school him on slipping the line, but the kid had already done so, giving Nazir his dollar admission fee and disappearing inside.

Hemmed in by supplicants, they knelt side by side like batters in an on-deck circle before the Virgin, the shrine-pile of offerings having tripled since Eric's previous visit.

His first thought was to approach one of the brothers, appeal to them to least reroute the line outside so it wouldn't screw up all the other businesses in the neighborhood, but he realized that the line was just that: outside, as in, out of their control. Which left asking them to lose the Virgin altogether, not likely given the cash coming in. Which left . . .

"Fuck me," Eric whispered, then to Ike: "Can I ask you something personal?" his voice feathery with tension.

"Absolutely."

"All those tattoos, what are you going to tell your kids someday?"

"My *kids*? I'm my own kid."

"My own kid," Eric said, massaging his chest as if to get more air in there. "I like that."

"Yeah? Good, it's true."

"Shit," Eric hissed. "How do you do this . . ."

"Do what?" Ike whispered, then casually reached for the glass door, opening it for a few seconds, then closing it back. "That?"

Within a minute the inrush of humid air had changed the condensation pattern and sent the Virgin packing. Fifteen minutes later, as the news shot back across Rivington, the *milagro* line was no more. And by noon, over at Café Berkmann, there was a twenty-minute wait for tables.


"See you din't live round here back in the heyday, so no way you'd know, but about ten, twelve years ago?" Little Dap Williams yakking away as he stopped to scoop up the next bunch of Bible pages from under a brick. "Man, it was, there was some bad dudes up in here. The Purples on Avenue C, Hernandez brothers on A and B, Delta Force in the Cahans, nigger name Maquetumba right in the Lemlichs. Half a them got snatched up by RICO for long bids, the other half is dead, all the hardcores, so now it's like just the Old Heads out there sippin' forties and telling stories about yesteryear, them and a bunch of Similac niggers, stoop boys, everybody out for themselves with their itty-bitty eight balls, nobody runnin' the show."

"Maquetumba?" Tristan's pillowcase was nearly full.

"Dominican dude. Dead now. My brother told me him and his crew had the Lemlichs sewed tight."

"What kind of name is that."

"I just said. Dominican."

"What's it mean, though."

"Maquetumba? Man, you should know, you Dominican."

"Puerto Rican."

"Same shit, ain't it?"

Tristan shrugged.

"Sss," Little Dap sucked his teeth. "Like, 'he who drops the most,' some shit like that."

"Drops what?"

Little Dap just stared at him.

"Right." Pretending like he got it. Tristan was just glad to be hanging with Little Dap, glad to be hanging with anybody, with him having to live 24/7 with his ex-stepfather, the guy's new wife, kids, rules, and fists. Even how he got here, picking up Bible paper on this shitpile, seemed a little bit of a miracle; after having dropped off the hamsters—his not-really brothers and sisters—at their schools this morning, he hadn't felt like going to school himself.

So he'd been sitting outside Seward Park High School at ten, not knowing what to do or having anyone around to do it with, when Little Dap cut out of the building, passed him by with a nod, then shrugging, walked back and asked him if he wanted to make some change at the Jew cave-in.

It always seemed like whenever he chose to cut school, everybody else picked that day to go in and vice versa; if he didn't have to be dropping off the hamsters first thing every morning, he could just hang out in the candy store by Seward having a Coca-Cola and Ring Ding breakfast with everybody from the Lemlichs when they decided what to do that day, but he could never make it there in time; same for the afternoon, everybody coming together after last class and deciding whose place to go to; Tristan once again stuck doing the reverse hamster run and not having a clue where they went. And his ex-stepfather wouldn't allow him a cell phone.

"Yeah, the PJ's wide-open now," Little Dap said again.

"What about your brother?"

Tristan knew all about Big Dap, everybody did, the only nigger in history to ever get into a fight with a police in an elevator, wind up shooting the guy in the leg with his own gun, and beat the case.

"Dap? Pfff . . . Nigger's too lazy. I mean, he *could* run the Lemlichs, at least if he wanted to, got everybody up in there so scared a him, you know, if he put in the effort? But shit, all *he* wants is get the cheese easiest way he could. Go up on a corner, 'Yo Shorty you slingin'? It's a hundred a week.' Collect, go back to Shyanne's crib, smoke his brains out and watch the TV. That ain't no life."

"Times ten corners?"

Tristan only made $25, $30 on a delivery for Smoov, and Smoov only came to him if nobody else was around.

"Wide-open . . ." Little Dap shaking his head like it was a tragedy.

"So, what. You gonna go all kingpin out there?"

"Hell no. And wind up in some underground supermax? This Old Head round the way said them joints age you ten years for each real one, guys be laying there twenty-four/seven daydreaming 'bout how to kill themselves."

"For real?"

"I'll take another bid in gladiator school over that anytime."

"For real."

Tristan had never been to either juvie or, since he turned seventeen last year, the Tombs, just ROR'ed a few times like everybody else for the usual shit: possession, trespassing—aka hanging in the park after curfew—for fighting that one time, pissing out the bedroom window.

"I tell you what I *am* gonna do, though," Little Dap said. "Get up on a package tonight? Work it, sleep in tomorrow and party."

"Pay your own brother corner rent?"

"He ain't charge me."

"You got the money for a package?" Tristan asked.

Dap did what Tristan did, deliver, maybe more often because he was more popular, but he also got money from his grandmother and occasionally made collections for his brother.

"Not right now as such, but I'll get it tonight. Come back out here to the midlands, jux me a head, and I'm good to go."

"All right." Tristan not really following.

"There's this barbershop up in Washington Heights? If you're an *hermano dominicano*, they sell you a gram for twenty dollars, so I'm thinking let's snatch us a head out here, take the kibble, go up there, let you do the talking, come back down around Tompkins Park, resell the g for a hundred to the white boys coming out the bars, you know what I'm sayin'? We go up with, say, two hundred for ten grams, come back out here, sell for a grand, you do the math."

We . . .

"Yeah, huh?"

"Oh hell yeah."

But Washington Heights. Or even just back out here. They were only five or six blocks from the Lemlichs, but Tristan could almost count the times he'd been this deep away from home when he wasn't making a delivery. He didn't like going north of Houston or west of Essex, and he hated delivering dope to the doctors and nurses up at Bellevue or NYU Special Joints, both so far uptown they might as well be in another country. In fact the only place he didn't mind delivering to was the lawyer's office on Hester Street, close enough, although that redheaded lawyer there, Danny, sometimes when he got his head on, he'd start calling Tristan "Che" because of his goatee, Tristan having no idea how to tell him to quit it.

It was amazing to him how Smoov, only a year older than him, had the confidence to go into all those uptown bars by the hospitals and chat up all those doctors, nurses, and lawyers and whoever to drum up new customers. Shit, he wouldn't even be here in this junk field now if Little Dap hadn't just said, C'mon.

"So you up for this?"

"I don't know." Thinking about his curfew, those fists. "I might got to watch the kids."

"See?" Little Dap addressed the rubble. "Similac niggers, everywhere I look."

"Maybe I can get out of it," Tristan murmured.

"Ey, yo," Little Dap called out to the rabbi or whatever he was. "What you gonna do with them candlesticks back there?"

"That's not your concern."

"*What?*" Little Dap starting to trip.

The bearded guy, back on his cell now, ignored him.

"I *ast* you a civilized question. You think I'm gonna *steal* them or something?"

The guy smiled, briefly taking the phone from under his jaw. "They'll go in the new temple."

"Who gives a fuck," Little Dap said, tossing his pillowcase.

Tristan looked out at the rubberneckers on the roped-off sidewalk—sand niggers, flat-face Chinese, *blancos*, other kids—imagining that they were all there to stare at him, to see what his goatee was hiding, the lightening underneath, knowing it wasn't really true but not liking the idea anyhow, and so he put his eyes to the task he was getting paid for. A big $20.

When he looked up again, the rabbi or whatever was staring at him, a pained smile on his face.

"What?" Tristan flushed, then tracked the guy's eyes down to his own feet, seeing the Bible page he was standing on.


During the late-afternoon lull, Eric wandered behind the bar and made himself a light club soda and Hennessy. He wasn't a daytime drinker as a rule, but he'd been feeling amorphously anxious ever since they booted the Virgin. The boss hadn't even thanked him, not so much as a knowing nod, although it was probably more prudent for Steele to go all Don't Ask, Don't Tell on it if you were in his position.

Having watched the two new bartenders get through the lunch crush, Eric thought they'd both work out. Cleveland, the black one, was no artiste with a cocktail shaker, but was a warm conversationalist, far more important; and Ike, good enough with the drinks, had an easy laugh. Eric imagined that both would build up considerable followings within a month.

He was not amused at the stunt Ike had pulled. Not that he hadn't been thinking of doing the same thing, but the kid didn't even have the patience to look around and size up the pilgrims present to see if they'd wind up with a good ass-kicking before they could make it out the door. Fortunately there was just enough of a time delay before the Virgin evaporated, and they were almost out of earshot before the wailing started.

"Eric." Ike sidled up to him as he was putting back the cognac. "If you want, I'd be happy to make those for you."

"I'm good."

Despite three women coming in off a shopping spree to belly up to the bar, Ike lingered by Eric's side, anxiously toddling from foot to foot. "Can I tell you something?" His voice dropped. "I'm not superstitious or anything, but that thing I pulled this morning? I have a real bad feeling it's going to come back and bite me in the ass."

Touched by the kid's unprotected candor, Eric was about to say something dry and reassuring, but the nitwit beat him to it, grinning and punching his shoulder: "I'm just fuckin' with you, brother," then going off to serve the ladies.


Tristan took the offered joint and dug his feet into the gravel on the roof of their building in the Lemlichs, the both of them gazing at mile-high One Police Plaza only a few blocks away. Not only was he blowing off curfew tonight, but he never picked up the hamsters from their various schools this afternoon: a first. There'd be hell to pay, but there was always some kind of hell to pay in that house, and he couldn't believe Little Dap was still hanging with him, so fuck it.

"We going to the Heights?" he murmured.

"First things first."

"What."

"What do you mean, what . . ." Little Dap cocking his head. "Gotta get that cheese, podner."

"Oh," Tristan said. "Shit."

In his preoccupation with the big journey to Washington Heights, he had forgotten that part of it.

"What." Little Dap sipped deep. "You never . . ."

"Yeah, no, not like . . ."

Little Dap shrugged. "Ain't nothing to it," passing him the joint.

Tristan in his embarrassment was unable to stop grinning.

"But I can't do it without my *dol*gier." Little Dap slow-poking him in the chest. "You know what I'm saying?"

A bloodred moon slipped out from behind 1PP.

"Why don't you just go to a couple corner boys," Tristan said, coughing out a cloud. "Say you collecting for Big Dap, we run uptown get the shit"—coughing again—"come back down here and turn it into something before he finds out, then just give him his money like normal."

It was the most words he had said all at one time in a year.

"Nah, unh-unh." Little Dap stretched his neck. "I tried that once, ran into some problems? That ain't a good idea. You don't ever get between Dap and his money. I mean, shit, you can send *me* to jail, I can handle that gladiator-school shit, in fact if truth be known, I could be like one of the instructors, but with Dap, he gets his hands on you when he goes off? Naw, unh-uh.

"And that's like the other, we got to be like deep cover on this, 'cause all them porkies from the Eighth? They always looking for a excuse to beat my brother's ass for that cop got shot, so they collar me, it's like, 'Oh, Little Dap, where's Big Dap?' Like he's my automatic mastermind on a caper, and so now they got another excuse to light him up from here to the river. But whatever they do to him? Comes back on me double."

Tristan dredged up a memory of Big Dap hauling off and slapping Little Dap in front of everybody on the street last year, the sound of it like a gunshot.

Then he thought of his ex-stepfather's eyes, the way they bulged when he was good and liquored, getting ready to knock one out of the park.

Tristan didn't want to go through with this anymore. "Maybe you shouldn't do it then," trying to come off as if he were saying it out of concern.

"Nah, it's good, I'm good with it."

They smoked in silence for a while, Tristan deciding the Manhattan Bridge was God's forearm, barring the way to Brooklyn.

"I tell you." Little Dap choked. "The one thing when we get out there? Stay off the Chinese, they get juxed so much, most times they never have nothing on them no more, and even when they do? You come up on them, they're like, 'Here,' hold out the money before you can even say something."

"What's wrong with that?"

"It's disrespectful."

"It's what?"

"How do they know what I got in mind before I even get up on them."

"Yeah."

"But them *white* kids?" Little Dap laughed, snorting smoke. "Ho' shit, they're like . . ." Doubling over, hand over his mouth. "I come up on this one guy last year, put the whistle in his mug? Motherfucker din't have no money on him so he asked if I wanted him to write a check, like, whom should I make it out to?"

"What?" Tristan laughing too now, like everybody up here was a fully blooded vet.

"Here." Little Dap went to his back pocket and pulled out a wrinkled pale blue check. It was from a bank in Traverse City, Michigan, dated six months ago and made out to cash for $100.

"You gonna cash it?" Tristan suddenly dizzy with friendship.

"Naw, man, if I cash this, then they can trace it. I just keep it for a joke."

"But if they find it on you, it's like evidence, right?" Tristan murmured. "Call this bank on here, ask who's this guy, was he robbed in New York . . ."

Another silence came down, Tristan worried that he had just disrespected Little Dap, made him out to be a fool.

But Little Dap was too wasted to catch it, his eyes like two cherries floating in buttermilk.

"So what do you say," passing Tristan the roach. "You gonna be my dolgier out there or what . . . I need to hear you say it."

Tristan took a last hit. "Yeah, OK." The words coming out like smoke signals.

"All right then." Little Dap offering his fist for a pound, Tristan fighting off another out-of-control smile, it felt so good, something did at any rate.

"Man, you are one grinny motherfucker," Little Dap said, popping the nub of the joint in his mouth, taking the gun out of his sweatshirt muff and attempting to hand it over.

Tristan reared back and laughed, if you could call it that.

"What." Little Dap blinked.

"Nah."

"*Nah?* What, you think you go out there and what, yell at a mother-fucker?" He took Tristan by the wrist. "It ain't like you *use* it, man," slapping it into his palm. "You just flash it."

At first Tristan tried to pass it back to him, but then got caught up with the feel of it in his hand, the giddy heft.

"Naw, man, this'll be good for you," Little Dap said. "Get you blooded, you know what I'm saying? First time's like first-time sex, you just do it to get it done with, then you can start concentratin' on getting better at it, havin' fun with it."

"All right." Tristan staring and staring at the thing in his hand. "Can I ask you something?"

Little Dap waited. And waited.

"What the fuck is a *dolgier*."

"A dolgier? A do-anything soldier."

"OK."

"OK?"

"OK." Grinning, grinning.

"You're in the game now, son." Little Dap studied him studying the gun. "Time to show and prove."

# TWO

# LIAR

**At 4:00 a.m., the first** to come on the scene were Lugo's Quality of Lifers on the back end of a double shift, still honeycombing the neighborhood in their bogus taxi, but as of 1:00 a.m. on loan to the Anti-Graffiti Task Force, a newly installed laptop mounted on their dashboard running a nonstop slide show of known local taggers.

What they saw in that limbo-hour stillness were two bodies, eyes to the sky, directly beneath a streetlight in front of 27 Eldridge Street, an old six-story walk-up.

As they cautiously stepped from the cab to investigate, a wild-eyed white man suddenly came charging out of the building towards them, something silver in his right hand.

Bellowing with adrenaline, they all drew down, and when he saw the four guns trained on his chest, the silver object, a cell phone, went sailing and cracked the window of the adjoining Sana'a market; within seconds, one of the Yemeni brothers erupting from the store, a sawed-off fishpriest cocked over his left shoulder like a baseball bat.

At 4:15 a.m., Matty Clark received a call from Bobby Oh of Night Watch: a shooting fatality in your precinct, thought you'd like to know, just as he was leaving, for the last time, his midnight-to-four-a.m., three-night-a-week security gig at a slender Chrystie Street bar that had no sign, no listed phone number, and whose clientele were admitted "by appointment only," buzzed in from behind a scarred narrow door on this obscure stretch of a Chinese-dominated side street; single-batch Cruzan rum, absinthe, and cocktails made with muddled ginger or ignited sugar cubes the specialties of the house.

He was a shovel-jawed, sandy-haired Irisher with the physique of an aging high school fullback, slope-shouldered and dense, his low center of gravity, despite his heaviness, making him appear to glide rather than walk. When he was asked a question, his eyes, already narrow, would screw down into slits and his lips disappear altogether as if speaking or maybe just thinking was painful. This gave the impression to some of his being slow, to others of being a sullen fumer; he was neither, although he could definitely live without ever feeling the need to verbalize the majority of his thoughts.

There wasn't a single evening in his time at the No Name when he hadn't been the oldest human in the room; the baby-faced bartender-proprietor, Josh, like a twelve-year-old in dress-up, sporting garter sleeves and suspendered pants, hair bowl-cut and pomade-parted, but as earnest as a Kinsey researcher, every drink chin-pondered before acted upon, advising his equally young patrons, "Tonight we're featuring . . . ," the entire rail-thin establishment smelling like the tea candles that were its sole source of illumination, smelling like specialness . . .

Although the clientele were primarily the Eloi of the Lower East Side and Williamsburg, an incident a month earlier had involved a platinumed-out crew of Bronx Morlocks: some words tossed around about coming back and lighting the place up, immediately after which a meet had been arranged through an ex-cop intermediary between the owner and Matty, and his off-the-books job for the last few weeks had been to sit quietly in the candlelit shadows, cultivate a taste for scratchy Edith Piaf recordings, not hit on any of the silky-looking mixologists, and not get too smashed in case something did actually jump off. It was a perfectly cushy gig, especially for someone who, at forty-four, still saw closing his eyes at night as a punishment, who liked the feel of unreported cash in his hand as much as any cop, and who enjoyed watching the making of drinks last seen, he imagined, at the Stork Club.

And now the gig was over, his only consolation on this last night the inadvertent violation of the hands-off-the-mixologists rule; inadvertent as in, she started; a new hire, tall, dark, and moody like a long twist of smoke, eyeing him all evening, slipping him samplers across the bar when the Baby King wasn't looking, then giving him the high sign on her 3:00 a.m. break; Matty following her out through the rear loading entrance into the hidden tenement-ringed courtyard. After he passed on her offered joint and watched her take a few hits, she just hopped on up, her arms around his neck, her legs locked over his hips, and he commenced, more for traction and for relief on his lower back than out of passion, whamming her against the brick wall. She had to be fifteen years younger than him, but he couldn't even relax enough to appreciate it, to go exploring, it was all about the hop up, the hoisting, the whamming, until alarmingly, she started weeping, at which point he started whamming her more tenderly, at which point she dried up on the spot: "What are you doing?"

"Sorry," going back to hard whamming like moving a credenza: Over here, lady? Like this, lady? The sex had been unnerving, not exactly fun, but still, it was sex. Besides, she seemed happy again, back to weeping.

So.

Regarding the call from Night Watch . . .

He could let them handle the investigation until his tour began at eight or jump in now; Matty deciding to jump because the bar was so close to the crime scene he could see the fluttering yellow tape from where he stood. What would be the point of going home for only a few hours' sleep?

Besides, his sons had come down for a few days to stay with him and he didn't particularly like them.

There were two: the one he always thought of as the Big One, a jerk of a small-town cop in upstate Lake George, where his ex-wife had moved after the divorce, and the younger one, whom he naturally thought of as the Other One, a mute teen who had still been in diapers when they broke up.

He was at best an indifferent parent but didn't know what to do about it; and the boys themselves were pretty conditioned to think of him as a distant relative down in New York City, some guy obliged by blood to let them crash now and then.

Additionally, about a month earlier, his ex-wife had called to tell him that she was pretty sure the Other One was dealing weed at his high school. Matty's response was to call the Big One at his upstate precinct house; who said, "I'll take care of it," a little too quickly, Matty knowing then that they were in it together, and letting it be.

Better to keep working . . .

When he made it to the scene at 4:35, twenty minutes after the call, it was still dark, although the first bird of the day could be heard chittering in a low tree somewhere close, and the ancient tenement rooftops of Eldridge Street were beginning to outline themselves against the sky.

Directly beneath the streetlight in front of the building, a yellow plastic evidence cone was next to a spent shell, Matty guessing a .22 or .25, but the two bodies were gone: one whisked away by an ambulance, leaving an almost acrylic-bright runnel of blood worming its way to the curb; the other now upright and puking over the siding of a stoop a few doors south, his eyelids askew with liquor. A uniform stood babysitting discreetly downwind, smoking a cigarette.

Matty preferred his outdoor crimes to come about in the wee hours, the eerie repose of the street allowing for a deeper dialogue with the scene; and so he now pondered the shell casing, .22 or 25, thinking, Amateurs, 4:00 a.m. the desperado hour, the shooter or shooters young, probably junkies looking for a few bucks, didn't mean to use that piece of shit, now they'll hole up for a little, look at each other, "Oh, man, did we just . . . ," shrug it off, get high, then come back out for more, Matty telling himself, Look at who just got out, talk to Parole, to Housing, hit the dope spots, the dealers.

Nazir, one of the two Yemenis who worked the twenty-four-hour mini-mart, was back inside his store, sitting glumly behind his just-cracked front-window display of hangover-themed pharmaceuticals, the rarely used riot gate pulled down over the narrow door, Matty assumed, at the request of the cops.

He counted six uniforms, four sweatshirts, but no sport jackets.

Then Bobby Oh, the Night Watch supervisor who had called him, came out of the vestibule of 27 Eldridge.

"It's just you?" Matty asked, shaking his hand.

"I'm stretched like piano wire tonight," Bobby said. He was a short, trim middle-aged Korean with an all-business manner and hectic eyes. "We had a bar shooting in Inwood, a rape in Tudor City, a hit-and-run in Chelsea . . ."

". . . a Scout troop short a child, Khrushchev's due at Idlewild . . ."

". . . and a cop beaned with a marble up in Harlem."

"With a what?" Matty began scanning the street for surveillance cameras.

"Guy was a lieutenant." Bobby shrugged.

"So what's the story," pulling a steno pad from the inside of his jacket.

"Story is . . ." Bobby flipped open his own pad. "Three white males, after a couple of hours barhopping, last stop Café Berkmann on Rivington and Norfolk, walking from that location west on Rivington, then south on Eldridge, are accosted by two males, black and/or Hispanic in front of Twenty-seven here, one of whom produces a gun, says, 'I want all of it.' One guy, our witness, Eric Cash, hands over his wallet, then steps off. The second guy, Steven Boulware"—Bobby pen-pointed to the puker hugging himself on the stoop—"is so boxed, his response is to take a little power nap on the sidewalk. But the *third* guy, Isaac Marcus? *He* responds by stepping to the gunman, saying, quote, 'Not tonight, my man.' "

" 'Not tonight, my man,' " Matty marveled, shaking his head.

"Suicide by mouth. In any event, one shot," pen-pointing to the shell casing by the yellow cone. "Home run to the heart, the shooter and his partner book east on Delancey."

East on Delancey: Matty glancing towards the two possibilities, the multiple projects there or the subways, the Lower East Side too isolated, too Byzantine, for anybody other than local kids from the PJs or Brooklyn rollers taking advantage of the hop-on, hop-off BMT.

"Quality of Life shows up five minutes later, a bus from Gouverneur a minute after that, Marcus is pronounced on arrival, I talked to the doc myself."

"Got a name?" Matty head down, writing every word.

Bobby consulted his notes. "Prahash. Samram Prahash."

"Nine-eleven calls?'"

"Nope."

Matty continued to scan the street for security cameras, didn't think he'd find any, eyed the tenement windows, wondering how much of a canvass, if any, he could manage before the squad came in at eight. Despite the limbo hour, the block was alive with an intersection of two parties: the last of the young kids still on their way home from the lounges and music bars just like the homicide and his friends; and the pre-land-rush old-timers, the Chinese, Puerto Ricans, Dominicans, and Bangladeshi just starting their day, either leaning out those weathered stone windowsills or going off to work.

Many of the homebound kids lingered behind the tape, but the crime scene barely seemed to register on the ethnics, especially the undocumenteds, heading off for the market terminals, restaurants, and sweatshops around town.

The sky continued to almost imperceptibly lighten, the birds coming on in earnest now, dozens of them barreling low from tree to tree over the crime scene as if they were stringing beads.

Matty nodded towards Nazir in his quarantined shop, the guy smacking himself with frustration, both the kids ending their day and the workers starting theirs usually coming in for his bathwater coffee and a roll about now.

"Anybody talk to my man Naz?"

"The Arab? Yeah, me. Didn't see or hear shit."

Matty then gestured to the slack-lipped drunk on the stoop. "Boulware, you said, right? Why is he still here?"

"The EMTs said he's just intox."

"No, I mean why isn't he at the house?"

"We tried to get him over there, he threw up all over the back of two patrol cars, so I figured keep him around, flood him with coffee, see if he has something to say."

"And?"

"He's still so zotzed he's going to need a past-life regression therapist just to remember his name."

"Then I don't want him here. Can we get somebody to walk him over? It's only a few blocks. Maybe it'll clear his head. And the talker?"

"Cash? Around the corner in a squad car. I figured maybe you'd want to have him walk you through it, so . . ."

Night Watch tended to go light on the interviewing, not wanting to back somebody into a corner an hour before the local squad clocked in, handing over either a witness or a suspect already lawyered up before they could even get a crack at him.

Matty had made that mistake the first time he volunteered for the constantly revolving night pool, being too aggressive with a likely shooter, and the stony looks he got from the locals as he handed over a perp already with representation stayed with him for weeks.

"CSU coming?"

"About an hour out."

"Who else you call?"

"You, the bureau captain."

"Chief of Ds?"

"That's your call."

Matty checked the time, almost five. The chief of detectives got a daily 6:00 a.m. report, Matty wondering if this merited a one-hour-earlier wake-up call, then thought, white vic, dark-skinned shooter in this Candyland of a neighborhood: a media shitstorm if there ever was one.

"Yeah, have the Wheel call him now." Matty thinking, Cover your ass by covering his, then, "Wait, hold off on that," wanting at least an hour's clear work before everybody began breathing down his neck.

"And of course you had somebody notify the family."

"Gee, I was just about to, then you showed up."

It wasn't Oh's job, but . . .

A tap on the shoulder turned him to face a deliveryman, cigarette dangling, his arms filled with long brown bags of rolls and bagels.

Nazir slapped his broken window, extended his arms as if the guy were holding his children.

"May I?" The man obese, bearded, and bored, the smoke stream from the corner of his mouth curling directly into his eye.

Matty signaled for a uniform to let the guy make his delivery. "Then I want that gate down again."

Just as he was about to make some calls, wake a few of his own squad, two sedans rolled up, more Night Watch, down from Harlem, from Inwood.

"S'up, boss?" addressing Bobby.

"Matty?" Bobby deferring to the local.

He was being offered four, two men, two women, three of them Hispanic, which was lucky given where they found themselves. "OK, canvass," waving at the tenements, seeing now that some of the doors to the street were slightly ajar, probably jimmied that way permanently, a sign of Fujianese overcrowding, dozens of men crammed together in the same apartment, needing to come and go at all hours. "You know, as much as realistic. I don't think there's any street-facing security cameras around here, but maybe the subway cameras caught them if they booked to Brooklyn. The nearest station is Delancey and Chrystie, talk to the porters, the token clerk, you know the drill," then to Bobby, "Where's this other guy again?"

Matty stood hunched over, a hand on the roof of the patrol car in order to be on eye level with the victim/witness sitting motionless in the backseat.

"Eric?" As he opened the door, Eric Cash turned to him with shock-starred eyes. A slight tang of alcohol was in the air, although Matty was fairly certain that the kid had the drink chased out of him a while ago. "I'm Detective Clark. I'm very sorry for what happened to your friend."

"Can I go home now?" Eric said brightly.

"Absolutely, in a little bit. I was wondering though, it would be of tremendous help to us . . . Do you think you could maybe come back around the corner and show me exactly what happened?"

"You know," Eric continued to speak in that lively dissociated tone, "I always heard people say, 'I thought it was a firecracker going off.' And that's exactly what it sounded like. It's like, I don't remember how many years ago, I read this novel, whatever one, and the character is in some city and he witnesses a stabbing, and he says it was like the stabber, I'm paraphrasing here, the stabber just like, tapped the other guy on the chest with the knife, just a pat, really soft, and the stabbed guy just carefully laid himself down on the cobblestones and, that was it."

Eric looked at Matty, then quickly looked away. "That's what it was like, 'Pop,' so soft. And that was it."

Coming around the corner back onto Eldridge Street, Eric Cash did a little baby-step shuffle of distress when he saw the blood still there, Matty supporting him by the elbow.

Day was breaking faster now, fresh and soft, the street a madhouse of birds. A dawnish breeze made Nazir's tattered pennants snap above his shop as if they were strung from a mast, and the tenements themselves seemed to be rolling forward beneath the scudding clouds.

Every cop on the scene, every Night Watch, every plainclothes and uniform, was either on a cell phone calling in, calling out, calling up, or else feeding each other's steno pad; Matty always taken by that, how you could literally see the narrative building right before your eyes in a cross-chorus of data: names, times, actions, quotes, addresses, phone numbers, run numbers, shield numbers.

By now the La Bohèmers had mostly packed it in, but they were being replaced by another group, the video freelancers hopping out of vans, one of them even rolling up on a ten-speed bike, a police scanner lashed to his handlebars.

"OK," Cash began, wincing and tugging on his hair as if he had forgotten something critical. "OK."

"Take your time," Matty said.

Bobby Oh had stepped off to direct a canvass of those kids who remained on the scene, see if anything personal out here was keeping them from their beds.

"OK, so . . . We were walking across Rivington from Berkmann's, the three of us, heading for Steve's apartment here?" pointing to the tenement next to 27. "He was, we had to get him up there, he was shit-faced, I don't really know him, I think he went to college with Ike, I don't really know Ike either, and . . ." He started to drift, whirling a little as if looking for someone.

"And . . ." Matty nudged.

"And these two guys, they come out of the dark like two wolves, put a gun on us, say, 'Give it up.' And I'm, I immediately hand over my wallet, I had to let go of Steve to do it, he just flops to the sidewalk, but then Ike, I don't know, Ike, he like steps to them, says, 'You picked the wrong guy,' like he's ready to fight, then 'Pop,' just 'Pop,' and they're gone."

" 'You picked the wrong guy.' " Matty wrote it down. The kid had told Bobby Oh his friend said, "Not tonight, my man."

"They didn't say anything else?"

"I think one might have said, 'Oh.' "

" 'Oh'?"

"Like 'Oh shit,' then maybe the other said, 'Go.' "

"Nothing else?"

" 'Oh' and 'Go.' I think."

"And which way did they go."

"That way," pointing south. "But I'm not sure."

South now, not east, which is what he told Bobby. South presented a whole new set of projects but no subway stations, making the shooters local, most likely from the massive Clara Lemlich Houses. Unless this guy had been right the first time and they ran east . . .

Finished with their canvass, two Night Watch detectives exited the tenement directly across the street from the scene, one of them making slant eyes with her fingertips, i.e., crammed to the rafters with Fooks.

Matty saw Bobby Oh catch the gesture, his expression, Matty hating to admit it, inscrutable.

"And just one more time," he said to Cash. "Describe them for me?"

"I don't know. Black. Hispanic. I'm not trying to be racist, but in my mind? I close my eyes and see wolves."

Matty noticed that Nazir in his store was studying this guy as he spoke, giving him a hard eye.

"Other than wolves . . ."

"I don't know. Lean, they were lean, with a goatee."

"Both had goatees?"

"One of them. I think. I don't know, I was mostly looking down. Hey, listen," he said, unconsciously doing the Twist again as he blindly scanned Eldridge. "I already told all this to the Asian detective earlier, at this point my memory's getting worse, not better—"

"All right, look, this is got to be hard for you. I understand, but—"

"I didn't do anything *wrong*," his voice starting to break.

"No one said you did," Matty said carefully.

**44**

Nazir rapped on his window to get Matty's attention. He looked furious.

"Just bear with me, Eric. I know you want to catch these guys who shot your friend as much—"

"I *told* you, he isn't my friend. I don't even really know him."

Matty noted Eric's use of the present tense, wondered if this kid knew that Marcus was dead. Cash had yet to ask how the other guy, friend or not, was doing.

"Can you describe the gun at all?"

Eric sagged, took a deep breath. "I think it was a .22."

"You know your guns?"

"I know my .22s. My father made me take one when I moved to New York. I ditched it the minute I got here."

"OK," Matty said after a pause, "then what happened."

"What?"

"They shot Ike and ran off. Then what happened."

"I tried to call 911 on my cell, but I couldn't get any reception, so I ran into the, the vestibule there to try indoors."

"You ran indoors."

"It must've been dead altogether, so then I ran back out to the street to get help, and all of a sudden there's these four cops pointing guns at me." Eric took another breath. *"Huh."*

"What?"

"I just realized . . . I've had five guns pointed at me in the last two hours."


As a patrol car took a weakly protesting Eric Cash back to the Eighth Precinct, Nazir rapped angrily on his glass again, beckoned for Matty.

Bobby Oh said the guy hadn't seen anything, but the store was in Matty's bailiwick so he would give him a few minutes to complain about being shut down, rail about how he was going to make the city pay for his broken window.

As he stepped to the storefront, the Yemeni raised his riot gate from inside the shop.

"Nazir, Crime Scenes is a little backed up, but I'll have you opened as soon as I can, buddy."

"No. That too, but I want to tell you something. That son of a bitch you were talking to? Whatever he said to you, don't trust him. He's no damned good."

"Oh yeah?" Matty eyed the jagged branches of the window fracture. "Why is that?"

"We had the Virgin Mary in here yesterday, did you know that?"

"Yeah, I heard. Congratulations."

"Congratulations? That bastard came in with a friend and they wiped her out like this." He snapped his fingers. "Broke everybody's heart."

"Disappointed a lot of her fans, huh?" Matty said, then, glancing at his watch, "All right, boss, I'll get you open as fast as I can."

"Hold on," Nazir said, digging in his pocket and pulling out a cell phone. "This is what that bastard threw at my window," handing it over. "I'll be goddamned if I give it back to him."

Flipping it open, Matty discovered that not only was Eric Cash's phone fully charged, not only wasn't the last outgoing call to 911, but, as Matty scrolled down the Recent Calls screen, none of the others were either. When he pressed the send button, the phone rang through to the last number dialed, Café Berkmann, getting a recorded message at this nonhour, but the reception clear as a bell.

OK, maybe the guy in shock had just imagined he called. Or maybe there was a temporary power glitch, or a signal glitch. Or Matty hadn't heard him right, or . . .

Daley, one of the Quality of Lifers, a weight lifter made twice as big by the bulk of the vest under his sweatshirt, caught his eye and waved him over to where he stood with two kids, a tall, husky carrothead, his long frizzy hair pulled back in a bushy ponytail, and an equally tall black girl, slender as a gymnast, her chopped hair laquered down into pixie bangs.

"He's the guy you talk to." Daley gestured to Matty.

"What's up?" Matty asked.

"As I was just saying to this officer, me and my girlfriend were listening to that guy tell you what happened?" the redhead said. "In fact, we hung around specifically to hear what he was going to say because we were right here on this side of the street when it all went down."

"Hold on," Matty cut him off, then pointed out Oh in the crowd. "Tommy, can you get him over here?"

Daley made his way through the crowd as Matty rested his hand on the redhead's arm to keep him quiet until Bobby could come over and they could separate the couple. The kid seemed jagged with the hour but sober, his girlfriend a little jittery but clear-eyed too.

A moment later Matty was walking the kid around the corner, his girlfriend looking over her shoulder at him as Oh swept her along in the opposite direction.

"OK," Matty said when they were finally alone in front of a ramshackle *shteibel*, a Talmudic reading room on Allen. "What's up?"

"Like I said already, my girlfriend and I were right there when it all went down."

"When all what went down."

"The shooting."

"OK."

"What that guy said to you about two black guys, Dominican guys, or whatever coming up on them out of the blue?" The kid lit a cigarette, then blew a brisk stream. "He's a fuckin' liar."


At 5:30 a.m. Eric Cash rose stiffly from the back of the squad car and turned to face the Eighth Precinct station house, an octagonal Lindsay-era, siege-mentality fortress set down on razed lung-block acreage like a spiked fist aimed at the surrounding projects—Lemlich, Riis, Wald, Cahan, and Gompers—the rest of the neighborhood squat and dumpy and far east enough to be a world of pre-land-rush lasts: the last Hebrew old-age home, the last bulletproof liquor store, the last Chinese take-out hole in the wall, and the last live-poultry market, everything and everyone cast in permanent gloom beneath the massive stone arches of the Williamsburg Bridge.

As he was being escorted up the short steps to the main entrance, the front doors abruptly flew open, two EMTs luge-racing a gurney directly at him, then at the last moment taking a sharp left to hit the handicapped ramp along the side of the building, Ike's friend Steven Boulware looking up at him with sunken eyes, his head lolling with every bump and jostle.

• • •

At the same hour two Night Watch detectives crossed the chipped octagonal tile of the front foyer of 27 Eldridge, then began trudging up the saddle-backed marble stairs to the top floor to begin their canvass.

There were three apartments to a floor, each with its own paint-slathered century-old husk of a mezuzah, the front doors painted the same dull carmine as the embossed tin that lined the bottom half of the stairways from lobby to roof.

Each took a door, turning the ancient twist-knob ringers like tweaking a nose, the resulting sound tinny and minute. At first, no one responded on the top floor, but when they were halfway down the stairs to the next level, one of the tenants, a small Asian woman, by what anyone could see of her, peeked out through the crack of her door.

"Excuse me, ma'am?" Kendra Walker trotted back up the stairs, flashing her ID as she came.

It had been a warm night and she carried her sport jacket over her arm, revealing a male name tattooed beneath her fleshy shoulder in a script as jazzy as a team logo.

"Do you speak English?" she asked, talking as if volume enhanced comprehension.

"English?" the woman repeated.

Behind her, the cluttered apartment, lit by a lone overhead fluorescent halo, was not much more than a high-ceilinged single room with attached nooks and crannies.

"No English?"

"No." The woman couldn't take her eyes from Kendra's tattoo.

"That's my son's name," Kendra said, then saw the boy come out of a bathroom. "Hi." She smiled, the kid freezing in midzip. "Do you speak English?"

"Yes," he answered briskly as if a little insulted. He came to the door without prompting.

"Is this your mom?"

"My aunt," he said, then, "Kevin," reading Kendra's arm.

"What's your aunt's name?"

"An Lu."

"An Lu." Writing down *Lou*. "Can you ask her . . ." Kendra hesitated, the boy not more than ten or so. "There was a shooting downstairs a few hours ago. A man was killed."

"Killed?" He winced, baring his teeth.

"Could you ask your aunt if she saw—"

"How was he killed?" the kid asked.

An Lu turned from speaker to speaker without blinking.

"Like I said, he was shot."

"Shot?"

"Yes, shot," she said slowly. "Can you ask your . . ."

The kid translated to his aunt, the woman taking it in with a neutral expression, then turning to Kendra, she shook her head no.

"OK, can you ask her if maybe she heard anything?"

Again the boy translated, this time the woman having something to say.

"She heard people yelling at each other, but she doesn't speak English so . . ."

"These people she heard, what did they sound like, white, black, Spanish . . ."

Another quick exchange, then, "She says American."

"She wouldn't be able to pick out any words, maybe a name."

The kid waved off the question as hopeless. "Why don't you ask me?"

Kendra hesitated, no time for games, but if the kid maybe heard something . . .

"OK." Flourishing her pen like a baton, giving him a show. "What's your name?"

"Winston Ciu."

"OK, Winston Ciu. How about you? Did you see or hear something?"

"No," he said. "But I wish I did."


On the third floor the Dominican woman who came to the door jumped back, hand to chest, when she saw the detective standing there.

"Jeez, do I really look that bad?" Gloria Rodriguez said, patting her hair. "Sorry to bother you so early, but there was a shooting right outside."

"An hour ago," the woman said. She wore spin-rack reading glasses, a floral housedress, and vinyl slippers.

"You saw it?"

"Heard. I was in bed."

"What you hear?"

"Like a shot, shots."

"Which."

"One, like a firecracker, like 'pop pop.' "

"That's two."

"Yeah, no, just one."

Gloria could hear Kendra knocking on a door below her, getting a nibble.

"OK, so, you heard the shot, the pop. You look out the window?"

"No, I don't do that."

"You overhear any talking? Arguing?"

"I don't do that either. If I hear something? I don't listen."

"Maybe you couldn't help it. Maybe . . ."

"I heard arguing, maybe. Maybe I was dreaming it."

"What were they arguing about?"

"In my dream?"

"Sure."

"I don't remember my dreams."

Gloria looked at the woman. "You know there's still some bad people around here we're trying to get off the street."

"Good."

"You probably see them every day, right?"

The woman shrugged.

"Who am I talking about . . ."

The woman shrugged.

"Who's got a gun around here."

She tilted her chin to Gloria's hip. "You do."

On her way down the stairs, Gloria could hear another tenant also talking about an argument out on the street, but when she got to the floor, she saw that the person she was talking to wasn't Kendra but a reporter.


At a quarter to six, Bobby Oh stood across the street from the still-bustling crime scene with Nikki Williams, the redhead's girlfriend.

"I still can't believe, it's like, it's like your life. I mean all you have to do is walk down the wrong street . . ." The tall, slender kid was shivering, her eyes stark in her head.

"Nikki . . ."

"It was like nothing. It was like God snapped his fingers."

"Nikki"—Bobby gave a little wave—"you need to tell me what you saw."

"There's a famous line in this poem, 'the world will end not with a bang but with a whimper.' "

Bobby took a breath, spoke to her eyes. " 'This is the way the world ends. Not with a bang but a whimper.' "

Nikki stared at him with naked surprise.

"Now please, time is everything. Tell me what you saw."

She took a deep, shuddery breath, palmed her heart, followed the arc of a pigeon scouting the commotion.

"Nikki."

"OK. Me and Randal we were walking towards each other on Eldridge?"

"Towards each other?" Bobby cocked his head. "I thought you were together."

Nikki took a moment to smile at him. "How do you know T. S. Eliot?"

"The apes that raised me were surprisingly intelligent. So you were walking towards each other?"

"Well, yeah, I mean originally we had come around the corner from Delancey together, but I guess he stopped to light a cigarette or something and I didn't notice, because all of a sudden I'm halfway down Eldridge by myself, so I turned to see where he was and he had like, just rounded the bend *onto* Eldridge, which was when I started walking *back* to him, and on my way back, I saw three guys across the street

SPRINGDALE PUBLIC LIBRARY
405 South Pleasant
Springdale, Arkansas 72764

kind of in between us? They were just standing there, then all of a sudden I heard this sharp pop or snap sound and then there's like this flurry of movement like they were all jumping away from something, then two of them fell down and the third one ran into the building with something metallic in his hand."

"Metallic." Bobby needed to rear back a little, Nikki having a good four inches on him.

"I figured a gun because the two of them were laying there, but I just saw the shine of it in his hand, so . . ."

"And you first saw the three of them on your way back down to rejoin your boyfriend?"

"Yeah."

"Were they facing you?"

"No, more like with their backs to me, like facing the building."

"Did you see any other people with them?"

"I didn't. No one else on the street even, just Randal." Then: "I can't believe I'm just standing here like this," running her thumb lightly across the ridges of her lips.

"And how long would you say you were aware of them before you heard the shot?"

"I don't know. As long as it took to walk back towards Randal with him walking towards me? What's that, ten seconds? Twenty seconds? I don't have a very good sense of time."

"And were you watching them for all that time?"

"Not like, staring at them, just seeing them out the corner of my eye because it was just us and them out here."

"Did you happen to hear anything?"

"From them?"

"Yeah."

"You mean like conversation?"

"Anything. Conversation, random words, a name, some kind of outburst . . ."

"I don't think so. I would've remembered, I think."

"Some of the tenants around here said they heard arguing or shouting before the shot was fired. But you didn't hear anything?"

Nikki hesitated, cocked her head as if thinking something through;

began to say something, then said something else. "Did I offend you by acting so surprised that you knew that T. S. Eliot line?"

"Absolutely not," Bobby said. "So you didn't hear any arguing?"

"Not from them."

"What . . ." Bobby said.

"I mean, when those cops came out of that taxi a few minutes later with their guns out, they were shouting like crazy, you know, 'Police. Put it down. Don't fuckin' move. Drop the fucking gun.' *That* was pretty loud, and then the guy from that little grocery store came out, they broke his window, somebody did, and he was shouting pretty good too for a while. Maybe those people heard that, but, no, I didn't hear anything from those three guys."

"And you didn't see anybody else with them. Anybody that might have been facing them, maybe they were talking to . . ."

"No. I mean, like I said, I wasn't studying them, but no."

"And you and Randal, where were you relative to each other when the shot was fired."

"I would say I was right here," she said, hugging herself and staring down at her shoes. "And Randal was maybe by that building down there with the mermaid heads carved on it?"—pointing to a tenement maybe a hundred feet south, three doorways up from the corner with Delancey, two reporters standing there now, both on cell phones.

"I have a distinct mental picture of him and I walking towards each other with those three across the street between us so that we all made kind of a triangle, and then all of a sudden hearing that sharp pop and seeing the two of them fall away and the third guy with the silver in his hand run into the building. Next thing I know Randal's on top of me trying to push me down below this car," nodding to a parked Lexus. "Sir Galahad," she added drily.

"What's that?" Bobby smiled.

"Nikki, you OK?" A young couple still dressed in their evening clothes but carrying coffee and newspapers got in between Bobby and his interview as if he weren't there at all. The girl was blond, the boy light-skinned black like Nikki.

"I just saw someone get shot," she blurted.

"What?" the girl gasped.

"It was like nothing. It was like they slipped on ice."

"Yeah, well, that's how it is," the black kid said sagely, Bobby thinking, Straight Outta Scarsdale.

"Shot dead?"

Nikki leaned around her friend to get the answer from Bobby, who tapped his watch.

"I'll call you." Nikki stepped away from them.

"Be careful what you say," the boy murmured as they walked off.

"What?" Nikki looked after him. "Why?"

The boy cast a chary eye Bobby's way, then kept walking.

"Why?" Nikki looked anxiously to Bobby.

Bobby shrugged. "Your friend there watches too much TV. Why did you just call your boyfriend Sir Galahad like that?"

"Did what?" Still distracted, then pursing her mouth and staring over Bobby's head. "It's . . . I was joking."

Bobby gave it a second, was about to push for more, when the abrupt racket of a security gate going up over a storefront Buddhist temple made her levitate.

"Am I putting myself in any kind of danger talking to you?"

"None whatsoever," he said without blinking. "So where were you both coming from before you separated?"

"My girlfriend's birthday party at this club Rose of Sharon on Essex?"

"Were you drinking?"

"I can't. I'm allergic to alcohol."

"Were you altered in any other way?"

"Was I stoned?"

Bobby waited.

"I had a few tokes earlier, but way earlier, like midnight, and it was just to be sociable and so that everybody would get off my back for not drinking. So, four hours later?" She shrugged. "I was just tired."

"All right." Bobby nodded. "All right." Then, "Look, I'm obliged to ask. Have you ever had any history with the police?"

"Like, have I ever been arrested?" Cocking her head.

Bobby waited.

"Would you ask me that if I were white?"

"On something like this? I would ask you that if you were Korean."

"No, I haven't any history with the police," she said tersely. "Now. Can I ask *you* something?"

"Absolutely," Bobby said, his eyes on to the next thing.

"OK, it's like, the cops are pointing guns at you, and they're yelling for you to drop the gun, put it down, put it the fuck down, but they're *also* yelling for you to freeze. So, which one do you do?"

"Which do you think?" he said. "But slowly."

A moment later Matty came back from his interview around the corner with the boyfriend, Bobby seeing the new story in his eyes too.


The first order of business now was finding the gun Eric Cash had dumped. After putting in a request for a search team from Emergency Services to give 27 Eldridge a top-to-bottom toss, Matty went back to the squad room, sat quietly at his desk for a minute to gather himself, then started working the request lines for more manpower.

When he was done with that, he called Bobby back at the scene to have him steer Crime Scenes, if and when they ever showed up, directly to the precinct before processing the street. He then got up and glanced through the window of the interview room at Eric Cash, slumped with his cheek resting on the edge of the scarred table in there, an untouched cup of coffee inches from his face. Matty wanted CSU to come here first to give this guy a gunshot-residue test, without which, if he truly was the shooter and the murder weapon remained unfound, they could possibly be screwed, depending on how tough he would hang during the interviews; how quick he'd lawyer up.

Matty put a hand to the door, then backed off; let him stew.

Back at his desk he started to call his most immediate boss, Lieutenant Carmody, but hung up middial. The guy was supposed to be informed 24/7 whenever anything of this magnitude went down in the precinct, but he was new, would only get in the way, and wouldn't want to know about it anyhow.

Instead, he called Bobby Oh again.

"Where the fuck's CSU?"

"What can I tell you."

"No gun?"

"You'd know." Then, "You better call them."

Matty gave himself one last moment to breathe, to think of a bamboo forest or an alpine brook, whatever they might look or sound like, then put in the call to Crime Scenes, praying he wouldn't get the Goalie.

"Baumgartner."

"Yeah, hey, Sarge," Matty thinking, Fuck me, "this is Matty Clark, Eighth Squad? I have a homicide down here, a possible perp in custody but no gun, and I need a paraffin test."

"Homicide?"

"Yes."

"Confirmed?"

"Yes."

"At."

"Gouverneur's."

"Doctor's name?"

Matty checked his notes. "Prahash, Samram Prahash."

"And he's the perp why?"

"We have two wits."

"Any visible residue on clothing or hands?"

"I believe so, yes," Matty lied.

"What time was the shooting?"

Matty took a breath, knowing where this was going. "Roughly oh-four-thirty," making it later by half an hour.

"And what time is it now?"

Look at the fucking wall clock; Matty envisioning Baumgartner sitting there, the guy as big as a sea lion with a mustache to match.

"Sarge?" Baumgartner singsonged. "What time is it now?"

"Oh-six-thirty, about." Pedantic douche.

"All right," the Goalie sighed, "I'll have to reach out to my boss for this, but I'll tell you, as I'm sure you know already, once you're past two hours a paraffin test's inconclusive."

"Look," Matty said through his teeth, "when you get your boss on the horn, tell him that the chiefs are already all over this," he lied again. "Tell him we already have more news trucks than residents down there. Tell him we got a major shitstorm on our hands."

"All right," Baumgartner said, "I'll get back to you."

"Call me direct." Matty gave him his cell number.

"Name again?"

"Clark. Sergeant Matthew Clark. Eighth Squad."

At 7:00 a.m., two of Matty's detectives, Yolonda Bello and John Mullins, were at 2030 Henry Hudson Parkway in Riverdale, a white-brick twenty-five-story monstrosity overlooking the river with a near-primordial view of the Jersey Palisades. It was not Isaac Marcus's current address, that would be a five-man crash pad in Cobble Hill, an Our Gang, pot-stanky garden apartment in which none of his just woken roomies could even tell the detectives where Ike originally hailed from. Riverdale was the address on his driver's license, also home to a William Marcus, presumably the father or at least a blood relation.

The two cops assigned to the visit were chosen because the Riverdale address was pretty much on their way in to work: Yolonda living only three blocks away, Mullins ten minutes north in Yonkers. John tended to come off as an impassive hulk, not his fault really, but Yolonda, when in the mood, was the best at this, with huge liquid eyes that seemed perpetually on the verge of tears and a voice like a hug. When they identified themselves as detectives to the fortyish barefoot woman who met them at the door, she went from sleepy to irate in a heartbeat.

"Oh, for Christ sakes, did that psycho file a complaint or something?"

"What?" an alarmed teenage girl announced her presence in the dining alcove. "What do you mean a complaint. What's a complaint?"

"That kid had been beating the crap out of her all game and she got what was coming to her. The ref didn't even call a flagrant," the woman went at Yolonda. "*She* was the one tripping, throwing elbows, talking all kinds of shit, and there's a hundred witnesses that'll back that up. I mean, Jesus Christ, did you take a look at the *size* of her?"

The woman was wearing a carefully ripped pair of jeans and a freshly ironed white T-shirt.

"I go in today, I'm dead." The girl in a straight-out panic now. "I *told* you!"

"Calm down, Nina. Nobody's dead," the woman said, then turned back to the silent detectives. "This is complete and utter horseshit."

Whatever these two were talking about, it was either relevant or not, Yolonda thought, but it would have to keep for at least a few minutes.

"Does Isaac Marcus live here?" she finally asked.

"Isaac?" Yolonda's soft, apologetic tone immediately slowed the woman down. "No, he lives in Brooklyn I think." Then, "What do you want with Ike?"

"No way I'm going to school today," the girl moaned to herself.

"What do you want with Ike?" the woman repeated, her voice getting smaller.

"Are you his mother?"

"No. Yeah. No, no." Stark-eyed now, she began stepping in place, raised a finger like a saint. "I'm married. To his father. Remarried. What's wrong."

"I'm sorry, what's your name?"

"Mine?"

Yolonda waited, thinking, She's there already.

"Minette. Minette Davidson."

"Minette," Yolonda said, then without asking eased herself across the threshold and steered the woman to her own couch, Mullins following silently, his gaze straying to the prehistoric bluffs across the river.

Lost in her own panic, the young girl did everyone a favor by marching out of the dining area. A moment later a door slammed.

"Please," Minette said, an open-ended entreaty.

"Is his father home?" Yolonda asked, following the script.

"He's upstate."

Yolonda and John glanced at each other, *upstate* to them a euphemism.

"At a conference. He'll be back tonight. What is it . . . "

"Do you know how we can reach him?"

"Oh, *please!*"

Enough.

"Minette . . ." The woman tried to rise but Yolonda put a hand on her shoulder, then squatted on her haunches to be on eye level. "We have some really bad news."

Minette shot to her feet despite Yolonda's staying hand, then, not waiting for the details, swirled to the floor like a leaf.

Unwilling to leave Minette Davidson alone with her daughter, Yolonda called in to Matty, then she and John stayed in the apartment for the thirty minutes it took until Minette's sister finally showed up. During that time, no one approached the girl, oblivious behind her closed bedroom door.

According to Yolonda via the guy's wife, a high school Spanish teacher at a prep school in Riverdale, the dead kid's father worked for Con Ed, a project manager on toxic remediation sites, whatever the hell those were, and was currently up at a Marriott near Tarrytown for a two-day seminar on hot-spot removal, whatever the hell that was.

Matty was about to ring the Tarrytown PD to request a notification when Kendra Walker, one of the Night Watch detectives, came in to use the bathroom, her belt half-undone before she even knew where it was located.

"That way." Matty pointed from his desk. "Hey, did CSU ever show?"

"Yeah, they just got there when I was leaving. Bobby's talking to them now, trying to get 'em to come by for that GSR test you wanted? But I think I heard one guy say they never got an order to do that, so . . ."

"Never *what*?"

"Yeah, sorry there, Sarge." Kendra shrugged and headed for the bathroom.

"Baumgartner."

"You talk to your boss yet?"

"Who's this?"

"Matty Clark, Eighth Squad."

"He gets in at eight."

"I thought you were gonna reach out for him right after we talked?

*Eight?* You didn't tell me that." Matty tried to curb his anger, there being no percentage in pissing off this guy, who would only put you at the back of the line the next time you needed CSU fast.

"Well, I can tell you right now what he's gonna say." Baumgartner chewing something. "Which is that for something like this, the request's got to come from higher up than you, division captain at least."

"Hey"—Matty grinning with rage—"couldn't you tell me that the first time? You know, with us playing beat the clock here?"

"I'm just telling you how it is."


"This better be good." The voice of Mangini, the division captain, came over the line like crusted glue.

"Cap"—Matty wincing—"Matty Clark from the Eighth, are you up?"

"Am now." Mangini coughed.

"Sorry there, boss. What time you due in?"

"Noon."

"Yeah, we have a situation down here, a homicide, we maybe got the shooter, two eyewits say he's the shooter, but we haven't found the gun as yet, and I need CSU to do a paraffin test."

"So?"

"I need a boss to make the call."

"The fuck, it's not even seven yet."

"It's seven-thirty. The thing is, I need this done now, it's already going on three and a half hours."

The captain abruptly smothered his receiver, Matty stuck paradiddling a pencil on his blotter as he endured the muffled halftones of Mangini arguing with his wife, whom he had probably just woken up by taking this call in bed.

"All right, what?" The cap back on the line.

"How about this . . ." Matty sitting there, palms up and out. "How about I have one of my guys call over there and just *say* they're you."

"Sure, whatever." Then, "Wait. For a paraffin test?"

"Yeah."

"Didn't you just tell me you got two eyewits?"

"I did, but—"

"Then what do you need a paraffin test for?"

"Because I want one. Because I'm thinking better safe than sorry."

The cap sighed. Matty envisioned him lying there, his hair sticking up against his pillow.

"All right, look." Mangini coughed, sniffed. "You want to do me a favor? Call the DI for this, clear it with him."

"Berkowitz?" Matty pinching his brows. "What time's he get in?"

"Eight, about."

With bosses, eight could mean eight, could mean nine, could mean ten; ten o'clock, six hours after the shooting.

Matty hung up, rang up Deputy Inspector Berkowitz, got the machine, left his situation and cell number, and that was all he could do.

He got up to check on Eric Cash again, then stopped, what was he forgetting . . .

Sitting back down, he finally called the Tarrytown cops to notify Isaac Marcus's father at his hotel, although by now the guy's wife in Riverdale had to have given him the news.

No one had a clue as to where to find the kid's mother.

The moment he hung up, his cell went off, Matty hoping for Berkowitz, for Bobby Oh.

"Hey, Matty." The squad boss, Carmody, on the line. "I was just watching the news. What the hell's going on down there?"

"Yeah, hey, Lieutenant, I didn't want to bother you, we got it under control."

"You need me to come in?"

"We're good, boss, thanks."

"All right, call me if something changes."

"Absolutely, boss."

From his desk he saw Eric Cash being escorted to the bathroom, walking from the interview room as if he should be wearing an open-backed hospital gown.


At seven-thirty, roughly three and a half hours after the murder, the redheaded witness, Randal Condo, was, for the third time since coming forward, once again standing across the street from 27 Eldridge, this time with Kevin Flaherty, an assistant district attorney from the Prosecutor's Office.

". . . the three of them arm in arm in arm like a chorus line. They were right under the streetlight. It was like they were on a stage."

By now the crime scene was down to the tape, a bloodstained sidewalk, a pair of discarded inside-out surgical gloves, and a scatter of lesser reporters like boys at a dance trying to figure out the best way to approach the prosecutor and the witness across the street.

"They were facing you?" The ADA, a still-young ex-cop, offered up some gum, his now regrettably tattooed wrist, a trompe l'oeil ring of barbed wire, peeking out from beneath his stiff white shirt cuff like a bracelet.

"No, with their backs to me. I was walking up from the corner towards Nikki."

"Your girlfriend."

For a brief moment they both took five as a tall blond girl on a bicycle stopped directly in front of them to watch the action, the tattoo at the base of her spine drifting up from the ass of her jeans like blue smoke.

"Your girlfriend," Flaherty repeated.

"Yeah, and she was walking down towards me and they were like in between us, across the street, so . . ."

"You hear anything they said?"

"Not really." Randal shielded his eyes from the daylight, their whites now as red as his hair.

"A lot of people on the block said they heard arguing."

"I didn't hear any, maybe Nikki did. Anybody giving her the third degree?"

"I'm sure they are. So, arm in arm in arm, backs to you . . ."

"Yeah, and we were coming at each other, me and Nikki, then a shot goes off, the guy in the middle like, crumples to the ground, the guy on the left falls straight back with his arms out, and the third guy runs into the building."

"Did you see a gun?"

"No, at that point Nikki and I kind of met from where we both started walking towards each other, fortunately, and I just went on automatic pilot, you know, pulling her down right behind this car here," touching the passenger door of a battered Lexus, "so I wasn't looking."

"So you never actually saw a gun."

"No, but I'm pretty damned sure as I was walking towards Nikki I saw the guy that ran into the building raise his arm beforehand, and I bet you the dead guy had a bullet in him."

"And you didn't see anybody else with them."

"Nope. Just those three."

"Just those three." The ADA popped some gum. "Any people walking by?"

"Nobody here but us chickens."

"But who?"

"It's a song."

The ADA stared at him.

"Never mind." Condo looked off, half smiling then. "No. No other people."

"And nothing was blocking your view, no parked cars, no moving traffic."

"It was like a ghost town."

The ADA took a beat to shift gears, the both of them watching as a gray-haired Chinese woman carrying two plastic bags of vegetables walked obliviously through the blood.

"I understand you overheard that guy telling the detective his version of what happened."

"I did."

"So you know he's claiming two black or Hispanic guys did the shooting."

"Yeah, well, what did you expect him to say?"

"How do you feel about that?"

"You're asking me that why, because my girlfriend's black?"

Flaherty waited.

"Are you asking me if I would lie and try to screw some guy because he's a knee-jerk racist? Or are you asking me if I would lie to cover for two scumbags because they're the same color as the woman I sleep with?"

"Either."

"Neither."

"Just between us." The ADA waved off a reporter before he could even get halfway across the street. "Walking around here four in the morning, you weren't stoned or anything?"

"I haven't gotten high in nine months."

"Have anything to drink?"

"Why are you asking me all this like I'm the bad guy?"

"Better me than a defense attorney, trust me. Have anything to drink?"

"A few beers." Condo shrugged. "These days? Basically, I'm into clarity."

"You ever been arrested?"

Randal stared at him. "I have two master's degrees, one from the Berklee College of Music, the other from Columbia University."

The ADA shielded his eyes from the sun again. "So, were you or weren't you?"

Thirty minutes later, back in the squad room, the ADA stole a peek at Randal's girlfriend, Nikki Williams, through the three-quarter-lowered venetian blinds of the otherwise vacant lieutenant's office as she waited for someone from the Prosecutor's Office to take her through it again.

"The guy was pretty confident," he said. "How was the girl?"

Matty shrugged, folded his arms across his chest. "Bobby Oh says solid. Sober, good sight lines, says she saw everything out the corner of her eye beforehand because they were the only ones on the street. So it was like, peripheral, bang, focus, see two down, one running into the building with something in his hand. Plus apparently they were walking towards each other, him up from Eldridge and Delancey and her coming down Eldridge towards Delancey, so it was two completely different angles of vision, so . . ."

"Yeah, that's what he said. She hear any arguing?"

"Nope," Matty said. "No arguing."

"So what's with everybody hearing arguing except these two?"

"I don't know." Matty shrugged. "New York at night, ambient noise, or maybe what everybody heard was Lugo and his crew yelling afterwards, or the Arab bugling about his broken window, you know, got their timelines all inside out."

"And how was Lost Weekend boy?"

"Boulware? Useless," Matty said. "They wound up taking him to Gouverneur to pump his stomach."

"So where's this Cash guy now?"

"Here." Matty steered the ADA down the corridor to the observation nook outside the interview room, where they could see Eric Cash once again slumped over the edge of the table, his forehead resting on his forearm.

Flaherty glanced at the wall clock: 8:00.

"You have a go at him yet?"

"No. I want to do him with Yolonda."

"Learn from the master, huh?"

"Get fucked," Matty said without heat. "She's on her way in from making the notification."

"I understand he's got a little something of a sheet?"

"Took a collar about six years ago up in Broome County for slinging coke," Matty said. "Drew a suspended sentence. I'm not sure what to make of it."

"He didn't ask for a lawyer?"

"Didn't even ask to make a phone call." Matty put his hands in his pockets, suddenly so tired he could feel the dewlaps growing along his jawline. "It would be nice if I had some notion of a motive."

"So go in and get one," the ADA said.

"Nice to have that gun in hand too."

"Sarge." One of the fresh day-tour detectives waved him in from the hall. "Deputy Inspector Berkowitz, line three."

"I agree, better safe than sorry," Berkowitz said. "On the other hand, with your two wits, it sounds like you got a slam dunk on your hands."

"No, I hear you." Matty starting to fade on the paraffin request as the hours piled on. "I'm just saying, if we can't find that gun . . ."

"You go at him yet?"

"Going in now."

"Is he hard? Soft?"

"My gut says soft, but . . ." There was no real eyeball test for that; some of the roughest-looking ghettoheads would cry like a baby after one go-round in there, and the creamiest of college boys wind up giving you a thousand-yard stare that could bore through a mountain.

"All right, look, how about this," Berkowitz said. "Go in, see what you got on your hands, and if you still feel like you need the test, it's probably not a bad idea, so call my boss, let him reach out for you."

"Upshaw?" Matty's face hurt.

"Upshaw."

Thinking, Fuck the first go-round, Matty rang Upshaw, the chief of Manhattan detectives, got the machine, sang his song, and hung up.

A moment later he dragged his ass back into the hall and sang his song to Kevin Flaherty.

"Well, gun, no gun, test, no test, I'll tell you right now what *my* boss is gonna say." The ADA studied Cash though the glass. "How often do we get two eyewits to a murder?"


A moment later Yolonda Bello came bustling into the room. "Hey, Kevin!" Stepping to the ADA and hugging him. "What are you, lifting weights now?" Taking a step back and palming his pecs. "You look so good." Then to Matty: "Doesn't he look good? I always tell him when I first came on the job I used to ball his old man, he never believes me."

When Yolonda went on like this, Matty just smiled politely until it ran its course.

"So, OK, I talked to the dead kid's father's wife, it was pretty rough, they have this other kid, cute, the vic's half sister or something. Mullins is gonna bring them down when they can get their shit together. So . . ." Rubbing her hands as she peered through the blinds. "What do we got in there. Hard? Soft?"


"You all right, Eric?" Yolonda led the way into the interview room, she and Matty taking seats on either side of him. "You need anything? Coffee, soda, a sandwich? There's this new Cuban takeout right on Ridge . . ."

"I feel like I should be cuffed to that," he murmured, turning to eye the low steel restraint bar that ran the width of one short cinder-block wall.

"Oh yeah?" Matty said mildly, looking down and smiling as he shuffled his notes. "Why would you feel that?"

"I don't know." Eric hunched his shoulders and looked away.

"Listen to me," Yolonda said, putting her hand atop his and giving him the big soul-eye. "You need to know that what happened wasn't your fault. You guys were out having a good time, you got a little drunk, but you didn't do anything wrong, OK? The guy who did it? Did it."

"OK," Eric said. "Thank you."

"All right. First off, we need another description of the actors from you as best, and in as much detail, as possible."

"Ah, Jesus," he softly wailed, "I did that at least three times already." His eyes were puffed blisters.

"I know, I know." Yolonda touched her fingertips to her temples as if the request were driving her mad too. "But sometimes the more you go over something, details just pop out of nowhere, OK? I cannot *tell* you how often we've sat at this table with some witness or other going over it, over it, over it, and then all of a sudden it's 'Oh yeah, oh wait, oh my God.'"

"All the time," Matty said.

"OK." Eric nodded at his own clasped hands. "OK."

"Look, the fact of the matter is the tip line's been ringing off the hook on this," Matty lied. "Plus these guys, they booked on foot, no car, so we're definitely talking local hood rats, probably holed up somewheres in the projects, ESU's already going through doors, all of which is to say that there is no doubt in my mind that they're as good as got. But, Eric." Matty's turn to get in his eyes. "Here's what we worry about . . . According to you, they're armed, and that kind of foreknowledge puts cops in a whole different kind of headset, can make them a little too quick on the draw, you know what I'm saying? And if they come up on some unlucky stiff out there fits the vague description and that guy should make a quick move for his wallet, his ID, his green card—"

"Wait." Eric sat up, a vein pulsing in the hollow of a temple. "According to *me* they're armed? Like maybe they weren't?"

"No, no, no, Eric." Yolonda again. "What he's saying is you're our only eyewitness, ESU's out there based on *your* words, and we need as precise a description as possible because no one wants to draw down on the wrong guy and God forbid we have a tragedy on our hands."

"OK."

"Think what almost happened to you when you came busting out of that building just holding a cell phone."

"OK."

"Those cops would have to live with that the rest of their lives. As would the poor guy's family. As, I hate to say it, would you."

"No, yeah, OK."

"So . . . Two guys."

"Yes."

"Both black?"

"Black and/or Hispanic, one guy a little lighter than the other, but I don't know for sure."

"Which one had the gun?"

"The lighter one."

"The one you think was Hispanic?"

"I guess so."

"Gun was a .25?"

"No," Eric said carefully. "I already told you. It was a .22."

"Hang on." Matty fingerwalked his notes. "Right. And you knew that because"—squinting, rearing back from his own writing—"your dad made you take one with you when you moved to New York?"

"Yes." Eric's tone increasingly wary.

"But you got rid of it as soon as you got here."

"As soon as I got here." Eric's body began to settle in on itself like a slow leak.

"I'm just, how'd you go about doing that?"

He took a beat to study their faces. "This precinct right here was running a cash-for-guns drive back then. I gave it to you, you gave me a hundred bucks, no questions asked."

"No questions asked," Matty repeated, Eric looking at him.

"I'm glad *some*body took advantage of that thing," Yolonda said, capping a yawn.

"OK, so. The guy with the .22 . . . Is there anything other than relative skin tone that made you think he was Hispanic rather than black?"

"I don't know." Eric shrugged. "Why does someone strike you as Irish rather than Italian?"

"Because they'd rather drink than fuck," Yolonda said.

Startled by the blunt profanity, Eric turned to Matty as if waiting for him to wink or toss off a second quip, but Matty just kept staring at him as if Yolonda had commented on the weather.

"Hispanic was just an impression I got," Eric finally said. "Nothing specific."

"OK, well, maybe we can help you here." Yolonda's turn. "The shooter. What kind of hair did he have? Straight, shaved, kinky"—then reaching out to touch his—"curly like yours."

"I don't remember." Flushing at her touch.

"How about facial hair?" Matty asked.

"I think I said a goatee. It's in your notes."

"Forget my notes. Close your eyes and see it again."

Eric dutifully did as he was told and immediately drifted off into a hypnagogic limbo. Yolonda and Matty looked at each other.

"Eric," Yolonda softly saying his name, and he quivered back to the moment. "You OK?"

"What." Wiping his mouth.

"How about clothes."

"Clothes?" Fighting for alertness. "I don't know. What did I say. Hoodies?"

"Both had hoodies?"

"I don't know. One did."

"What color?"

"Darkish, black or gray. I'm, I don't . . ."

"Any words?"

"Words?"

"On the chest, the sleeves."

"I don't know."

"Slogans, logos, graphics?"

Eric shook his head, stared at his knotted fingers.

"Shoes? Sneakers?"

"Sneakers, I think. Yeah. Sneakers, white sneakers." All the way back now. "I don't know brands or styles or whatever? But definitely white sneakers."

Matty leaned back in his chair, intoned, "Male black or Hispanic in a dark hoodie and white sneakers," making a show of massaging his forehead as if another Diallo were a gimme.

"You have to understand," Eric said, offering them his upturned hands. "When I saw that gun, I handed over my wallet *purposely* not looking at him. I kept my eyes *down*, because I didn't want him getting worried that I would remember his *face*. I didn't want to *die*."

"That's very clever of you," Matty said.

"Clever?" Eric looked slapped.

"As in street-smart," Yolonda said quickly.

"At least we're clear on how you remembered the footwear," Matty said.

The crack made Eric flinch, Yolonda glaring at Matty; way too early for that; but it was just a probe, Matty wanting to confirm his impression that the guy, for some reason, found his calculated displeasure near unbearable.

"All right, so you didn't see much," Yolonda said, still eyeing Matty. "But you couldn't shut down your hearing, right? So . . . When he spoke, what kind of accent did you hear, Nuyorican, black, foreign . . ."

"I have no idea."

"And what did he say again exactly?" Matty asked.

"Please," Eric begged. "Just look at your notes."

"I thought we were going to forget my notes."

"Eric?" Yolonda ducking and bobbing to find his eyes. "You want to take a breather?"

"Look," Matty said, "I'm sorry if I sound persistent or aggressive or however I'm coming off to you, but like I told you before, repetitive questioning—"

"Sometimes stirs new memories, and you're racing the clock out there with a too vague description," Eric near-snapped at the table. "I'm *try*ing, OK?"

There was an unnerving moment of silence, Yolonda half-smiling as if she were proud of him, Matty frowning as he made a show of reluctantly opening his pad.

"I'm trying," Eric repeated in a smaller, more apologetic voice.

"We can see that," Yolonda said.

"OK, you told me he said"—Matty squinted at his own scrawl— " 'Give it up'?"

"If that's what I said."

"Not"—checking his notes again—" 'I want all of it'? Which is what you told Night Watch."

"Whatever I said he said," Eric pleaded.

"And then your friend Ike said to him, 'You picked the wrong guy'?"

"Ike? Yeah. Yes."

"Or did he say, 'Not tonight, my man,' because once again, you gave us two different versions."

Eric stared at Matty.

"Any other exchanges come to mind?" Yolonda said.

"No."

"Between Ike and the bad guys, the bad guys among themselves . . . anything. Words, threats, curses . . ."

"No."

"Don't just say no," Matty said. "Think for a minute."

"You mean like 'Hey, Jose Cruz!' 'Yeah, Satchmo Jones?' 'Let's shoot this guy, then throw the gun down that sewer at the corner of Eldridge and Delancey, after which we'll withdraw to our hideout at 433 . . .' " Eric cut himself off, looking suddenly winded.

They stared at him.

"Sorry," he said, his lids turtling down.

"This must be like a nightmare for you," Matty said.

"I'm so tired." Eric looked at them with ragged eyes. "When can I go home?"

"I promise, soon as we get to the bottom of this?" Yolonda said in her mournful voice. "You are out of here."

"Bottom of *what* . . ."

"Let's talk a little more about the actual shooting."

Eric cupped his temples, stared bug-eyed at the table.

"The guy who throws the shot."

"What?"

"Shoots," Yolonda said.

"Yes."

"How was he holding the gun?"

"How?" Eric closed his eyes and, after a moment's hesitation, extended his arm, his gun hand turned sideways, his elbow slightly higher than his shoulder, so that the bullet would have a downward trajectory.

"That gangsta style from the movies?" Matty asked.

"I guess, yeah."

The coroner would verify the accuracy of that.

"OK. Then what."

"They take off."

"They take off. And you did what."

"Me? I tried to call 911."

"From where exactly."

"First I tried right on the sidewalk, but I couldn't get any reception, which I told you before, so I ran into the building to try in there."

"No luck?"

"No."

"But you definitely tried. Punched in 911?" Matty asked.

"Yes." Searching their faces. "Of course."

"How long would you say you were in the building for?"

"I don't know. As long as it took to try a few times?"

"A few times."

"Yes."

"So, guess."

"A minute?"

"A minute," Matty echoed, thinking of all the possibilities for stashing a small gun in a broke-down walk-up with sixty seconds at your disposal.

"And where in the building were you exactly?"

Again, with each new question, Eric's responses became both more tentative and more alert.

"In the lobby, you know, the ground-floor hallway."

"Anyplace else?"

Eric faltered then. "Maybe up the stairs."

"Up the stairs? Why would you go up the stairs?"

"To see if I could possibly get better reception higher up?" The exhaustion leaving his eyes altogether.

"Do you know anybody in the building?" Yolonda asked.

"No." Eric again looking from face to face.

"I'm just asking," she said, "because most buildings, the street doors are locked, so unless you know someone to buzz you in, or . . ."

"Well, this one was open."

"OK."

"Probably a boat building."

"A boat building?"

"You know, two hundred Chinese guys sharing an apartment, you have to keep the front door open or make a million keys."

"A boat building." Matty turned to Yolonda. "I never heard that one before."

The door opened, Fenton Ma, cap in hand, popping his head in.

"Excuse me, I'm looking for the witnesses they brought in on the shooting last night?"

"Who, him?" Yolonda chucked a thumb.

Ma recognized him, Matty could tell, his expression of naked surprise making Eric Cash feel both humiliated and lost.

"No," Ma said. "The, the Chinese people from the canvass? I'm supposed to interpret, they said to check with you."

"We don't have them." Yolonda shrugged.

"They're somewheres around," Matty said. "Ask the desk."

"All right." Ma giving Eric one last look. "Thanks."

"Canvass came up with a couple of people in some of the buildings near 27 Eldridge claimed they saw the whole thing from their windows," Yolonda said.

Eric didn't respond, most likely, Matty thought, either too busy rejigging his story or still lost in the Chinese cop's eyes.

"My guess, however," Matty said, "is the most we'll get out of them are aerial head counts, you know, how many people were there when the shot went off."

"That would be five, right?" Yolonda said.

"Yes," Eric said carefully, "that would be five."

"Good," Matty said, then settled into himself without losing eye contact, as if it were Eric's obligation to keep the conversation going.

"I didn't think . . ." Eric finally said just to say something. "Can you guys just barge in on each other in rooms like this?"

"Why not?" Yolonda shrugged. "It's not like we're in the middle of an interrogation or anything."

A knock on the door brought round one to an end, a detective waiting for Matty's "Yeah" to stick his head in.

"Sarge, Chief Upshaw?"

Leaving Yolonda to small-talk her way out of the interview room, Matty eyed the time as he walked to his desk: 9:00. Five hours since the shooting, not great in regards to the test, but . . .

"Yeah, hey, Chief, thanks for getting back to me." Matty taking the call standing up in order to stay up.

"What's this about a paraffin test?" The chief of Manhattan detectives not sounding too happy.

"Well, here's what we got—"

"I know what you got, and the answer's no."

"Chief, it's only been five hours, we still have a shot at a positive, otherwise . . ."

"Well, at this point, if in fact he is the shooter, which with your two wits it sounds like he is, you got a better chance of getting a false negative."

"Boss—"

"False negatives, false positives, too easy to screw up a case from the door on in. Look, the bottom line here is that Chief Mangold doesn't trust that test under the best of circumstances. Any of those others you talked to before me this morning could have told you the same."

Matty and Yolonda stood behind one-way glass watching Eric Cash work with a tech on the digital photo manager, Eric staring pie-eyed at the computerized mug shots coming up on the screen six at a time.

"Bottom line?" Matty said. "Mangold hates the test, wouldn't've OK'd it two minutes after the shooting. Baumgartner, Mangini, Berkowitz, Upshaw, it was like the pass-the-buck Olympics."

"Fuck it." Yolonda shrugged, studying Cash through the window. "He was like a cornered rat in there."

"Or like he didn't know where we were coming from," Matty said.

"Right. What I said."

"Well, he's lying about calling 911."

"No kidding."

"I don't know. Maybe he was in shock and just thought he did."

"Thought he tried it over and over?" she said.

"Can I be honest with you?" Matty began, then let the rest of it go.

"He never asked how Marcus was doing," Yolonda said. "Or did I miss that."

"No, he didn't."

"He doesn't know the guy's dead, does he?"

"I don't think so," Matty said.

"Good." Then, "Check it out," tilting her chin at Eric, his eyes at half-mast as he sat slightly rocking before the computer screen. "He's not even looking at the thing."

"Let's just go nice and easy until they find the gun," Matty said.

Fenton Ma stepped to them, his cap in his hand. "Was I OK?"

"You were great," Matty said. "Thank you."

"You were so convincing, you should be an actor," Yolonda said, looking into his eyes. "Matty, don't you think he'd be a great actor?"

"It looked like you recognized him in there," Matty said.

"Yeah, Eric something. Works at that restaurant nobody can get a table at over on Rivington." Then, rearing back a little, "*He's* the perp?"

"We're just talking," Matty said. "Anything you can tell us about him?"

"Let me jump the line once with my girl." Ma shrugged. "Good guy by me."

"Well, like I said, we're just talking."

"Thanks again," Yolonda said.

Ma continued to stand there.

"What?" Matty said.

"Just . . ." Ma fidgeted. "So, there *are* no Chinese witnesses, right?"

"And so handsome too," Yolonda said, patting his cheek.


"You catch anybody?" Eric Cash asked almost listlessly as Matty and Yolonda walked back into the room thirty minutes after they had left him.

"Not as yet," Matty said, dropping into his chair.

Whether it was the tediousness of the photo manager or just the interlude itself, the guy seemed transformed: emotionally flattened and near-agog with fatigue.

Matty had seen that before in here; sometimes the first go-round did no more than set up the physical and mental plummet of the break, which in turn yielded a much less artful customer for round two; it was the interrogation equivalent of rope-a-dope.

"Eric?" Yolonda briefly covered one of his hands. "We need for you to run us through the night."

"To what?" He raised his eyes to her as if they were attached to sinkers. "From when?"

"I don't know. From knocking off work, say."

"From *me* knocking off work?"

"Why not?"

Eric hesitated, then, with his forehead supported by a splay of fingers, he addressed the tabletop before him. "I don't know, I left Berkmann's at eight, went home, took a shower, then I went to this coffeehouse on my corner."

"Which one?" Yolonda asked.

"Kid Dropper's on Allen. You know, everybody's in there with a big mug and a laptop. Except me, I like a martini after work. They have a bar, so . . ."

"What time are we talking?"

"Eight-thirty, eight-forty-five? They were having some kind of open-mike thing in the back room. I take a look and I see Ike at the podium, and he's reading."

"Reading out loud?" Yolonda asked.

Eric stared at her. "That's what the microphone was for."

"What was he reading?"

"I guess it was poetry because it had that pronouncement thing, you know, where you say each word like you're angry at it?"

"OK," Matty said, clocking the new tone.

"I just looked around, then went to the bar up front, had my drink, and a half hour later there's this big clapping and everybody comes out of the back room. Ike sees me at the bar, says he's going over to the Congee Palace with his buddy for dinner, do I want to come."

"So you're friends?"

"With Ike? No. I told you that. We just work under the same roof."

"So you never hung out before?" Matty asked.

"No . . . But so I go with him, it's him, me, and that guy Steve that, that was with us last night." Eric faltered, his jaw working.

"What," Yolonda said.

"Nothing."

"So . . ."

"So . . . We go over to the Congee on Allen." Eric hesitated, working his jaw again. "I mean that asshole was already half-wasted at the reading. And who the hell orders mojitos at a Chinese restaurant?"

"You're talking Ike?"

"No. Steve . . . *Stevie*." The fatigue starting to lead now, as it often did, to a sloppy, sullen candidness.

"What time was this?"

"Nine-thirty or so."

"What did you guys talk about?"

"Me? I didn't say much. But they're all irons in the fire, like, apparently Steve had just gotten a callback for a movie, right? His first callback, you know, like next stop the Oscars, then it's Ike's turn, gonna start up some online literary magazine, raise money for a documentary, we're all gonna collaborate on a screenplay, la-la, la-la, the usual bullshit." Matty and Yolonda solemnly nodding, neither of them wanting to stem the flow.

"Anybody have problems with anybody?" Matty asked.

"You mean between them?"

"Between them, you, anyone else . . ."

Eric hesitated. "No."

"What was that." Yolonda smiled.

"What was what," he said, then, "I just get so fucking tired of hearing all of that, you know? Everybody's big plans around here."

"Sure."

"I have mine too, you know. I just don't . . ."

"Don't . . ."

Eric held up a hand, turned profile to the table.

"So where'd you go next?"

"Next?" Eric's voice suddenly bright with anger. "*Steve*, because he wasn't quite hammered enough, took us to this top-secret bar on Chrystie. You're supposed to have a reservation, but if you have any kind of name down here, they just let you in. I didn't think either one of them would have even heard of it."

"How'd that go?" Matty asked, thinking they had to have been there and gone before his own shift.

"Well, they both started drinking absinthe. And I got a little lecture about how it isn't real absinthe unless it's from Czechoslovakia, and how even if it was from Czechoslovakia, it had to have wormwood in it or tapeworms or whatever . . ."

"You sound like you weren't having a very good time with these guys," Yolonda said.

"I don't know. Sometimes it feels like everybody I know down here went to the same fucking art camp or something." Eyes brimming, he stared at his hands, then added as if ashamed, "Ike was OK."

"So the top-secret bar was from when to when?" she asked.

"We were out of there probably by eleven or so."

"Everybody still getting along?"

"Yeah, I guess. I think I told you they got their MFAs together something like three months ago, now Steve's all night, I'm not moving to L.A., man, L.A.'s ass. New York feeds me, feeds my soul. They want me, they gotta come *here*. And I'm *not* doing any studio bullshit.'

"And Ike's like, 'And I'm not writing any.'

"Then everybody, all together now, 'I'll fuckin' *starve* first, man.'

"I mean, what are they, two years old? Christ, he got one fucking callback. Do you have any idea how many . . ."

The room was a silent for a beat, Yolonda nodding in sympathy.

"What's an MFA again?" Matty asked.

"Master of fine arts."

"Right."

"So then where'd you go after that?" Yolonda asked.

"After that it was Ike's turn, he took us to some poetry bar on the Bowery, beatnik bar, or something."

"What's it called?"

"Zeno's Conscience."

"They can get that all on the sign?"

"He said they had a midnight puppet porno show we couldn't miss."

"A what?" Yolonda smiled.

"The thing is? These guys, the both of them, they just moved downtown maybe what, a month ago? Two months? We walk in, they know everybody in the place. Ike, he's like the street mayor or something. A real operator. I mean, shit, if a guy's big enough a hustler, maybe he's got a future for himself, who knows."

"My sister was like that," Yolonda said. "My mother's all like, 'Yolonda! Would it kill you to smile? Why can't you be nice to people? Why can't you be more like Gloria?' Made me want to slaughter the both of them."

"So how was the puppet show?" Matty asked.

"The what?" Eric yawned, a spastic ripple streaking through his body. "He had the wrong night."

There was another knock at the door; Matty and Yolonda looking at each other.

"Excuse me," Matty said, and slipped out to see Deputy Inspector Berkowitz standing there, short, trim, and remarkably clear-skinned, like a teenager with gray hair.

"How's it going in there?" he asked.

"It's going," Matty said.

"Let me just ask, the other guy, Steven Boulware, is he shaping up as a perp in this at all?"

"Not, no, so far he's maybe a witness, if that. He was pretty intox."

"OK." Berkowitz slipped his hands in his suit pockets as if they had all the time in the world. "Just so you know, Boulware's dad was apparently in the same Ranger unit with the police commissioner in 'Nam."

"Like I said"—Matty stared—"he was mainly intox."

"All right." Berkowitz turned on his heel. "If something changes with that? Call me."


"Sorry," Matty said, retaking his seat, then jerking his fist under the table, Yolonda catching it without changing her expression.

"So the puppet bar, beatnik bar . . ." Matty faltered, looked to Yolonda, who looked at her notes.

"Zeno's Conscience," Eric said slowly.

"Right," Matty said.

"Anything happen there? Run into anybody memorable?" Yolonda asked.

"No. I don't know. I was probably smashed myself at that point. But, no, I don't think so."

"All right, then . . ."

"Then we're supposed to call it a night, *should* have called it a night"—his face abruptly graying—"obviously."

"What did I say to you about blaming yourself?" Yolonda warned.

"Right . . . In any event, at that point Captain Callback had already gotten sick on the sidewalk . . . "

"Steve."

". . . is talking at about a word an hour, but somehow we wind up at Cry."

"The bar on Grand?"

"Right."

"What time are we talking?"

"I don't know, had to be one o'clock or so."

"How'd that go?"

"How'd it go? We're in there five minutes, Ike disappears with this girl at the bar."

"Disappeared where?" Yolonda asked.

Eric looked at her again. "That's why they call it 'disappeared.' "

"For how long?"

"Just long enough. Fifteen, twenty minutes, left me with Steve, the guy is squinting at me like, 'Who the fuck are you?' "

"Did you know the girl?"

"Actually? Yeah. She works at Grouchie's on Ludlow. Been around here forever. A real old-timer."

"Just curious," Matty asked. "How old's an old-timer?"

"Well, her, she's got to be in her thirties by now, mid-thirties. I think at first she was some kind of performance-artist-slash-barmaid. Now she's just a barmaid. It's like . . ." Eric cut himself off again.

"Like . . ."

"I don't know, people *say* they're one thing or another? Then at some point, they just are what they are."

"I hear you," Matty said.

"You hear me?"

"You OK, Eric?" Yolonda said. "Anytime you want to take five, just say so."

Eric didn't respond.

"So what was her name?" Matty asked.

"Whose?"

"The girl."

"I'm not sure. Sarah something. Sarah . . . I don't know."

Matty didn't know her last name either. Grouchie's was a cop bar, one of the few places on the Lower East Side that made you feel like you were drinking in Queens.

"She has a tattoo," Eric added grudgingly. "A cartoon character. One of the seven dwarfs maybe? I'm not sure."

"Tattoo where?" Yolonda asked.

He hesitated. "On her leg, the inside of her leg."

"Inside of her leg. You mean like her thigh?"

"In that neighborhood . . ." Looking away from them.

"Eric," Yolonda said, "you know she has Sneezy or Grumpy or whoever 'in that neighborhood' but you're not sure of her name?"

"I said, Sarah something."

"Eric." Yolonda throwing a sad smirk.

"What."

"What," she gently aped him.

"It was one time." He shrugged. "Over a year ago."

"You sound like my husband."

"What do you want me say." The guy suddenly looking pounded.

Matty remembered her now; she actually had all seven dwarfs, like himself that night, whistling while they worked their way up her leg.

"Afterwards, when you all regrouped, did anything come up about him being with her?" Matty asked.

"Come up between who, me and Ike? No. He doesn't know me. And why would I ever volunteer information about myself like that? To be humiliated?"

"So he didn't comment on it at all. Maybe to his asshole buddy Steve. You know, just to brag, make a crack, not realizing that you and her . . . "

"No, but even if he did, what would that have to do with anything?"

They gave it another beat of silence, a little test run to see if he knew where this was ultimately heading.

"So what time did you leave Cry?" she finally asked.

"I don't know if you heard me," Eric said, some of the first go-round's anxious alertness returning to his eyes. "What would that have to do with anything?"

Matty casually looked to Yolonda, who, staring at the table, briefly shook her head no; too early to risk him asking for a lawyer.

"We're just trying to get a handle on his personality," Matty said. "See if maybe he was the type of guy who tended to rub people the wrong way."

"So what time did you leave Cry?"

"What do you think, I just kept checking my watch after every drink?" Eric said in a sulky but retreating tone, as if not quite ready to pursue his suspicions about what was going on in here.

"Well, how long do you think you stayed there?" Matty asked.

"All I can tell you is we got to Berkmann's right at last call. So it had to be two, two-thirty."

"What's that, about a three-block walk?"

"Three-block stagger. Well, no," palming his face. "Actually, I was all the way around to sober again. I think Ike was too. And I didn't have anything to drink at Berkmann's. I don't like socializing where I work. And I certainly didn't want to show up at my own place of business with some shitface already dragging his toes, but Ike sort of braced him up, it was right on the way, they had a nightcap, and that was it. When we left there, we were just going to carry him back to his apartment on Eldridge, then go our separate ways, but obviously . . . "

They waited.

"You know," Eric finally said, his eyes suddenly shining as if jelled, "I'm probably an alcoholic? But I don't get incapacitated in front of other people. I don't make a spectacle or, or a burden of myself. People like that . . . they wreak such havoc and then they go home. Then somebody takes them home. Fucker." Eric went off somewhere behind his teeth, then came back, his voice a passionate burble. "*He's* the one should have caught that bullet."

Matty and Yolonda straightened in their seats.

There was another knock at the door, the cops tensing, Eric oblivious.

"And you know what?" offering them a livid, teary grimace.

Yolonda and Matty waited, the blood whistling in their veins, until the knocking became so persistent that Eric finally became distracted and the moment passed.

"What, Eric," Yolonda pushed nonetheless.

"When he wakes up today?" addressing the table. "He won't even know what happened. No memories, no pictures . . . Not one fucking clue."


Matty almost tore the door off the hinges, Lieutenant Carmody on the other side reflexively stepping back.

"I just got in," he said. "So how's it going in there?"


"Eric," Yolonda said, when Matty came back in. "We need to do some more legwork. I know you're beat six ways to Sunday, but do you think you could possibly hang around a little while longer? Money in the bank, we're going to need to come back to you a half-dozen more times today."

"For what?"

"For anything, look at more photo arrays, view a lineup if we get lucky, or maybe just to clarify a few things here and there. It's hard to say right now."

"Clarify what?"

"Whatever," Matty said, rising. "We just need to see where the day takes us."

"Can't I just go home?" Looking from one to the other.

"Sure, but . . ."

"I mean, if I were to get up and walk out the door, it's not like you can keep me here against my will, right?"

"Is that what you really want to do?" Yolonda said softly, she and Matty staring at him, the guy somewhere knowing what was going on, but still afraid to let it into the forefront of his brain.


After sticking Cash with a sketch artist to buy more time on the weapons search, Matty and Yolonda went up to the roof for a smoke.

It was hot up there, and Yolonda, the mother of two half-Irish boys, pulled off her turtleneck to reveal a T-shirt that read I'M NOT THE NANNY.

"Oh my God," she said. "I thought we had him for sure."

"Can I tell you something?" Matty so tired now that he found the sunlight dancing on the East River oppressive. "I'd feel a lot more solid about this guy if we had that gun."

"They'll find it," Yolonda said, lighting up.

Matty rocked his head from shoulder to shoulder, hearing the gristle roll in his neck. "Nice to have a why too."

"Three drunks on an all-night bender, the one with a chip on his shoulder's packing? Why ask why?" Yolonda stifled another yawn. "We got him lying about the call to 911, lying about never hanging out with the vic before, tried to lie about having fucked the same girl but only fucked her once, as in, was probably dumped, so jealous, in general a bitter motherfucker, *still* hasn't asked how the dead kid's doing. And, oh yeah, I almost forgot. Two witnesses."

Matty closed his eyes for a second, fell asleep on his feet.

"Nice to have a why," Yolonda muttered. "Why'd that Salgado kid get shot last year, remember? Borrowed an iPod, gave it back without recharging it."

"C'mon, that was in the Cahans."

"Oh. Right. Excuse me. I forgot. This guy's white. Sorry. What was I thinking."

"Give me a break."

"You're such a redneck asshole sometimes, I swear to God."

Matty's inside coat pocket began to tremble.

"Clark."

"Yeah, Sarge, this is Captain Langolier from DCPI? The chief wants to know where you're at."

"Well, right now it's either a robbery or a dispute, two wits giving his friend as the shooter, but the guy himself, for whatever it's worth, is claiming they were jacked at gunpoint."

*He, killed, him,* Yolonda mouthed, Matty waving her off. "We need some time to sort things out."

"There's word they were out there last night tripping the light fantastic?"

"There was a certain amount of barhopping, yeah," Matty said carefully. The chiefs in Public Information often got their information as much from reporters calling up to confirm some fact or rumor as they did their own detectives. And when they called down like this to confirm what the reporters had brought them, the circle came complete.

"Listen, you get anything about the vic having some kind of confrontation with Colin Farrell?"

"Colin Farrell, the actor?" Matty massaged his temples.

"The same."

"And where would this have taken place?" Matty looked at Yolonda, then to the heavens.

"We were hoping you could help us with that."

"I got nothing on that so far, but I'll get right on it, boss."

"Get back to me."

Matty hung up.

"Colin Farrell?" Yolonda said, flicking her butt off the roof. "He was great in that movie *Phone Booth*, you see that?"

"Fuckin' guy."

"Who was it?" Yolonda flicked her butt. "That gimpy kid from the *Post*?"

"Who else?" Matty dialing, then, "Hey, Mayer. Matty Clark. Do me a favor, stop calling Langolier and gassing up his head with all the bullshit you hear on the street. He hangs up with you and right away he's in my ear with every stupid little rumor and it's like a wrecking ball coming through the window. You have any questions on this, you come to me, not Langolier, or I swear to God anything you need to know I will refer you *to* Langolier, you hear me? . . . *Excuse* me? Say again?"

Matty held out the phone so Yolonda could hear too.

"Is it true the shooter was an army Ranger in 'Nam?"

"Jesus Christ . . ."

"What I do now?" the reporter squawked. "I'm asking you, aren't I?"

"Do me a favor, stick to writing about the victim for now, OK?"

"Fine, what do you got?"

"I'll get back to you."

Matty hung up and looked out over the neighborhood, could almost see 27 Eldridge if not for a stack of add-on floors going up atop some tenement on Delancey that weren't there the last time he was on this roof.

He wanted the gun.

"OK, so we've got people out there, reconstructing the night," Yolonda said, opening up round three. "Interviewing some of the people at the bars you mentioned."

"What would you do that for?" Eric's voice started to climb. "It was a mugging."

"Most likely. But we just want to make sure that no one was staking you guys out, maybe some bartender noticed somebody not quite right, or Ike got into something that you were unawares of."

"And?"

"And nothing. Well, those neighbors, the Chinese people who were waiting around for that translator? They all pretty much said that when they looked out the window, they saw *three* people down there, not five."

"What? No, no. They must've looked out after the gun went off."

"Thing is, they all came from different buildings on Eldridge, north of the scene, south of the scene, directly across the street."

"They all must've looked out after. I don't know what else to say."

"Maybe," Yolonda said faintly.

"All those eyes, though," Matty jumped in. "All those angles of vision. The shooter and his buddy, they must've been bookin', huh?"

"Everything happened so fast." Eric palmed his heart. "You have no idea."

"You told me that they ran south, correct?" Matty asked, looking at his notes.

Eric closed his eyes, reenvisioning. "South. Yeah."

"Because we had our people check all the street-facing security cameras along Eldridge from Delancey to Henry," Matty said. "We didn't catch anybody running at that time on any of them."

"Maybe they hung a quick left and went west. Or east," Eric said. "I wasn't standing around tracking their progress."

"Right. You were busy trying to call 911."

"Yes," he said, looking stricken. "What. Was I supposed to chase them or something?"

"That would have been stupid," Yolonda said. "By the way, Sarah Bowen was pretty shaken up."

Eric looked at them blankly.

"The tattooed lady that hooked up with Ike at Cry? You know, one minute she's having sex with a guy, next thing she hears . . ."

Eric reddened, looked away.

"And by the way, it seems like she remembers you a lot more than you remembered her."

"What's that supposed to mean?"

"She said you were kind of hung up on her last year."

"What?"

"Kept calling her."

"No, wait, hang on. That's because she kept saying to me whenever I called, tonight wasn't a good night, like *another* night would be." Eric near gobbling his words as he searched their faces. "If she had ever said to me straight up, 'I don't want to *see* you, I am not interested in *seeing* you,' that would've been the end of it. I mean, what the hell, what did she say, I was stalking her or something? Jesus."

"All I'm saying is, when we talked before, you damn well knew right off the bat exactly who Ike was with last night, right? Because you were kind of playing it, you know . . ."

"I was embarrassed, so . . ." Then, "What's going on here?" His alarm cranked too high again, the both of them suddenly scrambling to deflect the flow, Yolonda the first in.

"What . . ." she said down low with a smile. "Afraid we were gonna tell your girlfriend?"

"How do you even know I have one?"

"Don't you?"

Still lost in consternation, Eric stared at the table as if there were writing on it.

"Don't you?"

"Don't I what?"

"Have a girlfriend."

"Yes," he said emphatically. "Of course."

"Well, it's not a gimme or anything," Yolonda said. "What's her name?"

"Alessandra. Why?"

"She's from around here?"

"Yeah. We live together, but she's in the Philippines now, why?"

"She's Filipino?"

"No. She's doing research for her master's over there. Are you going to tell me why you're asking all this?"

"We're just trying to get a fully rounded picture."

"Of me?"

"Sometimes with investigations?" Yolonda shrugged. "There's a lot of hurry up and wait. Right now, before we can go forward we need for some people to come in from the field. These are just killing-time-type questions."

"Master's in what?" Matty asked.

"Gender studies. She's doing research on the movement to organize sex workers in Manila."

"Sex workers," Yolonda said.

"How long has she been over there?" Matty asked.

"Nine months or so," Eric said as if embarrassed.

"You guys talk much? Or do you e-mail?"

"A little of both."

He was lying, Matty could tell, their relationship most likely pretty thin soup.

"Excuse me."

He got up, left the interview room, and stepped to a detective. "Jimmy, in about fifteen, twenty minutes? Knock on the door, say there's a phone call."

"You got it." Then, "Hey," waving Matty closer. "The PC's driver Halloran called?"

"And?"

"The PC wants to know if you're bringing in Phillip Boulware."

"Who?"

"The father of the drunk kid. Apparently they were on the same high school football team."

"Sorry," Matty said, stepping back inside.

"So, Eric," Yolonda said, "we understand you spent some time in Binghamton?"

"I was born there, why?"

"OK, don't take this the wrong way?" She laid a hand on him again. "But we had to do a background check, anybody we talk to in an investigation like this it's mandatory, and . . ."

"And you saw I was arrested."

"It reads like bullshit," she apologized. "Do you want to tell us what happened?"

"Do I have to?"

"That's completely up to you," Matty said.

"Look, again, I'm sorry, I don't understand, what does this have to do with anything?"

"I think we just explained what's going on now, but if you prefer, we can just sit around and stare at each other," Matty said.

"Look, it's not . . ." Eric tried to resist, but once again Matty's irritation was too much for him. "I wouldn't even know where to start."

"What the hell," Matty said. "Give it a shot."

"I don't know," Eric began, sounding embarrassed by his inability to hang tough. "Something like fifteen years ago? I went to the same college as Harry Steele up there. SUNY Binghamton. I was a freshman, he was a senior, and he had this idea, he was looking for someone in the dorms who would be willing to convert their room into a cocktail lounge . . . My dad owned a bar and grill in Endicott, one town over, so I kind of grew up around all that, and I said I'd do it. Put in some stock, some colored lights, a few card tables, hired a bouncer from the wrestling team . . ."

"Are you serious?" Matty sat up straighter, cocking his head.

"Oh yeah." Eric tentatively smiled, Matty again sensing the power he had been granted in here, the guy's mood rising and falling with the tone of Matty's voice. "Cleared about five hundred a week."

"So how long before you got caught?" Yolonda asked.

"About a month."

"And you took a collar for *that*?"

"No, no. The college said if I immediately withdrew from school, they wouldn't press criminal charges. So I did."

"What happened to Steele?" Matty asked.

"Nothing. He was just the bankroller, never set foot in the place, and I never mentioned his name. So . . ."

Eric went off somewhere, came back. "I didn't even really give a shit about school all that much except . . ."

"Except . . ." Yolonda leaned forward, giving him her sad smile.

"Nothing, I mean, I was a theater major? And I had just landed the lead in *The Caucasian Chalk Circle*, so with rehearsals starting, I would've had to shut down the bar anyhow in a week or two, so . . ."

"The *Chalk Circle*, that's a play?"

"Yeah, a play," Eric said quietly. "And they almost never gave parts out to freshmen either, let alone the lead, so I wasn't, you know, without talent."

"That sucks," Yolonda said.

"Yeah, well, I was heading for New York anyways, so, I came down, and, it wasn't easy, but I actually got stuff. Some children's theater, a few basement plays, a commercial for Big Apple Tours, another for Gallagher's Steak House . . ."

"Can I ask you an actor's question?" Yolonda said.

Eric looked at her.

"Did you ever have any dealings with Colin Farrell?"

Eric continued to stare, then, "What on earth would make you ask that?"

"Never mind."

"So there you were, doing commercials," Matty said.

"Barely . . . And then Steele came to town to open up this lounge on Amsterdam Avenue, and he owned, *owed* me, and you have to eat, right? So I started working for him, worked about seven, eight years, but then I was, I felt like my time, my moment was just, like coming and going, so I quit, borrowed some money, went back home to Binghamton, and I actually bought this restaurant that, years ago, was the first place Steele opened right after he graduated from up there. It was going through a foreclosure and I figured, you know, maybe I could follow in his footsteps or something."

"Turn, turn, turn . . ." Yolonda said solemnly, and Matty had to look away.

"What kind of menu are we talking?" Matty asked.

"Eclectic . . . you know, steak, crepes, lo mein."

"I thought that was fusion," Yolonda said.

"More like con-fusion, a total bust from the door on in," Eric said, starting to relax a little, Matty getting a feel for how he was when everything was going OK.

"Anyways, I never did any business except at the bar, and, in those days, blow was making a huge comeback up there, you couldn't keep it out of the place, always a line to the bathroom, and some of my customers would ask if I knew where to score, which I did . . . so, I got into the habit of keeping some behind the bar, just quarters to keep everybody coming in. And it's not like I made any money off it. Any extra cash went right up my own nose, but I liked all the happy faces at the bar." Eric then abruptly went off into his thoughts, his lips still moving like the last actions of a decapitated head.

"I like coming through for people sometimes?" He stared directly at them, but without any kind of challenge in it. "No matter what the, you know, consequences, I guess."

"I'm exactly the same way," Yolonda said so softly and sympathetically that Eric looked at her with something akin to desire.

"Anyways," Eric continued unprodded, "the restaurant was still going down the tubes, then the guy that I scored from gets busted, gives *me* up straight out of the box, I wind up selling to an undercover at my bar, the place gets padlocked, I'm in cuffs." Eric drifting again, then, "They give you that one phone call, right? . . . You know who I made it to? I couldn't possibly call my father, that would have been . . . No. So, I called Steele in New York. I was so ashamed, I mean it used to be his place, plus he was not happy when I quit on him to begin with."

Yolonda grunted in sympathy.

"But you know what he did? He wired me the bail money within an hour. I spent one night in jail, got off with a suspended sentence, which I'm pretty sure he was behind too. So, I filed for bankruptcy within the week, and within the month I was back down in the city working for him again, helping him open Berkmann's."

"Wow," Yolonda said, her eyes flicking to the wall clock.

"The thing is," Eric said, speaking to his hands, "what's it now, seven, eight years? I'm *still* waiting for him to say something about it. But I find some way to thank him every day."

"So you're like a Harry Steele lifer, huh?"

"I'm a what?" Eric flushed.

"Didn't you hear one word of what he said?" Yolonda carped at Matty.

"What do you mean, about the acting?" Matty leaned back, rubbed his eyes. "Yeah, every word. But that sounds like it's over, right?"

"I never said that. When did you hear me say that?"

"You know, you're right, you didn't, sorry. So what are you doing with it now?"

"Now?" Eric leaned his cheek on his palm, closed his eyes. "Now I'm, actually, mostly writing."

"Oh yeah? What kind?"

"Just writing." The guy shutting down.

"Detective stuff?" Yolonda asked.

"Why would you assume that?" Eric snapped.

"I don't know." She shrugged. "That's what I would write if I could."

Eric put his face in the crook of his arm.

"I'm working on a screenplay." Saying it like he was embarrassed.

"For a movie?"

"For money."

"What, like a personal star vehicle?"

"A what?" Eric raised his head, his face a blur.

"A personal star vehicle," Yolonda said. "That's what Sylvester Stallone did. Guy couldn't get to first base as an actor, so he wrote *Rocky* as a personal star vehicle for himself. They were going to buy the script from him but for Steve McQueen to play the guy? Stallone said no way, it's me as Rocky or you can go shit in a hat. And look at him now."

Eric looked as if he were going to cry.

"You should think about it."

"Well, what's it about?" Matty asked. "You got us curious."

"It doesn't matter." Eric put his head back on his arm.

Yolonda looked at Matty: *Push.*

"Eric," Matty said in a flatter tone. "What's it about?"

Eric raised up again, took a breath, his mouth hanging open.

"It's historical, about the neighborhood."

"Yeah . . ." Waiting.

"It's kind of like a ghost story. But not about *ghost* ghosts? It's more like, metaphorical ghosts, like, I don't know, I can't . . ."

"So it's scary?" Yolonda asked. "Or not."

Her question seemed to sink him further.

"Eric?" she repeated. "Is it—"

"It's stupid," he cut her off, in a voice not much more than a whisper. "Utterly fucking stupid."

"Anyways," she said. "So how'd you meet Ike?"

Eric was still so gone in his depression that she had to repeat the question, and when she did, his eyes became dull and wary again.

"For the tenth time. He was just hired last week. I didn't do the hiring. There's a lot of turnover. One day one guy's behind the bar, the day after, it's somebody else."

"So other than last night, you guys never hung out before, never socialized . . ."

"I told you that too."

"Never went out on a break to have a cigarette, shoot the shit."

"No."

"Did you go into the Sana'a Deli together yesterday?"

"Where?"

"The corner store on Rivington and Eldridge."

"Wait. Hold on. That was a coincidence."

"We hear you wiped out the Virgin Mary."

"*I* didn't. He did."

"So you *were* together? Or not."

"It was a bump-in, that's all."

"The Virgin Mary thing. How'd you feel about that?"

"How did I *feel*?" Eric offered his palms again. "It was frost on glass. What are you asking?"

"Some people take that stuff very seriously."

"Me?"

"Well, not you, but maybe someone there got very upset. If so . . ."

"Yeah, there was. The guy who was getting a dollar a head from the neighborhood nitwits. Check him out."

"We did."

"Eric, speaking of that, we found your cell phone in front of the guy's place."

"What?" Patting himself down. "I lost it?"

"Can I just ask—" Matty began.

"How did I lose it?"

"You said you called 911, correct?"

"I said I tried to."

"OK. It's . . . But there's no 911 on your send log."

"I told you about this. I couldn't get through. That's why I ran into the building."

"For better reception."

"Right." Eric's expression an agitated gawk. "What are you saying?"

"I'm just wondering why there's nothing on the log," Matty said. "Because on my phone—"

"What am I, Thomas Edison?" Eric squawked. "I'm lucky I know how to say hello on that thing."

"All right, all right," Matty pulled back.

"Eric, let me ask you something else." Yolonda leaned in. "Last night, is there the slightest chance that during the, the encounter, you might have touched the gun? You know, reached out to grab it or deflect it or maybe when you handed over your wallet there was some accidental contact . . ."

"Are you serious?"

"The reason she's asking," Matty said, "is that we're required to give you a paraffin test for gunshot residue." Still furious that they couldn't. "Just standard operating procedure."

"And we need to ask you now because if in fact you *did* touch that gun, or any *other* gun in the last twenty-four hours? You're gonna come up positive, and if we don't know why beforehand . . . surprises, at this point . . ."

"I didn't." Eric faltered, then, "Wait. What the hell's going on here?"

There was a knock on the door, Jimmy Iacone peering in. "Phone."

Matty looked to Yolonda. "You take this one." Then waited until she left the room.

"You OK there, Eric? You look kind of stricken."

"Am I in some kind of trouble?"

"Not to my knowledge."

"When do I take this test?"

"Relax. It's not like you have to study for it," Matty said. "As long as you've been truthful with us about not having touched a gun in the last twenty-four hours, you have nothing to worry about."

"Well, I haven't."

"Well then, there you go . . . But let me ask you this. Just out of my own curiosity . . . When *was* the last time you had your hands on a gun?"

"What?" Eric cocked his head, Matty instantly pissed at himself. "Hang on. Do I need . . ." he began, then to Matty's great relief, faltered, started breathing through his mouth.

Yolonda reentered. "Great news."

They both turned to her.

"Your friend Ike?" She beamed at Eric. "Just came out of surgery. Looks like he's gonna pull through."

Eric looked stunned.

"There you go." Matty bobbed his head, then turned to Yolonda. "Who's at the hospital?"

"Mander and Stucky." Yolonda made a face.

"Well then, we should go over there, right? Is he good to talk?"

"Will be, soon enough."

Matty rose to his feet. "It's a good thing the Virgin Mary wasn't *too* pissed at your pal, huh?"

Eric stared at him, throttle-faced.

"You OK there, Eric?"

"What? No, yeah, I'm just really tired."

"I'll bet," Matty said, smiling down at him.

"We're heading over there now," Yolonda said. "But before we go, is there anything you want to tell us? Anything we didn't get to?"

"No, I just . . . He's going to make it?"

"Apparently so," Matty said, one hand on the doorknob but otherwise staying put.

Eric's eyes roved without focus.

"What's up, Eric?"

"What . . ."

"You look like you want to say something."

"Does this . . ."

"Does this what?"

"Does this mean I can go home now?"

No one said anything for a moment, Yolonda half smiling at him in that way of hers.

"If you can bear with us a little bit longer," Matty said, "we'd really appreciate it if you could stick around until we get back from the hospital."

Eric stared at air, patted himself down as if looking for his cell phone again.

"I'd offer you a cot in the bunk room," Matty said, "but frankly that place is so disgusting you'd probably be more comfortable in the cell."

"Why don't you just put your head down right where you are," Yolonda said. "We can have someone scare you up a pillow if you want."

Eric didn't respond.

"If Ike's alert," Matty said, "is there anything you want us to say to him? Any messages?"

"Messages?" Eric repeated mindlessly.

"All right, let's go." Matty began to steer Yolonda to the door, but she sidestepped him, came back to the table.

"Can I ask you something?" she said almost timidly. "Not to sound hard or critical, and I know he was just an acquaintance from work . . . But how come, in all this time in here, you never once asked us how he was doing, or even just whether he was dead or alive."

She waited on his answer.

"I *didn't*?" Eric finally said, his eyes wildly searching the blank cinder-block room.

"No."

They stared at him.

"No. How could . . . I *didn't*?"

"Just put your head down," Yolonda said softly. "We'll try to be quick."


"That there is all the proof I need," she said on the other side of the glass as they watched Eric twitching in his sleep like a dreaming dog.

"Maybe he's just exhausted," Matty said.

"Yeah, that must be it," Yolonda said.

"C'mon, he didn't even ask for a lawyer," Matty said. Then, "Well, he almost did. I think he was afraid that if he actually asked for one he'd come off guilty. But that's the thing, what kind of hang-tough hard boy thinks like that?"

"He just hadn't done it before. He doesn't know how to play it. So what."

"Give me a single plausible motive."

"You want a motive?" Yolonda said crisply. "Here's a motive. Men, overreact, to *pain*. And when they do? They take everybody with them."

"What the hell does that mean?"

"It means motherfuck a motive. I'm good with it."


As Matty came downstairs, intending to use the remainder of this breather to return to 27 Eldridge to backseat-drive the gun search, he reflexively checked out the customers in the waiting area below: an elderly Chinese couple, the man sporting fresh blood-blackened stitches down the side of his face; a young East Indian woman clutching a car impound voucher; and a middle-aged, agitated-looking white guy wearing a suit jacket over sweatpants. The usual neighborhood mix, more or less.

As he hit the front door, his cell phone rang, the incoming number vaguely familiar.

"Detective Clark."

"Yeah, hey."

Matty was chagrined to hear his oldest son on the other end.

"Hey, you guys are awake? It's not even noon."

"Where the hell is Audubon Avenue. Me and Eddie been driving around here for an hour."

"You're in Washington Heights? What are you doing in Washington Heights?"

"Looking up a friend."

"You have a friend from Lake George who lives in Washington Heights?" Matty's stomach fluttered.

"A friend of Eddie's."

"*Eddie* has a friend . . . " Matty put the phone to his chest, exhaled. "Put your brother on."

"He's not here."

"You just said to me 'me and Eddie.' "

"Dad, Audubon Avenue. Do you know where it is or not."

Matty felt sick, with anger, with self-disgust.

"I can't help you there, Matty," he finally said. "Ask a cop."

Rattled, telling himself not to jump to conclusions, he stepped to the handicapped ramp that ran along the side of the building to have a smoke before heading over to the crime scene and saw the Toyota Sequoia, sitting almost in the middle of Pitt Street, unoccupied, driver door open, exhaust fumes curling, no sign of the driver. Then, almost without thinking, he ditched the cigarette and reentered the vestibule to take a second look at the white guy, sitting there hunched forward, elbows to knees, squinting at the wall-mounted bas-relief memorial plaques as if to memorize them. He had the cloudy red complexion of a stew bum, but Matty didn't think that was his problem.

"Mr. Marcus?"

The guy whipped his head to the voice, then just as quickly stood up.

"Yes," extending his hand. His gaze was both alert and unfocused.

"Detective Clark." Matty took his hand and felt a tremor running beneath the overly firm grip.

"You're the detective whose name they gave me?"

"Yeah, yes, I am. How long have you been waiting down here?"

"I don't know."

"Did anybody call up to the squad?"

Marcus didn't answer. Matty stared at the cop at the reception nook still nose-down in his *Post*, then decided to drop it. "Look, I'm very sorry we have to meet under these circumstances." Sounding to himself like a kindly robot.

"Well, I would have been here earlier," Marcus said, "but I couldn't find it."

"Yeah, no, the streets are tricky down here, but if I had known you were coming, I would have sent—"

"No, no, I couldn't find the, the *city*, the whole fucking New York City. I took the Saw Mill instead of the Thruway, and I wound up at the Whitestone Bridge somehow, then—"

"You came down from . . ."

"Tarrytown, the Con Ed remediation seminar, but you know if this had happened a day earlier, I would have been coming from Riverdale, which is just like thirty minutes away."

Matty nodded as if everything he was hearing now was both reasonable and interesting.

"Are you here by yourself?"

"Myself, yeah."

"You drove in by yourself."

"Yeah, but it wasn't . . ."

Sliding his hand inside Marcus's arm, Matty steered him out to the street and gestured to the thrumming SUV in the middle of the block.

Marcus gave a start like he was falling out of a tree.

"Keys are still in there?"

"I can't believe . . ."

Matty flagged Jimmy Iacone, coming out of the building for a smoke. "Hey, Jimmy? Would you park Mr. Marcus's car for him?"

Iacone reared up a little at the request, then Matty watched the name register in his eyes.

"Just put it in the lot." Then, turning to Marcus, "Look, like I said, I'm sorry to have to meet you under these circumstances."

"Well, you know they woke me this morning, the cops up there, actually it was this VP from Con Ed, I guess for the personal touch, and, I don't know, honestly? I think I'm handling it pretty well so far, but I need to ask you something, and this is the main . . ." Marcus looked off for a second, palming his mouth. "Do you have his driver's license?"

"We have his effects," Matty said cautiously, wishing it were Yolonda here instead of him.

"OK. Did you notice . . . Did he happen to check the box for organ donation? And if he did, could I, as his father, override that? I really don't want anybody harvesting his organs. Really don't."

"No, no. We can take care of that."

Two young Latino cops in matching black and blue NYPD windbreakers and fiberglass helmets came through the front door and walked their patrol bikes past Matty and Marcus down the handicapped ramp. Jimmy Iacone, on his way back from parking Marcus's car, drawled, "You guys look like twin centerfolds for *Blueboy*."

"Yo, bitch, you said nobody here'd see that thing," one bike cop vamped to the other, all three low-key laughing like life is life is life, then going about their business.

"Mr. Marcus, do you want to come upstairs? We can sit and talk."

"Sure," bobbing his head.

Matty turned to the building, but sensed that Marcus was suddenly no longer with him. Turning back, he saw him transfixed by the sight of John Mullins escorting a teary red-haired woman and a stunned-looking teenage girl towards the house.

He started to ask Marcus if they were his wife and daughter, but the guy abruptly took off towards the building without him, and by the time Matty made it back inside, all he could see of Marcus were his unlaced shoes high-stepping up the open stairs, the reception cop finally on his feet but doing nothing.

Marcus wasn't on the second floor in any of the assorted squad rooms or bathrooms, nor on the third, in the half-assed gym or locker rooms, but on the unpopulated fourth, which was empty save for storage rooms and weapons cabinets, the guy having apparently just climbed blind until he ran out of stairs.

Matty came on him pacing between the bolted gun racks and the wall-pegged hazmat suits.

"Mr. Marcus."

"Please." He gulped for breath. "I don't want to see them now."

"Was that your family?"

"Can you get them out of here?"

Matty couldn't tell if Marcus was distraught or just winded.

"I'm begging you."

The captain's office downstairs was undergoing renovations, and Carmody was on the phone in the lieutenant's office, so the best Matty could offer the father in terms of privacy was the squad's eating alcove, half-hidden from the cramped sea of desks by a chest-high partition.

He seated Marcus behind the salvaged Formica desk that served as a dining table, turned off the portable TV before they could run any news footage of the murder, stacked and discarded the multiple partial copies of the *Post* and the *News* strewn about the tabletop. He could do nothing about the mingled ghost-reeks of Chinese and Dominican takeout or about the bathroom a few feet away, someone in there now having a splashy time of it.

He would have done anything to have Yolonda in his place right now. At least cosmetically, though, he was probably the better choice. Most families found more reassurance in the big, lantern-jawed Irishman, all ass-kick and unrelentingness, than the Bambi-eyed Latina; no matter that for all her touchy-feely vibes Yolonda was a better hunter than he'd ever be.

Marcus seemed less babbly now, more dazed, although he tended to jump at everything, the sound of the toilet flushing a few feet away, the scattered telephone rings and disembodied call-outs, the sudden appearance of a detective who leaned in from around the bend of the partition and, seeing that the bathroom was occupied, palmed his tie to his gut and without ceremony spit a stream of mouthwash into the newspaper-filled garbage can.

When the bathroom door finally swung open, Jimmy Iacone stood there still adjusting his belt, at first startled, then embarrassed, to see Marcus sitting just a few feet away. Whisper-coughing, "Excuse me," he turned back to make sure the bathroom door was closed, then as he sidled past, murmured to Matty, "Give me a heads-up or something."

"I apologize for the mess, we're not—" Matty cut himself off and twisted around, tracking Marcus's distracted gaze to a baseball cap that sat atop the TV, its legend, scripted in red on the brim, NYPD CRIME SCENE UNIT, beneath which read WE SEE DEAD PEOPLE.

"Sorry," Matty said. "Unfortunately that's how we cope."

"Gallows humor," Marcus said evenly.

As Matty got up to stow the hat, he glanced out the window and saw John Mullins escorting Marcus's distraught wife and kid back to his car.

"All due respect?" Matty said, turning back to the table. "I think you're making a mistake not being with your family right now."

"It was a robbery?" Marcus asked lightly, the red creeping back into his face.

Matty hesitated, wanting to keep campaigning for at least the wife being here, but got caught up in the trickiness of the question. "Well, at this point we don't think so." He hesitated, then forged ahead. "In fact, let me tell you exactly what's going on. Right now we have two credible witnesses who're telling us they saw three white males standing in front of a building, one of which takes out a gun, fires at your son, then runs into the lobby."

"OK," Marcus said, his eyes wandering.

"When, when the first officers responded to the scene, that same white male who ran inside was back out there and told them that he and his buddies had been robbed at gunpoint by two black or Hispanic males, one of whom fired the shot. But, as I said, our two eyewitnesses say otherwise."

Matty wasn't sure if anything he'd just said had registered in the slightest on Marcus, but he knew there was a good chance that this nutshell of a scenario could come to take over the man's life until his own death.

"Mr. Marcus, would you like some water?"

"Why'd he do it?"

"Honestly? We're not sure. They were all drinking pretty heavily, there could have been some kind of argument, possibly involving a girl, but basically—"

"They were friends?"

"They worked together at Café Berkmann, his name is Eric Cash. Did you ever hear your son mention that name?"

"No." Then, "He's here?"

"He hasn't been charged yet but we're talking to him."

"Here."

"Yes."

"Can I see him?"

"That we can't do."

"I just want to ask him—"

"We can't do that, Mr. Marcus, try to understand."

"OK. I just thought, you know, both for your sake and mine I could . . ."

"It's not . . ."

"I understand," Marcus said reasonably. Then, "Where was he shot?"

Again, Matty hesitated. "The upper-body region."

"Did I *ask* you that!" Marcus shouted, the unseen squad room beyond the partition suddenly quiet.

"I'm sorry," Matty said carefully, "I misunderstood the question."

"*Where*, out *there*, in New *York*."

"On Eldridge Street, a few blocks south of—"

"I'm . . . Eldridge? Can I ask what number Eldridge?"

"Twenty-seven."

"We're from Eldridge, Houston and Eldridge . . . Ike's great-grandfather." It was the first time Matty had heard him utter his son's name, and Marcus took a moment to catch his breath, the ambient clamor filling the void.

"Twenty-seven Eldridge," Marcus finally said, nodding to himself. "Did he suffer?" Then before Matty could respond, "No. Of course not. How could you possibly tell me yes."

"He did not suffer," Matty said nonetheless, hoping it was true.

"It was instantaneous?" The question was real, Marcus unable to hold on to his ironic edge.

"Instantaneous."

They sat there for a moment, Matty seeing the beginnings of a slightly less shell-shocked pain seep into the man's face.

"Look," Matty plowed on. "I know now is a bad time, but honestly we have some real problems figuring out the why of things, so if there's anything you can tell us about your son . . ."

"I can't remember when I talked to him last," Marcus said. "When I saw him last. Hang on." His mouth hung open as he searched the ceiling. "Hold on."

And Matty knew there was no way this guy could help the investigation. The thing to do now was get him with his people.

"Is there anything I can do for you, Mr. Marcus."

"Do for me."

"If you don't want to be with your family, which, as I said, I think is a mistake, is there someone else I can call?"

Marcus didn't respond.

"Do you need a place to stay?"

"To stay?"

"We can arrange—"

Marcus jumped as Yolonda abruptly materialized alongside him, leaning against the partition.

She touched his shoulder in sympathy, gave him her sad face, and he finally started to cry.

Matty's cell went off: Bobby Oh. Leaving Yolonda to babysit the father, he took the call around the corner.

"Mr. Bobby, tell me something good."

"Nothing from nothing," Oh said, then yawned.

Matty could just see him after eight hours on the scene, pink-eyed, shirttails flapping, the sparse hair rimming his scalp shooting straight up like frozen fire.

"Nobody in the building knew him or ever saw him before, so I can't imagine he passed it off to some in-house confederate, the roof's clean, so's the neighboring roofs, the fire escapes, drainpipes, stairwells, basement, we went through the garbage cans on six corners, tracked down the sanitation truck which makes the nighttime pickups around here, holding that for a go-through, got EPA coming in to dredge manholes and sewer grates . . . Anything we missed?"


"This guy's a regular fuckin' Rip van Winkle," Yolonda said, tilting her chin at Eric Cash through the glass. "If I got that much sleep, I'd look ten years younger."

"I'm just not feeling him for this."

"I do."

"And I'll tell you something else. If he's telling us the truth about last night, he was six inches from catching a bullet. And with what we're putting him through?"

"You're such a good person," Yolonda said. "So how do you want to play it?"

"I don't know. Give him one last run for his money, then let the DA call it."

"OK. So how do you want to play it?"

"Let me go at him hard."

"Why you? You say you don't even like him for it."

"Yeah, I know, but he gets real upset when I come off disappointed in him."

Deputy Inspector Berkowitz materialized alongside them, his London Fog draped over his arm.

"Where we at?" Going into a half dip to eyeball Cash through the glass. "The natives are getting seriously restless."

Matty and Yolonda started arguing again like an old couple with a road map.

"Well, I'll tell you." Berkowitz straightened up and checked his watch: 12:45. "I were you, I'd be getting ready to wrap this guy up."

"You got it, boss," Yolonda said, looking at Matty as if she were dying to stick out her tongue in triumph.


With Billy Marcus in no shape to drive and, in any event, unwilling to return to his family in Riverdale, Matty had booked him a room at the Landsman, a new hotel on Rivington that had a goodwill arrangement with the precinct, offering a cheap rate for drug-sting suites, and economy singles for out-of-town testifiers, victims, and on occasion family members waiting for the release of a body. The Landsman would have gotten out of the deal if it could. The owners had panicked midway during construction and started scrambling for long-term commitments within the community, fearing that they had overestimated the allure of the neighborhood, but in fact the place had been a hit from the door on in.

Jimmy Iacone drew the job of handling the check-in. Since there was no luggage to carry and the hunt for a parking space could take half an hour, Iacone decided to walk Marcus the seven short blocks from Pitt to Ludlow. It was slow going, the guy moving as if he were walking through a neighborhood in the wake of a bombing, its storefronts in flames and bodies littering the pavement; and he couldn't take his eyes off any of the kids coming their way, male, female, straight, freak, black, or white. Then, on the corner of Rivington and Suffolk, he stopped dead and turned to stare hang-jawed after someone or other they had passed, and Iacone knew that Marcus had just seen his son, most of them did; and that's why he hated being a squad detective: he would rather go through the reinforced door of a dope house, roll in the dirt with a 250-pound ED off his meds, buy crank from a tweeking biker—anything but deal with the parent of a freshly murdered child.

Because the hotel was nearly full, they had no choice but to give Marcus a room fit for a photo shoot, a sixteenth-floor glass-walled corner aerie, more perch than shelter, all white: white furniture, fixtures, wall-mounted flatscreen, and a king-size bed covered in synthetic white fur.

Despite its stark opulence, the place was the size of a shoe box, with barely a foot clearance between that huge bed and the three-sided terrace, which offered an imperial overview of the area: a sea of cramped and huddled walk-ups and century-old elementary schools, the only structures out there aspiring to any kind of height the randomly sprouting bright yellow Tyvek-wrapped multistory add-ons, and farther out, superimposed against the river, the housing projects and union-built co-ops that flanked the east side of this grubby vista like siege towers.

Marcus sat slumped on the edge of the polar bed, Iacone fidgeting before him as if they were breaking up and he didn't know how to leave without provoking a scene.

"Do you need anything, Mr. Marcus?"

"Like what."

"Food, medication, fresh clothes . . ."

"No. I'm OK now, thanks."

"Yeah?"

"Yeah. Thanks, thank you." Reaching out and shaking his hand.

Iacone extracted a card from the side pocket of his sport jacket, laid it on the night table, then continued to two-step for a minute, feeling a little guilty about how easily he was getting out of there.

An hour after they had left Eric, they reentered the interview room, Matty whacking the door into the cinder block to wake him up.

"What." He jerked upright, his mouth white with sleep. "Is he OK?"

"*Now* you ask?"

"We haven't gone over there yet. Something came up." Yolonda took her chair and slid it so close that their kneecaps intersected.

"What."

"Eric, are you sure everything you told us is to the best of your memory?" she asked, leaning in even farther.

"Considering that I was drunk," he said carefully.

"Well, you're sober now," Matty drawled, pushing himself upright off the wall.

"What?" Eric repeated, his eyes ticking from face to face.

"Almost the first thing you said to me walking into this room, you looked at *that* rail," Matty barked, leaning on the table now, his shoulders humped higher than his head, "and you said, 'I feel like I should be cuffed to that.'"

"What were you trying to tell us?" Yolonda asked.

"Nothing." Rearing back from them. "I was feeling bad."

"Feeling bad. Bad for Ike, or for yourself?"

"What?"

"Here's the latest." Matty straightened up. "We now have two witnesses just came in the house, said they were right across the street last night when the shot went off. And guess what. They saw you, and Steve and Ike, and no one else. Explain that to me."

"No. That's not right."

"They heard the shot, saw Ike go down, and you take off into the building."

"No."

"No, huh?" Fuming. "No."

"Look, we're not here to hurt you," Yolonda said. "There's a million reasons why shit happens. You guys were horsing around, drunk off your ass, and the goddamn thing just went off."

"What?" Eric started to tremble, seemed embarrassed that he couldn't control his own body.

"Hey, for all we know, Ike grabbed it from you, or maybe the other guy did, whatsit, Steve," Yolonda offered. "We have no idea, that's for you to clear up, but I am *telling* you, Eric, as stupid as you were for bringing a gun with you on an all-night crawl like that? You are one lucky bastard because the jam you're in could be a hell of a lot worse. Ike could be lying on a slab right now and *you* could be looking at a murder charge."

"No. Hold on . . ." Sounding as if he were shouting in his sleep.

"Eric, listen, Matty and me? Every day we're up to our ass in human garbage. Psychos and sociopaths and common household scum. Every, day. Does that even remotely sound like you? Doesn't to me. As far as I'm concerned? You're almost as much a victim in this as Ike, so here's the deal. You tell us how it went down, tell us where the gun is, and we'll make this as close to a cakewalk for you as we can. Will be *happy* to. But the first move here has got to be yours."

Eric frowned at the blank table, then abruptly jerked back, chin into chest.

"C'mon now, Eric, work with us."

"Work with you . . ."

"Use your *head*," Matty snapped. "When we go talk to Ike, he's going to tell us what really happened anyhow, right?"

"I hope he does," Eric said, small-voiced, his eyes still trained on the table.

"You what?" Matty cupped an ear.

Eric didn't repeat himself.

"Why do you think we're holding off on going to the hospital right now?" Yolonda's eyes shining with emotion.

Eric stared at her.

"If he lays it out for us with you still holding on to this story of yours? What do think that's gonna look like? To us, to the DA, to a judge. We're holding off to give you one last chance to help yourself."

"I don't understand." Eric near grinning in disbelief.

"Look, I know you're scared, but please, trust me on this." Yolonda palmed her heart. "Nothing good will come of you sticking to a lie."

"It's not a lie."

"No? Well, let me tell you something," Matty said. "If I was, like you claim to be, an innocent man? Right about now I'd be hopping around this fucking room like my ass was on fire. *Any* innocent person would. That would be the natural instinctual reaction. But you've been sitting here all morning, you're coming off a little bored, a little depressed, a little nervous. It's like you're at a dentist's office. You went to *sleep*, for Christ's sakes. In twenty years, I have *never* seen an innocent man just rack out like that. Twenty, years. *Never.*"

At first, given the lack of eye contact, Matty thought Eric was literally shrugging off the barrage; then he realized that his body was spasming.

"Eric," Yolonda said. "Tell us what happened before Ike does."

"I did."

"Did *what*," Matty snapped.

"Tell you what happened."

Yolonda shook her bowed head in grievous surrender.

"You're a terrible actor, you know that?" Matty yanked at his tie. "No wonder you wound up working at a restaurant."

"Look, what if, God forbid, Ike doesn't pull through?" Yolonda again. "Do you think that's somehow better for you? All we have then is your version and the witnesses' version. Where does that leave you?"

"It leaves me wherever you want me left." His voice still small, but with a shaky touch of defiance.

This is costing him, Matty thought. This man is a mouse, and hanging tough here is taking everything he has in him, is taking everything out of him.

"All that shit about running into the building to get better phone reception," Matty said. "You never even *tried* to call 911, did you."

Eric hunched his shoulders as if waiting for a blow.

"Admit *that* at least, for God's sakes."

Silence, then, "No, I didn't."

"Your buddy is lying there with a bullet in his chest, and innocent man that you are, you refuse to dial the three numbers that could save his *life*? How can that be? Even if you were telling us the truth about this, this Afro-Hispanic stickup team, which you're *not*, the question remains, what kind of human being would refuse to do that for a friend? Or, no, excuse me, an ac*quaint*ance from work."

"I just wanted to get away," Eric said minutely, addressing the space between his hands. "I was scared."

"Was *what*?" Matty squinted in disbelief, then turned to Yolonda. "He was *what*?"

Yolonda looked helpless and grief-stricken, a powerless mother watching her child being beaten by her husband.

Eric finally raised his face, stared at Matty, gape-mouthed.

"Yeah, you look me right in the eye, you fucking ant."

"Matty . . ." Yolonda finally put out her hand.

"I have listened to your shit in here all day. You are a self-centered, self-pitying, cowardly, envious, resentful, failed-ass career waiter. That's your everyday jacket. Now, add to that a gun and a gutful of vodka? I don't believe that shooting last night was an accident. I think you were a walking time bomb and last night you finally went off."

Eric sat there in a rapture of attention, chin uptilted as if for a kiss, his eyes never leaving Matty's.

"We are giving you one last chance to tell us what happened. Save your own skin and give us any version you want to justify your own part in it, but you get the ball rolling right here, right now . . . And I swear to fucking Christ, if you hand us *one* more time that pernicious horse-shit about a, a Hispanic *and, or, and, or* some, some *black* guy coming out the shadows or wherever, I will make *sure* this goes down for you in the worst possible way."

They waited, Eric shimmering in his seat, Yolonda giving him the mournful big eye, Matty glaring at him, but praying that he was even vaguely justified in laying into the guy like this.

"All I can say is what happened," Eric finally said, his voice infinitesimal, his eyes still fixed on Matty's.

And there you have it.


Jimmy Iacone walked back towards the Landsman in a funk; Matty didn't have to say anything, just give him that what-the-fuck-is-wrong-with-you stare, and he had made an about-face in the squad room without a word.

Still, a block from the hotel, he was surprised to come upon Billy Marcus in the street, standing across from the hilly guts of the recently collapsed synagogue on Rivington, gawking at the devastation as if he couldn't tell whether what he was looking at was really there or just a hallucinatory extension of his new eyes.

And whether it was due to the weight of the two overflowing shopping bags in his arms, emotional exhaustion, or just the sun chopping at the back of his knees, he repeatedly half dipped, then quickly straightened up, looking to all the world, if you didn't know his deal, like a junkie on the nod.

"Mr. Marcus?"

Billy wheeled, a quart bottle of hair conditioner bouncing on the sidewalk.

Jimmy stooped to retrieve it, carefully wedged it back into one of the overfull shopping bags.

"I'm sorry, I forgot to ask you. Are you going to need someone to take you for the identification? Or is another family member dealing with that."

. . .

Matty, Yolonda, ADA Kevin Flaherty, and Deputy Inspector Berkowitz, the designated point man on this for the chief of Manhattan detectives, all stood by the one-way again, watching Eric Cash tilted forward in his chair, his forehead on the edge of the table, his hands clasped between his knees.

Both Flaherty and Berkowitz had been wandering around the squad room talking to their respective bosses for hours.

"This stinks," Matty said.

"Why," Yolonda said, "because you made him feel bad and he didn't confess?"

"He's too guileless to be hanging tough like this. We hit him with the eyewits and he *still* doesn't ask for a lawyer? Doesn't even ask for a *phone* call? What is that, some kind of reverse psychology?"

Berkowitz kept his peace, observing them like a parent letting his kids work it out for themselves.

Flaherty's cell phone rang and he stepped away, a finger in his free ear.

"Yeah, well, about those eyewits."

"Hey." Matty raised his hands. "I don't know what to say about that. But I will tell you, if somehow, some way they're wrong and this poor bastard here's telling us the truth?" Wheeling to Berkowitz, "Boss, we're completely fucking ourselves, wasting all this time while the real shooter goes Running Man with something like a twelve-hour head start."

"Kevin." Yolonda snapped her fingers to get the ADA's eyes. "How many times did you reinterview those two?"

"You see me on the phone here?" he snapped, palming the mouthpiece.

"Look." Yolonda punched Matty's arm. "He went right back to sleep again."

"DA says charge him?" Matty asked Flaherty, fresh off the phone.

"Says we have problems, but we also have probable cause."

"This stinks," Matty said again.

"I'm not nuts about it either," Flaherty said, "but it's what I told you from the jump. Two eyewits trumps no physical evidence. If we let that guy walk out of here and he decides to go skiing in Switzerland before we can clear him for sure? Can't chance it."

"Switzerland? The guy's a fucking waiter."

"What can I say."

"You want me to do the honors?" Yolonda asked. "He likes me."

"I'll do it," Matty said.

"Whoever," Berkowitz said. "Just pull the goddamn plug already. Jesus Christ."


Besides Marcus and Iacone, only two other people were in the ground-floor waiting area of the medical examiner's office, a stone-faced black couple, both younger than Marcus, sitting side by side but not touching, the woman clutching a crumpled but dry Kleenex.

And after twenty minutes of silence, of sitting there breathing in the faintly refrigerated, vaguely skunky air and staring at the large city-owned oil painting of a golden sunset that hung directly above their heads, Marcus abruptly stood up, crossed the room, and, standing with his hands on his knees to be on eye level with them, said, "I'm very sorry for your loss," sounding like he owned the place, then returned to his seat.

A few minutes later, a powerfully built detective with the dropped shoulders of a boxer emerged from a side door, murmured, "William Marcus?" Billy popped up again as if goosed. After introducing himself as Detective Fortgang of the Identification Unit and nodding to Iacone—they had played on the NYPD football team together before Iacone blew out his knee and gained seventy-five pounds—escorted them back through that same door down two flights of cement stairs, the smell of disinfectant intensifying with each step.

Traveling along a cinder-block corridor, Fortgang's extended arm behind but not touching Marcus's back all the way, they were ushered into the room Iacone hated more than any other in the city of New York, large yet barren with only a single desk and two chairs. A long, rectangular viewing window, covered by thin metallic venetian blinds, was set into one of the walls.

Remaining on his feet as the father was offered the chair alongside Fortgang's desk, Iacone watched Marcus tensely scan the clutter there: a photo of Fortgang in sweats standing next to a teenage girls' softball team, a coffee mug with NEVER FORGET and NYPD superimposed over a drawing of the Twin Towers, and a stack of manila envelopes labeled in ballpoint with names, dates, and an initialed shorthand that didn't seem as if it would be too hard for anyone to decode.

Looking off, Iacone noticed a Polaroid wedged under a leg of the desk, a headshot of a middle-aged Latino, his eyeballs bulging from their sockets like a horny cartoon wolf, the butt of a plastic airway tube still taped into his mouth. Then he saw that Marcus was staring at it too.

"Sorry," Fortgang said, then leaned down to retrieve it, slip it into a drawer.

Marcus exhaled in a tremulous huff, then nodded to the long, shuttered window.

"The body's behind there?"

"No, that's not really necessary."

"OK."

Fortgang teased an envelope from the middle of the deck, *Isaac Marcus* scripted in a looping feminine hand followed by *GSW Hom. 10/8/02.*

"Mr. Marcus, we have an individual here"—the detective's voice sonorous—"may or may not be your son. All we need for you to do is to look at these photos, there's two of them and, if in fact it is, you know . . . You just sign the back of each and we're done."

"OK."

"Before . . . I just need to tell you that Polaroids like this, sometimes they're a little gritty."

"Gritty?"

"You're not seeing the person in their best light."

"OK."

"Are you OK?" Fortgang's hand on the envelope clasp.

"What?"

"Do you want some water?"

"Water? No."

Fortgang hesitated, glanced up at Iacone, nodding for him to get ready, then took out two three-by-five Polaroids, carefully laying them side by side facing the father. In the first, Ike Marcus was faceup, slack-mouthed, one eye peeking dimly from beneath a three-quarter-drooped lid, Iacone wondering why they wouldn't at least close that eye all the way before taking the picture; you were most likely going to be showing it to a parent, and it made their kid look retarded.

Marcus frowned as he studied the photos, as if perhaps the tattoos on the arms, the mermaid, panther, and devil's head, were unfamiliar and throwing off his concentration. The entry wound seemed inconsequential, a third nipple slightly off-center between the other two.

Fortgang waited, watching his eyes.

The second photo was of the kid lying on his stomach, his face profiled to the left, eyes lightly shut beneath arched eyebrows as if the radio alarm had just gone off and he was fighting waking up. His shoulders were hunched upwards towards his ears, and his hands were turned backwards so that his palms lay facing the camera. Marcus took in the stubble-cut hair and the backside of the tattoo that encircled the upper left arm, a vaguely Celtic-Navajo patterned band, and shook his head as if disappointed by the generic mystico-horseshit; as if he thought his kid had more irony to him than that. The exit wound in the lower back, once again, seemed hardly worth the hassle, no bigger than a strawberry.

Marcus picked up one of the photos, then put it down.

"It's not him."

Iacone winced, but Fortgang didn't seem surprised or put out.

"Would you prefer some other family member to come down?"

"Why? If it's not him, then you have the wrong family, so what's the point? I'm his father, wouldn't I know?"

Fortgang nodded. "I understand."

"I'm sorry."

"That's OK. We can make the ID some other way."

"What other way?"

"Dental."

"But if it's not him, why would you go to his dentist? Again, you're not making any sense."

Fortgang took a breath, glanced up at Iacone, then shrugged. "All right, Mr. Marcus, I'll take it from here. Thanks for coming."

Marcus stood up, shook the detective's hand, straightened his shirt, took a step to the door, then wheeled back around and let loose with a single whooping sob that should have been heard all through the building but was swallowed by the acoustically tiled walls: specifically installed, Iacone had once been told, in anticipation of moments such as this.

"We've got some bad news, Eric," Matty said in an almost apologetic tone while he slid his chair as close as he could without actually touching.

Eric sat up straighter, waited.

"Ike died."

"Oh." His eyes starred with chaos.

"And, after consulting with the district attorney, given the testimony of those two witnesses, we have no choice at this point but to charge you."

"Charge me. You mean arrest me?"

"Yes."

"Eric," Yolonda called him out in a heartbroken voice. "You can still help yourself. Tell us what happened."

But instead, he did something that genuinely shocked Matty.

With his mouth locked in a rictus grin, he rose to his feet and extended his wrists.

Matty could feel Yolonda's *I told you so* right through the back of his head.

"Relax," Matty said, reaching out and lightly pressing down on Eric's shoulder, "it'll be a while yet."

"Eric, please," Yolonda moaned, but then, taking in his vacant expression, just dropped it.

As Matty came up on 27 Eldridge again, he sensed, by looking at the reporters, that something had happened out here. They were mostly quiet now, both focused and hesitant, staring at a middle-aged woman standing with her back to them just outside the tape, her hands resting with a light tension on the weightless plastic as if it were the keyboard of a piano.

Oblivious to the attention she was drawing, she stared at the tenement without seeing it, her head tilted to one shoulder. Sporadically, one of the shooters would venture forward to capture her, the solitary snap, the whirring of videotape too loud in the tentative street.

Like most of them, Matty was guessing that this was the mother, although how she got here or even who gave her the news was a mystery since even the boy's father had no idea where she could be found, what country, what continent.

In her mid-forties, dressed in a silk blouse and black skirt, she had the effortless bearing and frame of a young athlete, but her face, from what he could see, carried the years, weathered and puffy.

Matty mentally set himself, then approached her from behind.

"Did he say anything?" she asked him without turning around, without any introduction.

"I'm sorry?"

"What was the last thing he said." She had an accent that he couldn't place.

"We're still gathering that." He began to offer his automatic condolences, then curbed himself; she wouldn't hear them anyhow.

"Where was he standing. Exactly," she quietly demanded, finally turning to him. She had jagged blue eyes, like cracked crystal.

Matty glanced reflexively at the dried blood, the woman tracking his gaze, then abruptly hooting, the sound flutelike, a musical sob.

"Idiot." She brusquely swiped at her eyes as if slapping herself.

Matty couldn't remember her name, first or last.

"Do you have people here?" he asked.

"People? What do you mean, people."

"Family."

"Yes." Pointing to the blood without looking at it again.

"This is not a good place for you right now," he said.

"Elena?"

They both turned to see Billy Marcus stumbling towards the crime-scene tape as if it were a finish line.

At the sight of him, her face inflated with rage, and for a second Matty thought she was going to attack him. Marcus apparently did too, stopping dead and lightly closing his eyes as if bracing for it, but then she started to cry, and he first tentatively, then more emphatically, wrapped his arms around her, sobbing himself, the shooters having a field day until Matty and some others chased them off.

"It's OK," Marcus said, then, putting his arm around his ex-wife, began to walk her out of there, both looking decades older than they were.

Bobby Oh emerged from the building, caught Matty's eye, then shrugged apologetically: no gun.

When prisoner transport finally arrived, ninety minutes after they were called, Yolanda and Matty reentered the interview room, Eric again rising and extending his wrists.

"Actually," Matty murmured, turning him by his shoulders and cuffing him so that his curled hands rested on the small of his back.

"Huh," Eric said. "Up in Binghamton they did it from in front."

The door to Billy Marcus's hotel room at the Landsman was unlocked, but there was no response to Matty's knocks, so calling out a tentative greeting, he let himself inside. It was like walking into a cave, the curtains having been drawn all the way around against the sun.

The first thing to catch Matty's attention in this murk was the smell: alcohol-infused sweat, and a hint of something alkaloid beneath that. The second thing, when his eyes began to adjust, was the king-size bed, its great synthetic polar-bear spread humped and bunched, the pillows and sheets beneath rumpled or cast to the floor altogether.

The third was the silence: a silence so complete that he assumed he was alone until a brief slish of stockings drew his attention first to one shadowed corner, a huff of breath to another.

"May I?" Matty said, then carefully parted just enough of one curtain to not disrespect the desire for dark.

They were sitting on opposite ends of the room, the mother in a hard plastic easy chair, the father on the radiator, their clothes in disarray; Elena wearing only one shoe, Marcus barefoot, the both of them staring at him with the unself-conciousness of animals, with unblinking pie-eyed shock.

The floor was equally chaotic, littered with splayed luggage and jumbles of trance-snatched personal items: clothing and slippers, prescription bottles and a travel iron, a quart bottle of Herbal Essences conditioner and a pint bottle of baby oil, which, upended, slowly pooled on the rug, adding its own nutlike scent to the atmosphere. He counted three plastic bathroom cups around the room, filled with varying amounts of melted ice and what he guessed was vodka, then spotted a fourth on the night table, using an open Gideons Bible as a coaster.

Pulling out a chair from beneath a small desk, he positioned himself midpoint between them and leaned into the infused air. "I came here to tell you that we've arrested Eric Cash."

"OK," the father said neutrally.

"But he still hasn't confessed and I'm not going to lie. Like I told you before, Mr. Marcus, there's still a huge amount of work to be done for the charges to hold up."

"He's arrested?"

"He's . . . yes, he is."

"In court?" Marcus sounded like he was talking in his sleep.

"He's in Central Booking being processed."

The mother had been looking directly at him since he entered the room, but he was pretty sure she hadn't heard a word he'd said.

"Why'd he do it again?" Marcus asked.

"That's one of the elements we're still trying to put together right now."

"But he's in court?"

Matty took a breath. "Going in that direction, yes."

"OK, good," Marcus said faintly. "Thank you."

Another silence came down, Matty obliquely studying the mother, looking off glassy now, lightly stroking her right temple with a fingertip.

And once again he was taken by the contrast between her face and body; the feline ease and coiled readiness of a woman twenty years her junior, but those eyes carried the years, and an unhappiness that he didn't think began in the last few days.

"Is there anything else I can do for either of you. Anything you need."

"No, no thanks," Marcus said. "Thank you."

Matty hesitated. "How about some fresh ice."

"No. Thank you."

Matty tilted forward to rise. "I understand you've already been to the medical examiner's office. Do you have any—"

"No!" the mother shouted, out of her seat in a blur, flying at Marcus. "*He's* been!" Swiping at his face, the guy listlessly raising a hand to shield himself. "*He's* been!"

Marcus's eyes sagged in their sockets.

Matty stayed put.

"I go there, to see Isaac, and they say *no*. They say the father has been and we don't show twice.

"I say, I am his mother, please, let me see him, please, what kind of a rule is this? No. Sorry. No."

"How was I supposed to know?" Marcus said without heat.

"*He's* been!" She caught him on the cheek with a nail, a line in the flesh there blooming from blanched to pink to dripping like a fast-forwarded film.

"Elena, I told you, all they show is a photo," Marcus pleaded. "You wouldn't have—"

"Don't you say to me *wouldn't*! You don't say to me *any*thing!"

She turned, stalked across the room, flung open the door, and left. Matty couldn't tell if the unsteadiness of her stride was from the drinking or from her only wearing one shoe.

Marcus drifted from the radiator to the edge of the unmade bed and distractedly wiped his cheek with a corner of the top sheet. He seemed to notice the massive disarray for the first time.

"Do you want me to catch up with her, make sure she's OK?"

"No," Marcus said. "She's . . ."

"You know, I could probably cash in a favor at the medical examiner's, you know, if she really needs to see . . ."

"Don't," Marcus said with a flare of sudden energy. "You don't know her, she doesn't need, she . . . Just, don't. Please. Thank you."

"No problem."

Marcus took a long, exhausted breath, then gestured to the rumpled sex-damp sheets.

"She said we should make another one right away," plucking at the synthetic fur. Then after a moment's hesitation, "That's crazy, right?"

The intake entrance to the Tombs was surprisingly funky for a prison so well known: a small, rackety roll-down gate on a narrow backstreet in Chinatown. Inside the building itself, all of the bureaucratic way stations leading to the holding cells maintained the same grubby proportion: gun locker for the accompanying officers, paperwork submission, fingerprinting, photographing, medical interview, and finally, body search, each stop bookended by its own modest wire-mesh security gate, its own low air-duct-cramped ceiling; this massive institution as far as Eric could tell a claustrophobic multileveled maze of stairs and short hallways, a life-size game board of Chutes and Ladders. He had been inside for half an hour so far, escorted every step by the two detectives who had taken him from the precinct just a few blocks away, and he had yet to see another prisoner. Those detectives, while impersonally polite and even-tempered in their dealings with him on the way over, once inside the gate became increasingly on edge, more so than he was; probably, he figured, fearing some procedural snag that would trap them in here for hours.

He himself wasn't afraid; more like inordinately preoccupied, still vibrating with fragments of things said or unsaid by him, to him; things done or not done, again by him, to him; and lastly, sneaking up on him like a recurring bout of fever, what he'd seen.

Matty walked into Berkmann's in the midst of its late-afternoon sunbath and took a seat at the empty bar. The place was as quiet as a library save for the staff meeting going on, Harry Steele addressing his managers at a back banquette.

"Unfortunately, at this point, we need to talk about hiring a new bartender."

There was an uncomfortable silence.

"I know, I'm sorry," he murmured, "but . . ."

"Handsome Dan?" one of the managers finally said.

"The waiter?" Steele half smiled. "He'd want a little wind machine back there for his hair."

"Well then, we should get that English guy from Le Zinc, looks like he got bit by a crocodile."

"Too far the other way."

"How about that kid I was telling you about, the cafeteria cashier from NYU, spiked his Hawaiian Punch dispenser with vodka, had a tray line around the block."

"No," Steele said, "I don't like operators."

"Never got caught."

"Exactly."

Not sure Steele knew he was waiting, Matty briefly stepped away from the bar to catch his eye, the owner holding up a finger, one more minute, without looking at him.

"You know what?" one of the female managers said quietly. "I don't really think I can talk about this right now."

The table descended into another silence, until Steele nodded. "No, you're right."

There was another reflective pause, people nodding to themselves, chewing knuckles, staring into their coffees until Steele finally said, "OK, then."

As they began to rise and collect themselves, Steele remained sitting there in a glassy-eyed brood.

"Lisa," he said, freezing one of his people midrise in a high-eyebrowed smile, waited for the others to walk away, then gestured for her to sit back down. "Why did you put that solo at the table next to me yesterday morning," wincing as he spoke. "The entire restaurant was empty. It was embarrassing, two men alone that close. You *never* put solos of the same sex next to each other. It's like an ad for loneliness. Like a bad Hopper painting."

"The guy wanted a window seat," she said.

"Are you hearing me?"

Through the windows, Matty counted four detectives out there canvassing Rivington.

Three others entered the café in a flourish of topcoats, nodding to Matty, then eyeing the staff, mentally divvying up the room.

Matty took the place of the dispersed managers at the back banquette, accepted the French press from the busboy with a nod. Across the floor there were more tables full of detectives and employees than there were of customers, those tall glass cylinders of roasted coffee floating around the room like helicopters.

"Terrible," Steele said softly, the pouches under his restless eyes looking like thumbed clay. "Half the business today was reporters."

"You tell them anything you should've told me first?" The two of them had known each other since the café opened for business eight years ago and Matty had handled the discreet off-the-premises arrest of a waiter for selling meat out of the kitchen to other restaurants.

"Did you get to know him at all?" Matty asked.

"Marcus?" Steele shrugged. "In all honesty, I just hired him because he looked right."

"Did he have any problems with people?"

"After two days?"

"Who would have known him the best in here?" Matty asked.

"No idea." Steele shrugged. "You have any leads?"

"We've made an arrest," Matty said reluctantly, then, "Tell me about Eric Cash."

"Eric?" Steele smiled with a combination of affection and something less, then, *"Eric?"*

Matty drank more coffee.

"You can*not* be serious," Steele said. "Why would he do something like that?"

"He's been with you a long time?"

"From a pup."

Matty waited for more.

"You're out of your mind."

"There's a headline. Tell me about him."

*"Eric?"*

Matty waited.

"He's very good at what he's good at." Steele curved his palms around the coffee press, frowned, and signaled for a fresh one. "Terrific reader."

"Reader . . ."

"You know. Faces. Unhappy tables, cokey waiters, who's passing by out there"—Steele tilted his chin at Rivington—"which of our neighborly neighbors is gearing up for another offensive at the next Liquor Board hearing. Great reader, great anticipator, alert as hell. There's got to be some mistake."

"What else?"

"Loyal? I'm not sure what you're looking for."

"Did he have any issues with Marcus? A run-in?"

"I have no idea. I doubt it, though."

"He says they were in here together last night about two-thirty."

"I'm never here past nine myself. Check out the tapes if you want."

"What do you know about the Virgin Mary incident yesterday?"

"The what?" Steele blinked.

Matty stared at him but didn't pursue.

"So this what, makes no sense to you?"

"Eric Cash . . ." Steele shook his head as if to clear it, then leaned forward. "Listen, speaking of the Liquor Board, how do you feel about maybe getting up there next month, saying a few words on our behalf?"

"Like what?"

"You know, what good neighbors we are, how we helped you out with the Lam murder."

"I'll check with my boss, but I can't imagine him having a problem with it."

Two months earlier, when an elderly Chinaman had been shot and robbed on Rivington Street in the middle of the night three blocks from Berkmann's, no witnesses, the cops had spent hours looking at the café's security tapes, both internal and street-facing, and caught an image of the perp, briskly walking past the place a few minutes after the deed.

They also caught footage of one of the cooks bending a busboy over the slop sink and two waiters in the locker room sharing a bottle of $250 Johnnie Walker Blue Label, that one never leaving the restaurant, although the word was that Steele screened it at a full staff meeting, busboys to managers, before firing the stars.

"I'm sure it's no problem. Just give me a day or two heads-up," Matty said, beginning to rise.

"You hear what happened at the last meeting?" Steele asked, making no move to rise himself. "They tried to get the board to revoke our liquor license because we sell alcohol within five hundred feet of a school." Steele looked out the window at the nineteenth-century junior high across the street. "You ever see the kids that go there? I mean, Jesus, we need protection from *them*. I mean, who do *you* deal with out here, right?"

"I hear you," Matty said neutrally.

"And you know who does all the complaining at these meetings, don't you?"

"Who?" Matty sank back down, thinking, Here we go, thinking, Five minutes.

"The whites. The, the 'pioneers' . . . The Latinos? The Chinese? The ones been living here since the Flood? Couldn't be nicer. Happy for the jobs. The thing is, the complainers? *They're* the ones that started all this. We just follow them. Always have, always will. Come down here, buy some smack squat from the city, do a little fix-up, have a nice big studio, rent out the extra space, mix it up with the ethnics, feel all good and politically righteous about yourself. But those lofts now? Those buildings? Twenty-five hundred square feet, fourth floor, no elevator, Orchard and Broome. Two point four mil just last week."

Matty saw three police techs walk in, heading directly for the office downstairs where they kept the tapes.

"Bunch of middle-aged, talentless artistes and armchair socialists complaining about the very people who made them rich. Sitting there saying they have a right to perfect peace and quiet in their own neighborhood . . . No. You *don't*. This is New *York*. You have a right to *reasonable* peace and quiet.

"I mean *I* live here too. I live with the noise, the drunks, the tour buses. It's called revitalization.

"Do you remember it down here when we first opened? A hellhole. A dope souk. You guys were suiting up like you were in Baghdad."

"Remember it well," Matty said distractedly, this diatribe an oldie.

"It's called resur*rec*tion."

"All right then," Matty repeated, rising and shrugging on his coat.

"I swear to God"—Steele glared out the window—"I wish they'd all put their shit on the market, take the money, and move to Woodstock."

"Let me just ask." Matty stood over him. "What happened with Eric Cash in Binghamton a few years ago. Losing the restaurant and that drug collar. I heard you helped him out around that?"

Steele looked off, gave up a tight smile. "Like I said, Eric is very good at what he's good at. But sometimes you have to give people their head." Then, looking directly at Matty, being the teacher now, "Trust me, it comes back to you in spades."

On his way out, Matty ran into Clarence Howard, the bouncer-doorman, on his way in to work and was embraced in a backslappy hug before he could set himself. Howard was a weight lifter and an ex-cop who had been fired his first year in uniform for walking out of an in-door crime scene he was safeguarding in possession of a stamp, an upside-down 1918 "Flying Jenny" misprint worth hundreds of thousands of dollars. They'd have brought criminal charges, but the thing was found stuck to the inseam of his pants, not inside his pocket; room for doubt regarding intent. Matty thought the kid got a bad deal and helped secure him this gig with Steele, only to find out a year later, as they drank their way south on Ludlow one night, that Clarence had been not only the youngest but also the first African-American president in the history of the Forest Hills Philatelists Club.

Matty still liked the guy.

"Some sad shit," Clarence said, sipping from a cup of take-out coffee.

"You knew him?"

"Who, Eric?"

"The vic."

"Nah. He just started on days. I'm nights."

"How about last night?"

"I was about to say, although I did see the three of them at last call."

"And . . ."

"The fat guy was shitfaced, the vic was like halfway back to sober."

"How about Cash."

"Cash . . ." Clarence shook his head, blew on his coffee. "I tell you, man, I hope you got some hard evidence on him because, *Eric?* I don't get that."

Matty felt sick. "Does he ever carry a piece?"

"Not that I ever saw."

"And not last night."

"Not that I noticed."

"How'd he strike you coming out of here?"

"Unhappy. I mean, Eric's an OK guy, but he always struck me as an individual needs to have a little more fun in his life, you know?"

Clarence paused to watch a cab pull up, three women loaded down with shopping bags exiting from the rear seat.

"Although today don't seem like it's gonna be a good day for him to start, huh?"

Although still off-duty, Clarence held the door to the restaurant for the women, the last one inside turning back and dropping a quarter in his coffee cup, the liquid dancing above the rim.

White-faced with embarrassment, she turned on her heel and race-walked to her friends at the bar.

"Happens all the time," he murmured, pouring his drink into the gutter.

"So you're doing OK, Clarence?"

"I'm doing what I got to be doing, you know?" The kid hungry to say more, but then Yolonda rang.

"Hey, Matty," she said, "guess who's awake."


Walking into the hospital room, they came up on either side of Steven Boulware's bed.

Blood sick, stomach pumped, flat on his back, and sprouting IVs from both arms, the kid still managed to project an air of thick sensuality, his hooded eyes both vacant and on the prowl.

He scanned their IDs, then looked away, as if ashamed. "How's Ike?" His voice metallic with hangover.

"Ike?" Matty said.

"What happened last night?" Yolonda tilted her chin at him.

"Are you serious?"

They stared at him, waiting.

He stared back, as if the question were mined.

"What do you remember?" Matty said as placidly as he could.

Boulware slowly inhaled, exhaled, remained silent.

"I know," Yolonda said tenderly, smoothing back the hair on his forehead. "But talk to us."

"We were by my building, the three of us, late," he began. "And these two guys come out of nowhere, they must have been laying up for somebody. One had a gun, said something like, 'Give it up, fork it over.' I'm like, shit . . ."

Matty and Yolonda looked at each other, Matty's mind a scramble. "This older guy from Ike's restaurant that was with us, I can't remember his name, I think he just did what they said." Boulware paused. "But then Ike, Ike goes and gets all chesty about it, I heard him say to the guy, something like, 'Not tonight, my man.' Or, I don't know, something to the effect of get fucked . . . And then I think, I think he started to go for the guy." Boulware closed his eyes, then crossed his arms over his chest, a pharaoh in repose.

"What do you mean, you 'think,' " Yolonda said calmly, starting to balloon with anger.

Boulware continued to play corpse, long enough for Matty to want to rip the IVs out of his arms.

"We're going to need you to look at some photo arrays, sit down with a sketch artist," Yolonda said, glaring at Matty. "Like, today."

"Honestly?" Boulware winced, opened his eyes. "I don't think I can do that."

"We'll bring everything here," Yolonda said, making it sound like great fun. "You won't even have to get out of bed."

"No, it's not . . ." He craned his neck to the right, a yearning for escape in the upward roll of his eyes.

"What's the problem, Steve?" Matty asked, his bottled distress adding a little more zip to his tone than usual.

"Look. Last night? I have . . . I was off my nut. Ike and that other guy were actually kind of holding me up. But as soon as I saw that gun? I just hit the deck and stayed there. And my eyes were closed the whole time after that."

"Playin' possum, huh?" Yolonda said as if amused.

"I'm not going to lie to you. I was scared. I mean, I was off-my-ass drunk too, but I was really fuckin' scared." He paused, looking at them for sympathy. "So I went with the drunk thing."

"The drunk thing."

"I wasn't faking, ask anybody here, but sometimes, when I'm good and rocked? I get into this zone where I can tell myself I'm physically more this, or more that, than I really am, and . . . it becomes true. And it's not just with making myself more drunk. It could be like, making myself stronger, faster, have a better voice, whatever."

"You ever tell yourself you can fly?" Yolonda asked.

"Look, I saw that gun and that thing I do just took over, like a survival reflex. For all I know, it just might've saved my life, but . . . I mean, it's not like I feel proud of myself about it. I don't feel . . . shit, I mean even after the cops came, I was still so ripped I couldn't talk. I couldn't . . ."

Again he looked to them for understanding, a free pass; got only stares.

"But you were definitely held up at gunpoint," Matty said.

"Oh yeah. Yes . . ."

"By two males."

"Yes." Then, "I'm pretty sure it was two, could have been more, but like I said . . ."

"Your eyes were closed."

"Well, how many voices do you remember?"

"Just what I said. Ike and the guy with the gun."

"Think on it again."

"Maybe you should close your eyes," Yolonda said. "You know, get in the mood."

Matty cut her a look, Yolonda twisting her lips.

"I think there was a girl there."

"A girl was with them?"

"No. Separate, like, behind us, across the street maybe, I'm not sure."

"What do you mean, a girl? A child?"

"No. Just young, like, my age? Like, arguing with someone, maybe?"

"Arguing about what?"

"I don't know."

"What did she sound like, white, black, Latino . . ." Yolonda's anger made her rattle through the litany as if she were bored.

"Black. She kind of sounded black."

"What do you mean 'kind of.' "

"Like, educated?"

"Nicely put," Yolonda said.

"What?"

"This, educated black girl, who was she arguing with, male or female?"

"I'm pretty sure male."

"White, black?"

"His voice?"

"Yes," Yolonda said, "his voice."

"White maybe? I'm not . . . I don't know."

Matty stared at Yolonda, the both of them thinking the same thing.

"No," Yolonda said to Matty, "no fucking way."

Matty was unable to respond, to put their troubles in size order as he tried to calculate the dozens, the hundreds, of warrants they would now be executing on the Lower East Side in the next twenty-four hours on the off chance that one of their homegrown skeeves out there knew someone who knew someone who knew someone who overheard someone; as he tried to calculate the hundreds of old robbery-pattern reports to be pored over, the reinterviewing to be done, the recanvassing, the threatening, the cajoling, the bargaining, the bullshitting, the bluffing, the whole hopeless pig-in-a-poke cluster fuck this was about to become if Boulware's account turned out to be accurate, which it probably would; if the witness accounts turned out to be flawed, as they probably would; as they tried to play catch-up with a robbery-homicide nearly fourteen hours after the horses had left the gate.

"So is Ike OK?" Boulware asked sheepishly.

"Your friend Ike?" Yolonda said brightly. "He's dead."

At six in the evening, Kevin Flaherty, the ADA who had reinterviewed Randal Condo on the street earlier that morning, went at him again, this time in one of the squad's small rooms, Matty pacing outside like an expectant father.

"Go back to right before you heard the shot. What were you doing?" Flaherty said.

"Walking up Eldridge towards Nikki while she's walking down Eldridge towards me." Condo looked like he hadn't ever gone to sleep from the night before.

"Talking to each other?"

"Most likely."

"With some fraction of a block between you?"

"I guess."

"That takes raised voices. You were raising your voice at each other?"

"I'm not sure."

"Arguing?"

"No."

"You sure about that?"

Condo took a moment, then shrugged. "Possibly."

"People say possibly to me they usually mean probably."

"So what if we were?" His voice smaller than the bellicose response would have suggested.

"Randal, dead of night, your girlfriend's walking a half a block ahead of you. You were having a fight, yes?"

He didn't answer, Flaherty cursing himself, this all so fucking obvious now.

"Now, I told you this morning we had a number of people told the canvass they heard shouting in the street around the time of the shooting, yeah? Voices raised loud enough to be heard in fourth-, fifth-, sixth-floor apartments, you remember me asking you about that?"

"We weren't that loud."

"Your girl's a half a block down the street and you're still going at it? Trust me, you were."

Condo breathed through his nose, looked off. "Possibly."

"And I'll tell you something else. People who get into arguments in the street? In public like that? You got to be pretty deep into it not to give a shit about who's watching. In fact, I'd say that there could be a three-ring circus twenty feet away, they'd barely know it."

Condo closed his eyes, rubbed his face.

"So, I'm thinking, if, when rounding Delancey onto Eldridge, you two are going at it so hot and heavy that she starts stomping away from you so that now you have to start *yelling* just to keep it going? There's no *way* you were watching that encounter develop across the street."

"I didn't make it up."

"And then it just gets worse. Because at some point you must've said something, yelled out something got this woman *so* pissed off that all of a sudden she does a one-eighty and starts coming *back* at you? Now, at *that* point there's no *way* she's not getting your undivided attention. No *way* you're checking out anything across the street. That'd be like the quarterback sizing up some blonde in the stands while a linebacker's coming for him straight up the middle. And *that* leads me to believe that what *first* got your attention over there was *hearing* that gun go off, and by the time you really gave them a good look-see, whatever had gone down was already a done deal. You might have seen the two of them falling and the third guy booking into the building, but I don't think you can honestly tell me if before that there were originally three, four, or five people, who actually had the gun, or if anybody else took off other than the guy running into the building." The ADA took a beat to let this sink in. "All they would have needed was a split-second lead on your eye and they're out into the shadows like they never existed."

"Look, I saw what I saw."

"That's my point."

Condo took a breath. "Can I smoke in here?"

"Not really, but go ahead."

Flaherty watched him fire up, watched him think.

"We have a guy in the Tombs right now pretty much based on what you told us," Flaherty said, then leaning forward, lowered his voice. "It's not criminal to be mistaken, Randal. Sometimes we confuse the words *see* and *hear*, especially when something goes down so fast and unexpected."

"OK," he said hoarsely.

"So." The ADA tapped Condo's crossed knee. "Are you still sure we have the right guy?"

"I saw what I saw."

"Just answer yes or no."

"No."

Flaherty sat back and finger-combed his hair, resisting the impulse to pull it out by the fistful.

"Just out of curiosity," his own voice growing hoarse now, "what exactly were you two fighting about?"

"The definition of a word."

"What word would that be?"

Condo closed his eyes. "Girlfriend."


"I specifically asked you if you heard arguing." Bobby Oh was not in the habit of raising his voice, so he didn't now, but it was all there in his bloodshot eyes.

"Well, if you're doing the arguing yourself, do you consider that 'hearing arguing'?" Nikki Williams responded queasily.

Bobby leaned forward in his chair so abruptly that she flinched. "Say again?"

"It's like, if you're already underwater, do you think of yourself as wet?"

He stared at her until she looked away.

"He always told me I was only the second woman of color he had ever had a relationship with, then somebody at the party tells me that actually I was the fifth." Nikki talking to her lap now, avoiding his eyes. "That's a very creepy kind of lie."

Bobby made himself look away from her.

"Then on the way home he goes and improves things by yelling out from halfway down the block that those other three were just about the sex."

Bobby Oh was Night Watch. He was here, he was *still* here, eighteen hours after his tour began, strictly as a favor to Matty Clark because he had developed a rapport with this witness, this bullshit witness. He could go home now and nobody would think the lesser of him even though he had helped screw the pooch on this one as much as anyone else.

"I didn't want to say anything about it," Nikki said, "because it was nobody else's business."

Then, "It was humiliating."

Then, tearing up, "I'm so sorry."


Eric had been standing in a corner of the holding cell for three hours. Four cells all directly faced the CO command desk, their capacity twenty prisoners each. In his particular cell, thirteen prisoners, most of them seeming to take being here in stride, were standing or sitting together and talking as if at a bar or in a barracks, the only swirl of action coming about when a new arrestee had made it through the maze and stood in front of the desk with his accompanying paperwork and escort. Most of the prisoners saw this as an occasion to drape themselves on the front bars and call out to the cops or COs that an innocent man was in here, that they were still waiting for that Tylenol or pay lawyer or asthma medicine or whatever came to mind. The only ones in the cell who didn't seem to know anybody else or join in this periodic rush to the bars were Eric and a blaze-eyed black man, slack-bellied and nuts, wearing his T-shirt around his neck like a dickey as he disjointedly paced the perimeter whispering to himself. For hours now this guy had been keying on Eric, approaching him in his corner every few minutes on his aimless journey though the cage and asking to borrow his E-ZPass, Eric just ignoring him and slipping back into his own inner static like slipping back into bed: The reason he ran into 27 Eldridge was because . . . The reason he didn't call 911 was because . . . The reason he never even thought to ask if Ike Marcus had survived was because . . . The reason he had lied about everything was because . . .

Lost as he was in his fractured and incomplete ruminations, not even the ambient stink of the cage got through to him; not even the occasional rush of phantom hands in his pockets, the mumbled threats; not even his own name being called over and over by a pregnant CO was enough to pull him out of the forest fire that was his head, until she finally barked, "Hey, *Cash*. Do you want to go home or *not*?"

When he looked up, he saw that the same two detectives who had brought him here three hours ago were back, looking jumpy as ever about getting the hell out.

• • •

The first car stop of the evening came right at sundown, the Quality of Life taxi just happening to be there as a Nissan Sentra ran a red light in front of the Dubinsky Co-ops on the eastern end of Grand; no need to justify the pullover.

Lugo and Daley, working as a solo team this tour, walked up on either side of the car, cross-beaming the front seats. When the driver, a beefy crew-cut white guy with an open box of KFC on his lap, rolled down his window, the weed stank curled out like steam from a sauna.

"You got to be shitting me." Lugo reared back, fanning the air. "Make my job a *little* hard at least."

"Sorry." The driver, still chewing, half-smiled, a glistening sliver of dark meat pasted to the corner of his mouth.

The passenger, also white, a vacant-faced teenager blinged out in triple-X-size threads and a sideways baseball cap from the Negro Leagues, stared directly into the beam of Daley's flashlight as if it were a movie screen.

"C'mon out." Lugo opened the driver's door, but instead of hopping to it, the driver purposefully wiped the grease from his fingers one at a time, then leaned across the lap of his passenger to open the glove compartment.

"Whoa!" Lugo lunged forward, seizing the man's wrist with one hand, fumbling for his gun with the other.

"OK, OK," the driver said easily. "I was just getting out my ID."

"Did I *ask* you to?" Lugo near shouted, his hand, still trembling, gripping the butt of his unpulled Glock.

The kid in the passenger seat was grinning now, his eyes red and waggling. Daley reached in and pulled him out by the back of his shirt, dropped him belly-down on the hood, and held him there.

"I said get the fuck out of the *car*," Lugo bellowed, yanking on the already open driver's door so violently that it slammed itself shut on the rebound.

The driver waited for Lugo to step back a little, then came out with his hands up. "I'm on the job, fellas," he said calmly, his jaw still rolling with chicken. "Check the glove box."

Daley went into the compartment, came out a moment later with a Lake George, New York, police ID, displaying it for Lugo across the roof of the car.

"The fuck is *wrong* with you, reaching for something like that," Lugo barked. "Of all people, you don't know better than that?"

"Sorry," the driver said. "We've been driving around all day, I'm a little spacey."

"Spacey, huh? It fuckin' *reeks* in there."

The teenager sniggered.

"Just a little somethin' somethin' for the drive," the upstate cop said.

"Somethin' somethin', huh?" Lugo hadn't heard that phrase in two years.

"Can I ask *you* somethin' somethin'?" Daley addressed the blinged-out kid. "What exactly *is* cow-tipping?"

"Fuck should I know," the kid sulked.

"Where are you headed now?" Lugo asked the driver.

"Right there." The driver pointed to the co-ops. "My father's apartment."

"Do me a favor." Lugo lit a cigarette, his hand still shaking. "You want to do your little somethin' somethin'? Do it up there."

"Yeah, Dad would love that," the younger kid said. "He's a cop too."

His brother threw him a look.

"Cop down here?" Daley asked.

"*Right* down here," the kid crowed, the driver coming off his buzz now, glowering a little.

Daley reread the guy's ID. "Huh," he grunted, then threw Lugo a look.


This time, with the drapes pulled back and the glass doors open, walking into room 1660 of the Landsman felt like walking up to the edge of a cliff. Billy Marcus, reduced to a silhouette, sat outside on the low railing, his back to the street sixteen floors below.

Matty walked out to join him.

"Derek Jeter got some hate mail," Marcus said, leaning backwards a little, turning his head and peering down at the street life. "That's the headline, today's headline."

"I hear you," Matty murmured, getting a casual grip on Marcus's elbow and easing him off the railing.

Actually it was yesterday's headline, but Matty wouldn't tell him that.

Matty maneuvered Marcus back into the room, then closed all the terrace doors.

"Where's Elena?"

"She left."

"To where?"

"I don't know."

"She's coming back?"

"I don't think so."

Surveying the clutter on the floor, Matty noted the absence of any obviously feminine items.

"I was hoping she would be here," Matty said, pulling up the desk chair.

"For what."

"I have some news."

And at the way the guy's face leapt, Matty knew that he had just made a mistake, the word *news* probably sounding to Marcus like a coy prelude to an announcement of a miraculous reversal of recent events, his son in some way having snapped out of it or finally stopped messing around, fucking with everybody's head.

"We had to cut Eric Cash loose. The third member of your son's party, Steven Boulware? He came to and basically backed Cash's version of events." Matty took a beat, let that sink in. "So we reinterviewed our eyewitnesses, and it turns out their testimony, unfortunately, is a lot more sketchy than we initially thought." Another beat. "So, without any solid testimony, without any physical evidence, without . . ."

"Who's Eric Cash?" Marcus said.

"The initial suspect," Matty said evenly. "The one we arrested."

"OK." Marcus nodded cautiously.

Matty stared at his hands. "Look, we had to move fast with what we believed to be a credible account."

"No, sure, you had to."

"But we're right back out there scouring the area for other possible witnesses, for the gun, for . . ."

Marcus continued to nod, as if to show Matty what a good attentive listener he was.

"Can I be honest with you?" Matty said. "We fucked up. We wasted a whole day throwing everything we had at the wrong suspect and . . . we fucked up. But we're going to move fast now and make this right."

"Good," Marcus said with a hollow forcefulness, then extended his hand. "Thank you."

Having been braced for an explosion of rage since the moment he walked into the room, Matty just felt saddened by this man's total lack of comprehension.

"Are you sure Elena won't be coming back here?"

"Who's to say, but, no, I don't."

"Mr. Marcus, I don't have a lot of discretionary time but . . ." Matty leaned into him a little. "Would you like me to reach out to your wife for you?"

"You know," Marcus said, addressing the middle distance, "when they're little, you love them, take pride in them, and when they grow up, you still do, but it's bizarre when other people, new people, see him and think, 'Well, here's this young man, here's this young adult who does such and such very well,' and you're witnessing this acceptance from others, this respect and seriousness, and you, I can't help laughing, thinking, that's, *what* young man, that's Ikey, you wouldn't believe the dopey shit he did as a kid, but there he is getting respect, and it's not like *I* don't have it for him, me of all people, but I always feel like laughing, not put-him-in-his-place laughing, just 'Aw, c'mon, that's *Ike* . . .'"

"Mr. Marcus . . ."

"Call me Billy, please?"

"OK, Billy, look, I understand you're distraught, but you have to believe me when I say you're making a serious mistake by being alone right now. This, this, what you're going through? You're going to be going through it for a long time, and your family? Your family can save your life."

"It's like . . ." Marcus stared at the terrace rail. "People try to convince you, they *do* convince you, that you can't make a child happy if you're miserable yourself. You want to take care of him? You take care of yourself first."

He shook his head in disbelief, then, tearing his eyes away from the railing, looked directly at Matty. "So with Ikey? . . . I just left." Then in an explosion of dry blubbering, the words coming out as if tumbling down stairs, "He was so little and I just left, you know?"

"Mr. Marcus, Billy"—Matty so bad at this—"were you ever contacted by victims' services?"

Unable to think what else to say, Matty found himself picking up random scatter from the floor: a towel, an empty vodka from the minibar, and at least a dozen reporters' cards from every media outlet in the tristate area.

"Look, Mr. Marcus, Billy, I have to go now."

"I understand," Marcus said. "I just need to lay down for a minute, get my head together."

"I'll try to come back, keep you abreast, see how you're doing."

Marcus stared off, whispering to himself.

But when Matty turned to the door, Marcus said, "Don't be too hard on yourself. You did what you thought was right," then eased his head to the pillow.


He needed to get Marcus moved to a lower room. On one hand, if someone intended to do himself in, dropping from a fourth-floor window would do the trick as neatly as a drop from the sixteenth, but that wraparound vista seemed a little too charismatic.

Walking out of the elevator into the lobby, Matty was surprised to see Billy Marcus's wife, in jeans and a wilted T-shirt, leaning across the front desk to get into the eyes of the clerk on duty, a spectacular blond kid in a bloodred Mandarin blouse that matched the hellish hue of the walls to the point of camouflage.

"He is my husband, he has lost his child, what am I *asking* you, just give me his *room* number."

Strangling beneath her innocent fabulousness, the clerk looked to Matty with openmouthed distress. "Miss, I'm sorry," her voice small and pleading. "I'd lose my job."

He began to step forward, then stopped; he'd been campaigning for this reunion all day, but now that he had husband and wife under the same roof, he reminded himself that the guy had just been up there a few hours ago fucking and fighting with the dead kid's mother, who could possibly return; that family reconciliations were not his job.

"Look." Marcus's wife extended her hands to the girl, took a breath. "I cannot imagine any decent person in the world penalizing someone in your position for doing the compassionate thing here."

Definitely take a pass on getting involved any further; nonetheless he found himself lingering, just to watch her.

This woman was something else: exhausted, distraught, probably hitting one wall after another since the morning, she was still somehow in possession of herself, mounting this latest assault without losing her composure, without allowing herself to degenerate into abusiveness or rage; in his eyes, a real high-hearted warrior.

"OK, how about . . ." the wife began, the long, slender fingers of one hand hovering over a decorative bowl of indestructible-looking green apples. "Is there someone you could call, someone that could take the weight off you."

The clerk, becoming with each passing moment more and more of a child, picked up the phone as directed. Matty waited until he heard a recorded voice on the other end of the line, then he left the hotel.


Out on the street he called Yolonda, found out that the autopsy had confirmed Eric Cash's description of how the gun had been held, raised overhead in a curled-wrist gangsta arc, the bullet having entered the heart and exited through the lower back; that the recovered shell casing had no connection to any other casing in the system; and that dredging twelve manholes and grates in a three-block radius of the crime scene produced six knives, eleven box cutters, the lower half of a samurai sword, but no gun.

He took the long way back to the precinct so he could go past the crime scene one more time and was not particularly surprised to see the first sproutings of a makeshift memorial: a few bodega-bought bouquets still in their stapled cellophane wraps, a few condolence cards, and two botanica candles, one featuring Santa Bárbara, the other San Lázaro.

He had forgotten to get Marcus moved to a lower floor.

He could have arranged the transfer by phone, should have arranged it by phone, but what he really should have done was push for a family reunion. With the guy in the state he was in, for Matty to conspire in keeping him away from a wife like that . . . He headed back to the hotel.

The lobby was empty save for the blond clerk standing stock-still behind her severe pyramid of apples.

"She went up?" Matty asked.

"She left," the girl said quickly. "I would have lost my job," her voice suddenly sticky with tears.

"Hey, no, I hear you." Matty nodded, masking his disappointment.

"She gave me a note for him," the clerk said.

"You send it up?"

"I was waiting for the bellhop."

"I'll take it for you."

He didn't even have to ID himself.

Riding the elevator back to sixteen with a young couple arguing in German, Matty resisted unfolding the sheet of hotel paper.

The front door was ajar, the ones to the wraparound terrace flung wide-open. Marcus was not there.

Flushed with dread, Matty stepped to the terrace, looked down to the street, and saw, nothing. People.

The guy was just gone.

The wife's note was short and to the point: BILLY PLEASE.


Even on the brightest of days the steel accordion grate that covered the front parlor window of Eric's three-room dumbbell made the dark train of rooms seem like a penitent's cell, looking out as it did on the identical grate of a window across the narrow street; but at night the flat came on like a straight-up tomb.

Eric had turned down the ride from the detectives, had walked in a daze from the jail to his building, through the small vestibule reeking of cat piss, damp, incense, and a hint of decomp, walls, stairs, doors, everything aslant to the earth, climbed the five flights to his floor, past the defunct hallway toilets, to his apartment, stepped inside, then he threw the double lock, took a shower without turning the lights on, puked in the toilet, took a second shower, brushed his teeth, came out into the parlor naked, turned on the TV, nothing on the screen register-ing but the gibber of voices as calming to him as a double vodka, which he got up and made for himself, then drained in a swallow before he could even get back to the couch, the shit-ass futon couch, then just sat there glass-faced, debating whether to get up and pour himself an-other. That was when he noticed the printout of his one-fifth-done screenplay, his bullshit screenplay, Pushcart Pauline meets the dybbuk on Delancey, which was lying atop the steamer trunk/coffee table. He picked up the first page, tried to read it, but the words just slid off his eyes incomprehensible, as meaningless and blithery as whatever was coming out of the television; what the world needs not; dropped it back onto the velvet shawl that served as a tablecloth or whatever the hell it was supposed to be other than his supposed girlfriend's way of mark-ing even this as somehow hers; got up, fell back down, got up, was abruptly revisited, saw, heard that deceptive pop, that sharp snap, the buzz of that steel bee, followed by the slow falling back of Ike, as slow as a flip-book, onto the pavement, Eric imitating it now and clipping a shoulder blade on the corner of the steamer trunk but no matter, he had it coming, that and more, got to his feet, walked past his girl-friend's bookshelves packed with literature both academic and sleazy on prostitution and bondage, with Southeast Asian phrase books and sex-tourist guides, with assorted fetish magazines and reproduced Ti-juana Bibles, every fuck book, textbook, eight-page comic and titty magazine bristling with her hand-scrawled notations; unhinged the se-curity grate on the window, went back to the bathroom, wrapped a towel around his waist, waded through the lone closet, the allegedly shared closet, jam-packed with zippered bags full of whatever they don't wear in Manila, found the hibachi on a high shelf lined with her boots, her shoes, brought it out to the fire escape, returned to the kitchenette, had another drink, rummaged through all the labeled pouches and widemouthed jars of her dried lentils and beans and spelt and fuckball until he found the small bag of briquettes, grabbed a box of kitchen matches. He was headed back to the fire escape when the sharp and sudden rap at his apartment door shot through him like an arrow, spun him like a top.

• • •

"Eric."

Yolonda stood there in the hallway, looking small and tired, her hands in her coat pockets.

He just stared at her, his legs trembling beneath the towel.

"I just came by to see how you were doing. I'm so sorry you had to go through that. I'm supposed to go home now, but I can't stop thinking about you. Are you OK? Tell me you're OK."

He nodded, unable to speak, to take his eyes off her.

"Listen, we need for you to come down to the house, help us try to ID these guys."

"Not now." His voice a hoarse whistle, the trembling getting worse.

"Are you cold? You want to put some clothes on?"

"Not now."

"Yeah, no, you must tired, I understand. But we got to get these guys, you know? Something like this, every minute is precious."

"I did that already." Sounding like he was gargling.

"What?" Yolonda squinted.

"I did, *that*."

"What . . ."

"Try, to *help* you."

"You know, you're shaking like a leaf. Please, I don't mean to mother you, but you're gonna get sick. Put something on, I won't even come in, I'll wait out here."

"Not"—closing his eyes—"now."

Yolonda took a breath. "Eric, listen to me. We know it wasn't you. We know that now. Why do you think of all people I'm the one coming here to knock on your door? Because this request needs to begin with an apology, and who needs to apologize to you more than me. There's nothing for you to be nervous about. I swear on my son's eyes."

Eric continued to stare at her, his body popping and rippling as if it belonged to someone else.

Yolonda took another moment. "OK, you know what? I'll come by, pick you up first thing in the morning, this way you can get some rest."

"I have to work tomorrow."

"No problem. What time do you need to be at work?"

He closed the door in her face.

・・・

Yolonda called Matty on her way down the stairs.

"I hate to say it? But I think we maybe good and fucked ourselves with this guy."

Out on the street, a small cluster of people were standing opposite Eric's building and looking up at his lone window.

Yolonda crossed over to see what they saw: Eric still in his bath towel, feeding sheets of paper to a small grill on his fire escape, each page catching and curling before floating off in the heated air, then drifting down to Stanton Street in a flurry of glowing black snow.


It was a tribute to Yolonda's reputation that after she'd spent all day trying to break the guy down, then had him arrested for something he didn't do, she was still regarded as the best choice for reeling him in as a witness so soon after his release from the Tombs. Matty knew he himself would have been a stone disaster, although a part of him had wanted to take a shot at it anyway, not so much to directly apologize to him, but at least to explain the day.

In any event, with Cash released and everybody back to square one, actually not even up to square one considering the nearly full-day head start they had given the shooter, at this late hour Matty was relegated to poring over Manhattan robbery-pattern reports from the last six months, the monthly All Sheets of unsolved crimes, keeping it close to home, though, the Eighth, the Fifth, and the Ninth, because a deer never travels more than a mile from where it was born and always walks in the path of its ancestors. The local housing projects were the best bet, but he still had to sift through volumes of computer spew in response to his punching in the categorizable details of the Marcus homicide: location of incident, number of perps, race of perps, weapon used, wording of threat, angle of approach on victim, mode of flight.

Then there were his personal in/out piles: his private photo stack of local knuckleheads divided into who at present was on the street, who in jail, who just released. Matty looked specifically at two categories of actors: muggers and gun-possession collars. No need to look at shoot-ers per se, since he didn't think the shooting was intentional, the victim having most likely taken a run at or in some way panicked the perp. Continuing to play sociopath solitaire, he eliminated those who, com-pared to Cash's vague descriptions, were too old or looked wrong or whose robbery preference was all wrong: home invaders, commercial specialists, any of those who preferred to do their thieving indoors. When his perp stack was down from fifty to twenty, he put together a flyer with each of their photos, MOs, and a list of known running bud-dies, then computer-posted the document—the Want Card—to all precincts citywide; if any of these guys were picked up, anywhere in the five boroughs, a red flag would pop up: notify Matty Clark of the Eighth Squad; the potential perp described as a possible witness, not a shooter, to keep all those citywide trigger fingers from itching.

More to do: check for locals with outstanding warrants; guys with swords dangling over their heads who'd talk word on the street to make that sword temporarily go back in its sheath; especially those who were facing three strikes, or even better, their softer partners in crime, the beta males living under that same three-strike shadow who'd been forced to go along on the caper in the first place; they were victims too, or at least that's how it would be put to them.

More to do: check with parole officers, find out who's having a hard time toeing the line out here, who's most likely to miss a curfew, to drop a dirty urine, to not show up at work; good people to squeeze, easy to violate.

More to do: put in the paperwork for the city's automatic $12,000 reward; for an additional $10,000 from the Mayor's Fund for media-sensitive homicides.

More to do, more to do, Matty shuffling, posting, keying up, punch-ing in, poring over, looking for someone, something to jump out at him.

At midnight a fresh wave of detectives came in, and the sight of them, relatively clear-eyed and crisp, made him finally head for the door.

As Matty was leaving the squad room, Lugo, standing in the door-way of his own Quality of Life office across the hall, quietly called his name, then signaled for him to head up the stairs.

. . .

Matty sat on a dusty window ledge in the long, gloomy hallway of the uninhabited fourth floor where earlier, God knew how many hours ago, he had caught up with Billy Marcus running away from what remained of his family.

"So, we were doing car stops tonight?" Lugo began, and Matty pretty much knew what was to follow. "And, we wound up pulling over your sons."

"And?" Matty asked calmly.

"And nothing." Lugo lit a cigarette. "But just so you know? That car stunk to high heaven with weed."

Matty nodded, nodded some more, then offered his hand. "I owe you one, Donnie."

"That's how we do, my brother."

"All right, then." Matty feeling ninety years old.

"Can I just ask . . ." Lugo spit out a fleck of tobacco. "Your kid, the older one, he tinned us, right? What kind of cop is he?"

"About what you'd expect," Matty said, and headed home to his one-bedroom sublet in the Dubinsky Co-ops on Grand, filled now with sleeping sons, the Big One sprawled on the couch, the Other One in a down-filled bag on the floor.

He poured himself two fingers of whatever his hand came to first, walked over to the pile of clothes draped on the arm of the couch, and lifted the car keys from the Big One's pants.

Searching the Sentra parked in his space beneath the building, Matty found a half-smoked joint in the glove compartment but nothing else to speak of. Then he opened the trunk and found two Lake George PD gym bags stuffed with grass already broken down into nickel and dime lids for sale back home.

A friend in Washington Heights . . .

Back in the apartment he sat in a chair and watched them sleep.

They were heading back upstate in the morning.

He put the car keys back in the Big One's jeans pocket, then left the apartment and headed back to the precinct.

An hour later, lying wide-eyed in the airless, fetid bunk room, Matty thought about the shooting death of Isaac Marcus.

Although a few pure athletes of evil did exist out there, most murderers, when he finally caught up to them, pretty much never met his expectations. For the most part, they were a stupid and fantastically self-centered lot; rarely did they come across, at least on first impression, as capable of the biblical enormity of what they had done.

Survivors, on the other hand, even those who were as thick and brutish as the killers who had done away with their spouses or children, almost always appeared to him as larger than life; and being in the service of that kind of suffering often left him feeling both humbled and anointed.

"Don't be too hard on yourself." The guy was in shock when he said it, but that only made it more potent, because what he had reverted to in his numbness, his horror trance, was empathy.

Trying not to think of his own sleeping boys back in the apartment, Matty stared into the darkness and continued to mull over the plight of Billy Marcus.

No matter how many times he had witnessed the externals of receiving a blow like that, the greater part of it would always remain, and blessedly so, unimaginable to him. But of all the unknowables, what Matty at this moment found most incomprehensible—and it wasn't like he couldn't understand the urge to hide—was why anyone, no matter the trauma, would flee the comfort of a woman like Marcus's wife.


At three-thirty in the morning, the scene in front of 27 Eldridge was fairly typical: the last of the last-call stagger-zoo, many of them walking as if it were their first time on ice skates; a kid in the back of an open-doored taxi staring at the knot of damp cash in his hands as he tried to make sense of the meter; and up the block a shirtless, bearded man sticking the top half of his body out of a sixth-floor tenement window and screaming at everybody to shut the fuck up and go back to New Jersey, then slamming his window down so hard that it rained glass, the people below whistling and applauding.

"Excuse me," the gaunt Night Watch detective addressed the disheveled man perched on the top step above the growing shrine. "How you doing?"

"Good." The guy looked like human soot.

"You live here?"

"Not right here."

"You from the area?"

"Originally."

"There was a shooting in front of this building about this time last night, you hear about it?"

"I did." Vigorously scratching the side of his neck.

"We're looking for people who might have been around then, maybe seen or heard something."

"Sorry."

"All right." The detective started to walk off, then came back. "Can I ask what you're doing here right now?"

"Me?" The guy shrugged. "I'm waiting for someone."


Yolonda, having volunteered for Night Watch to avoid either having to go back home or sleep in that repulsive bunk room, sat in a parked sedan across the street watching her partner walk back from talking to the dead kid's father, Marcus looking to her as if he'd just sit on the top step of that stoop until time found a way to reverse itself.

"That's so sad," she said to the detective sliding back into the car.

"What is?"

"It's like he's waiting for his son to come back, right?"

"That's the father?" He reared back. "Thanks for telling me."

"Poor guy," Yolonda said. "I just hope he's not going to wind up being a giant pain in the ass on this, you know?"

# THREE

# FIRST BIRD
# (A FEW BUTTERFLIES)

**The deal was this:** opposite sides of the street; if they saw a likely bunch of heads, the one across the street from them went up a block, then crossed over, then came back down so they got them in a pincer, but because Tristan had the whistle, Little Dap was always supposed to play it like he was getting juxed too, but stand slightly behind the real vics in case they tried to run or fight. That was the plan, and they spent hours walking down opposite sides of every street from the Bowery to Pitt, from Houston to Henry, both of them limping in order not to draw attention to the slow hunter's pace they had to maintain, then after a while getting bored and forgetting to limp, then remembering, then taking a break for pizza, whatever, for hours.

At first there were too many people, then no people, then that police taxi showed up and keyed in on Little Dap, motor-stalking him for blocks until he went into the Arab twenty-four-hour just to get them off his back.

Then at two, two-thirty, when the bars and clubs all began to empty, at first there were too many people again, then nobody again, until at three-thirty Little Dap had said fuckit, calling it a night; and the two of them started walking together back to the Lemlichs. Tristan, already worried about toe-sliding through the apartment past his ex-stepfather's door, was imagining what it would feel like to take the whistle home with him, when suddenly they saw the three white guys on Eldridge coming towards them, the one in the middle drunk, half-carried by the other two, and before they could even get it together, it was happening—Tristan, his heart slamming in his chest, putting the gun on them, the drunk hitting the deck as the two others separated to organize their individual responses to Little Dap's demand. The guy on the left did it right, passing over the wallet and backing away eyes to the ground; but then the other guy made it all go to shit, almost smiling as he stepped to him, to the gun, like he was in his favorite movie or something, saying, "Not tonight, my man."

When the white guy said whatever the fuck dumb thing he said, Little Dap saw Tristan go way too stiff and bughouse, Little Dap wishing he had the gun instead right then, in order to pistol-whip this hero into a different attitude. In fact, he was about to reach for the gun, take it from Tristan's knotty grip, but then—pop—too late, the guy chest-shot, looking up on impact as if someone had called his name from a window, then crumpling without ever looking back down, Tristan quick-stooping over him, like to take a bite out of his face, hissing, "Oh!" Little Dap hissing, "Go!" yanking him out of there, and then the two of them just flew straight south on Eldridge, booking so fast to the Lemlichs that Little Dap's side vision was just a blur of riot gates. They swooped around one drunk couple like white water past a rock, then came up on an old Chinese dude, the guy wide-eyed, automatically going for his wallet. But as soon as they hit the far side of Madison, Dap grabbed the back of Tristan's hoodie, pulling him to a stop, "Walk," the word a wheeze, then gasped, "Roof," before walking away from him a half block down Madison to the corner of Catherine so they'd cross over to the Lemlichs unrelated, the both of them breathing through their mouths, staring straight ahead as if blind to each other's existence, entering the grounds, then heading to 32 St. James, entering the lobby at the same time, fucked *that* up, then taking the separate stairwells on either side of the elevator bank, lunge-climbing the thirty half-flights up to the fifteenth floor, then together silently taking the sole stairway to the roof door, pushing through to the gravel and almost walking into the two housing cops who had their backs to them, hunched over the riverside railing, taking five after a vertical patrol, tapping cigarette ash while discussing the view: Wall Street, the bridges, the Brooklyn Promenade, the Heights. "A kick-ass Trump view," one cop said, then speculating how much it would go for on the open market. "All you got to do is lose the fifteen stories' worth of shit-skins living under it."

Little Dap and Tristan hid behind the now wide-open roof door breathless, Tristan's hand like a claw on the outside doorknob. The two of them remained in a frozen crouch until the cigarette butts were air-dropped over the edge and the cops turned, walking back, Little Dap praying they wouldn't notice that the roof door was wide open now, the two of them hunkered behind it; then at the last moment Little Dap had to yank Tristan's hand off the outside doorknob so the cops could pull the fucking thing shut behind them.

Still in that crouch, they listened to the shuffling echo of footsteps heading down, then finally bolted for the west edge of the roof to look back at where they had come from. They couldn't see through the snaggle of walk-ups, new green-glass high-rises, and towers of add-ons, nor could they hear sirens or any other sounds of alarm, but the body was out there, it was out there.


Tristan stood rooted in the pea gravel of the roof, his tongue leather-dry in his mouth, pictures and sensations jumping around in him; the small kick in his grip when he squeezed one off, the guy looking up on impact, the whites of his eyes all visible beneath, then again and again, that unexpected jolt in his hand like the snap of a dog as the .22 bucked. Did he mean to shoot? He didn't know. He was OK, though.

He surprised himself by going off into remembering when he was little and living in those other projects in Brooklyn with his grand-mother, the time that him and those kids were messing around inside the elevator shafts, jumping from the top of the one car that was going up, to the top of the other car that was going down, when that boy

Neville had slipped, got trapped between the cars going in opposite directions, how the feathers just exploded out of the back of his puffy coat when the edge of the up car slashed it open, slashed him open, then more feathers coming out later as the medics scissored it up the back, trying to get at whatever was left inside.

"Are you *deaf*?" Little Dap hissed without turning his head from the view. "I *said*, give me the motherfuckin' gun!"

Tristan reached into the pocket of his hoodie, panicking a second because there was nothing in there, then discovered that the .22 was still clutched in his right hand, *had* been in his right hand since he'd squeezed one off.

"OK." Little Dap took it, still looking straight ahead in the direction of the body. "OK. You say anything?" Shaking his head, wheezing. "You say, to like, *any*body?" Taking a breath. "I got this now," holding up the .22. "Got your prints all over it."

Tristan had the thought, Got your prints too with you holding it, but figured it had to be more complicated than that. Didn't it?

Then suddenly Little Dap had him from behind in a bear hug, was thrusting his crotch into the seat of his jeans and hissing in his ear, "You *like* this? It's all day, all night in there like this, you *hear* me? But you ain't even gonna *make* it that far." Tristan wanted to laugh at that, big gladiator-school man, but then Little Dap squatted behind Tristan's legs, brought his hands in another bear hug around his thighs, and lifted him off the gravel, tilting him almost upside down over the too low railing, Tristan mute with terror, the blood bubbling in his temples as he clawed for purchase on the outside metal grille that separated him from a fifteen-story drop.

"Nobody knows nothing. You don't say nothing, it's gonna *stay* that way," Little Dap hissed, his grip slipping a little. Tristan jerked a few inches closer to the earth, his mind a screech. "Now. You *know* they gonna come in here knocking on doors looking, so don't you give them a reason to knock on *your* door, look at *you*, you *hear* me? Because I am *not* going back to that *place*." Even in his white shock, Tristan could hear the blubbery catch in Little Dap's throat.

Little Dap hauled him back up, Tristan silently dropping to one knee just to feel the gravel beneath him.

"I'm goin' downstairs," Little Dap said, his voice still shaky. "You wait twenty minutes, then you come down." He started to walk to the roof door, then turned again. "And now on? You don't even *look* at me."

Half an hour later Tristan ninja-walked past his ex-stepfather's bedroom to the one he shared with the three hamsters, all four mattresses packed so close it was like one wall-to-wall bed. Tristan's bed was the third or the second in, depending if you were counting from the window side or the closet. The boy, Nelson, to his left was six; the girl, Sonia, to his right, five; the baby, Paloma, three.

There was a note on his pillow: DON'T THINK YOU WON'T PAY FOR THIS, written in the same painstakingly fancy print as the House Rules pushpinned to the bedroom wall.

Tristan went into the bathroom and looked at himself in the mirror. After a long moment, he turned on the hot water, running it as quietly as possible, reached inside the medicine chest for his stepfather's disposable, and started to shave for the first time since he was old enough to grow the goatee. When he was done, the fat white lightning bolt still ran in a jagged S-curve from his left cheek to the corner of his mouth then out the opposite corner and down to the right side of his jawline. The tight beard had covered enough so that at least it wasn't the first thing he saw whenever he caught his own reflection in a store window, but the sight of it now completely exposed after all this time was a raw shock, kicking up some more unasked-for memories.

Heading back to the bedroom, he pulled his spiral notebook out from beneath the mattress and tried to put down some lines.

*Touch me once ill touch you twice*

But nothing else came to mind so he put the notebook back in its hiding place.

A few minutes later, when he finally lay flat on his back, he heard the first bird out there, the first bird in the world, sunrise in a half hour, school business a half hour after that.

Closing his eyes, he once again felt the buck of the .22, saw the guy's eyes going up, up, then listened to that bird again, its insane tweety song. Turning his head to the window, he saw its trembling, magnified silhouette against the lightly flapping manila shade: monster bird.

He stared at the ceiling for a bit, then closed his eyes again.

He was OK.

FOUR

# LET IT DIE

**The next morning,** giving his back to the rumple and clutter left behind by his departed sons, Matty stood hunched over the railing of his AstroTurfed seventeenth-floor terrace, coffee cup in hand, and looked down on the neighboring streets to the west, an aerial checkerboard of demolition and rehabilitation, seemingly no lot, no tenement untouched; then looked south to the financial district, to the absence of the Towers. He always imagined the slick obsidian office building that as of last year dominated the view as embarrassed, like someone exposed by an abruptly yanked shower curtain.

He felt mildly embarrassed himself, for avoiding his sons again, for sleeping in the bunk room. At least it was just that one night; Jimmy Iacone, unable to get it together after his separation, and preferring to spend his disposable income in Ludlow Street bars, had been straight-up living in that windowless hamper for the last six months.

Matty's piano-legged neighbor stepped out onto the adjoining terrace and, ignoring him, started beating a throw rug like an intractable child. Hers was the only Orthodox family in the building willing to use the self-starting shabbos elevator as opposed to walking up the stairs from Friday sundown through Saturday, and therefore the only Orthodox family willing or able to live above the sixth floor. But they had only a two-bedroom and she was pregnant again, the third time in five years, so they'd probably be moving soon, selling for at least half a million, most likely to some young Wall Street couple who liked the idea of walking to work. Each December you could track the increase in gentile couples living in this formerly all-Jewish enclave simply by counting the new Christmas-light-trimmed terraces along the twenty-story building front; last year's influx finally enough to vote in a seven-foot Scotch pine in the lobby next to the perennial Hanukkah menorah.

The ringing of the cell phone set his shirt pocket trembling. He peered down at the number coming up, Berkowitz. And so it began.

"How you doing, Inspector."

"He wants to see you."

"Oh yeah?"

"You got a hell of a lot of explaining to do."

"I do, huh?" Matty rained the dregs of his coffee cup down onto Essex Street.

"How come you didn't tell us how weak this was?" Berkowitz said.

"How come *I* didn't?" Pacing the AstroTurf now. "How many times did you hear me say, 'I have some real problems with him being the perp on this.' How many times." The persistent pounding one terrace over was giving him a headache. "And all I ever heard back from you and everybody else was wrap him up, pull the plug, wrap him up, pull the plug. The DA too. I laid it out like carpet. Guy says, 'Two wits trumps no gun, we have probable cause with the wits.' The DA says go, when do we ever say no? Tell me *one* time."

"Eleven o'clock."


The chief of detectives' office in 1PP was like a cabin in the sky, the fifteenth-floor reception area tricked out like a banged-up precinct house complete with an old wood-scarred receiving desk, poorly maintained fish tanks, and paint-chipped newel-and-post barriers, walls covered with cheaply framed photos, petty administrative notices, and an American flag big enough to cover a king-size bed.

Once you got past the stage set, however, into the inner suites, it was all teak, hush, and power.

Which is where Matty found himself two hours later, standing already exhausted in his best suit directly outside the chief of detectives' conference room, Deputy Inspector Berkowitz beside him, one hand on the doorknob but going nowhere for the moment.

"This isn't good." Berkowitz's voice an urgent murmur.

"So you said."

"They're all trying to find a way out."

"I'll bet."

"My boss doesn't want to be embarrassed."

"I'll bet."

"So. Who authorized this arrest?"

"He did."

Exhaling through his nose, Berkowitz quickly scanned the barren corridor, then brought his face even closer.

"Who authorized this arrest?"

"You did?" Matty knowing what Berkowitz wanted to hear.

Another exhalation, another walleyed scan.

"One more time."

"Are you kidding me?"

Berkowitz glared at him, Matty thinking, Okeydoke.

"I did."

Berkowitz hesitated for a second, searching his face, then finally opened the door, taking his seat before Matty could even cross the threshold.

Despite his righteous truculence, Matty's first sight of the seven men waiting for him around the long, burnished table high above the East River momentarily turned him into a child.

The chief of detectives, Mangold, impeccable, telegenic, pissed, seated at the short end, flanked by Berkowitz and Upshaw, the chief of Manhattan detectives; the others included two full inspectors; Mangini, the division captain; and seated as far away from the other bosses as possible, Carmody, the Eighth Squad lieutenant.

"So." Mangold tilted his chin in Matty's general direction. "What the hell happened?"

For the thousandth time Matty gave his recitation: his concern about the absence of the gun, the absence of a motive, the ultimately prevailing counterbalance of two seemingly dead-on eyewits, the DA saying, Probable cause, saying, Better safe than sorry.

"Let me ask you a simple question," Mangold, said, squinting out at the East River, the mountain chain of rubbled lungblocks lurking beneath the dapple. "Did you at least do a paraffin test?"

Matty wanted to laugh, thinking this had to be some kind of *Candid Camera* thing, April Fools' thing, but no. Everybody was either glaring out the window or scowling at his nails.

"There was a time concern according to CSU," he finally said, setting himself up for the next shot.

"In that case I have another simple question." Mangold had yet to look at him directly. "Who was running this case, you or the techs?"

Matty could feel the color rushing into his face. "I was."

"And so you let them talk you out of a paraffin test. You've got no gun, no motive, a situation like that, we're talking the most elemental, the most basic . . ." Shaking his head in disbelief. "A detective of your experience."

"This is news to me, boss," the chief of Manhattan d's said, sounding both mournful and mind-boggled.

In a moment everyone at the table was doing the exasperated head shake, the entire phone tree plus Carmody, who was completely out of the loop on this one, who, on the simplest of jobs, couldn't find a lump of coal in a snowball.

"Don't you shake your head at me," Matty blew at the lieutenant before he could stop himself, Carmody the only one in the room almost safe enough to snap at. Almost, but not really.

They all had their eyes on him now—where's he going with this—until Mangold said, "All right, enough," as if bored. "Now you're gonna do things my way."

Everybody exhaled.

"You have Vice involved?" Mangold asked Matty.

"Vice?"

"Back in '92 we had a ton of pross in that area. Call Vice, see if they have any kites on that block, any informants, maybe it was a john from an encounter."

"We're on it," Berkowitz said.

A john . . .

"Hit any after-hours clubs, gambling activity." Mangold speaking to the river again. "Your robbery parolees in the Eighth, you know who they are?"

"Actually I do," Matty said. "Most of them are in their thirties and forties, nobody that fits."

"Get Parole involved anyhow. We had a PO down there when I was on foot patrol back in the eighties? Guy must've closed half a dozen cases for us. A human computer."

"The eighties?"

"Also that bar, the one they were last at?"

"Berkmann's."

"Somebody knows something there hasn't said it yet. I want Vice to do an underage ops, call Narcotics, see if they have any kites for that place. I want an all-out effort in there until somebody waves a flag."

Matty thought about opening a bar, teaching high school, junior high, anything. What did he know enough to teach . . .

"OK, next. Guy claimed to have a gun?"

"Who."

"The guy you locked up."

"Not anymore," Matty said. "Says he handed it in at one of the guns-for-cash exchanges at the Eighth a number of years back."

"OK, fine. Find out if he actually did that."

"We can't, Chief." Matty again. "We don't keep records for that."

Mangold finally looked at him directly, his eyes starred with marvel. "Man, you are nothing but trouble for me."

But then Berkowitz surprised Matty by stepping in, although all he did was state the obvious: "The whole point of cash for guns, Chief, is no names, no questions, that's the hook for it, otherwise . . ."

"Then go back to the Eighth, find out the year he supposedly gave it in, check the invoice log, and see if any .22s were vouchered at that time. Get me *some*thing makes me a little fucking happy here."

"That's a needle in a haystack, Chief." Matty in his despair actually starting to enjoy all his negative responses. "All due respect."

"Well, Jesus Christ, the guy lives in sneaker distance of the scene? Then go to his house, get in there and talk to him, rattle his cage, I want more on that gun. We're not done with him yet."

"Chief"—Matty flushed—"hang on, why are we burning bridges

here, the guy's our only witness and he already hates us. I don't see—"

Ignoring him, Mangold turned to Upshaw. "This is not good. With the press? This is a problem."

"In terms of that?" the chief of Manhattan d's said softly, as if discussing a patient just out of earshot. "I think we let it die, weather the storm."

Once again that ring of solemn nods, Matty seeing it all: a gag order on the press as of this moment. Then inevitably, after a day or two, a more media-friendly murder, with 90 percent of the detectives he'd commandeered quietly returned to their precincts; leaving Matty in the middle of the room with a cardboard box of 61s and 5s and no backup except, maybe out of pity, Yolanda; everyone else tacitly avoiding him on this one like a landlocked Ahab, like an ass-pain Ancient Mariner, like he had halitosis of the brain.

The ruminative silence that had come down on the conference room was finally broken by Mangold himself, giving Matty his eyes for the second and last time.

"A simple paraffin test," he said dreamily, his voice filled with withering amazement.

Matty found himself levitating into a half crouch, his fingers splayed red and white on the table, and for a swollen second or two it looked like he was going to lower the boom on every boss in the room, lay it all out for Mangold, phone call by phone call, all of them stone-faced now, reading his mind, but then, but then . . . he just ate it, any one of these career-long careerists having enough juice to deep-six his own career, send him to work via the Verrazano and its $7 toll every remaining day of his professional life.

As he sank back into his seat, he could palpably sense the relief behind the facades.

Fuck it. At least they all know.

"Look, just go to his place, knock on the door, apologize, and come back," Matty said to Iacone and Mullins, doing his best to follow orders without getting Eric Cash any more agitated than he already was.

"No search?"

"No search. No search." Then, grudgingly adding, "I don't know.

See if he has anything else to say about the gun, but tread light, then get the fuck out of there."

The lieutenant stalked past without looking at him.

Matty waited for Carmody's door to slam, then called a friend in Vice. "Hey. You're gonna get a call from 1PP to do an underage ops on this bar Berkmann's?"

"We did already."

"Hit it?"

"No. Got the call. We're going in sometime this week. Tomorrow, day after, like that."

"Look, the owner's a friend to the squad, never gave us trouble, always helped us out, so, I'm just curious, you have any idea who you're sending in?"

The friend from Vice hesitated for a beat, then, "I like this Dominican kid, a cadet still, but done it before."

"Oh yeah? Nice-looking?" Matty grabbed a pen.

"Not really, kind of short, on the chunky side, wears an earring through her left eyebrow."

"No kidding." Jotting this down.

"Has kind of a metallic red dye streak going."

"Kids today, huh?" Matty clucked, still writing. "You'll give me a heads-up before you roll?"

He wasn't exactly sure how this would pay itself back, but with the investigation about to die, having Harry Steele owe him a favor right now seemed like an instinctual good move.

When Eric opened his door, he was not surprised to see that the City of New York wasn't finished with him. He had been sitting on his folded-up futon sofa all morning, just waiting for something like this.

"Eric?" Jimmy Iacone offered his hand "I'm Detective Iacone, big guy here"—chucking a thumb over his shoulder—"is Detective Mullins. And basically we came by to see if you're OK, and you know, again, to extend our apologies for yesterday."

They were a dream come true: Mullins, huge, blond, and mute, his lightless eyes trained on the center of Eric's forehead; the other one fat and transparently unguent, like the villain in a spaghetti western.

"Fortunately," Iacone went on, "we never stopped working for you. Just kept at it until we could find someone to support your story . . . *Un*fortunately, we have one loose end left."

Eric's shoulders began to do that pop and ripple thing again, drawing Mullins's gaze from the sweet spot above his eyes.

Iacone took a cheerful step forward, making Eric back up. "May we come in?"

The place was doorless straight through to the window, and as Mullins strolled into the book-lined front parlor, Iacone steered Eric into the dining nook/kitchenette, then turned him so that his back was to his partner.

"You mentioned you had a .22?"

"Yeah, I told the detective, what's it . . ." Eric's fingers chittered through his wallet until he found Matty's card. "Clark. Detective Clark. That I did a cash-for-guns exchange." He could hear Mullins prowling behind him.

"Right," Iacone said, laying a light hand on Eric's arm to keep him from turning around. "Can anyone verify that you actually . . ."

"Did it? Well, the cop who took it from me gave me the cash receipt, it was years ago, I have no idea his name, and, hang on, I believe I went with a friend, Jeff Sanford."

Iacone wrote down the name. "How we can get in touch with Jeff?"

"To make sure I'm not lying?"

"This is just how we do." Iacone shrugged apologetically, his pen poised over the notepad.

"He's somewheres upstate, Elmira?"

"The correctional facility?"

"The what?" Eric reared back. "No. The city. He's a teacher in the high school." Then, at the sound of a fallen book, "What's he doing?" Finally wheeling to the parlor, where Mullins was going through the bookshelves packed with Alessandra's research material.

"It's not what it looks like," Eric said. "All that's my girlfriend's, it's for her master's degree, you can ask Detective Clark, we, this is all research material, every . . ."

With an Arabic sex-tour guide for Thailand in one hand and a German spanking magazine in the other, Mullins gave Eric a look that pulverized whatever was left of him.

"Please." His voice breaking.

"Johnny," Iacone said softly.

Mullins made a show of replacing each item to the slot from which he had taken it, but the shelves were overstuffed, and with each put-back, other books and magazines spilled out, each freakier than the last.

"I'll get it. I'll get it." Eric knelt before Mullins and began stacking the spillage with shaking hands.

"What's in there?" Mullins asked, gesturing to the padlocked steamer trunk covered with a fringed brocade shawl between the futon couch and the TV.

"You know something?" Eric looked up at him from the floor. "I have no idea. It was locked when I moved in here, she never gave me the key, and I never saw her open it. Probably something really embarrassing, but it's hers. Everything in here is hers, look."

Springing to his feet, he marched into the kitchenette and flung open the cabinets, displaying the shelves stuffed with beans and lentils and supplements. "Hers." Then striding to the lone shared closet exploding with zippered bags full of coats, sweaters, and dresses. "Hers."

Then to the bathroom, where he pulled back the shower curtain to reveal the dozens of dolphin, giant squid, and whale decals glued to the wall tiles. "All hers. And you know what? I don't even know when, or even if she's coming back, OK?"

"All right, all right," Iacone said, hands up in retreat. "Like I said, we just came by to tie up loose ends."

"And to apologize," Mullins added.


Eric could hear them as they went trudging down the stairs.

"We should get a warrant for that trunk, you know?" Mullins said.

"Fuck it," Iacone said, then: "Research."


"You should have seen them in there, Yoli." Matty was sitting on the edge of her desk. "Like roaches with the lights just turned on. 'I never *knew* that,' 'You never *told* us that,' 'News to me, boss,' 'Great idea, boss,' and I just had to eat it. Everybody like, skittering under the stove and I just had to eat it."

"Yeah, see, that's why I never took the sergeant's test," she said. "It's the first step to being that way. It's like a gateway drug."

Mullins and Iacone returned to the squad room.

"So how'd it go?" Matty dreading the answer.

"Good," Iacone said.

"You think he'll be up for helping us with this?"

"I don't see why not."


Occupying his new client's old hot seat in the Eighth Squad's interview room, Danny Fein, aka Danny the Red, of the Hester Street Legal Initiative, his thick, square teeth glinting like old mah-jongg tiles through his ruddy beard, sat facing Matty, Yolonda, and Kevin Flaherty, the ADA.

"Look," Flaherty said, "we have a basic description of the perps, we know who most of the local bad guys are, we just want Eric to browse through some photo arrays, maybe sit down with a sketch artist again so we can get a better likeness and make something good happen."

" 'A better likeness.' You mean get a sketch that's not just a stall to buy you time to build a case against him?"

"Exactly," Flaherty said.

"Sure, no problem." Danny hauled one leg across the other. "Like I said, soon's I get a signed waiver says he's immune from prosecution."

"You're not . . ." Flaherty looked off, laughed through his teeth. "C'mon, Danny, all indications say he's not the perp, but we can't do that and you know it. It's an open investigation."

"I'm sorry to hear that."

Matty and Yolonda exchanged tight glances, Matty sitting there already with a few array folders in his lap like a visual aid.

Rumor had it that Danny had just moved out on his black wife, Haley, and two sons, Koufax and Mays, to live with his Jewish ex-girlfriend from college and that no one in the Legal Initiative was talking to him.

"What are we asking for," Yolonda said softly, "descriptions of clothing, facial hair . . ."

Danny made a show of cocking his head in amazement. "You grilled him for eight hours and you didn't get all that?" Then, leaning forward, "Show me the waiver."

"Could we have been any more up-front about how it went down?" Flaherty said. "They were out there all day trying to bolster his story."

"Bolster, huh? You're lucky he's not filing a suit."

"No one's sorrier about how it went down than us," Matty finally chimed in, "but we had two eyewits. What would *you* have done? We cut him loose the minute we could. But now he's our only real witness, and simple human decency says he needs to step up."

"Show me the waiver."

"This boy, Isaac Marcus, has parents," Yolanda said. "You know why I say *has* instead of *had*? Because when a child is killed and somewheres down the line someone innocently asks, 'So, how many kids you folks have?' they always include the lost child in the number. Never fails. They're like phantom limbs."

"Yolonda," Flaherty warned. She was the only one who had never met Fein before this conversation.

"You ever spend any time with the parents of a murdered child, Mr. Fein?"

"Ah shit," Flaherty murmured, Matty thinking, Here we go.

"Yeah actually," Danny said brightly, "Patrick Dorismond's among others."

A silent sigh filled the room.

"I'm sorry," Yolonda again, "did we shoot your client yesterday?"

"Show me, the waiver."

"C'mon, Danny," Flaherty tried to jump back in. "Ike Marcus and Eric Cash were friends. They were work—"

"Show me the waiver."

The ADA finally lost it. "You don't think we won't go to the media with this? How's he ever going to show his face?"

"You interrogate him for eight hours, throw him in the Tombs groundless, and now you're what . . . threatening to publicly humiliate him?" Danny leaned back in his chair as if to see them better. "It never ceases to amaze me, the balls on you people."

"You people?" Yolonda tried to look insulted.

"Look, you can put any kind of spin on this you want," Matty said, "but you know what we're asking for here is the right thing."

"Show me, the waiver."

. . .

Matty followed Danny out of the building, spoke to him on the handicap ramp.

"I heard you and Haley split up."

"Yeah, but amicable-like."

Two uniforms escorted a cuffed Latino, one eye swollen and already turning a metallic purple, up the ramp, Danny slipping his card in the guy's front jeans pocket as they passed.

"Let me ask," Matty said, "not to be personal, but what's worse for a black woman. Your white husband leaves you for another black woman? Or he goes back to his own kind."

"I hate generalizing like that," Danny said. "How the fuck do I know. Leaves her for another guy."

"So who's happier, her in-laws or yours?"

"Actually? Neither. We all got along great."

"Yeah?" Matty lit a cigarette. "How are the kids?"

"Insane."

"Sorry."

"No, sorry would have been us staying together."

They took five to watch a bum fight start up in front of the bulletproof liquor store on the far side of the Williamsbridge Bridge supports, two young-old men windmilling ineffectually at each other.

"You know that whole 'show me the waiver' thing you pulled in there?" Matty said. "You could have just as easily told Flaherty all that over the phone."

"Yeah, I guess."

"So what did you come in for, a little Danny in the lion's den?"

The lawyer snorted, looked off smiling.

"Or you just didn't want to miss out on seeing our faces when you said it."

Danny squinted up at the Brooklyn-bound traffic on the Williamsburg. "Both."

"C'mon, Danny," Matty said, "you're just using this kid to stick it to us."

"And, so, what," Danny said as he began to walk down the ramp, heading back to his office a few blocks away. "You don't think the police need an occasional sticking to?"

"Cut the crap. From your heart, what's the right thing here."

"The right thing?" Danny walking backwards now. "How about keeping you guys accountable."

"Fuck yourself, you commie rat bastard," Matty said absently.

"Hey, if I could, I'd never leave the house."


Tristan needed to go to the bathroom, but from the bedroom he heard the dragging of the chair and then the crowd noise on the TV, the Yankees announcer saying, "Bottom of the fourth," and he knew he was trapped. His ex-stepfather had played in Yankee Stadium in the PSAL championship game of 1984, shortstop for James Monroe, no errors and a single off a pitcher from DeWitt Clinton who was later drafted by the Expos, and now he was a waiter in Dino's Bronx café, where a lot of the Yankees and visiting teams brought their girlfriends for dinner, and even though he had too much self-respect to ever mention it to any of them, they knew he wasn't just some plate monkey; Bernie Williams and El Duque always greeted him by name, and if it wasn't for the pooling of the tips, most nights during the season he'd come home with more in his pocket than anybody else; all of which was to say that whenever he was off and the Yankees were on, he would drag his chair from its spot in the corner to the center of the room, *his* chair, sit in it and die, and everybody else had to tread light for the next few hours, and you better believe they did. By the third inning he was usually dangerously drunk, still alert enough to use those wicked-quick infielder's hands; by the sixth he was too wobbly to do any real damage, but that wouldn't stop him from trying to go for you if you got in his eyes or ears, so you pretty much had to wait until after the seventh-inning stretch, his snoring in the eighth like an all-clear signal for everybody to come out and go about their business. But being that the game wasn't even out of the fourth yet, Tristan had no choice but to piss out the bedroom window.

After checking the facing buildings to see if anyone was looking out and might call the housing cops on him like last year, he went up on his toes, unzipped, and thrust his hips forward to get the stream to clear the outside sill. He thought he was doing pretty good, until he heard, felt, and smelled pee-splash bouncing off the wall; Tristan looking down to see the six-year-old boy imitating him, looking up with his little thing in his hands and laughing as his own stream spread across the bedroom floor, rimming Tristan's shoes.

After four hours spent rescouring the All Sheets, spent pulling the last two years of District Arrest Books, Matty stepped out onto the ramp again for a smoke. As he did, the driver's door of a Mini Cooper swung open across the street, and Mayer Beck, the young clubfooted reporter from the *New York Post*, struggled to his feet, a sheepish I'm-not-really-here half-grin on his face.

Beck's self-consciousness was painfully obvious as he corkscrewed across Pitt to the ramp in front of an audience, Matty looking away to lighten his embarrassment, shaking his head as if he'd had it with these media vultures. In fact, he kind of liked the kid.

"No comment, right?" Beck said as he adjusted his football yarmulke. "Let it die a pressless death?"

"Not at all," Matty said. "In fact, here's an exclusive. Colin Farrell did it."

"Sorry about that." Beck half-smiled. "Seriously, can you talk?"

Matty flicked his butt into the gutter. "I'll see you around, Mayer," turning to head back inside.

"You sure about that?" the reporter said, his reflection caught in the swing of the glass doors. "Last chance."

It was ten in the evening and Eric was hiding again, this time in his sanctuary of last resort, the fungal coal cellar, former coal cellar, that lay two stories beneath Café Berkmann like a crypt. The sketchy illumination that came from the four worklights scattered about the earthen floor highlighted both the long, irregular brickwork of the walls, brickwork the likes of which hadn't been seen in this city since the Civil War, and the four crude hearths that still stood like neolithic kilns, one in each corner of the room, the source of both heat and light for the ones who had once lived down here, all that remained of them now the names and Yiddish phrases, some in Roman letters, some in Hebrew, carved into the blackened joists not even an arm's length overhead.

Upstairs, Café Berkmann was in full effect, packed at the bar and at the tables with the usual 30 percent overbookings and unpredictable number of walk-ins spilling out the door.

Most times when the place was thrumming like this, it operated more smoothly than when it was half-empty, clamor having a way of making everyone go on automatic pilot, do what they were hired to do; no spacing out, drifting, hanging. If you want good service, go to a busy restaurant, Steele liked to say, but with Eric Cash running the show tonight, the room was pure hell; he could feel himself provoking a chain reaction of surliness and dysfunction that extended from the door to the tables to the kitchen, starting with the customers, Eric personally putting them in an ass mood all night by showing them to their tables as if it weren't his job, dropping the menus, then giving them his back, the oblivious waiter now a sitting duck; doing a further number on the waiters by occasionally taking an order himself and wordlessly handing it to them on their way over as if they were too slow to live, pulling the same on the busboys by clearing tables himself, ignoring staff complaints about the lack of flow with the kitchen, about wrong orders coming out altogether, about customer bitching, the lame-ass tips.

And the bartender Steele had hired to replace Ike Marcus had been straight-up giving him fits; anytime Eric looked over there, he had seen the same shit attitude on display; the guy stone-faced and forbearing as if he actually thought he was the only one working here who envisioned a higher calling for himself; talking to his customers as if each word cost him blood, meditating on his fingernails during the lulls . . .

Eric had taken the shift only at Steele's suggestion; get right back in the saddle; and to his credit he was trying: all evening he'd been attempting to duck out and get himself together, but always the question was where, where, he couldn't *leave* leave, and he'd already been down to the bathrooms under the pretext of restocking the toilet paper, the paper towels, the liquid-soap dispensers, had already gone out into the stairwell to check on the extra-chair stacks, as if chairs were prone to wandering off by themselves, had been to the prefab supply shed in the small rear courtyard to ogle the lightbulbs and backup silverware, and so now, here he was in the cellar . . .

All he wanted was ten minutes, five minutes to have a smoke, be alone, *alone* being a relative term around here with all the surveillance cameras, but each time he went AWOL, he had only come back upstairs in a deeper funk because quiet time below invariably meant heightening chaos above, so all evening, after a taut minute or two in some musty nook, it was back to the floor, the door, the mob at the reservations pulpit having doubled in his absence, no one even able to squeeze inside from the sidewalk, forcing him to do triage; Eric speed-reading faces, sending some straight back to New Jersey, Long Island, the Upper West Side, or wherever, others over to the three-deep bar with a false promise of just a few minutes' wait, that fucking bartender there . . .

And so now it was time again, Eric crushing his butt into the moldy earth and taking a last look at the word gallery above his head, finding his favorite, one of the few Yiddishisms that he understood: GOLDENEH MEDINA, City of Gold; someone down here back then having had one hell of a sense of humor.

"I don't just grieve for my friend and his family," Steven Boulware said, his alcohol-softened face framed by the TV in the Eighth Squad eating alcove, "I grieve for the murderers, for their own human degradation. We as a society need to take a hard look at ourselves, at our culture of violence, of unfeelingness . . ."

Yolanda came out of the adjoining bathroom, sliding her holster back onto her belt.

"As long as our legislators continue to pocket handouts from the NRA, as long as they continue to condone a way of doing business that readily puts guns in the hands of the marginalized and the desperate, of children who see no other access to their share of the American dream . . ."

"Didn't we ask that asshole not to talk to the press?" Tossing a shredded paper towel in the garbage can.

"Yeah, but can I tell you something?" Matty wiped his mouth free of tomato sauce, then ditched the heel of his slice. "Right now I don't really give a shit, because as long as it's still on the tube, in the papers? They can't pretend it never happened."

It had all gone down as he knew it would. The only way a detective caught talking to the press wouldn't be transferred to Staten Island was if he already lived there, in which case he'd be transferred to the Bronx. And with 90 percent of his dragooned manpower already returned to their home squads not forty-eight hours into the investigation—the hell with a cosmetic grace period—a near absolute state of Neverwas had descended upon the Marcus homicide with record speed.

Four days from now they'd at least have the mandatory seven-day recanvass; Borough Patrol would flood every corner near the crime scene, canvassing for habitual walk-by witnesses who had possibly passed through the area on the same day and hour one week before. They were obliged to give him at least that; but until then his squad was pretty much on its own.

For all the time Matty spent poring over the Lower Manhattan All Sheets, only three unsolved street robberies in the area had jumped out at him: the victims, two Chinese, one Israeli, all held up at gunpoint on the Lower East Side by young black and/or Latino tag teams. Unless someone off one of his Want Cards got pinched and offered up the shooters, all they could really do was go out and take a shot at reinterviewing those complainants.


"Look, I know it's my first night, and I know you don't know me, so you just have to believe me when I say I'm not a complainer." The new waitress, Bree, had Irish eyes like damp stars and a way of angling her face that made her seem as if she were perpetually on the verge of ecstatic surrender. "But I just had my ass grabbed again."

"Again, huh?" Eric tried to stop himself, but . . . "By a new customer? Or the same one from an hour ago."

She faltered, turned a bright pink, then mumbled, "A new one."

Well, it could be true.

The Quality of Life taxi rocketed past the big picture window on Norfolk, Eric tamping down a surge of panic as the lazy wash of its misery lights briefly played on the new waitress's delicate face.

It could be true . . .

"All right, switch tables with Amos," he said, unable to look at her anymore.

He watched her go to the service station at the short end of the bar to pick up a tray full of novelty martinis and speak briefly to Amos, who shot Eric a what-the-fuck glance from across the room, Eric gesturing for him to just do it, creating another happy camper in here, then turning and almost walking nose-first into a familiar-looking guy in a bright green skullcap.

"Just you?"

"Just me."

"We're kind of jammed, you want to eat at the bar?"

"Sure." Smiling at Eric like he knew something delicious. "So how you holding up, man?"

"Holding up?" Eric at first thrown, then, "Oh, fuck no."

"No?"

"No comment."

"No, I just . . . It must've been a hell of an ordeal."

"Do you want to order at the bar or not?"

"Sure, I'm just . . . I kind of seen you around. I'm from the neighborhood."

"Half the country's from the neighborhood."

"True dat," Beck allowed, taking a stool, lightly slapping a nervous riffle on the bartop, then signaling to the new bartender, who at first simply gave him the once-over as he continued to wipe a few wineglasses, then stepped to him as if picking his way barefoot through broken glass.

And Eric just flipped, flinging himself nearly halfway across the zinc. "Can I speak to you?"

"I'll be with you in a minute," the bartender said as if Eric was out of line.

Cleveland, the other bartender, the dreadlocked one, stepped in to take Eric's order. "What you need, boss."

Eric waved him away. "You." Pointing at the new guy, now drawing a draft beer for the reporter. "Right now."

"May I finish serving this first?"

Eric waited, embracing the stall to stoke his fury.

"What's your name again?"

"Eric," the bartender said.

"Eric, huh? No kidding, so's mine. So what's your problem, Eric, you think you're destined for better things?"

"Excuse me?"

"How utterly, utterly unique."

"Excuse me?"

"Let me tell you something. This right here isn't about researching your next role. It's a *job*. In fact, we're *pay*ing you. And I'm gonna tell you something else. It's pro*active*. Customers don't come to a bar for the drinks, they come for the bartender. Any bartender worth a shit knows this, but you, you stand there, got a one-word answer for everything: *huh, uh, duh, yes, no, maybe.* You make people feel like losers, like they're your punishment from a jealous God or something. I swear, Cleveland?" Nodding to the Rastahead at the far end now. "The guy makes a martini like he's got hooks for hands, but he's *twice* the bartender you are because he works it. Everybody's a regular with that guy, and he never stops moving, never comes off like this gig is some demeaning station of the cross on his way to the Obies. I mean, watching the two of you back here tonight? It's like a blur and a boulder. And to be honest, right now even with the traffic the way it is, I'd rather cash you out on the spot, have him work a solo, or draft one of the waiters or even come back there myself than let you pull this 'I'd rather be in rehearsals' crap *ten* more minutes, you *hear* me?"

"Yeah." The guy had gone pale.

"I'm sorry, say what?" Cupping an ear.

"Yes." Wide-eyed. "I hear you."

"Excellent. Just remember. No energy? No gig. Talk. Smile. Do it. You're hanging by a thread."

"Can I say one thing?" Half-raising his hand.

Eric waited.

"I happen to be in med school."

"Same difference," Eric said, thinking, Sort of, yeah, no, most definitely, even worse, *I happen to be,* like Little Lord Fauntleroy, Eric turning away, then seeing Yarmulke head down the bar, obviously having overheard the whole thing, fuck him too, then bumping into that waitress again, starry-eyed Stella, Eric fending off an anarchic pulse of desire. "*Now* what," he said. "We have a *third* ass-grabber on our hands?"

She reared back as if slapped. "I just came to thank you for the table switch," giving him a flush-faced once-over. "It's working out well."

"Good," he said, waited until she turned away, then returned to the coal cellar.


One of few remaining pre-tenement rookeries in the city, 24 East Broadway was squat and rambling, on a block filled with similarly ancient and amorphous buildings, the door to the street at this late hour kept open via a strip of duct tape blocking the lock.

Matty and Yolonda began trudging up the stairs to the top floor with a copy of an assault complaint signed by the victim Paul Ng, which had been filed three weeks earlier; two dark men and a gun, three blocks from the Marcus homicide and at roughly the same time of night. Ng, a Fujianese restaurant worker less than two years in-country, had made the complaint, Matty guessed, most likely against his will, but had no choice in the matter because he had almost been run over by Quality of Life as he stood dazed in the middle of Madison Street five minutes after the deed, his pants pockets turned out like elephant ears and blood dripping from a corner of his pistol-whipped mouth. If Matty had to guess what happened next that night, he'd say Ng had spent half an hour cruising the neighborhood in the back of the bogus taxi looking for the perps, a fruitless exercise because one dark-skinned kid looked like another to him, the cops themselves probably halfhearted about it too given their own experience with dozens of other Paul Ngs in that backseat.

Then, Matty still guessing here, as Quality of Life headed back to the precinct to hand him over to the detectives, Ng probably really began to wish they'd never come across him, maybe because of a sketchy immigrant status, or because he lived in an illegal squat, or because of bad associations with cops back home, but most likely in addition to some or all of the above, because the time spent reporting the stealing of money was time away from the making of money, which was the only realistic way to start recouping your losses, so . . .

But Matty was only guessing.

The top floor of 24 East Broadway had only one apartment, this door slightly ajar too, Matty looking at Yolonda, then pushing it wide as he knocked and droned, "Hello, police," his ID curled in his hand. The first thing they saw stepping inside was a rough pyramid of men's shoes, maybe two dozen pairs, either black slip-ons or plastic shower clogs stacked beneath a department-store still life of buckshot pheasants and a powder horn. No one came to the door, but Asian pop drifted from down the hall.

"Hello, police," another desultory shout-out, and then they began walking towards the music. The place was a modified railroad flat, basically a long central corridor flanked by rooms, most of which had been divided and divided again with Sheetrock into cells, each with a foam mattress topped by a twist of sheets, save for two larger rooms, one on either side of the hallway, both bare of furniture other than what looked like extrawide bookshelves bracketed into the walls in vertical stacks of three. On a few of these planks men were either smoking in the dark or asleep, each man still awake slowly rolling to face the wall as the detectives shadowed their doorway. The railroad ended in a wider kitchen, where four other men were sitting around a table eating something nesting in tiny shells and a broccoli-like green off sheets of newspaper, and a fifth was singing into a microphone while facing the monitor of a karaoke machine. On a Formica counter behind the dining table sat a fish tank holding a single carp so large that it couldn't turn around, Matty thinking the fucking thing must have lost its mind years ago.

"How you doing," he said, unnecessarily flashing his ID.

The men nodded in greeting, as if two police just strolling through the flat unannounced was business as usual, then turned their attention back to the singer. Only one short-limbed, compact guy, beaming and vigorous, flew out of the kitchen and returned with two more chairs. "Sit," pointing at the seats, then gesturing for them to check out the pipes on the guy with the mike. "Sit."

"Not now," Matty said, slow and loud. "We need to talk to Paul Ng." Then, "He's not in trouble."

The karaoke song came to an end, the guy with the mike passing it to one of the others.

"Sit," the energetic guy repeated, still beaming like the sun.

"Where's Paul, Ng," Matty blared flatly.

"No."

"No what."

The next man began his song, which sounded like a Chinese cover of Roy Orbison's "Dream Baby."

"No *what*."

"Maybe you're pronouncing it wrong," Yolonda offered.

"No, I'm not. That's how that kid Fenton says it." Then blaring, "Paul *Eng*."

"Jesus, you don't have to yell," Yolonda snapped, "they're not deaf."

"Fellas, stay with me on this. Who's Paul Ng."

The men had no reaction except to look from the singer to the cops with expectant grins as if to see whether they dug him.

"What's *your* name?" Yolonda asked the chair carrier.

"Me?" The guy laughed. "No."

"No? Your name is No?"

"Huh?"

"Dr. No," Yolonda said.

"What's *his* name." Matty pointed to the singer.

"Good, huh?"

Matty turned to Yolonda. "Are they playing us?"

She shrugged, squinted at the fish.

"Look, we're gonna come back and come back and come back until . . ."

"OK." The chair carrier waved goodbye, still smiling.

"Let's just come back with Bobby Oh," Yolonda said.

"Oh's Korean."

"OK. We'll bring that kid Fenton, then."

They left the apartment without another word, but before they could start down the stairs, that compact chair carrier came out into the hallway and, grabbing Matty's arm, beckoned for them to follow him up the short stairs that led to the roof door, the landing up there wedge-shaped beneath the slant of the eaves and littered with discarded vials, matches, burnt spoons, and hypes. Standing a few steps above the police, the guy then went into a brisk, efficient mime of shooting up, stabbing a forearm with his thumb, saying "Psssht!" then acting out the woozy stagger of some kind of bellicose junkie. "Arrgh! You fight me! Pssht! Arrgh!"

"What the hell does he expect," Matty said, "keeping the street door open like that."

"You come more!" the guy said.

"Yeah, we'll keep an eye out," Yolonda said mildly. "Have a good night, now."

Steven Boulware walked into Berkmann's by himself and with an air of peripheral alertness headed directly for the bar.

Eric hadn't thought about the guy since the murder. Disoriented, a little frightened even, he had no idea what to say or how to act. As Boulware brushed past the pulpit, however, it became apparent that he didn't recognize Eric at all.

But he could bank on people recognizing him, his face having been on the cover or in the first few pages of all the dailies hanging on the café's newspaper dowels. Both the local TV stations and CNN had been replaying sound bites from his earlier presser all evening.

Standing sideways at the packed bar, he signaled for a drink from Cleveland, Eric seeing the recognition come into the bartender's eyes, seeing the recognition of the recognition come into Boulware's eyes, the quickening in his face, Boulware hunkering in for a gratifying evening.

Waiting until Boulware was served, Eric left his post and signaled for Cleveland to come to the short end of the bar.

"Listen to me." Laying a hand on his arm. "That guy? From the news? Whenever he's close to finished, serve him up another. Don't wait. I don't want him to have to ask for a drink or see an empty glass in front of him all night."

"You want me to say it's on you?"

"No."

"All right." Cleveland nodding, almost smiling, misinterpreting Eric's anonymous largesse.

Matty was leaning against a car hood a few doors down from the urban still-life that had blossomed in front of 27 Eldridge. The shrine was a few days old now and threatened to span the width of the sidewalk from stoop to curb.

The offerings, as far as he could tell, represented three of the worlds that made up the universe down here: Latino; Young, Gifted, and White; and Geezer/Crackpot/Hippie—no word from the Chinese.

There were dozens of lit botanica candles, a scattering of coins on a velvet cloth, a reed cross laid flat on a large round stone, a CD player running Jeff Buckley's "Hallelujah" on an endless loop, a videocassette of Mel Gibson's *The Passion* still sealed in its box, a paperback of *Black Elk Speaks*, some kind of unidentifiable white pelt, a few petrified-looking joints, bags of assorted herbs, coils of still-smoldering incense that gave off competing scents, and a jar of olive oil. Taped to the brick directly above all this was the front-page headshot of a smiling Isaac Marcus from the first day's *New York Post*, the headline his now notorious last words: NOT TONIGHT MY MAN (Matty had no idea who fed that to the papers), alongside of which someone had cryptically put up an old tabloid photo of Willie Bosket, the fifteen-year-old urban boogie boy of the 1970s who famously killed someone on the subway "just to see what it felt like," and next to that, a homemade handwritten rant, "Amerikkka's war on poverty is a war AGAINST the Poor," the rest of it illegible. There were even memorial tokens anchored to the tenement facade from flagpole-like riggings so that they dangled directly above the murder spot: an open umbrella suspended upside down like a buttercup in which nestled a teddy bear and a beanbag eagle; and a home-crafted tubular-steel mobile whose desultory clanging on this nearly windless night truly sounded like mourning.

Matty was here on his own time, on the off chance someone known to the squad would show up to admire or fret over the results of his handiwork; or maybe he'd overhear something, a street tag, a rumor; all serious long shots, but he could already sense that this would become a nightly ritual until the shrine dissolved maybe a week from now.

Most people passing by couldn't help but stop, although usually for only a few seconds, their comments equally divided into sad and sarcastic; the local male teens the worst, as if this whole display was a throw-down challenge for them to be instantly hard-ass funny in front of their friends. Some people truly lingered, their faces pinched with sadness, but no one of interest to him; middle-aged Latinas, a few of the twentyish newcomers.

"What this was?" A short, muscle-humped Puerto Rican holding a mason jar of tobacco-colored liquid was standing next to him now. "A Bloods initiation. Those motherfuckers who did him was Bloods, and I know because my daughter is with a Blood right now carrying his baby, which is also an initiation rite, and *I'm* the one locked up for child abuse?" Punching himself in the chest.

"Oh yeah?"

"Twenty-five hundred dollars bail on me with no record, no proof, but you know what that's about?" The guy looking right through Matty now. "It's because they're scared of me, the police, of what I know about that precinct, about what's really going on. I would never lay a hand on my daughter, you ask anyone in that building, the walls are like paper. There was no abuse, they just needed to shut me up. Twenty-five hundred dollars first-time bail for something I never did? Please . . ."

The bulked-up PR turned to walk away, couldn't, wheeled back to Matty, and started in again. "But this right here?" Waggling his finger at the shrine. "It's up to you, the whites, you got to wipe out the gangs so this shit don't happen again. The gangs, the projects, this whole area, all of it." Marching away again, his back to Matty. "All of it!" Bellowing to the rooftops, then disappearing into the shadows in two strides, highlighting the one thing that had become painfully obvious this evening—how easily two rollers could attempt to snatch a wallet, throw a shot, then just vanish into the darkness in the span of a heart-beat.

Berkmann's was emptying earlier than usual this evening, not even 1:00 a.m. and the waiters were starting to look like loiterers. Eric could follow the conversations at the bar as clearly as if he were right up there with them.

Boulware was on his seventh or eighth complimentary Grey Goose and tonic; nearly off his stool now, his mouth a curtain of saliva as he held court with two, count 'em, two girls at once, one of whose thumb was a loving metronome on the back of his hand.

Cleveland was dying to cut him off, but Eric wouldn't allow it.

"The, the irony is, if Ike . . ." Boulware faltered, blanched, briefly palmed his eyes, maybe his conscience starting to slap the shit out of him, Eric hoped. "If Ike could walk through that door? Could put his two cents in? He'd be the first to stand up for those guys. Not, not for what they did, but that, that, no one is born with a gun in his hand . . . That, that there's this, this culture of violence, of inequity, of unfeeling-ness . . ."

Unable to bear another word, Eric caught Cleveland's eye and finally ran his hand across his throat.

Just as the street seemed to be settling in for the night, three young black women came walking past the shrine and, caught up by the display, stopped to absorb the narrative, two of them automatically raising a hand to their face in a gesture of awed distress. The third one, who had a sleeping toddler draped over her shoulder, slowly shook her head.

"My God, he was just a child." Her voice high, on the edge of breaking.

"What are you talking about?" one of the others said.

"Look at him." She pointed at the old photo of Willie Bosket.

"That ain't him," her friend said, then pointed to Ike Marcus. "That's the dead boy. Don't you watch the news?"

The third woman grunted, shrugged the sleeping kid to her other shoulder. "Him?" she drawled. "Now all this shit here makes a lot more sense."

As Boulware stood hunched over, barking up cocktails in front of the riot gate of a Dominican jewelry store on Clinton Street, Eric came up from behind and hooked him in the ribs. Because he had never swung on anyone in his adult life, the punch probably hurt him as much as it did the other guy; nonetheless it felt so good, so right, that he didn't, couldn't stop swinging until his knuckles were the size of gumballs and Boulware was snuggled up atop his own spatter.

Squatting on his hams, Eric addressed the one eye that was somewhat still open. "Do you know me?" The smell was making him tear up. "Do you remember me? I should've done that the minute you walked in tonight, but you're twice my size and I don't give a fuck about 'fair' anymore."

Boulware's good eye started to settle like a sunset.

"So. What do you want to do, press charges? Maybe you should press charges, what do you think?"

Boulware had passed out.

"Seriously . . ."


As the rising sun began to tint the upper floors of the towers that edged the East River, Quality of Life walked into the Sana'a for their end-of-tour breakfasts, Nazir giving them a half salute, then sidling the six feet from his phone-card-trimmed register to the griddle.

"So," reaching for the white bread, "I hear you arrested that bastard who broke our window."

"Actually?" Lugo's eyes strayed to the miniature TV propped behind the counter. "I believe they cut him loose."

"What?" Nazir straightened up. "Why?"

"Something about him not having done it."

"Bullshit."

"Be that as it may."

"They don't tell us shit," Scharf said.

"They don't like us getting in their business," Daley said.

"Upstairs is upstairs," Geohagan said. "We're just infantry."

"But that's stupid." Nazir waved a bread knife. "Who spends all the time on the street, you or them?"

"Tell me about it," Lugo said.

The store descended into a momentary silence as they watched a girl eat a slug sandwich on a rerun of *Fear Factor*.

"What the fuck's that got to do with fear?" Daley said. "That's just disgusting."

"If you want to see good *Fear Factor* contestants, you have to come to my part of the world," Nazir said, wrapping the first bacon-and-egg sandwich. "We'd do great on that show."

A kid with a stitched cheek came barreling into the store so tricked out in Crip blue that no one took him seriously.

"I need four quarter," thrusting a dollar across the unoccupied register counter, his head turned to the street as if something was out there.

"Oh!" Lugo reared back, wincing. "Where'd you get slashed like that?"

"Hah?" the kid said, then, "On my cheek."

Daley gave him change for the dollar.

As Nazir scooped another fried egg off the griddle, the 6:00 a.m. news came on, the president rolling in grainy waves on the screen.

"He's coming into the city this week, right?" Daley asked.

"The day after next or something," Lugo said. "Naz, you hear his speech last night?"

"Yes, but on the radio."

Lugo and Daley looked at each other.

"Everything he said I agree with." Speed-wrapping the second grease bomb. "My brother too."

"Good," Lugo said. "Glad to hear it, man."

"Yemenis like a strong father. We respond to a strong father. The young people who come in here, they're very mocking about him and what he has to do now."

"In *this* neighborhood?" Scharf lit a cigarette. "Tell me about it."

"Sometimes your father does things you don't understand, but a father doesn't need to explain all his actions to you," Nazir said. "You need to have faith and trust that behind every act is love. Then later you look back or you sit quietly and it becomes clear that these things which seemed harsh at the time saved you. You were just too much a child to understand, but now you are a man with health and prosperity and all you can say is thank you."

"Fair enough." Lugo took a wolf bite out of his sandwich.

Preceded by his smell, Boulware stumbled in, misbuttoned, his face waffled with abrasions.

"Do you have an ATM?" he asked Nazir.

"Whoa, bro." Lugo straightened up. "That just happen?"

"What . . ." Boulware blinking.

"It's like the fuckin' knife and gun club in here tonight, Naz," Daley said.

"Where'd you get the tune-up?" Lugo asked.

"Where?" Boulware absently frisked himself.

"No ATM," Nazir lied.

Boulware wandered back out into the street, Quality of Life eating their breakfast sandwiches as they watched him negotiate the early-morning traffic.

**"Hey." Minette Davidson came** into the squad room carrying the weather, flush-faced and breathless.

"Hey, how are you?" Matty shot to his feet, flattening his tie and offering her the chair sidesaddle to his own.

"I'm Minette Davidson, Billy Marcus's wife?"

"Sure, I know. Detective Clark. Matty Clark."

"I know," mechanically shaking his offered hand. "Has, has Billy been in touch with you?" The corners of her eyes were creased with sleeplessness, her reddish hair carelessly brushed.

"Billy? No."

"So you don't know where he is . . ."

"Do I?" Then, "What's going on?"

"Nothing. He finally came home yesterday morning, then left again last night, never came back. I was thinking, I just thought, maybe he was down here somewhere, came in to see you."

"You try to call him?"

"He didn't take his phone." She unconsciously began touching random objects on his desk.

Matty willfully kept his eyes from watching her restless fingers.

"But you think he's somewheres down here."

"Why." Her smile a twitch. "Where do *you* think he is?"

"Me?" Matty thinking, The hell would I know, then, "My guess he's probably off somewheres trying to hash things out."

Minette stared at him bright-eyed, as if waiting for more.

More.

"Personally, if I were in his shoes? I'd want to be with my family right now, but with these kind of situations, in my experience, people, they just . . . they can go every which way, you know?"

Minette continued to stare at him avidly, as if each word were a key to something.

Then, snapping out of it, she went into her purse, took out pen and pad, and wrote down her number.

"I need to ask you two things." Handing him the sheet. "If he comes in to see you or you come across him, could you please let me know?"

"Of course." He tucked her number in the upper corner of his blotter.

"The other is, if there's any developments . . ." She whipped her head around as Yolonda entered the room. "If you could keep me in the loop."

"Absolutely."

"And on my end . . ." She trailed off.

"You OK?"

"I think . . . OK. I hope it's just, I believe it's what you said, he's probably off somewheres trying to clear his head."

"Good." Matty glanced at Yolonda at her desk, going through the District Arrest Books again but listening.

"Because he felt like, he feels like, if he had only . . . I don't know . . . If he had done *this* instead of that, or *that* instead of this . . ."

"I can't tell you how many parents put themselves through that hell."

"So you're saying that's meaningless, right?" she asked gingerly, her fingers back to handling the objects on his desk.

"Let me tell you something," Yolonda chimed in, Minette wheeling to her voice. "If you're the parent in a situation like this, and you're intent on blaming yourself? You can just pick a reason out of a hat."

"Right. Yes." Minette bobbing her head.

"It's like your mind becomes this vicious warehouse, you know?"

"Yes." Minette all hers now.

"Although it doesn't help very much to say that, does it."

"No, no, everything, anything."

"Do you think he's maybe trying to find the guy himself?" Matty asked, making Minette wheel back to him.

"How would he even know how to *do* that?" Her face twisting with incredulity.

Matty said nothing, just watched her eyes.

"That's insane."

"OK."

"That's a movie."

"Good."

Then she was gone again, something making her draw deeper breaths, her lips slightly parted.

"Minette . . ."

"What?"

"Are you worried he might hurt himself?"

"Hurt himself?"

Matty waited, then lightly touched her hand. "It's not a trick question."

"I don't think . . . No. No."

Yolonda half-turned, studying them.

"OK. Good." He took his hand back. "To be honest, we don't really have the time to track him down and also do the work we have to do on the other."

"I understand."

"But I'll get the word out."

"Thank you."

"Everyone here knows what he looks like."

"Thank you."

"Anticrime cruises these streets twenty-four seven," Yolonda said. "If he's walking around, they'll pick him up."

"Thank you."

"I didn't mean to spook you like that," Matty said.

"You didn't." Then, after a long moment of silence, "You didn't," her voice husky and distant.

She closed her eyes and immediately nodded off, her chin dropping, then jerking up.

"Whoa," she said. "Sorry."

There was nothing, no real business left, but Minette continued to sit and Matty wasn't inclined to rush her out of there.

"Can I get you something?" he asked. "Coffee?"

"You know, when Billy left his wife and moved in with me and my daughter, Ike was what, ten, maybe?" looking to Matty as if for verification. "He lived with Elena, but he came over every weekend, and when he did, it was like, me, Billy, and Nina would be watching television and Ike would be watching us. I mean, oh my God, we'd go to a restaurant, a movie, a basketball game, always the same thing. Never smiled, never spoke unless spoken to, and never took his eyes off us."

Minette went off with the recollection, Matty just looking and looking at her.

"But, it wasn't sulking, it was more like, observing. I swear to God, I'd never felt so observed in my life." Smiling at him, through him.

"I mean Nina was a little hinky towards Ike and Billy too, but she was a lot younger than him, more babyish, and her I could talk to, but that first year with Ike? That was not fun. I did everything I could to make him feel at home with us. And Billy did too, of course, but the distance that kid maintained, that watching, it was like *Children of the Damned*, you know?"

"That movie scared the hell out of me," Yolonda said.

"Then, like maybe after a whole year of that, one Sunday we all go to Van Cortlandt Park, the two kids and us. Billy's trying to get Ike to have a catch, he won't take his nose out of some book, you know, got the spycam up, but Billy gets him on his feet, Ike's catching and throwing like it's a two-ton medicine ball, then all of a sudden, he sees something over his dad's shoulder, drops his glove, and breaks into a dead run, yelling, 'Hey! Hey!'

"We're like, what the hell? Take off after him. It turns out that a couple of older kids had my daughter cornered by some trees, were trying to take all her little stuff, earrings, charm bracelet, play purse, she must've been too scared to cry for help, but Ike, Ike he just like, *launched* himself at them, and they were bigger kids too, came in on them like a buzz saw, but before they could get it together to kick his narrow little ass, they see me and Billy bringing up the rear, so they had to take off. But Ike, he's not done, he chases them halfway across the green, then stands there, shouts out, 'You keep your fucking hands off my sister!'

"His sister." Minette went off somewheres, came back laughing. "And my daughter, she hears him, turns to me, says, 'Ike's got a sister?' "

"Wow." Matty ran his fingers across his lips.

"Yeah. And that kind of broke it open. By the time we got married two years later? The kids gave us a toast together."

Matty just sat there, his face smeared into his hand.

"You know the thing I loved about Ike the most? He was a good kid and all, but the best thing about him was that he always seemed so *ready*. Does that even make sense?"

"Sure," Matty said.

"And the, the irony is, Billy always kicked himself for having to leave Ike behind, but the truth of the matter? That kid turned out good to go. A big heart and happy. A lot happier than either of his parents."

Minette hoisted her bag to her shoulder and wiped her eyes. "It just works out that way sometimes, you know?"

A moment after she left, Yolonda murmured to her computer screen, "If the kid had been a little less 'ready,' he might still be alive, you know what I'm saying?" Looking up at Matty, who was still looking at the door.


Eric sat alone in Café Berkmann's cramped cellar-level office, the narrow plank desk before him covered with neat stacks of cash and empty envelopes.

Despite his knuckles having continued to swell overnight to the point of splitting the skin, his fingers skittered across the face of the calculator in a controlled frenzy. And as always when stealing from the tip pool, he not only moved his lips but whispered the numbers out loud as if the TI-36 were in on the scam.

As a manager as opposed to, say, a bartender, he found it hard to steal or, as he preferred to think of it, shave, but Eric did what he could.

In divvying up the nightly tip pool, it was all about the cash value of a "point," which changed every night, and what fraction of that point your job was assigned.

Managers, hostesses, and waiters earned a full point per hour, jobs of lesser status, three-quarters to a quarter of a point.

Last night, the house took in $2,400 in tips, which, divided by 77, the accumulated number of points working the floor, gave a point value of $31.16.

So a waiter working eight hours was owed $31.16 times his full eight points, or $249.28; a busboy, getting one-third of a point, was due roughly $83 for putting in the same amount of time.

But, but . . . If Eric "miscalculated" and declared the point value for the evening not to have been $31.16 but, say $29.60 (no one ever checked up on him), then that waiter took home only $236.80, the busboy $78.93, and Eric would pocket $13 and $4 respectively, times ten waiters, seven busboys, plus everyone else in the pool equaled Eric walking out the door with an extra few hundred in cash every week.

The key to not getting caught was self-control; he never shaved more than $1.50 off the true value of a point and rarely pulled the scam more than once a week; never more than twice.

But since the shooting, he'd been dipping into that pool every day and yesterday had increased his shave to $2.50 a point, a new high or low for him.

Something furry ran past the office on its way to the storage room, and Eric scribbled a note to himself to call the exterminator. Then he saw the damned thing again, running in reverse this time—a trick of the eyes. Since his release from the Tombs, he hadn't been able to sleep for more than a few hours at a time, a combination of free-fall dreams and late-night alcohol. So in the subterranean quiet of the office right now he briefly laid his head between the cash and the envelopes, closed his eyes, and drifted off. When he woke, Matty and Yolonda were seated across the plank desk from him, Yolonda's eyes filled with that pitiless pity of hers, Matty unreadable . . . When he woke, he was on his feet staring at the brick wall. Shaking it off as best he could, he applied himself to the stuffing of envelopes, today's skim surpassing for the first time $3 a point; suicidal most likely, but he just needed to leave; this city, this life, and he would do what he had to do to make it happen.

. . .

Avner Polaner, a tall, bony Ashkenazi-Yemeni Israeli, sat before the digital photo manager, staring listlessly at the mug shots coming up at him six to the screen, droning, "No, no, no," his head aslant on the heel of his palm.

Of the three robberies on the All Sheets featuring two dark-skinned males and a handgun, Polaner's mugging coincided most neatly with that of Ike Marcus; three in the morning and took place only a few blocks away on Delancey and Clinton. The downside was the incident had happened ten days ago, and he had never been interviewed on it because five hours after the encounter he was on a plane to Tel Aviv. But with Eric Cash out of the loop, Avner was the closest thing Matty and Yolonda had to a best hope.

"No, no, no." The guy bored out of his mind.

Yolonda, operating the monitor, threw Matty a look.

Polaner appeared to be in his early thirties, basketball tall, his long, kinky hair bound up in an urban samurai topknot. An hour earlier, when he had come into the squad room shoulder-carrying a bike as long and thin as himself, Matty thought he had moved with the geeky grace of a flamingo.

"No, no, no." Then, plunging his face into his hands, "OK, stop," rearing back. "Look, a dark kid with a gun is a dark kid with a gun. That's the price of living here, is every now and then it's going to happen, so you don't do anything stupid like the guy you just told me about, you just shrug it off and go about your business. You go on."

"Are you worried about some kind of payback?"

"Please. I was stationed on the Lebanese border for two years, I don't sweat the occasional stickup. Besides which, as I told you already, I knew better than to give him a good look right in his face, so really, this here is a waste of everybody's time." He took a deep breath, reset himself. "That being said, I have a question."

They waited.

"What would it take to arrest Harry Steele?"

"Backtrack a little there, Avner."

"Do you know *why* I went to Tel Aviv right after the holdup instead of coming in here to look at this stuff? To get some *sleep*."

"Avner," Matty said, "backtrack."

"Of all his tenants I pay top dollar, sixteen hundred for an apartment so small I have to leave the room to change my mind because everybody else in the building has been living there since the Flood. The welfare queen below me pays six hundred, the hippie spinster on top a thousand, and the millionaire, an eighty-five-year-old man who remembers shaking hands with Fiorello La Guardia in the lobby, remembers the seltzer man, the iceman, toilets in the hallway, who owns three hot-sheet motels in the Bronx and half the town of Kerhonkson, New York, *he* pays three hundred and fifty dollars.

"And you should see how they keep their places, crusted food on the stoves, shower curtains that could grow penicillin, cat piss on the carpets, roaches, mice . . . You know what I have on my floors? Wide-board pumpkin pine. I installed it myself, paid for it myself. And when I move? I'm going to take it with me so Steele doesn't have another reason to jack up the rent on the next poor sucker."

"This is in the Berkmann's building?" Yolonda asked, slowly rolling her head from ear to ear.

"Worse. I'm across the street, so not only do I get to *hear* all the drunken assholes who have to go outside for their smokes until three in the morning *every* morning, not only do I *hear* all the pukers, the cab whistlers, the moon howlers, but I have the proper angle of vision to *see* them as well. And you know what he has the nerve to say to me, Steele? He says, 'Avi, nobody ever complains but you.' He says I'm an 'environmental hypochondriac.' Can you imagine that?"

"Huh."

"I have friends run restaurants and shops in the neighborhood, everybody says to me, 'Avi, you got to roll with it. The guy is running his business just like you. Be realistic, be sympathetic.' But no. *Not* just like me. I own two delis around here. One on Eldridge and Rivington—"

"The Sana'a?"

"That's one, yes."

"I thought the brothers ran that."

"The Two Stooges? Those guys couldn't run a race. They work for me."

"So how'd you like the Virgin Mary showing up there the other day?" Yolonda asked.

"The who?"

"The Virgin Mary."

Avner shrugged. "Did she buy anything?"

"Excuse me." Matty got up and took a short walk around himself.

The thought of returning to the house of Babel with a Chinese uniform to once again try to track down Paul Ng made him want to drop to his knees with despair.

And the only other vic on the All Sheets who seemed like a possible match to the Marcus shooters was a guy named Ming Lam, also Chinese, also reluctant to file his complaint, and with the added bonus of old age—seventy-six, according to the report.

They were fucked without Eric Cash; he just knew it.

"My point is," Avner said, "never has one of my stores ever got a public-nuisance citation. So I go to all the state Liquor Board hearings every month, I file noise complaint after noise complaint. 'Avi, nobody complains but you.' Oh yeah? I get so many names on petitions I could start my own political party. I go in there and talk to them about the fact that he's selling alcohol less than five hundred feet from a school, I talk about the exhaust pollution from the delivery trucks, how his sign is too bright, too big. I research everything, I try everything. At this point I know every state Liquor Board member by their first name, but he's Harry Steele, they all live in his ass and that's that."

Matty toyed with the idea of making a backdoor plea to Danny the Red; beg him to call off this waiver-of-immunity pissing match.

"He says he'll pay me ten thousand if I move. Says he'll pay for the moving van, help me find another apartment in the neighborhood, he'll even throw in the key money on the new place, says I'm paying close to market value already, so what's the big deal. The big deal, Mister Hot Shit Harry Steele, is I was here *before* you opened the restaurant, I was here *first. You* move."

"Why don't you just go back to Israel?" Yolonda said, more out of boredom than anything else.

"If I was a black man complaining like this"—Avner smiled—"would you tell me to go back to Africa?"

"I would if that's where you grew up."

"I love Israel, I go back all the time. I just love New York a little more. My workers are Arabs, my best friend is a black man from Alabama, my girlfriend's a Puerto Rican, and my landlord is a half-Jew bastard. You know what I did this morning? I read in the paper yesterday that the circus is setting up in the Madison Square Garden, they said the elephants would be walking through the Holland Tunnel at dawn. I'm a photographer a little too, you know? So I get up at five o'clock, bike over to the tunnel, and wait. It turns out the paper got it wrong, they came through the Lincoln, but still, you know? This is a hell of a place."

"Avner." Yolanda leaned forward, elbows on knees. "I want you to keep looking at these faces."

"It's a waste of time."

"It's a homicide," Matty snapped. "The shooters are still out there, and the victim could have just as easily been *you*."

Avner seemed to think on that, went off somewheres behind those raccoon eyes, then abruptly came back. "You want to hear the worst?" He leaned into them, smiled softly. "Now he's pushing for sidewalk tables."

Eric sat the bar with a brandy and soda, the last of the sun slashing at him through the venetian blinds.

He surprised himself by recognizing Bree's silhouette through the Rivington Street window shades and had her tip envelope in hand before she came through the door.

She stood near the pulpit looking around for him, Eric once again thinking "Irish eyes," half song title, all cliché.

She was maybe twenty, twenty-one, fourteen–fifteen years younger than him, wearing a hippie-vintage light orange Indian blouse and a worn pair of jeans a size too big in the seat. He could imagine her rising this morning and grabbing them from the rumpled pile of clothes that lay alongside her flat-to-the-floor mattress.

"Hey." She stepped to him at the bar, accepted her envelope, then took a deep breath as if drawing herself together. "Look."

And he did. Her face was so white it was pale blue, like skim milk.

What did that drunk cop once call it? Cheap Irish skin.

Hardly.

"I don't know who you think I am, or who you think you are, but the tone you took with me last night was totally uncalled for."

It sounded worked on, sounded like it wasn't easy for her to say that, and it slayed him.

"Totally uncalled for," he agreed, training his eyes on the hands that held the envelope. "I'm sorry." Then, impulsively added, "It was on my mind all night last night. I couldn't sleep." The words coming out with a husky catch that he didn't trust in himself these days, but there it was.

She stood there for a moment, sizing him up, then slowly said, "Me neither."

And just like that they were talking about something else.

"So, we're good?" he asked, forcing himself to raise his eyes to hers.

"Sure."

She was supposed to go about her business now, head down to the lockers, but she hesitated, took an extra second to lag behind herself, Eric knowing all about that extra-second lag, everything in the world contained in that extra-second lag.

"So where are you from?"

"Me?" The question seemed to relieve her, the both of them on the same page. "You never heard of it."

"Try me."

"Tofte, Minnesota?"

"You sure?" Making her laugh.

Fourteen, thirteen years difference, maybe less.

"So, how long you been here?"

"Here, New York?"

"Here New York."

"Six weeks?" Her eyes on fire with the insanity of it all.

Six weeks . . .

"And what are you . . ." Suddenly, alarmingly, he felt himself beginning to fade.

"What *am* I? Like, what religion?"

"No, no. What do you want . . ." He had trouble finishing the question, could barely get out the "to be."

"Ideally?" she began, and he didn't hear what she said after.

"Interesting," he said automatically, then, "So."

She caught the dismissal in his tone, and projecting both disappointment and confusion, she stepped off for the lockers downstairs.

"Hang on," he called after her, and when she turned with those unbearable bright eyes, he put his hand out for her envelope. "Let me check that for a sec, make sure you got the right one."

He took the envelope into the kitchen, stared at it without opening it, then came back out and returned it to her still $29 light.

"Good to go." Taking one last look at that rice-powder throat, those pearly hands, thinking, No prisoners.


They were all sitting on Irma Nieves's bed: Crystal, Little Dap, David, Irma, Fredro, Tristan, and Devon, passing the blunt and eating chips, when Fredro just had to fucking start.

*"Bzzt."* The others looking to him.

"What?"

Fredro nodded to Tristan's exposed chin and did it again. *"Bzzt."* Like the sound of an electrical zap: like the sound of Tristan's zigzagged cross-mouthed scar.

Most of them in their stoned way got it, saw it, and just fell out bawling; Tristan once again feeling the resigned heaviness that came with being the natural target of others. Well, if it wasn't the scar, it would have been something else; it didn't take much and it had soaked into everybody's routine; what's Tristan doing or not doing, saying or not saying, today; people counting on him for entertainment like welfare heads count on the mailman.

The alternative, though, was home; was hamster watch.

"Oh, nigger." Fredro with tears in his eyes, rearing back in mock-horror. *"Please* grow that motherfucker back."

"Oh!" The bed trembling with sniggers.

"Put like a ban*danna* on, someshit." Devon's turn.

"Nigger *never* get no dugout now."

"I get bookoo dugout," Tristan said, couldn't help saying, knowing that the worst thing he could do was give them any kind of response.

" 'Bookoo dugout . . .' " Irma snorting out smoke, provoking another round of howls.

He liked Irma anyway, liked the way her teeth bucked out, the way she kept her hands curled palms-up in her lap when she wasn't doing anything.

"Motherfucker got to put a pork chop round his neck just to get the *dog* to play with him." Devon again, Tristan seeing that white boy's eyes going up, up, as he went down, down, then pretending it was Devon that night instead, it was Fredro, it was all of them; except Irma.

"Ain't you scare those little kids with that?" Fredro got off the bed to imitate one of Tristan's hamsters, raising his arms and looking up.

"Unca Tristan, pick me up, wipe my ass—*whoa, shit!*" Like the kid just saw the scar for the first time, everybody crying again, the cramped room dense with smoke.

Only Little Dap was holding himself together, but scowling at him, hating him for the burden of it.

"Yo, I'm sorry, man," Fredro said between howls, tears running down his face. "I just can't . . ." Howling again.

"Oh, man, I'm outa here." And within a minute most everybody was up off the unmade bed and still snorting and whooing, filing out of the sticky, filthy apartment.

Only he and Irma remained, Tristan at the head of the big bed, buzzing with alertness, Irma at the foot still puffing on that blunt until she finally looked up and realized it was just the two of them.

"You forget where the door's at?"

At least his ex-stepfather insisted on a clean house.


She thought the mermaid would be the easiest. She wasn't a bad copier, even if it was just from memory, and at first when all she intended to do was draw, it was coming out pretty good, but when the point of the pen started pressing in a little more than she intended, when it started to break the skin, when it started to hurt like hell but not so bad that she wanted to stop, it became increasingly hard to keep a steady hand.

And an hour later, when her mother came in without knocking, took one look at all the bloody towels piled at her feet and started screaming like a lunatic, Nina knew that Ike's panther and devil's head would have to wait for another day.

"Where's he live?" Fenton Ma asked.

"Twenty-four East Broadway."

"Fook?"

"I have no idea," Matty said.

"I don't speak Fook. You better hope he speaks Mandarin."

"You're Mandarin?"

"Mandarin's the language. I'm Cantonese. From Flushing. But East Broadway's Fook. Bottom dogs get to live in the bottoms."

It was a hot night, and beneath the iron shadow of the Manhattan Bridge's looping overpasses, East Broadway reeked of the iced fish that lined the sidewalks, Fenton Ma getting more and more stressed with each blabbing gaggle of women they passed.

"They're all speaking that hillbilly shit. I'm telling you, man, I don't understand a single word."

Once again they walked straight up from the street and into the top-floor apartment without encountering a single locked door. As they headed for the communal kitchen at the far end of the flat, they peered into the makeshift bedrooms and cubicles, saw the men lying on the bunks and planks, their cigarettes jerking in the dark like fire-flies.

In the empty kitchen, the dining table sat spotless, the karaoke machine was turned off, and the carp tank was empty.

"Hello, police," Matty said to no one.

The young, compact guy who'd followed them into the hallway last night emerged from a bathroom.

"I think that's the go-to guy here," Matty said to Fenton, then stepped off to let the two men talk.

"They ate that fish?" Yolonda whispered, nodding to the empty tank.

After a moment's conversation the manager led Fenton past Matty and Yolonda back down the hall to one of the larger bedrooms, said something to one of the smokers lying in the dark, then left them to it.

The guy's plank was the third one up from the bottom, so although flat on his back, he was on eye level with Ma, both of their faces intermittently illuminated by the flare of his inhalations.

A moment later Fenton came out, muttering, "Fucking eeba-geebas," and signaled for the manager to come in and translate for him.

"Is that our guy?" Yolonda asked.

"No," Fenton said, then returned with the manager to his conversation.

After a while the mingled odors of sweat and smoke coming from the bedroom made them retreat to the kitchen, where they waited in silence until Fenton came back out into the hallway and signaled for them to head on out.

"That wasn't Paul Ng?" Matty asked, leading the way down the stairs.

"That was his tenant."

"Whose tenant?"

"Paul Ng's."

"Tenant of what?"

"The plank."

"The what?"

Fenton stopped on the second-floor landing.

"Ng rents that plank for a hundred and fifty a month from the guy in the kitchen, who leased the whole apartment, but three days a week they got Ng working in a restaurant up in New Paltz, so he sublets his plank to that guy laying there now for seventy-five bucks."

"Jesus."

"Hey, between the seventy grand he's probably working off to the snakehead that got him over here and sending a little something back to his family on the mainland? He's kicking back about eighty percent of whatever shit salary they're paying him, all of which is to say you sublet that fucking plank."

"You get the name of the place in New Paltz?"

"Golden Wok."

"We should send somebody up there," Yolonda said.

"I guess." Matty shrugged, no one all that hopeful about something coming from it, or Paul Ng in general.

"So you guys need help with anybody else? I'm kind of liking the change of pace here."

"Actually," Matty said, "we have one more possible on the robbery pattern, also Chinese."

"I'm there."

"Guy is"—checking his notes—"Ming Lam."

"OK."

"You up for this?"

"Hell yeah. Another boat house?"

"No, he lives with his wife."

"Down here?"

"One fifty-five Bowery."

"With his wife? How old?"

"Seventy-six."

"Oh, forget it." Fenton suddenly blushing with projected failure. "Those old dudes never talk."

"That's because they never had someone like you ask them to before." Yolonda going eyes into eyes with the kid, Fenton blushing all over again. "Don't be so negative all the time."

As they came back out on East Broadway, Quality of Life was parked right in front of the building, misery lights revolving, a beat-up Toyota with tinted windows pulled over and waiting a few car lengths ahead.

Matty leaned into the front passenger window as Lugo ran the Toyota's plates on the dashboard-mounted computer.

"C'mon, fucking thing." Scharf whacking it as they waited for the information to kick back.

"So how much dope you take off the street tonight?" Matty asked.

"About six hours' worth?" Geohagan said drily.

A blowup of Billy Marcus's driver's license photo was taped over the glove compartment.

"Hair nor hide?"

"You'll be first to know," Lugo said.


Thinking the kid needed some fortification before the next interview, they grabbed a table in the Grand Street kosher pizzeria around the corner from Ming Lam's apartment and ordered a few slices.

The place was large and near empty at this hour, a sea of indoor picnic tables, just one other party across the room, a heavy, gray-bearded Orthodox in shirtsleeves sitting with a younger man in an elegant three-piece suit, this second guy tanned and groomed as if for a press conference.

Yolonda leaned into the table, whispered to Fenton, "That guy there? He wiggles his fingers, five people die in Oklahoma."

"He looks it."

"Not him. The fat one."

The pizza came, three slices floating in a clear orange fluid.

"You want to hear something?" Matty's turn to whisper. "I'd been trying to get a place down here for years, right? You know the Dubinsky Co-ops down the block? Three-year waiting list. I was like fifty names from the top. Not that I could ever afford it, but anyways, the reb over there, two years ago his son gets picked up in a john sweep on Allen. They bring him in, and I know him from the neighborhood, know he's got a wife, three kids, the wife's sick. Anyways, they haul everybody into the Eighth for processing, I see him in cuffs, looks like he's going to kill himself. My guy in Vice is there, owes me a favor, make a long story short, he lets me cull the herd a little, hustle him out the back door, say, sin no more."

" 'Sin no more,' " Yolonda clucked.

"Sin no more. My good deed for the night, right? The next morning, I get called down to the captain's office, I'm thinking, 'What did I do now?' Go in there, the old man, the rabbi? He's sitting with the captain plus, *plus*, Deputy Inspector Berkowitz from 1PP. I go in, both the cap and the DI give me this look, then just leave the office. The rabbi stays, offers me a seat, says, 'I hear you've been looking for an apartment.' I say, 'How'd you hear that?' The guy shrugs, I remember then who he is down here, say, 'Well, yeah, in fact I'm on the waiting list for Dubinsky.' He says, 'Interestingly enough, a couple of sunbirds in there, they decided they're getting a little too old for all the back-and-forth to Florida, and they're looking for a responsible year-round subletter for up here. Very reasonable rent too.' . . . A week later I'm standing on my new terrace, corner view, can see all three bridges, got three and a half rooms behind me, fourteen hundred a month."

"You hear that?" Yolonda said. "I follow that guy's kid around every day hoping he screws up again so I can save his ass and move out of the fucking Bronx."

"The thing is, the guy never once mentioned his son to me, what happened. Just, 'I hear you've been looking.'"

"This is all from being a rabbi?"

"This is all from saying vote for so-and-so and fifteen thousand people down here do it."

"Of course Matty has to keep the guy's kid out of trouble as long as he lives there, but . . ."

"A mere bag o' shells," Matty said, then, opening his cell, "Hello?"

"Detective Clark?"

"Speaking."

There was a moment's hesitation, Matty thinking it might be Marcus's wife but waiting.

"Yeah, hey, this is Minette Davidson?" as if she wasn't sure.

"Minette." Thrown for a second by the last name.

Yolonda recognized the voice before he did, giving him the eye as she used a napkin to blot up some of the grease on her second slice.

"Billy Marcus's wife?" Minette said.

"Of course. Sorry, hey."

He could hear the drone of a voice over a PA in the background: airport or hospital.

"Hey. Is anything . . ." She trailed off.

"We're interviewing possible wits, witnesses, as we speak, but . . ."

Fenton got up for a third slice, sauntering past the rabbi, studying him.

"And nothing on Billy?"

"He hasn't contacted me. They're out there looking, though."

Another amplified drone in the background, someone being paged.

"Minette, where are you."

"Where?"

Another voice, in the room with her this time, tentatively calling out for a Miguel Pinto as if reading the name off someone else's handwriting.

"Are you in a hospital?"

"Yeah, no, it's nothing."

"What's nothing. Are you OK?"

"Me? Yeah." Then, muffling the receiver and calling out, "Excuse me, miss?" Coming back to him. "I have to go." And hanging up.

Fenton came back with his slice.

"Your girlfriend?" Yolanda asked wide-eyed.

"She called from some hospital."

"Is she all right?" Yolanda asked flatly.

"I have no idea."

Matty hit Received Calls, got back *Restricted*.

"Shit."

"Didn't you take her number in the office?"

"I left it there."

"Maybe you should run back and get it," she said straight-faced.

Then his phone died altogether.

"So, what hospital is she in?"

"I just told you. I have no idea."

"Is she all right?"

"I just said, I don't know."

"So, what hospital is she in?"

"Why are you fucking with me?"

"Me?"

Fenton dug into his third slice.

The rabbi got to his feet, wiped his lips, shook hands with his dining partner, then walked towards the door, squeezing Matty's shoulder without looking at him as he passed the table.

"Rabbi," Matty said.

Fenton tilted into the aisle to track him out onto Grand Street. "Yeah, we got guys like him down in Chinatown," he said, straightening up. "But I was in Brooklyn North until six months ago, so I don't really know them yet."

"Make it your business," Yolanda said.

"Jesus." Matty glared at his dead phone.

As it turned out, Ming Lam did speak English, not that it mattered much given that the first half of the interview took place on the street through an intercom, the old man needing twenty minutes of coaxing before he would even let them up.

He lived in one and a half rooms with his wife, the half tub in the kitchen covered with a wooden board to double as a dining table.

Again Matty and Yolonda stepped off to let Fenton do the talking, Ming Lam's wife, a small woman the exact size and shape of her husband, reluctantly offering them seats on a bedsheet-covered couch half-piled with Chinese newspapers.

They could tell right away that Fenton wasn't going to get anywhere with this guy despite the old man's obvious pleasure at seeing a Chinese kid in uniform.

"You have to help us."

"Oh yeah?" Ming Lam said. They were standing toe-to-toe in the middle of the small room. "And when you catch him, what are you do, cut off his hands? Give him a beating? *No.* He'll be out on the street next day. Then he come after me."

"No, he won't. Not if you help us put him away. If you don't help us? Then, *yes,* maybe he comes after you again. You give off that kind of vibration to these guys."

Matty knew that he and Yolonda were making it harder on the kid just by being there.

"You *never* put them away. I got rob twelve times, told the police about the first three, then gave up on you. You arrest *one* guy for *one* day, and then he out here again, and I had to hide because he knew it was me told the police."

"Well, now it's different."

"Oh yeah?"

"Yeah. Now you have me."

"What the big deal about you?"

"That last guy that robbed you? I know he's still watching you, thinking about doing you again. But you know what? *I'm* watching you too. You were on Essex Street yesterday, right? Right?" The kid winging it. "I saw you but you didn't see me, did you. And you didn't see him. I *already* look out for you. And I promise, I will put this guy away if you help me."

"No. He'll come out next day and kill me."

"You know what?" Fenton said, starting to sputter. "If you don't help me get him off the street, maybe he *will* kill you. *Or* your wife. *Or* your children. How are you gonna feel, I'm saying to you help me and you didn't, and then he goes and hurts someone in your family, huh?"

"No."

Feeling bad for the kid, Matty sat up to pitch in, but Yolonda touched his arm and he settled back.

"Look, we can subpeona you, *make* you help us. Do you want that?"

"I'm not scared of you."

"All we're talking about is looking at some pictures, maybe a lineup, no lawyers, no court."

"No."

Fenton turned to Matty and Yolonda on the couch, flashing them quick I-told-you-so eyes.

"But you know what?" The old guy's voice turned Fenton back around. "This," patting his chest, his uniform, then smiling, "makes me happy."

Matty sat there on the musty couch; we are fucked.


On the way down the stairs Matty put his arm around Fenton's shoulder. "Can I tell you something in confidence?" walking him out of Yolonda's hearing range even though he knew she knew what he was about to say. "You know that story I told you about saving the rabbi's son from an arrest that night? It was bullshit. I always knew about that guy and his thing for pross, everybody did, and my connect in Vice knew to give me a heads-up if he ever got collared, you know why? Because I *also* knew that if I ever had the opportunity to save his bacon, his old man would probably swing something to get me into the Dubinskys." Matty stopped walking and reared back to see how the kid was taking the story. "It's a nightmare down here, real estate."

Matty had told him the truth as sort of a consolation prize for the old guy shaming him up there, but Fenton Ma was still obviously burning and hadn't heard a word.


It had rained hard for a few hours earlier in the day, and on this, the fourth night since the murder, the shrine felt all wrong, sodden and charred, sardonic and vaguely threatening; as if to say, this is what time does, what becomes of us mere hours after the tears and flowers. Someone had repositioned the teddy bear so that it now appeared to be buggering the stuffed eagle, the other plush animals lay on their sides like drowned rats, the coin offerings set before Lazarus and Saint Barbara had been all swiped, the incense reduced to spoorlike heaps and coils of ash. The tubular-steel mobile that formerly hung from a home-made flagpole had been scavenged and was now reduced to a single rod jammed into a gap in a pulled-down riot gate and acted as a divider between the shrine and a mound of garbage bags in front of the neighboring Sana'a Deli. The only leaving that seemed untainted was a white T-shirt emblazoned with the Hells Angels logo, crisply folded and placed on the ground like a cold offer of revenge.

Of all the images and messages taped to the overlooking tenement exterior, only Ike's last words, NOT TONIGHT MY MAN, seemed untouched by graffiti and the elements, as bold and untattered as if they had been carved into the wall.

Not Tonight My Man . . . Every fifth or sixth person passing by took the time to read the words, some silently; you could track their eyes scanning the print, some whispering it, others saying it aloud and shaking their heads, twisting their lips, smirking in marvel, What a dope. Some even saying it directly to Eric, standing at the edge of the shrine: Am I right or am I right?

They told him other stuff too; who did the deed: the Albanian Mafia, the Ghost Shadows, Rikers-based Five Percenters, Brooklyn-based jihadists, the po-po's, the government; and why: as payback for fucking a Latin King's queen, to keep him from telling what he knew about Cheney and the Trilateral Commission, the Illuminati, the Klan, to keep him from blowing the whistle on Sputnik and Skeezix, two Alphabet City detectives who had burned him in a drug deal; all these inside tipsters aimlessly jumpy, skittery-eyed, addressing Eric specifically because even though he could barely follow anything being said to him, he didn't move away from them, he looked like he was paying attention, like he genuinely wanted to know.

Not tonight my man . . .

He was filled with a livid despair when he heard the drawled recitations of Ike's last words, the jokes about verbal suicide, suicide by mouth, suicide by beer; in a white rage that he had to be immersed in this study, he didn't ask for this; this was thrust upon him by that naive jerk who decided to go out on a punch line that Eric would have laughed at if it hadn't so violently thrown him up against himself; hadn't turned his life inside out.

After all was said and done, he didn't really know why he wasn't at least going through the motions of helping out, if for no other reason than to get everybody off his back . . . But he did know this: the guy was dead and it wouldn't help bring him back or get him justice if Eric didn't see any faces or overhear any telling talk. And he knew this: after the shooters broke him in half that night, those bastards in the interview room had finished the job, removing every shred of innocence or inspiration or optimism that still clung to him after all these years, extracting whatever was left in him of hope or illusion, whatever amorphous yearning had managed to remain in him to shine, to *be* something; he'd been hanging on by his fingernails at best anyway, and now, and now, he was just saying No. He just didn't want to go along to get along anymore. He didn't want to break anymore. He'd picked maybe the worst thing to say No to, but there you are.

"Coward."

Eric looked up to see a middle-aged, blurry-faced man standing directly across the perimeter of streetlight from him.

"Fucking coward."

It was Ike's father, who else could it be; standing there crook-necked staring into the shrine pile as if it were a campfire. Entranced, Eric started to walk to him; to explain, to plead his case.

"Fucking cunt."

And then he stopped, backed away; the guy was oblivious to Eric's presence, was addressing himself.

A stork-thin nutter in a homemade burnoose came out of the shadows race-walking a shopping cart past the shrine. "Not tonight, my man. *Yes* tonight, you dumb motherfucker, slip a the lip sink a ship, well it's too late now." Nearly mowing Eric down.

**With the dark, skinny** mixologist from the No Name having done it to him again last night, weeping all the way through sex but with the added bonus of wailing through hiccuping sobs afterwards, "It's nothing personal, it's not you," Matty was the first one in the squad room Sunday morning, the peal of competing church bells—Spanish Catholic from Pitt, black Episcopalian from Henry—agitating the dust motes drifting above the sea of vacant cluttered desks. He sat in the stillness, his hands clasped in front of him, looking down at the front page of that day's *Post*. The photo beneath the banner was of Steven Boulware, looking somewhat pounded on, solemnly leaving a floral arrangement in front of the increasingly ratty-looking makeshift shrine on Eldridge Street, the caption, *Remembering a friend after a brush with death.*

But the headline itself was given over to a Sanitation Department scandal, the Marcus homicide pushed back to page five and basically saying nothing.

Let it die; five days after the murder, and Matty had zip: no leads and no real manpower save for Yolonda, Iacone, and Mullins, but Yolonda mainly, because she owed him for hanging in on one of her own hopeless let-it-die homicides a year before.

Two days more until the seventh-day recanvass, but it already felt to him like a last hurrah. In fact, given the albatross vibes he'd been getting from 1PP, he had a growing suspicion that it might not even come to pass.

Ignoring the mountain range of paperwork on his desk, he pulled out his local-perp stack and began reviewing the ones that were sent out as Want Cards, reassessing those that he had previously thought didn't fit the bill.

Then he spied Minette Davidson's phone number wedged into a corner of his blotter.

"She cut herself making a sandwich," Minette said.

"Oh yeah?" Matty didn't buy it. "She take stitches?"

"A few. We had to wait almost six hours for the plastic surgeon to show up, but finally."

"Good."

"You couldn't have called anybody at the hospital to speed things up last night, could you? Please say no so I don't kick myself."

"No."

"Thank you."

"She's OK?"

"Yeah. Sort of."

"Good." Matty's cell started to ring, his friend in Vice. "And I assume Mr. Marcus doesn't know about this?"

"Mr. Marcus?" she said, Matty picking up the edge. "How could he?"

"Right," he said, then, "Look, I know it seems a lot longer, but it's barely forty-eight hours," mulling over whether to initiate a morgue search.

"I know." She sounded too drained to care right now. "All right, then."

"Yeah, I'm sorry I couldn't help you out last night."

"Thanks. Thank you."

"And, as you know, my heart goes out to you and yours."

There was a moment's hesitation, then, "Thanks."

· · ·

*As you know, my heart goes out to you and yours;* Matty wincing as he returned the call to Vice, which in turn triggered a call to Harry Steele.

"Professor Steele." Matty held his cell in the crook of his neck as he reached for an upright half-full coffee cup in his wastebasket from yesterday, drank the rest. "I have it from an impeccable source that they'll be running an underage ops on you tonight. You'll be needing to keep an eye out for a short Hispanic, red dye streak, pierced eyebrow, on the chunky side. Make sure you check her ID. Tell Clarence and work the door with him."

Out on Pitt Street a car drove by with a bass system so powerful that his pencils rolled across the blotter.

"I have no idea what time. It's not like a dinner reservation. Just invest in the vigilance, all right? Now . . . I need something from you . . ." Matty about to ask him for help with Eric Cash when a commotion on the floor below made him hang up, the downstairs desk cop barking, "Hey, whoa!" followed by a rush of feet coming up the stairs, the desk cop in pursuit. "I said fucking *halt!*" Matty up and braced as the squad-room door whacked into the wall and Billy Marcus blew in, wheezing, stark-eyed, his liquored breath preceding him, announcing, "I know who did it," before being wrapped in a flying bear hug from behind, the desk cop's forward momentum toppling the both of them, Billy falling face-first with his arms pinned to his sides, his unprotected nose spraying blood across the floor as the enraged, winded 220-pounder landed on top of him.

"I know who did it," Billy said again, the words this time coming out flattened and adenoidal as he sat in a tipped-back chair at the makeshift dining table, eyes to the ceiling, Matty standing behind him and holding a fistful of paper towels to his nose. "I know who did it."

"OK, good. Just take it easy." The 10:00 a.m. Scotch fumes rising into Matty's face made his eyelids flutter.

"'OK, good. Take it easy,'" Marcus mimicked, wheezing like a radiator.

"Mr. Marcus, do you have asthma?"

"Billy. My name is Billy. I told you that"—he paused to draw breath—"the last time. Yeah, I do. A little."

Matty took Billy's hand and placed it atop the paper towels, went to one of the empty desks, and took the Advair inhaler from the overnight kit John Mullins kept in his bottom drawer.

"You know how to use one of these?" Shaking it up before handing it over.

"Yeah, thank you." He took a hit with his free hand.

As he stared at Billy now from less than a foot away, it dawned on Matty that for all their encounters over the last few days, he had never gotten a good fix on Marcus's face. His features seemed both half-erased and constantly fluctuating, as if the trauma had blurred him physically as well as mentally; his face normally nowhere near this puffy or gaunt, complexion this blanched or ruddy, eyes this muddy or fiery, hair this lank or wild. He seemed both older and younger than he was, his body slim and nimble, yet Matty had seen him move with the geriatric tentativeness of someone crossing an unfamiliar room in the dark; the bottom line here being that even from this close range and concentrating on the task, Matty still couldn't say what Billy Marcus looked like.

One thing he did know for sure, though, was that the guy was still wearing the same clothes from three days ago.

"God knows I'm not passing judgment, but are you drunk?"

Marcus ignored the question, dug a hand into his pants pocket, pulling out a crumpled page of that day's *Post*.

"Please." Offering it to Matty.

It was a page from the sports section, an editorial about the immaturity of the new point guard for the Knicks, then he saw the ballpoint scrawl running in the margin: *22 Oliver skinny caramel lat pink vel zip track st wash niks black.*

"What's this?"

Marcus palmed his chest, then lowered his head between his knees.

"What is this."

Marcus lifted up, eyes to the ceiling. "I was," taking a breath, "I was at a newsstand, and there's the papers, and, the front page? If you saw, today, it had the building on Eldridge with the flowers and all? That picture there, on your desk?" He spoke with a chattering quickness now, as if the room were freezing. "And, standing next to me, is this girl, Latin girl, and she picks up the paper, looks at the photo, and her eyes got like, huge. And then she says, 'Oh, *shit*. I thought them niggers was *bull*shitting.' Then she puts the paper down and walks away, so, I follow her to see where she's going, because she said it like she had heard the guys who did it bragging about it, don't you think?"

Or had friends who told her about a neighborhood shooting that they had seen on TV. There had been a dozen half-assed leads like this.

"So you follow her."

"Yeah. A block into it I realized I should have bought the paper she was holding, you know, because it had her fingerprints? But . . . I follow her to . . . What?" Trying to read his notes upside down now in Matty's hand.

"Twenty-two Oliver?" Matty said.

"Yes."

"The Lemlich projects?"

"Some projects, yeah. I can't believe I didn't catch the name."

"We know it."

"And so, she went into the building, I didn't think it was smart to follow her past that, so I wrote down what she was wearing, as you see, and I came straight here."

Marcus hadn't blinked once since Matty and the other cop had lifted him off the floor.

On the other hand, 22 Oliver wasn't a bad address for this; it lay in the general direction of the shooters' flight pattern, and they'd been guessing the Lemlichs from the jump.

"And this is her description."

"Yes."

"Can you read it for me?" Handing him back his writing.

"Skinny, caramel Latina in a pink velour zippered tracktop, stonewashed jeans, and black Nikes."

"How old about?"

"High school."

"And where was this newsstand?"

"Eldridge and Broome? You know, right around the corner from . . ." Marcus shook up the inhaler but forgot to take another hit. "Don't you think this is a good lead?"

"We'll check it out. But can I ask . . ." Matty hesitated, then, "Billy, why are you still down there?"

"Why?" He gawked incredulously.

Matty retreated.

"So when are you going over?"

"To?"

"Find that girl."

"Soon."

"How soon?"

"As soon as I get you squared away."

"Come again?"

"Get you home."

"No."

"Your wife's been here. She's out of her mind trying to find you."

Billy looked away.

"And your daughter was in the hospital last night."

"What? What happened?"

"She cut herself."

"Cut herself?"

"I believe she's OK," Matty said, "but she did take some stitches. You should go home and find out, don't you think? I can have someone drive you."

"But you say she's OK?"

Matty felt like smacking him. He gestured to the phone on his desk. "Call your wife, tell her where you're at."

"I will." Looking away, his hands in his lap.

Fuck it, Matty would call her himself later.

"I need to go with you," Billy said.

"Go where?"

"On this." Nodding to his writing.

"Mr. Marcus, we don't do that."

"You *have* to. That description I gave you is a million kids. I'm your eyes."

Matty often wondered what was worse, knowing who killed your son, your wife, your daughter, or not. Having a name and a face to go with your demon, or not.

"You *have* to." Billy nearly lunged out of his seat. "Grant me my . . ." Then, losing track of what he wanted to say, he finally blinked, then seemed unable to stop blinking. "I'm not as drunk as you think. And I'm not as crazy."

"I never said any of that."

"It's a good lead. I know it. I'm *begging* you."

Yolonda walked into the office carrying a café con leche.

"I miss anything?" Then seeing Marcus: "Oh my God," her voice automatically shifting to high and tender. "How are you doing?"

"I overheard a girl talking about the shooting and I followed her to a building."

Yolonda looked to Matty, who shrugged and said, "I was just telling Mr. Marcus here that we'd check it out, but that he can't really come with us."

Yolonda blew on her coffee. "Why not?"

Matty picked up the phone and handed it to Billy. "Call home." Then took Yolonda by the elbow and walked her around to the dining alcove.

"What's wrong with you?" His face inches from hers.

"Oh, big deal, let him go for the ride."

"He hasn't been in contact with his family for days."

"Sounds like you."

"Funny. The guy is out of his mind."

"Of course he's out of his mind. I take one look at him and I see he needs to do something, feel like he's doing something, or he's gonna kill himself."

"Then let him take care of his family. That's doing something."

Yolonda shrugged, sipped her coffee.

Jimmy Iacone, preceded by a swirl of night funk, came toddling out of the bunk room, a towel and a toothbrush in his left hand.

"Do you have any idea how loud you're talking?"

Matty looked out into the big room, Billy hanging up the phone after having talked to his wife, supposedly talked to his wife. He then grabbed a notepad off Mullins's desk and began writing.

Matty walked in a tight circle as Yolonda sipped her coffee. "He does not leave the car."

"So Mr. Marcus." Yolonda twisted around, hooking an elbow over the seatback. "I know this is a loaded question, but how are you holding up?"

"Not . . . I'm trying to, to, you need to use your mind, to, to battle this?"

"That's good," she said, squeezing his wrist. "But you need to be patient. This isn't some ladder you climb, every day better than the next, do you know what I'm saying?"

But Marcus had already tuned out and was lifelessly staring at the world running past his side window. Sitting across from him, Jimmy Iacone was doing pretty much the same, the both of them looking for the moment like bored kids on a long trip. The car was suffused with the smell of alcohol coming through someone's pores, but it could easily have been Jimmy's.

"And your family," Matty said, trying to hold Marcus's eyes in the mirror. "How are they holding up?"

"They understand," Marcus said distantly.

"What," Matty said. "They understand what."

Yolonda touched Matty's arm. The steno pad Marcus had liberated from the office was lying open in his lap, Matty reading what was written there via the rearview:

### HAVE I EVER BEEN A COMFORT TO YOU

"And your daughter?" he kept it up. "How's she doing? How was the hospital?"

"I have, I used to have childhood asthma?" Marcus said to Yolonda. "It's back. Thirty years and it's back."

"That's the stress," Yolonda said.

"No, I know that, I know . . ."

"Trust me, it's the stress. I had this lady once? Her son—" Yolonda cut herself off. "Anyways."

• • •

As they pulled up on the Madison Street side of the Lemlich Houses, Marcus stared at every passing tenant as if he couldn't quite get his eyes to open wide enough.

"Here's the drill." Matty twisted around. "We have your description of the girl, we have the address. Detective Bello and I are going in and trying to find her. Detective Iacone will stay here with you. If we come across anybody who looks likely, we'll walk them past the car. You make your ID to Detective Iacone. Under no circumstances are you to leave this vehicle. Do you understand?"

Still wobble-mouthed with concentration, Billy continued to search every face that came past the car, every set of nickel-plated eyes.

"Do, you, understand."

"Is this a bad projects?" Billy said lightly, his chest laboring.

"Not too," Yolonda said.

"Hey." Matty stared at him.

"I understand."

As Matty transcribed Billy's description into his own notebook, Yolonda turned to the backseat again.

"You know why this isn't too bad a place? The kids are so close to all walks of life around here, you know? Most projects are kind of like, that's all they know, but you go two blocks in any direction from here, you got Wall Street, Chinatown, the Lower East Side, they're like release valves, you know? They give you the confidence to mix it up in the world—"

"And jux everybody in sight," Iacone murmured.

"You're so cynical, I swear to God," Yolonda said. "*I* was a projects kid, *I* didn't jux anybody." Then, to Billy again: "I *hate* that, people say projects kid, projects girl, like everybody's got your number."

"Ready?" Matty said to her.

Once outside, Yolonda circled around to Jimmy Iacone's window, gestured for him to roll it down, and whispered in his ear, "Fuck yourself, you fat homeless guinea prick."

The Clara E. Lemlich Houses were a grubby sprawl of fifty-year-old high-rises sandwiched between two centuries. To the west, the fourteen-story buildings were towered over by One Police Plaza and

Verizon headquarters, massive futuristic structures without any distinguishing features other than their blind climbing endlessness; and to the east, the buildings in turn towered over the Civil War–era brick walk-ups of Madison Street.

As Matty and Yolanda entered the grounds on this dead gray Sunday heading for 22 Oliver, many of the young men hanging out in front of the buildings in their path wandered off flat-faced at their approach, then casually regrouped behind them once they had passed.

"The Nature Channel," Matty muttered.

"What's your problem, today?"

"He's fucking lying."

"Who is?"

"Marcus. He didn't call home."

"So he didn't call home. What are you, his mother?"

Matty walked in silence, trying to work it out. "Last week I promised him we'd make it right, and now it's all going south so fast . . ."

"So you take it out on him?"

"When did you ever hear me make a promise like that. Who with more than two minutes on this fucking job ever makes a promise like that."

"So you take it out on him?"

"You should have seen them in there, Yoli. Like fucking roaches with the lights just turned on."

Yolanda took over the spiel, doing Matty flawlessly: " 'I never *knew* that.' 'You never *told* us that.' 'How could you not give him a paraffin test?' And I just had to eat it. Everybody running under the stove and I just had to eat it."

Three kids in hoodies were sitting on the wood-slat bench before the entrance to 22 Oliver, one black, one white, one Latino, like the advance guard of a UN youth brigade, all fixedly staring at the ground with half-mast eyes.

"Hey, how you guys doing?" Yolanda stepped up, Matty always deferring to her on the street. "You see a girl go in maybe an hour ago, light-skinned Latina, fifteen, sixteen, wearing a pink zip-up, a little on the skinny side."

They kept their heads down and grunted, Matty thinking they were probably OK kids given the overdramatic quality of their stonewall.

"No?" Yolonda smiled. "How about you?" Addressing the black kid, three hundred pounds and a Neolithic thrusting brow. "No one you know?"

"Nuh-uh," he said, without looking up. He held both *Carlito's Way* 3 and *Danger Mouse: Likely to Die* game boxes in his lap.

"That doesn't sound like anybody in the building? Nobody around here?"

All three shook their cowled heads like grieving monks.

"She's not in trouble or anything . . ."

A girl came out of the building looking more or less like the one Yolonda had just described.

"Hey, how you doing?" Yolonda stepped in her path. "Listen, who's that girl here looks kind of like you, lives here, maybe visits friends in here, wears a pink velour zip-up. She's not in trouble or anything."

"Looks like me?" the girl said slowly.

"Yeah, not as pretty maybe . . ."

Yolonda hooked her arm and started walking her towards the car.

"Irma, maybe?" the girl drawled.

"Irma who?"

"I don't know her name."

"Lives in here?"

"I don't know. She might."

"About how old?"

"Eleventh grade? But I don't really know."

"Who does she live with?"

"I don't know her like that."

"What's your name?"

"Crystal."

Yolonda waited.

"Santos."

They were back on Madison Street.

Yolonda looked to the car. Iacone leaned into Billy, then shook his head no.

"You make your family proud of you, Crystal?"

"I don't know."

"Make your family proud, OK?"

"Right now?"

"In general. Every day."

"OK."

When Yolonda returned to the front of 22 Oliver, the three boys were still scowling and squinting as if in pain, each looking off in a different direction, Matty standing before the bench with his hands clasped behind his back.

"Irma," Yolonda said to Matty, then turning to the three, "Which apartment's Irma's?" The kids looking back at her like she was speaking Urdu.

"They all fucking know," Yolonda muttered. "Call the Housing Wheel."

The Housing Police information line had three Irmas on file for 22 Oliver: Rivera, forty-six; Lozado, eleven; and Nieves, fifteen.

"Give me the fifteen," Matty said, getting the apartment number. "Any history on the door?"

According to the Wheel, no outstanding warrants lived in 8G, no one who would answer the bell and suddenly go all fight-or-flight on them.


The elevator smelled like fried chicken and piss, its walls lined in what looked like dented aluminum foil. It was a crowded ride; an African mother and her three children, the woman in her bright, intricate headwrap roughly straightening their jackets and caps as if fed up with something, and an elderly Chinese couple shrink-wrapped around their shopping cart.

On the dimly lit eighth floor there were raised voices or TV tracks behind at least three doors, but when Matty rang the bell for 8G, as he expected, it all fell silent. He looked to Yolonda, then started banging with the side of his fist. Nothing.

"Fucking drag," she muttered, and started to ring all the doorbells, nothing doing.

As they turned for the elevators, though, 8F cracked a sliver.

"Hey, how are you." Yolonda stepped to the eye peeping out, flashed her tin. "I'm Detective Bello?"

The woman opened the door wider, standing there in a housedress and sweater.

"Let me ask, we're trying to reach the Nieves girl, Irma? Next door? You know her, right? She's not in trouble or anything, could I—"

"Anna!" the woman abruptly bellowed, the door to 8G opening slightly, the woman who stood there stooped over in shapeless stretch pants and an oversize T-shirt, squinting at them, no teeth on the left side of her head.

"¿Tú eres la abuela de Irma?" Again, Yolonda flashed tin.

The woman immediately went wide-eyed, clapping her hands over her mouth.

"No, no, no, no es nada malo." Yolonda lightly touched her arm. "Ella no tiene ningún problema, solamente tenemos que hablar con ella. Tenemos que preguntarle algo de su amiga."

The old lady sank into herself, eyelids fluttering with relief.

"¿Está ella en la casa?"

"Entra." Widening her door.

The apartment was greasy and narrow, the linoleum sticking to the bottom of their shoes. In the small front room where she left them to get her granddaughter, piles of clothing were everywhere, on the couches, chairs, in open garbage bags on the floor, and spilling over the lips of stacked plastic storage bins. A few magazine tear-outs of Jesus were pushpinned into the otherwise bare walls.

Two little boys wandered in from a room in the back to stare at them.

"What's she doing?" Matty asked. "She's waking the kid up?"

"I think so," Yolonda said.

"If she's still asleep, it's not her." He shrugged, heading for the door.

"Well, hang on." Yolonda touched his arm. "We're here, so . . ."

Matty stared out the lone living room window, the view probably once upon a time bucolic, broad river and the Brooklyn shore, but barely a slap of lead-colored water was visible now through the weave of high-rises and the stone-and-steel expanse of the Manhattan Bridge.

The grandmother came back in and gestured for them to follow.

Irma Nieves's room was small and cramped, three-quarters of it taken up by a triple stack of queen-size mattresses. The girl was sitting slumped on a corner of the unmade bed in pj bottoms and a baby T, her hands palms up in her lap. She was sloe-eyed, which accentuated her midday sleepiness, and slim-pretty save for crocodilian buckteeth and a narrow strip of dark pimples on one side of her face.

"Hey, Irma, I'm Detective Bello. We're looking for a girl looks a little like you in this building, maybe just visits here, light-skinned Latina, your age, wears a pink velour tracktop. She's not in any trouble, we just need to talk to her."

The two little boys came flying into the room and leaped up onto the bed, Irma clucking in languid annoyance.

"Looks like me?" she finally said, then seemed to drift off.

"It wouldn't be Crystal Santos, would it?"

"Crystal? Crystal don't look like me."

Yolonda shot a look to Matty: What did I tell you?

The grandmother hovered anxious and uncomprehending in the doorway.

Matty took in the rest of the room: a small dresser topped with jars of baby oil, Vaseline, a half-eaten Big Mac, and a paperback of *The Bluest Eye* sporting a Seward Park High School sticker; a mirror trimmed with photos of Latino and black teens hanging in an amusement park; and pristine pairs of sneakers parked wherever space permitted. The view out the lone window was nearly abstract, a sky-blotting crosshatch of those monoliths to the west: 1PP and Verizon.

"Somebody's got to look like you around here," Yolonda said. "Maybe not as pretty."

"Tania?" Irma said. "But I don't know."

"Tania lives here?"

"With me?"

"In this building."

"I think so, but I don't know."

The two boys started wrestling. Irma clucked her tongue again, then looked to her grandmother in the doorway to do something, but the woman seemed afraid to step over the threshold.

"What's Tania's last name again?"

"I don't know."

"Where's this, Rye Playland?" Yolonda pointed to the photos around the mirror.

"Yeah, uh-huh."

"Is she on here?"

"No, I don't know her like that."

"She's a wild kid, good kid . . ."

"Wild?" Then, "I couldn't say."

"So this Tania, who else knows her?"

A third little boy came flying into the room, a kitten under each arm.

"Who else knows Tania, Irma?"

"She hangs with this fat boy Damien sometimes?"

*"Moreno?"*

"Nigger, yeah, uh-huh."

Matty thought of that big kid on the bench.

"What's Damien like?"

"To eat."

"No. As a person."

"Nice, I guess."

"Who else does she run with?"

"This boy, I think his name's True Life?"

"Good kid? Bad kid?"

"I don't know him, but, yeah, he's most definitely from the dark side."

*"Moreno?"*

*"Dominicano.* No. Well, like, half?"

"Half and half?"

"Looks like it, but I don't know."

"Ever locked up?"

"I think so."

"You know his name?"

"True Life."

"No, his name."

"Not really."

"Where's he live?"

"I don't know."

"How old is he?"

"Like, eighteen? Twenty? But I don't know."

"But he's dark side."

"Oh yeah."

"Like, what's his thing?"

Irma shrugged. "I couldn't say."

"He's got a gun?"

"Could."

"How about a running buddy? Somebody he likes to jux heads with out there."

Irma shrugged.

"Can you come down to the precinct, look at some photos?"

"The make-a-face?" She smiled. "OK."

"In about an hour?"

"An hour? I'm supposed to see somebody."

"Who."

"My boyfriend. We're going over to my cousin's in Brooklyn."

"Can you go to Brooklyn later?"

"I don't know."

"I think you can," Matty said. "Come down to us in an hour and get it over with, OK?"

"You hear about that shooting on Eldridge Street last week?" Yolonda asked.

"The white boy got shot?"

"You hear anything about that?"

"Not really."

"We're looking for some bad people, here," Matty said.

"OK."

"You're not in any trouble," Yolonda said.

"OK."

Yolonda turned to the grandmother. "*Ella no tiene ningún problema.*"

"OK," the grandmother said.

"You have a nice family," Yolonda said to the girl. "Your *abuela* takes care of a lot of kids."

"Thank you," Irma said.

"You ever make her worry for you?"

"She's just a nervous-type person," Irma said, then nodded to one of the little boys. "He's the bad one here."


"Girl's got a touch of Gump to her, huh?" Yolonda said as they came out of the elevator.

"Grandma too, maybe," Matty said. "Keeps a nice house, though."

The three kids were still on the bench, and Yolanda went straight for the fat boy, his game boxes propped on his thigh. "Hey."

Caught by surprise, the kid actually looked right at her, his eyes beneath that browridge like something peering out of a cave.

"You're Damien, right?"

His wounded reaction was impossible to mask, the other two instantly dropping their heads to mask their sniggers.

"Naw," he said, his voice surprisingly high. "That's the other one."

"Other one what?"

"Other fat nigger," the Latino bawled, almost in tears.

The big kid exhaled through his nose, forbearing.

"So what's your name?" Yolanda played through.

"Donald."

"Like in Trump?" she said kindly.

"You know where we can find him, Donald?" Matty asked.

"No." The boy winced. "I just know him from . . ." He looked down at himself, his explosive girth.

"Ho." The white kid was struggling so hard not to laugh that his hood was trembling.

"How about a girl Tania, you know her?" Yolanda asked the white kid directly to stop the laughing.

"Tania?" he drawled. "I know *mad* Tanias around here, yo." Slapping palms with the Latino kid.

"How about a guy True Life, you know True Life?"

"True Life? I don't know, like, maybe, I'm not sure."

"How can you be not sure if you know someone named True Life?" Matty asked.

"I know a boy Blue Light," the white kid said.

"True Life," Yolanda repeated.

"I don't know."

"How about you?" she asked the Latino kid.

"Hah?"

"You?" She brought it back around to Donald, still clutching his game boxes.

But he was deaf to the question, unnerved as he was by the sight of Billy Marcus, who had escaped from the car and was now standing there staring at him, his face streaming tears.

Iacone, bringing up the rear, looked to them and shrugged: I tried.

Yolonda glanced at Matty, You win, lose him.

"OK then," she said.

The three boys got up as one, turned, and began to lumber-toddle away with an over-the-shoulder wall-eyed self-consciousness, with Sunday-afternoon boredom.

Iacone mimed pulling a hood over his face, made his voice go high. "They killed Kenny, those bastards."

"I'll meet you back at the house?" Yolonda asked Matty, quick-tilting her chin towards the weeping Billy, Get him out of here.

"What did I ask of you?" Matty said as he headed back uptown, Billy Marcus raw-eyed in the passenger seat.

"I'm not a child," he muttered, staring straight ahead.

Matty started to say something more on the subject, then just dropped it.

They crossed Canal Street into the Lower East Side, the names of long-gone hosiery wholesalers still readable through flaking paint above boarded-up doors.

"Did I help at all?" Billy's breathing was still faintly labored, a wheeze like a distant teakettle seeping from his mouth between words.

"I hope so," Matty said, squelching an impulse to tell him about Eric Cash going south on them, about Let It Die.

"Do you think it's True Life?"

"Honestly? No, I don't."

"True Life," Marcus repeated, then as Matty turned west on Houston towards the West Side Highway, "Where are we going?"

"I'm driving you home."

"Stop." Marcus put out a hand. "I'm not there."

Matty pulled to the curb by a twenty-four-hour kebab house.

"So where are you."

Marcus rested his head on his fist, his eyes pinking up again. "You know . . . I wake up every morning, and, for a second everything's OK . . ."

"Mr. Marcus, where are you staying?"

". . . which makes it worse. Can't you just call me Billy? For Christ's sake."

"Billy, where are you staying?"

"I keep thinking I see him, you know? Not *him*, but like, his walk, say, walking away from me, then last night I smelled him in this bodega on Chrystie, but really faint, like I had just missed him by a second."

"Billy, let me take you home."

"No. Not just . . ." Marcus cut himself off, his eyes filled with agenda. A faint humming was coming from beneath his wheeze, a Master Plan vibration, but Matty was pretty sure it was nothing, a sugar castle spun out of madness.

"This is not good." Matty nodded grimly.

Billy stared out the side window, knees jiggling furiously.

"Look, I'm sorry, it's just, you're adding to your own torture and you're torturing them. I hate to—"

"No, you're right," Billy said, continuing to stare out that window as if looking for someone.

"Your wife is breaking down my door every day, 'Where is he. Where is he.' Your daughter, I can't even imagine—"

"I *said*, you're *right*. You're right. You're right. You're right."

Matty took a moment, then, "Give me your address again?"

"Henry Hudson into Riverdale," Billy said after a long pause. "I'll direct you from there."


Sunday afternoons were the casual Fridays in the squad room, the usual jacket and tie replaced by a precinct-logo T-shirt and jeans underneath the preponderance of all-week military brush cuts.

"Anybody know a guy, True Life?" Yolonda called out, tossing her bag on her desk.

"I know a guy, Half Life," John Mullins said.

"I know a guy, Twenty-five to Life."

"I know a guy, Blue Light."

Yolonda sat down at a digital photo manager and punched in True Life; no one in the system popping up with that tag. She then started cross-feeding factors for Irma Nieves's viewing: race, age, hunting grounds.

· · ·

They were in Riverdale, sitting in the car by the entrance to Billy's building on Henry Hudson Parkway.

"I apologize for my bluntness earlier."

"No problem," Billy said distantly, squinting at the canopy over the building's entrance.

Again Matty debated whether to tell him how leprous this investigation had become; families often fed on even the bad news; deemed precious any scrap of new information, newness its own virtue. He understood that but could never get behind it. Besides, even here, in front of his home, even now after the long day together, Matty still felt like he hadn't quite gotten the guy's attention.

"You hanging around down there shadowing people at newsstands, following them back to their lairs, that's gonna stop now, yes?"

"I didn't even mean to do that," Marcus said, still squinting at his building. "It just happened."

"That's going to stop now, yes?" Matty stared at the side of Marcus's face, the bruised bags under his left eye. "Because I cannot work this in full effect if I have to be worried about you too."

"OK."

"Excuse me?"

"OK. Yes." Then, turning to Matty full-on, "I get it."

Marcus made it halfway to the building, then came back, leaned into the driver's window. "You know, all day you keep saying 'your family, your family.' You should understand something. I love Nina, but she's not mine. When I met Minette, she was already six years old." Then, "Ike is mine."


Irma Nieves sauntered into the squad room two hours later than she said she would, but no later than what Yolonda had expected.

"I'm gonna punch up six faces at a time," Yolonda said after she got the kid seated in front of the screen. "You don't recognize anybody, just say no and we'll move on, OK?"

Irma ripped open a bag of Cheetos. "OK."

Yolonda brought up the first array.

"No," Irma said, blindly bringing the Cheetos from her lap to her mouth. The screen went gray, read PLEASE WAIT.

"You come from a nice family," Yolonda said.

Six new faces popped up.

"No."

"All boys are liars, you know that, right?"

Another PLEASE WAIT, another set of six.

"No."

"You're pretty, but smart is better."

"No."

"You cut out of school a lot?"

"No." Then, "No."

"You're lucky you have a good *abuela*, you better not break her heart."

"No." Two of the faces in this last set were both bloody and over fifty.

"Don't ever let a guy you just met hand you a drink."

"No."

"You use protection?"

"No." Then looking at Yolonda for the first time, "What?"

"Don't wind up a pregnant stereotype, your poor grandmother gets stuck taking care of your kids too."

"Him."

"What?"

"Him." Pointing. "True Life."

Yolonda read the printout: *Shawn Tucker, aka Blue Light.*


"Button those things up, I'm freezing my balls off just looking at you guys," Lugo said to the two young Latinos perched on their own rear bumper as Daley rooted around the rear seats.

"Yeah, it got cold," the driver murmured with resigned civility.

"What a night, right?" Lugo lit a cigarette. "Where you from?" he asked the driver.

"Maspeth?"

"You?" Asking the other kid, who sported an eye patch.

"D.R."

"D.R. Dominican Republic? I was just there last year. Bet you wish you were there now, huh? I know I do. What part?"

"Playa?"

"Oh, fuckin' beautiful, right? We stayed at the Capitán, you know that?"

"My uncle works there."

"Excuse please?" Daley moved them off the rear bumper, then popped the trunk.

"Capitán's the best, right?" Lugo said. "The girls. We had this kind of bodyguard, tour guide for the city? Guy took us everywhere, did our talking for us, showed us the highlights . . . And packed a piece."

"That's smart," the driver said with a little more life, maybe seeing himself driving away from this in a few minutes. "How much?"

"Fifty a day," Lugo said, absently swinging his arms, fist into palm.

"Pesos or dollars?"

"*Dólares*, baby."

"That's a lot down there," the passenger said.

"You only live once, right? What happened to your eye?"

"My cousin poked me with a wire when we was kids."

Lugo flinched. "Took it out?"

"Just blinded it."

"That sucks." Then addressing the driver, "Don't that suck?"

The driver shrugged, smiled shyly at his shoes.

The kid with the eye patch laughed. "He's the one that did it."

"And you still run with him?" Lugo squawked.

"He's my cousin." He shrugged.

"Look at this." Daley brought over a cardboard temporary license plate from the trunk. "Somebody fucked with these numbers here, see?"

They all crowded around to look, Daley holding it out with both hands like a newborn. "See the seven turned to a nine? That makes this a forged instrument."

"A what?" the kid with the eye patch said.

"I just bought this car," the driver said. "That was in the trunk?"

Lugo and Daley stepped off a few feet to confer.

"What do you want to do?"

Lugo looked at his watch: 10:00. "Let's do it."

They returned to the cousins at the rear of the car.

"That was in the trunk?" the driver said again, his eyes drawn down with anxiety. "That ain't even the one on the car, look for yourselves."

"Turn around, please?"

"Oh, c'mon, Officer," the driver said. "I bought the car from a guy yesterday. I never even looked in there. I don't even know what that is."

"Not my call," Lugo said distantly.

"But for what is this?" The driver's voice continuing to climb.

"Damn, you got some wrists on you, brother," Daley said.


Two beds over, the littlest one, Paloma, had woken up, third time tonight, crying some nonsense about the man in her ear, and Tristan had to checker-jump the bed between them and start rubbing her back until she went down again. But this time she was more awake, flipped over, and stared at him, her eyes like X-ray beams in the dark.

"Just go to sleep, man."

But she just kept staring at him with this adult look on her three-year-old face, Tristan repeatedly having to look away as he kept up the massage like the mother had told him to.

"*Mami,*" the kid bawled, although the wail didn't reach her eyes, which creeped him out.

"Just shut up, man."

"*Mami!*" A flat blaring.

"Damn . . ." Tristan hissed.

"*MAMI!*"

The bedroom door finally opened, the kid's mother in a swish of nightdress coming in, clucking her irritation.

"I don't *like* Tristan now."

"Sssh." Moving between them like he wasn't even there.

"I don't *like* Tristan."

"Good, you little bitch," he murmured, "fuck I care."

The mother turned rigid when he said that, then picked her daughter up to bring her back to her own bed, the kid giving him those calm adult eyes over her mother's shoulder.

"I ain't *do* nothing." Tristan's face in the moonlight red as a berry.

Snatching his beat book from under the mattress, he wrote furiously in the dark:

*The will to fill the bill*
*kill or thrill*
*a man stands up a man stands down*
*sits tight when its right*
*My no*
*is a blow*
*to your yes*
*my power*
*by the hour*
*grows like a tower*

"Hey, am I calling too late?" Matty said softly into his cell.

"Who is this?" Minette responded a little shakily.

"Mat— Detective Clark." Fending off a wave of embarrassment as he leaned on the railing of his terrace and took another sip of beer.

"Oh, hi," she said. "Any news?"

"Not . . . I was just calling to see how everything's going."

"Well . . ." she half-sang, such a loaded question.

"Your daughter's all right?"

"She's . . . We're watching a movie."

"Oh yeah?"

Seventeen stories below, two ambulances, one Hatzolah, the other from Cabrini, raced from opposite ends of Grand Street to the same collision, the combination of beer and altitude making them look like electric insects.

"And how's the mister doing?"

"Who?"

Matty hesitated. "Your husband."

There was a long silence on Minette's end, then, "What do you mean?"

"I brought him back this afternoon, remember?"

"What?" Minette's breathing a little more pronounced. "When?"

Matty started pacing the AstroTurf. "This afternoon."

"I was here all day." Her voice starting to climb. "He was *here?*"

He knew he should have hung in a few more minutes before driving off when that asshole entered the building.

"Well, he's in one piece, at least," Matty said as she started to cry. "I can tell you that much."

She continued to weep into his ear, the proximity of her frustration making him dizzy.

"So," he began, then lost track. "Is there anything else I can do for you?"


Twenty minutes after the wife took her hamster out of the bedroom, Tristan felt himself yanked to a sitting position on his bed by his ex-stepfather.

"What you say to my wife?"

"What?" Tristan reflexively grabbing the arms that had grabbed his.

*"What? What? What?"* The guy bughouse with eighty-proof eyes.

"Nestor." Hissing from somewheres in the shadows.

"You disrespect my *wife?*" Spraying him with spittle.

Tristan had grabbed his ex-stepfather to keep from getting hit, and now he noticed that his thumb and fingertips overlapped around the guy's wrists.

The ex-stepfather tried to free one hand to raise up and smack him, and just as an experiment, Tristan wouldn't let him, the guy's eyes protruding now like eggs.

Dizzy-thrilled, terrified, Tristan abruptly bellowed, "I'M POPEYE THE SAI-LOR MANN . . ."

The ex-stepfather tried to free his hand again, Tristan gripping harder, bleating louder, "I LIVE IN A GARR-BAGE CANN."

Then it became just too disorienting, how easy it was to hold the guy, and so he let go, knowing what would happen if he did.

A second later he was flat on his mattress again, the taste of copper trickling down the back of his throat.

The blows kept coming, each one singing behind his eyes, Tristan drifting off underneath, the sensation of his thumb and fingertips overlapping around the guy's wrists like that coming back and back to him.

Finally the wife said "Nestor" again and the hitting stopped, his ex-stepfather leaning over him now as if to kiss him goodnight. "You are a destroyer, but you will *not* destroy my home." Then rose up and stormed out of the room, his equally bug-eyed mopstick skeeve of a wife bringing up the rear.

In the dark, in the quiet, Tristan grinned through blood-rimmed teeth.

With the upstairs anticrime squad room working on three other collars at the present, the Dominican kid with the cardboard license plate found himself sitting handcuffed between Lugo and Daley in the minuscule juvenile interview room on the ground floor of the precinct.

"First, say goodbye to that car."

"What?" The kid reared back. "No. Why you got to take my car?"

"Auto Crime's gonna take it to pieces," Daley said.

"Oh, don't tell me that."

"Money in the bank they check the VIN, it's been switched with some long-gone junker. But in the eyes of the law? They're not gonna differentiate between you and the car-ring assholes you bought it from."

"Don't tell me that."

"Possession is nine-tenths of the jackpot."

"Criminalistically speaking? That forged plate automatically makes this a RICO charge. Twenty years mandatory."

"As in years."

"Do not *tell* me that." The kid whipping his head so fast his hair was a blur.

"That baby due in five months?" Lugo yawned.

"Gonna be calling some other guy Daddy," Daley finished.

"You'll be Uncle Plexiglas."

The room settled into a bruised silence.

"Thoughts?" Daley finally said. "Comments? Suggestions?"

"I don't understand why you got to take my car."

"Bro . . . Did you hear anything of what we just said?"

"Yeah, but why you got to take my car?"

Daley and Lugo stared at each other.

"Least of your problems, bro."

"If I lose that car, man, I swear to God . . ."

Lugo widened his eyes and delicately placed his fingertips to his temples. "Let me ask," he said softly. "When you were a kid and the teacher saw you walking into the classroom in the morning, did she used to go all white and start shaking?"

"What?"

"Look, between us?" Daley leaned in close. "We don't give a shit about that bogus plate. We're in here staying late with you because you seem like a decent guy and frankly, you're getting fucked."

"But like we told you, bro, all we can do is hope you get us a gun." Lugo sounding glum. "Otherwise we're powerless."

"And it's got to be in the next hour because that's all the time we're allowed to stay, so . . ."

"Hey, yo, I would help you if I could."

"No, you got it backwards, bro." Daley leaned back, clasped his hands over his belly. "We're the ones trying to help you."

"I don't *know* a gun."

"You don't have to know." Daley rushing back in on him. "A guy knows a guy knows a guy."

"You're not a bad person." Lugo completing the bookend. "We know that."

"That's why we're talking to you."

"The other times you got popped, did any of the other officers converse with you like this? Did they invest in conversation like this?"

"No."

"Listen." Daley touched his arm, looked into his eyes. "Me and him, we've done this forty times at least. Guy says, 'I don't know a gun,' we wind up with a piece."

"And they weren't bullshitting us," Lugo said.

"Well, some were."

"Granted, but most times? It's six degrees of separation. A guy calls a guy calls a guy and we're off to the races. The last guy sitting right where you are now? In deeper shit than you, frankly, came through for us? Walked out of here come sunup, rubbing his wrists, wondering where to get breakfast. It happens, bro. But in your case? Due to the exigencies of the service, it's got to be right now."

"I don't, know, a gun."

"We never said you did. Are you listening to us?"

Apparently not; the kid muttering to himself, staring at his lap.

Lugo and Daley looked at each other, then shrugging, shifted gears. "How 'bout cuz in there?"

"Benny? He's my best friend."

"We have best friends go south on each other all the time in here. But that's not even what we're asking."

"Benny don't know no guns."

"No? You don't think he can reach out to someone?"

"Naw, man, Benny's a busboy like six years at Berkmann's. He don't . . . He taught *me* about work."

"You sure about that?"

"Yeah."

"Then I hate to say this, bro, but you are done for."

The kid shook his head in sorrow, then looked to Lugo. "But why do you got to take my car?"


After loitering at the shrine for an hour, hoping to at least catch Billy if no one else, Matty had himself buzzed in at the No Name, thrashing his way through the double layer of thick, sound-muffling theater curtains that immediately confronted him once past the scarred industrial street door.

Despite the hour, the narrow room was full, both bartenders, the young lacquer-haired owner and the long Italianate author of his two most sexually depressing encounters of the year, working those silver shakers like maracas.

The new hostess, having never seen him before, began to ask him if he had a reservation, then thought better of it, gracefully gesturing towards the one free seat at the bar; not because she knew that he was a former employee but because she read him correctly and no bar or restaurant down here ever turned away a police.

Matty sat watching his morose off-again, off-again lover from inches away, her lean, dark, unsmiling face underlit by the low-watt bulbs installed discreetly beneath the four cocktail-specific ice containers: shaved, cubed, slabbed, and fjorded.

"How are you doing?" Speaking as quietly as he could without whispering.

"Good," she said briskly, eyes on her work, pouring equal amounts of liquefied ginger and fresh-squeezed apple juice over a double shot of potato vodka and a crag of ice.

"That looks good," he said.

"Sazerac and a sidecar?" the sole waiter requested as if paging someone in a plush hotel lobby.

Matty sat there in the sepia-toned room staring into the luminous tubs of ice.

The thing about Minette was that she was no kid, that she was—how else to put it—a woman, a strapping woman with presence; clear-eyed, mature, with a red-brown saddle of freckles across the bridge of her nose; Matty thinking, Does it still just come down to that? Eyes and vibes and freckles across a stongly defined nose? Yes and no, yes and no, but, yeah, yes, of course, until the deathbed; it's the visual triggers that kick off the daydreaming.

"You know what?" He leaned in towards his bartender, unconsciously speaking in the delicate tone the room seemed to demand. "It *is* personal. It *does* have something to do with me."

She neither looked his way nor stopped her furious industry; Matty thinking, Mixologist, gathering himself to leave when, still unsmiling and without any eye contact, she slid one of those apple-vodka-ginger things in front of him, Matty quietly grateful to her for this last-minute save of his dignity and wishing like anything he could remember her name.

# FIVE

# WANT CARDS

**The call from Kenny Chan,** a Robbery sergeant in the Ninth, came to Matty as he was handing a blowup of Billy Marcus's driver's license photo to the daytime bartender at Kid Dropper's.

"Mr. Matty, we picked up one of your guys this morning off the Want Cards, Shawn Tucker?"

"Who?"

"Tucker, goes by the tag Blue Light? Got ratted out by his partner on a robbery."

"*My* Want Card?" Not remembering. "Who's the partner?"

"Which robbery? We ran some lineups, got three hits on Tucker so far, but the vics are all describing a different second guy. Apparently ol' Blue Light's democracy in action, just grabs whoever's around, takes whatever's handy, gat, knife, stick, tomahawk, says, 'Let's snatch a head,' and off they go. We have seven more vics on their way in, it's like we're having a clearance sale with this douche. You want to wait until we're done or you want to talk to him now?"

"Wait. Let him rack up all the hits first."

"Actually one of the vics is from your neck of the woods."

"Yeah?"

"Old Chinese guy, Ming Lee?"

"Who?"

"Hang on." Muffling the phone to talk to someone, then, "Sorry. Ming Lam," then, "Fenton Ma says to say hello."

Matty had no idea who this Blue Light was, but with at least one of the comparable victims off the All Sheets having made a positive ID, Matty was desperate now to have Eric Cash eyeball this guy—a lineup, a photo array, a drive-by, anything—and so he finally called Danny the Red to make a behind-the-DA's-back plea for cooperation. He got a recorded greeting, first in Spanish, then English.

"Danny. Matty Clark. Call me. Please." Assuming that he wouldn't.

Hoping for a second Blue Light hit, he called the Israeli flamingo, Avner Polaner. Another machine: "If you are calling for information on the Stop Berkmann's Coalition, please go to the Sana'a Deli at 31 Rivington Street and ask for Nazir or Tariq. If you are calling to speak to me personally, Avner Polaner, I will be in Tel Aviv until the end of the month."

Nothing. Matty thought for a moment, then remembered Harry Steele; time to call in his marker.

"I need your help with somebody."

"Who's somebody."

"Eric Cash. He needs to get over himself. I assume you know what I'm talking about."

"Do you remember where I live?"

"The synagogue?"

"Come by in an hour. No. Hour and a half. That would be brilliant."

"What do you mean 'brilliant'?"

"It's just an expression."


"Who the fuck is Blue Light?" Matty asked Yolonda as they took the elevator, reeking of cleaning solvent, to the Robbery Squad on the third floor of the Ninth Precinct.

"Blue Light's True Life," she said. "Albertina Einstein got his name wrong. I put out the Want Card last night."

In the hallway outside the squad room, Ming Lam sat doubled over on a bench, his face freeze-dried with agitation. Fenton Ma, one arm draped possessively across the backrest, sat at his side, looking fiercely proud of himself.

When Lam saw Matty and Yolonda walking towards him, he nearly growled.

"This guy, Tucker, they're throwing away the key on him, right?" Ma said loudly.

"Absolutely," Yolonda said at the same volume, Ma repeating her one-word answer to the old guy, first in English, then more elaborately in Mandarin, provoking another half-utterance, equal parts fear and anger.

"You did good," Matty said quietly to Ma.


They spotted Shawn "Blue Light" Tucker the moment they entered the squad room; a rangy, light-skinned black kid barely out of his teens, sulking like The Thinker in one of the two small cells.

Kenny Chan came out of his office with an armful of incident reports. "Since we talked? Got four more hits on this guy, including two burglaries, which brings us to seven."

"Used a gun?" Matty asked.

"On the old Chinese guy out there and on the original one we picked him up for."

"What caliber?"

"His partner, the one who gave him up? He didn't even know Tucker was carrying until he whipped it out, and Tucker's mad at us, so he won't say."

"Who's the partner?"

"This kid from the Walds, Evan Ruiz?"

Matty and Yolonda looked at each other: black and tan.

"Hang on," Yolonda said, then wandered across the room, Tucker following her with his eyes. On her return trip she smiled briefly at him, the kid turning away.

"Sorry," she said. "Go ahead."

"But Ruiz says he was only in on the one we got him for. Like I told you on the horn, when it comes to teaming up, Tucker's a real impulse shopper."

"Projects kid?" Yolonda asked.

"Yeah, from Cahan, but apparently from an OK family. Father's a motorman, mom's a teller for Chase. He's like the black sheep or something."

"Got beautiful hair," Yolonda murmured.

"Well, I'll tell you, right now he's not talking to anybody."

"No?" Yolonda said, then turned to Matty. "Don't you think he's got beautiful hair?"


When Matty left, Yolonda remained in the Ninth Precinct squad room, commandeering a vacant desk to check her mail and do busywork on the computer. Periodically she would get up and cross the room to the coffee station, and each time she did, Tucker would saunter up to the bars to track her, but look away whenever she returned the eye contact or threw him a smile.

After an hour of this, she finally stepped directly to the cell and gestured for him to come to the bars.

"What's your story," she half-whispered. "Everybody around here says you come from a nice family. What happened, they treated you bad? You were the light-skinned one or something?"

Tucker smirked in dismissal.

"You got that nice café con leche skin," she said. "That's what we called it."

"Who's we."

"My family. I bet that was it. Your father's darker than you, right? Your brothers and sisters? Am I right?"

He clucked his tongue and returned to the bench, Yolonda lingering a beat, then walking away too.

A few minutes later she left the squad room, went to Katz's, and returned with a murderous six-inch-high triple-decker pastrami on rye held together by two extralong, cellophane-bowed toothpicks.

Unwrapping it at the desk, she announced, "What the hell was I thinking?" Split it into two, wrapped half in a paper towel, walked back to the cell, and passed it to him through the bars.

"You're a nice-looking kid, but you're too skinny."

"Whatever." But taking it before giving her his back.

"How'd you get the tag Blue Light?"

Tucker shrugged, muttered through a mouthful of deli, "How'd you get the tag Detective?"

Yolonda started to answer, it was an interesting story, then thought better of it.

"Ever go by True Life?"

"It gets misheard," he said.

"OK."

Back at the desk, she wolfed down her half of the sandwich, then stepped into Kenny Chan's office.

"Do me a favor? However it goes with the other lineups today, don't let them transport this Tucker kid. Just hold him here for me, OK? I'll be back tonight." Again she returned to the desk, ordered a few movies from Netflix for her kids in Riverdale, fired the dog trainer her husband had insisted on hiring the week before, then left without giving Tucker another look.


Harry Steele lived in a desanctified synagogue on Suffolk Street, which had itself been converted from a standard tenement ninety-five years earlier. And now it was a private palazzo, the huge stained-glass oval above the door, overlaid with a wooden Star of David, the only outward sign of its nearly century-long stint as a house of worship.

A young East Indian woman sporting a bull ring through her nose, one of those confusingly hip domestics Matty always seemed to be running into down here, met him at the door and after a moment's hesitation led him inside and up a flight of stairs to the wraparound gallery that overlooked the main floor.

The building was three stories tall, the two upper levels of apartments removed by the congregation to make one high, hollow hall, as narrow as it was long, with only that interior balcony at the top of the landing for the women to view the services.

Down below, rough paintings of the Hebrew zodiac ran six to a side along the ocher-plastered walls, and a built-in Torah ark held Harry Steele's collection of eighteenth- and nineteenth-century cookbooks interspersed with ancient pottery and cookware from Asia and the Middle East.

Matty had heard about the place from an Eighth Squad detective who had responded to an attempted break-in; had read about it too; but even if he hadn't, he could still feel the holy-of-holies aura that lingered here, no matter that the long-dead immigrant worshippers had today been replaced by a group of Berkmann managers, hosts, and bartenders bathed in the same rainbow wash of color from the great oval window as they sat around the freestanding granite cooking island that had replaced the cantor's platform as the center of the house.

Steele hadn't said anything about a meeting and certainly hadn't told him that Eric Cash himself would be there. Matty watched the poor bastard go ashen when he caught sight of his former interrogator leaning over the now childproofed and reinforced women's rail twenty feet above his head.

This was fucked. Legally he couldn't talk to Cash in any event, but even if he could, somebody fresh should be the go-to, not him.

Matty stepped back into the shadows.

"If anybody has forgotten that we live in a complicated city," Steele addressed the troops, "the tragic incident of a few days ago . . ." Everyone around the island reflexively looked to Cash, who started twisting his shoulders as if stabbed. Steele shifted gears.

"Look, let's be realistic. What happened wasn't a crime wave, wasn't a rash, wasn't an outbreak, but it did happen, and one of the stations of the cross on the way to disaster was our bar, which brings us to the subject of protecting our customers and protecting ourselves, so everybody . . ." Steele searched the faces. "You need to develop a sixth sense about trouble. You see a customer's not right? You go to the door and get Clarence." Gesturing to Matty's solemn-faced protégé, sitting alone at the far end of the island, his arms crossed in front of his absurd chest.

Matty could sense that Cash was desperately trying not to look up at him, the guy staring straight ahead and rocking in his seat as if channeling one of the long-dead Torah readers.

"A customer's slurring, sleeping, muttering, bothering other drinkers?" Steele said. "Get Clarence. He doesn't need to be at the door all the time. He's going to start coming in once an hour, ask how it's going. I mean, it's a delicate situation, we can't just have him hanging there eyeballing a customer, we'll work something out, but in general, for now, if it seems even vaguely like we have someone on our hands who won't be able to negotiate the street? Do not wait."

Steele paused as another domestic brought out a platter of what looked from above like assorted mini-tortillas, the managers waiting for the boss to grab one before reaching in themselves.

"The red zone for all this, of course"—Steele swallowed—"is last call. You have someone at last call, a woman especially, can't stand up, is trashed, is a temptation, is trouble waiting to happen, you get Clarence to help and pour her in a cab. You and Clarence pour her in a cab together so that you have each other to back your story. And make sure she has enough money. Take the cab's number. Make sure the driver *knows* you took the cab's number. Get her home safe."

"What if they won't go?"

"Use your judgment. They can't fend for themselves? You call the cops. Otherwise we're responsible. Pretend they're family. Treat them like family."

"An asshole relation is still a relation," one of the managers volunteered.

"Also," Eric Cash said hoarsely, "remind your bartenders that they have the power to cut people off. And they should use it."

The managers stared at him as if waiting for more, but Cash finally looked up, locked eyes with Matty, and lost his thread.

"Absolutely," Steele said, stepping into the breach. "And don't worry about hurting someone's feelings. If they're so far gone that you're even thinking about it, they're not going to remember the next day anyhow."

Eric's face, still lifted to Matty's, bore the same eerily yielding expression as it had that day in the interview room when he had called him a gutless self-pitying failure and, let's face it, a murderer.

Again Matty took himself out of sight, stepping back from the railing and absently wandering among the divans, leather easy chairs, and bookshelves that lined the back wall. Much like the cookbook ark below, the aged Mylar-wrapped hardbacks up here mingled with artifacts: a handwritten Eighth Precinct incident book from 1898, a leather medical case holding instruments used to examine immigrants for trachoma and other rejectable eye diseases at Ellis Island, an eighteenth-century Dutch clay pipe unearthed in Steele's backyard privy mounted alongside the twentieth-century glass crackpipe found lying in the grass next to it, a still-loaded revolver that once belonged to Dopey Benny Fein.

But for all this reborn carriage house's ingenuity, its artful attempt at appeasing its own history while declaring itself the newest of the new, it was the double layer of evicted ghosts—pauperish tenants, greenhorn parishioners—that still held sway for him, Matty having always been afflicted with Cop's Eyes; the compulsion to imagine the overlay of the dead wherever he went.

Soft-stepping around the horn of the gallery to the front of the building, Matty peered though the lower triangle of the Star of David out to the People's Park on the corner with Stanton, a fenced-in quarter acre of crackpot sculpture, plastic-bucket pyramids, and a flag of no nation but the one inside the head, a heavily tattooed biker down there doing jailhouse dips on some monkey bars, Matty laughing, then suddenly there was a breathy grunt in his ear, guttural but human, snatching at his heart, then gone, this fucking place haunted, he'd swear it.

Then another abrupt sound had him wheeling thick-tongued from the stained glass to see a young woman seemingly emerging right out of the wall across the gap of the gallery.

"Fuck," he hissed, a few of the managers glancing up to see what was happening.

But the woman was real, Matty noticing now the outlines of the door she had come through.

"Hey," he whispered.

"Hey." Walking over to join him at the window. "Are you the new security guy?"

"Something like that," the question an instant chasm, not that he'd mind at least a part-time gig like that. "Matty Clark," extending his hand.

"Kelley Steele."

At the sound of her voice Harry Steele briefly looked up, smiling, and gave a short wave.

"What's behind there?" Matty gestured to the hidden door.

"The other house."

"What other house."

"We used to have all our bedrooms in the basement here? The rabbi used to live down there with his family, but it was too damp, so we bought the house next door to sleep in."

She was great-looking, tall and gray-eyed, twenty-one, tops, Matty thinking, These guys . . .

"So what did you do with the basement?" Asking just to keep her here.

"It's a gym," leaning on the rail next to him.

"I like the zodiacs," he said, once again just to say something.

"Well, take a snapshot, because their days are numbered."

"You're painting them over?" trying to sound like he cared. "That's a shame."

"You think? They're a little creepy for me. It's like, for Jews, it's forbidden to paint faces, right? So the archer, what's it, Sagittarius?" She pointed. "Check it out, just a bow and an arm, a weapon and a body part. Same thing with Virgo, see? A woman's hand and a sheaf of wheat. And Taurus over there is a cow, because bulls are supposed to be pagan."

"No kidding."

Down below, Cash, after jerking a glance up to the empty side of the gallery, stood in a half-crouch to pass the empty platter to one of the domestics.

"You see that guy?" Kelley flicked a finger. "Eric?"

"Yeah."

"That's the guy was at that murder. You wouldn't believe what the cops put him through."

"Yeah?"

"What a bunch of assholes."

"I heard he's not cooperating now."

"The hell, would you?"

It was a stupid game, Matty dropping it with a shrug.

"You know what's my favorite?" she asked.

"Favorite what."

"Cancer."

"What?"

"That one." She pointed to a panel featuring what looked to him like a South African rock-tailed lobster.

"Cancer the crab, right? But the artist was kosher, he didn't even know what a crab looked like. Then some other kosher Jew shows him a lobster in a restaurant window, says, 'There's one,' and so there you go."

"Wow."

"Harry loves that one. He'll probably keep it, start a new restaurant around it."

Below, the meeting was finally winding down, dwindling into small talk and anecdotes, people leaning back, faces softening, ready to laugh at something. One of the managers, a wiry woman wearing a heavily starched and oversize man's white dress shirt, began telling a story about being trapped in the locker area while, in the next room, the Chinese chef and the Dominican prep man were having a grossly graphic conversation about fucking their wives. She described how she kept banging things and clearing her throat so they'd clam up and she could walk past the kitchen without anybody getting embarrassed, but how they just wouldn't take the hint.

"I was stuck for like half an hour."

"So what were they saying?" Steele asked.

"I'd rather not say."

"Aw, c'mon, don't do that to us," Cash said too loudly and with a strangely atonal jocularity, as if he were reading his line off a page.


As the meeting broke up, Matty waited until Cash left the house before coming downstairs.

"So." Steele offered him a seat at the island.

Between them hung three chandeliers constructed of full red Campari bottles arranged in rings around halogen bulbs, the support wires disappearing into the nebulous upper reaches of the building.

"Why didn't you tell me Cash was going to be here?"

"If I told him, I don't think he'd've showed up."

"No. Why didn't you tell me?"

"If I told you, I'd have to tell him."

Matty hesitated, Steele having a little too much fun right now.

"Well, look, in any event, I can't just step to the guy like that," he said. "Did you talk to him at all?"

"About what happened? Yeah." Steele half-laughed. "You guys really did a number, you know?"

"I know. That's why I was hoping you were going to help me bury the hatchet."

"Well, look, I thought, if you were here, he was here, it's someone's home . . . What else can I do?"

"Fact of the matter is," Matty said, "legally, I can't even approach the guy anymore. That's why I asked you."

"Can't approach . . . Because of the lawyer?" Steele said, then, sounding as if he were speaking more to himself, "I had no idea."

Matty studied him for a moment. "You're not . . . Aw shit. Are you the one set him up with that guy?"

Steele looked off. "That's not an appropriate question for you to ask."

Matty leaned back, took in the zodiac panels, the images both maidenly and warlike, the cookbook Torah nook.

"You're paying for him too, aren't you." Grinning as he said it.

Steele stared at him with his sad-sack eyes.

"I'll tell you who else is having a good time with this," Matty said. "That lawyer? I know that Kingston Trio–playing son of a bitch and he is having a ball. On your dime too. And I'm not going to stop pressing, so you better believe that meter will be running."

Steele shrugged helplessly.

And right now he was still the only conduit to Cash, so . . .

"They run that underage op on you last night?"

"Yeah." Steele yawned. "But not until after midnight. I was at the goddamned door for hours."

"Better that than the other, though, yeah?"

"True."

"Well, I'd really like to be able to give you a heads-up next time too, you know?"

"That would be brilliant."

"Wouldn't it. So talk to the guy. Please. And lose that fucking lawyer."

"It's his lawyer."

"It's your money."

Kelley Steele appeared again, this time from somewheres behind the ark, leaned into Steele's shoulder, and took a sip of his cold coffee before leaving the house.

"I don't know how you guys do it," Matty said, trying to make nice.

"Do what?"

"The last time I was with a twenty-one-year-old? I was twenty-two."

Steele jerked back a little, winced. "That's my daughter."

"Really." Matty colored. "I guess I'm not much of a detective, huh?"

But feeling a little better for it too.

Walking back to work from Harry Steele's house after the meeting, Eric stepped in front of a parked and unoccupied van at the corner of Rivington and Essex and, thinking it was still moving, jerked in terror.

The unexpected appearance of Matty Clark had paralyzed him and was, even now, throwing his perception of the physical world into chaos.

That fucking cop; whatever other reasons Eric had for not coming forward, and they switched up on him almost hourly, the one sure thing he had learned today was this: that he would rather slash his own throat than go behind a closed door with either him or his partner ever again. It would be quicker.

At seven that evening, Yolonda came back into the squad room of the Ninth bearing two grocery bags. Three other prisoners were in the cell with the kid now, and when she finished cooking in the kitchen nook, she had fried-egg sandwiches for all of them, neither singling him out nor even making eye contact.

After a half hour of feeling him staring at her back, she returned to the bars, Tucker stepping to her without prompting.

"You hanging in?" she asked in a conspiratorial murmur, her long brown fingers curled around the bars.

He shrugged.

"You still hungry? I have two eggs left."

Another shrug, but he remained at the bars.

"Well, sing out if you are." Yolonda sad-smiled, then returned to her desk.

"You were right," he said a few minutes later.

Yolonda turned in her chair, asked him from across the room, "About what?"

"They don't like me too much."

"Who's they?" Strolling back to the bars.

"My parents. My brothers, they look just like my father."

"Dark, right?"

He stared at her. "My mother was dark too."

"Oh yeah?"

Signaling to one of the desks, she had Tucker transferred from the cell to an interview room, the squad detective cuffing him to the restraint bar on the wall. "It's regulations," Yolonda said apologetically, then waited for the other cop to leave them alone.

"Shawn, how old are you?" Sliding as close to him as she could without sitting in his lap.

"Nineteen."

"Nineteen, and you got picked out for seven robberies." Leaning back as if overwhelmed, palms open to him in despair.

"Seven's what they got me for," he murmured, both braggy and bummed.

"And for what."

"I don't know . . . stupid shit. You're hungry, got no cash, call for takeout, pound on the delivery guy, take the food, take whatever's in his pocket." He shrugged. "Most times I can't even remember what I did, I was so high."

"I wish I'd've been your big sister." Yolonda made a fist. "I'd've read you like a comic book before you ever left the house. What the hell is wrong with you?"

He gave her another shrug, his eyes roaming the water-stained ceiling tiles.

"You know you're going to jail, right?"

"I'm in jail."

"No. *Jail* jail. You know what I'm talking about."

"You come visit me?" he asked without looking at her.

"I want you to promise me something." Putting a hand on his arm. "You're so young. Don't waste your time in there. Learn something, a trade, a skill."

"Yeah, I was thinking about being a locksmith."

"You're kidding me, right?"

He stared at her.

"You just got ID'd for two burglaries."

"So? That was then."

"No. Something like electrician, sheetrocking, plumbing. This whole area's blowing up. Your own neighborhood. Construction, rehabbing, demolition. You can't even sleep anymore down here. So you master a building trade in there? A year or two from now, when you come out, unless we got hit with a dirty bomb or something, you can walk to work."

"Yeah, OK."

Yolonda gave it a moment, the silence belonging to them alone, then put her hand back on his forearm. "Let me ask you something . . . You say seven is what we got you for. Any of the others on Eldridge Street?"

Tucker took a long moment, breathed deep. "Yeah. One. A white guy."

Yolonda nodded, gave them another bonding silence, then quietly asked, "What happened?"

"I think I shot him."

"You think?" Her hand still on his arm, the kid looking at the ceiling tiles again.

"I was high. I might of, I don't know."

"When was this."

"October eighth?"

Yolonda briefly closed her eyes in mild disappointment; nobody ever gave calendar dates; at best you'd be lucky to get the day of the week.

"About what time?" Her voice losing its juice.

"Four a.m.?"

"Exactly where on Eldridge." Barely interested enough now to even ask.

"Right in front of Twenty-seven."

"I thought you said you were high."

"I was."

"You remember the exact date, the time down to the minute, the building number, but you can't recall if you shot him or not? That some funny high."

"I did."

"Did what."

"Shot him. Shoot him. I didn't want to, but . . ."

"You did this by yourself?"

"Had my podner."

"Who's your podner."

"I'm telling you?" Snorting.

"But you were the shooter."

"Uh-huh."

"What kind of gun."

"What kind?"

"What kind." Then, "Forty-five, right?"

"Yeah."

"You're insulting me now. Did I do something to you to deserve that?"

"What are you talking about."

"Shawn, why are you lying to me about this?"

"Lying . . ." Jerking back.

"You're putting yourself in for a murder you didn't do." She had to duck and twist to get into his eyes. "Look at me."

"I might have." Looking away.

"Why?"

"Why what?"

"You're breaking my heart now." Yolonda making her eyes glisten. "You're killing me."

"I don't know." Pondering his knuckles. "I figured it would be good for you."

"For me?"

"You know, for your career."

She leaned in close enough to bite him. "My *career*?" Sometimes Yolonda was so good at her job that she made herself sick. "How'd you even know to bring this up?"

Tucker shrugged yet again, massaged the back of his neck with his free hand.

Not until she brought him back to the holding cell did she see the information-wanted poster for the Marcus homicide that was taped up on the wall in there, that was probably taped up on all the walls of all the prison cells, bull pens, intake centers, and parole offices in lower Manhattan by now, and that had been staring back at him all day long.

・ ・ ・

Alvin Anderson's parole officer had told John Mullins earlier in the day that Anderson tended to play fast and loose with his curfew, so when he finally walked into his mother's apartment in the Lemlich Houses at nine-fifteen in the evening, violating himself by fifteen minutes, Matty, Yolonda, and Mullins were there waiting. They sat in the living room on chairs dragged over from the dining nook and arranged in a loose horseshoe like a makeshift tribunal. His mother, who had unhappily let them in a few minutes before nine, was seated by herself on the plastic-covered couch.

"Hey." Alvin, shave-headed and round, stood there in the doorway, frantically trying to suss out the nature of his trouble. "What's up?"

"You tell us," Mullins said, leaning forward and flourishing his curled wrist to frown at the time.

He had arrested Anderson a little over a year ago.

"Hey. I been trying to make it home for the last hour. There's like some kind of transit strike goin' on."

His mother palmed her mouth and slowly shook her head in surrender.

Matty had come upon Alvin Anderson while poring over the District Arrest Books for the last two years; the situation that locked him up: three men, two guns, one tourist; Alvin quickly giving up the others in exchange for a lighter-than-light sentence; a soft target, according to Mullins.

"So what's happening," Matty asked from one of the other easy chairs.

"Nothing." Alvin continued to stand as if contemplating a dash out the door. "You here to violate me?"

"Rather not, but . . ."

"But . . ."

"Working?" Mullins asked.

"Looking."

"Where you looking?"

"Everywhere," Alvin said with an exhausted air. "Ask my mother, ask my PO. I was over at the Old Navy the other day? It's all good, going good, then they see I was at Cape Vincent, so . . ."

"Transit Authority's hiring porters right now," Yolonda said. "Your record doesn't weigh against you there."

"Yeah?" Alvin tried to sound helped. "OK, OK."

"How's your girl?" Mullins asked.

"Which one?" Straining to come off relaxed and devilish.

"You're so bad," Yolonda said.

"Gonna be a father again," he said to Mullins.

"Oh yeah?" Mullins offering what for him passed as a smile.

Alvin's mother looked off again, sighed, then got up and left the room, everyone watching her go.

"Have a seat," Matty said.

Alvin lowered himself into a chair at the dining table as if into a hot bath. "So, what ch'all here for?"

"What do you think?" Matty said.

"'Cause I'm fifteen minutes violated?" Screwing up his face. "Three officers?"

They sat there staring at him, waiting.

"Yo." He sat up. "If it's that thing went down last week? I don't care what you heard, man, I wasn't there. I ain't doing that no more. You can ask my mother where I was that night."

"We're talking about the same thing here then, right?" Matty said.

"Yeah. The Chinese wedding store, right?"

"So if not you," Yolonda said, "then who?"

"Some Messican dude."

"Who." Mullins's turn.

"Some guy."

"What guy."

"Messican guy. That's like the sum total of what I heard and no more, God's my witness." Then, gesturing to Big John, "You can ask Detective Mullins how I do."

"Well, who told you about it?" Mullins asked.

Alvin hesitated, then, "Reddy."

"Reddy Wilson?" Matty asked. "Reddy's out?"

"Like, last week."

If Matty had known Reddy Wilson was out, he'd have been an automatic Want Card. That was something, at least.

"Other than that"—Alvin looked from one detective to another—"I'm not too sure exactly how I can serve you officers."

"No?" Mullins gave him the stare.

"Hey, just say."

Yolonda moved her chair back to the dining nook and put her hand atop Alvin's as if to hold him to the table. "You know that homicide last week?"

"The white boy?"

Again, the pregnant silence, Alvin looking from one face to another. "Oh." Snorting, "Y'all can't be serious."

They continued to stare to keep him talking, although no one really thought he was involved.

"C'mon now." Alvin laughed nervously.

"Anything in the pipeline?" Matty asked.

"I ain't heard nothing except 'Damn, you hear about that?' " Alvin's face bathed in relief.

"Just so you know," Yolonda said, "there's a twenty-two-thousand-dollar reward up."

"Twenty-two?" Then, "Y'all got the extra ten thousand from the White Victims' Fund?"

"It's called the Mayor's Fund," Matty said, trying not to smile.

"Yeah, OK."

"The point is," Mullins said, "a guy like you could be in a good position to hear something, make a little kale for himself."

"OK," Anderson said. "It's in confidence, right?"

"Always."

"OK, then." Slapping his knees and half-rising, as if it were up to him when they left. "I'll keep an ear out."

"Good," Yolonda said, standing up. "And don't forget what I said about the Transit Authority."

"The Transit Authority?" Alvin blinked.


Outside the apartment they rang for the elevator and waited in silence.

"What Chinese wedding store?" Matty finally asked.

"I have no idea," said Mullins, impatiently pounding the call button, then putting his ear to the door to hear if the car was at least in motion. "Probably something in the Fifth."

When the elevator finally came, it was full of cops heading to a higher floor.

"Hey," Matty said, "what did we miss?"

Hitching a ride to the call, a domestic on fourteen, they barely had room to exit into the hallway, dozens of police already crowded into the narrow space between the apartment and elevator doors.

It was a typically slow night in the area, so anyone who could pick up the transmission had responded just for something to do: uniforms from the Eighth, from Housing, supervisors for both, Quality of Life and other anticrime units, and now Matty and two other detectives; the scrawny, goggle-eyed woman at the apartment door scared by the sheer numbers, saying over and over, "It's OK now. It's nothing."

"What's going on?" Matty asked Lugo.

"The fuck knows, some kind of family smackdown," he said, gesturing for his crew to head out. "Might as well do our vertical." Leading them through the mob to the fourteenth-floor stairwell.

Matty was ready to go too, but Yolonda, as was her wont, had already began burrowing her way through the bored mill of cops into the apartment.

"What's up, buddy?" Matty heard Lugo say to someone on the other side of the staircase door.

"Just sittin'." The voice sounded familiar.

"Sittin' and . . ."

"Thinking."

"You live here?"

"Not really."

"Can I see some ID?"

Matty stuck his head around the open door to see Billy Marcus sitting on the stairs between fourteen and thirteen, that pilfered steno book falling off his lap as he twisted around to offer up his driver's license.

"Are you kidding me?" John Mullins half-whispered to Matty as he joined him at the stairwell door.

Lugo handed back the license. "How about you sit and think up in Riverdale."

"My wife doesn't let me smoke."

"Well, you're not smoking now."

Matty put a hand on Lugo's shoulder. "I know the guy."

"All yours." Lugo shrugged and Quality of Life began their nightly vertical patrol, splitting up, two men for each stairway to catpaw it out on alternating floors all the way down to the lobby, Daley and Lugo sidling past Marcus, still on the stairs, and beginning their quiet descent.

Waiting until they had disappeared around the thirteenth-floor landing, Matty stepped into the stairwell and not quite gently pulled Marcus to his feet. "All due respect, I am really starting to get tired of you." Then patted him down for a weapon.


Yolonda finally fought her way into the apartment through the bottleneck of cops, some of whom, like sports fans in the last few minutes of a blowout, were moving in the opposite direction, trying to beat the traffic home.

There was no interior hallway, the front door opening directly into the living room, where a fortyish Latino, liquor-breathed and with a fresh, bright punch-induced gash on his cheekbone, stood dead center as if onstage, delivering a speech to the half-dozen cops still there. His small, pop-eyed wife stood in a corner now, her arms draped over two equally pop-eyed but otherwise impassive young kids, who leaned back into her housedress.

Yolonda had never seen a room so clean and squared away; clear plastic slipcases or coverlets on every piece of furniture, including the VCR and cable box. A Yankees game was on the TV, the sound muted.

"See, I blame his mother for the way he turned out," the guy declared, sounding as if he honestly believed anyone present gave a shit.

The woman in the corner didn't react; He's not talking about her, Yolonda thought. Tracking the man's jabbing finger, she discovered who she assumed was the *he* of this speech: a skinny, scar-mouthed teenager in the half-walled dining nook, a Housing cop with a hand lightly to his chest as if to restrain him. The woman in the corner definitely wasn't his mother.

"I blame her for not teaching him the basic principles of, of prudential responsibility, of prudential impulse management, prudential self-control."

"Sir, are you pressing charges here or not—" one of the other cops said.

The teenager stood calmly, one hand resting on the dining table, the uniform there to keep him in check but there was no real need, keenly absorbed as he was in just observing this older guy, studying his every word and gesture, something both defeated and quietly triumphant in the set of the kid's mouth, his eyes.

"See, my mother raised us right," the older man stalled. "I am forty-six years old, lived a lot longer than many men of my age that grew up in these houses, but as she told me—"

"Sir . . ." the housing cop droned.

The man wasn't going to do shit and the kid knew it but had, Yolonda intuited, just found that out; ergo the small smile. Yolonda took in the fresh cut on the guy's cheek again, the jangly scar that ran across the kid's mouth and lower face like a polygraph readout, thinking, First time he ever fought back.

She moved past the remaining cops, more of them leaving every second, and sidled up to the kid. "Show me your room."


After taking Billy by the elbow down two flights of stairs to get away from the crowd, Matty abruptly backed him up against the wall. "What are you doing here."

"I'm not afraid of this place," Billy said, bouncing the back of his head off the smoke-dinged cinder block and looking off to get out from under Matty's eyes.

"Answer my question," Matty said, pressing in closer and cocking his head.

"You should have seen the shithole projects where I grew up," addressing the stairs heading back up to fourteen.

"Were you looking for somebody?"

"Besides"—Billy shrugged—"what can they do to me now."

"Who's *they*. Who were you looking for."

Billy kept craning his neck to get out from under Matty's stare.

"Who, True Life?"

"I don't know."

"Were you looking for True Life?"

"I don't know."

"You don't know?"

"No."

"And what would you do if you found him?"

"I just want . . ."

"What. You want what."

"I just want someone to explain to me."

"You want True Life to explain to you? What would you like him to explain? You want explanations, you talk to your wife. Your priest. Your shrink. True Life's out of the explanation loop. So I'm asking you again, what are you doing here." Then, "Give me this," taking the open notebook from his unresisting fingers.

Half-expecting to find some kind of vendetta written there, some kind of violent manifesto, he found instead a to-do list.

*Accept*
*Find higher meaning*
*Family*
*Friends*
*Prayer (??)*
*Whatever strengths of character*
*Don't be second victim—vacations, hobbies etc.*

Matty reading it again: *hobbies.*

"I just want . . ." Billy addressed the empty stairs, "I'm here, I am here, because, I need to get located, you know, oriented, so I can begin to . . ."

"All right, stop," Matty said.

"I mean, where do I go now, what do I do with myself . . ." His face at right angles to Matty's. "I just want to get oriented, and then—"

"Stop."

And Billy finally did.

"All right." Matty scanned the stairway as if there were something not apparent to see. "C'mon, let's get out of here." Walking him down eleven flights to the lobby, then out into the street.

The children's bedroom was as trim and tidy as the front parlor despite the apparent crowd that slept in here. There were four twin beds mattress to mattress beneath the bald overhead light, a three- or four-year-old asleep in one, a row of battered dressers and a large wicker basket filled with the remains of dolls, remote-control cars, and some unidentifiable toy parts, not a stray bit of plastic on the floor, the room so cramped that Yolanda opted to remain in the doorway.

The teenager sat hunched over on the foot of one of the empty beds, his apparently, and stared at air.

"What's your name?" Yolanda asked.

"Tristan," he muttered.

"That's what they call you?"

"Hah?" Not looking at her.

"Your friends."

"I don't know," that ever-popular shrugging singsong.

Yolanda carefully made her way into the room for a more intimate talk, sat on the edge of the bed alongside him, and saw, from her new vantage point, the *HOUSE RULES*, written with Magic Marker on oak tag and pushpinned to the wall directly over the door:

1. CURFEW is ten o'clock on weekdays, midnight on weekends—Sunday night is a weekday because it emptys into MONDAY MORNING
2. School drop ofs—on TIME
3. School pick ups—on TIME
4. NO ONE IN HOUSE when I am at work. This includes when my wife is there but I am not
5. LIQUOR is FORBIDEN in this house including my private stock which is OFF LIMITS
6. NO DRUGS this should not even be necessary for me to say it

7. No loud or PROFANITY style music and no headphones where you cant hear if theres an EMERGENCY
8. CONTRIBUTE TO HOUSE EXPENSE one half your earnings—with FOOD and SHELTER automatically provided for you this is THE BARGAIN OF THE CENTURY
9. DISRESPECT equals INGRADITUDE

The handwriting was exquisite, filled with curlicues and swordlike flourishes, oppressive in its lavishness.

"Your father write that?"

"That's not my father." He kept his head down, refused to look at her.

"Stepfather?"

"Was."

"Took you off your mother's hands?"

"I guess." Glaring at his high-tops.

"Where is she?"

"I don't know."

"You sleep in here?"

"Yeah."

"You babysit the little ones."

"Oh yeah." A half-dead snort.

"And his wife out there, whenever you buck, she always takes his side, right?"

He shrugged moodily, those sneakers on his feet so riveting.

Yolonda inched closer. "So why . . ." Then, "What happened, your grandmother died?"

"Uh-huh." His narrow eyes getting a sheen.

"And no way you can live with your mother."

"Ain't nobody can no more." Still avoiding her eyes.

"Then what's wrong with you." She bumped his shoulder. "It's his house."

"I don't care."

"You want to be homeless?"

"I don't care."

"You can't hit him."

"He can't hit me neither." His voice near inaudible.

"He do that to you?" Eyeing his scar.

"No."

Yolonda gave it a minute, the kid motionless but alert as a bird.

"Listen to me," she said, then startled him by taking his hand. "My father used to beat the shit out of my brothers? I had three brothers, my father'd come home drunk? The one and only time my brother Ricky hit him back, he busted his jaw and my father had him arrested. He was in Spofford for six months. It's not fair but it is what it is."

He didn't respond but Yolonda knew he heard her.

"But you know what?" Her lips almost in his ear. "After tonight? I don't think he's going to hit you anymore."

Still studying his sneakers, he fought down a smile.

"You're a nice-looking kid," she said, rising. "Don't make me go home worrying about you, alright?"


"Look, it's not like I'm completely helpless," Billy said. "You know, without resources. I've been reading, I mean, and, for what it's worth, and from what I can gather, there's basically three things I need to do to start getting through this."

They sat facing each other on rattan easy chairs in the otherwise deserted back room of a club on Delancey, a sub club, Chinaman's Chance, within the larger club, Waxey's, the two of them peering at each other through the dim light of paper lanterns, the walls and ceiling painted a flat red so that everything appeared awash in blood.

"Three steps to grace, some state of grace," Billy said, "the key to, to not just surviving, but having some semblance of, or, or even possibly rising to be an even better person than I was before."

Matty had picked this spot because Chinaman's Chance was closed until midnight except for special friends, i.e., cops and preferred dealers, and he knew they'd have it to themselves. But Billy had gone from inarticulately distraught to talking his head off from the moment they sat down, and now Matty wasn't sure how to play it.

"One. Accept the fact that the murder can't be undone. Just accept it."

"OK." Matty knew pretty much what was coming, had heard variations of this spiel dozens of times before, from dozens of newly branded Billys.

"Two, find the higher meaning in it. See the tragedy as a part of the human condition, you know, like how every event has a purpose, or, or, something worse has been averted according to God's plan. OK? And, by the way, nothing says you can't keep the bond with the loved one."

"No."

"I mean they're still with you if you want them to be. In fact, maybe even more so now that they've been purified into spirit. And there's no real reason to stop talking to each other just because . . ."

"True."

"And of course they live on in your memories, your undying memories . . ."

Every time, this hapless eagerness that most viscerally suggested to him the essence not of the grieving adult but of the lost child, as if the parents were unconsciously performing an impersonation of child innocence, and at least fleetingly, no matter how distant Matty tried to be, it always knocked him back.

"And three, most importantly—"

"That all sounds very solid there, Billy," Matty, hunching forward, cut him off. "But I hope you know this stuff takes a long time to truly set up house in you."

"Yeah," he said drily, "that was in the literature too."

The waitress came in from the front room with their drinks. It was Sarah Bowen of the seven dwarfs, Ike Marcus's last hump, but Matty would keep that to himself; and on her end, sensing that Matty, an old one-night stand, was into something back here with this other guy, she refrained from acting familiar.

She leaned in between them to off-load her tray, and in the few seconds it took her to straighten up again, it was like the pass of a magician's hand, Billy coming back into Matty's view completely transformed: dark, dull-eyed, somewhere else.

"You OK?"

"You want to hear something?" Billy said, stroking the sides of his throat. "When Ike was seven . . . some older kid hit him at school and he came home crying. I said to him, 'Listen to me. You go back out there, and you don't come back to this house until you stand up for yourself. Until you show that kid he can't push you around, otherwise . . .'"

Billy looked at Matty.

"And he did it. He went back out there, gave and took a real beating but . . . And when he came back? I was so, so . . . *Yeah!*" Billy shook his fist. "You know?" Then looked away. "What was that. What the fuck was that."

"That's what dads do," Matty said carefully. "Mine too."

"Bullshit. It didn't even sound like me. I'm the most frightened man I know. Always have been. I must've been in a panic about that other kid, that Ike would turn out . . ."

Sarah Bowen stepped into Matty's sight line, tilted her chin quizzically.

He shook his head, Don't ask, and gestured for the check.

"So here's . . . Did I *make* my son into that boy who charged a gun last week? I did, didn't I."

"Listen, I've been meaning to tell you," Matty said, trying to get him away from himself. "Just so you know, True Life? We found the guy. He wasn't involved."

Billy raised his eyes to him at that. "So what happens now."

"Now? There's a lot of stuff to be done now. On something like this there's always a lot of stuff to be done. We have Want Cards out there, an open tipline, a seventh-day recanvass tomorrow night, but," hunkering in, "I won't ever be less than honest with you. What doesn't bode well here is that we have a twenty-two-thousand-dollar reward out there and no takers. No one's picking up a phone, and believe me, they would if they could. So, I would say that this is going to turn out to be one of those cases that's going to take a lot of patience."

"Patience."

"Waiting for guys who wouldn't talk to you the first time around all of a sudden getting in a jam. Cases like this always end with someone trying to get themselves out from under a rock."

Sarah Bowen came back with a check and her cell phone number written on a scrap of paper, Matty's heart lifting, inspiring in him another burst of information.

"It's like, for example, I have this other active case, robbery-homicide from last year, Chinese guy, was shot in the vestibule of his building by two black kids, the bullet a .38, and right now I'm waiting to go upstate to talk to a guy named D-block, was part of a robbery team liked to work indoors, not *the* robbery team, but he never told me who his partner was, OK? But D-block's wife was just arrested the other day, and if she goes in, Family Services will take away his kids, so now all of a sudden he's asking for me, he's ready to talk to keep her out of jail. All good and well, hope springs eternal and all that, but here's what's probably going to happen . . ."

Matty paused to see if this was the kind of talk that would bring Billy back into the world.

"We'll go up there, he'll give us his partner, we'll pick up his partner, his partner will say D-block's a lying motherfucker, will say, 'Look at me. I'm two twenty-five and ripped. I never had to use a gun in my life,' but he'll *also* tell us something, like the only guy *he* knows uses a .38, does inside-the-building holdups, is some character, let's call him E-Walk. OK. Let's go find E-Walk. Problem is, E-Walk is a solo operator, but E-Walk, it'll turn out, will know this *other* stickup team we never even heard of. Go track down *those* boneheads. Only problem with those guys once we find them is that one was locked up at the time of the homicide and the other was in the hospital. But! The one in the hospital? He'll know a guy uses a .38, sometimes works with a partner, except *that* guy, it'll turn out, is a light-skinned Dominican, looks almost white. But. But. But. The point of which is to say, Billy, that with your son, it'll have to do with luck, and it'll have to do with just plugging away, plugging away . . ."

"How did you know the stickup team was two black kids?" he asked soberly.

"A witness saw them running out of the building, but didn't see their faces."

"What about the witness with Ike? That was face-to-face."

"Eric Cash?"

"Was he the drunk one?"

"No. He was the other."

"And?"

"He won't cooperate."

"Won't . . . I don't understand. Why not? He was right there."

"He was a little too there. If you remember—" Matty cut himself off.

Of course the guy didn't remember; the day had been a fever dream and there had been nothing in the paper about it because of the press gag.

"Wait. You thought he did it?"

"We know now he didn't. Now. But we raked him over the coals a bit, and he did spend a few hours in the Tombs."

"A few hours?" Billy blinking. "And now he's not helping?"

"Not without written immunity, which . . . so, no."

"But if he didn't do it, why would he care about immunity?"

"That, I believe, is his lawyer's influence."

"I don't understand."

Billy looked more bewildered than angry, but it was one of those seeds that could bloom overnight into a redwood.

"Look, I don't want you worrying about this. We'll iron it out."

Sarah Bowen came back to pick up the check, Matty distractedly dropping dollars, worrying whether he'd just seriously messed up here. "Billy, we should go."

Billy just sat there, off into something.

"Billy . . ."

"No, I was just thinking about this other homicide you told me about, the Chinese guy."

"Yeah?"

"How do I make you, or anyone else, care about my son, not as a job, just as a person, as opposed to your own son, or anybody's son. I mean, why would I care about anyone else's son."

"You don't have to make me care," Matty said. "I work for him."

Billy looked at him with dog's eyes. "You know something?" His voice turning to water. "He would have liked you. Ikey. I know it. And you would have liked him."

"He sounds like a great kid."

"He is," Billy said, then abruptly stood up, his chair roaring backwards across the floor. "Can I show you something?"

They went out into the front room, pulsating now with a mixture of bridge and tunnel, Eighth Squad detectives, and some of the more gussied-up locals, but tonight there seemed to be more police than usual, Matty seeing why right away, the return of Lester McConnell, a detective transferred six months ago from the Lower East Side to the

Joint Terrorist Task Force and relocated to Washington, most likely here as part of an advance Dignitary Protection Unit detail for the president's visit to the UN. Lester was big, huge, six-five, 350 pounds, standing at the bar now drinking beer, tilting his chin to the ceiling and spewing cigarette smoke like a humpback. And new guys from the squad were still coming in, leaning in to greet Lester with hard, slappy hugs; the ones who had been there awhile sitting kind of sideways on their stools, still as Buddhas, drunk out of their skulls, eyelids rising to voices in their own sweet time or staring at the cell phones clipped sideways on their belts and praying for peace on earth.

Matty had always liked McConnell. He moved towards the bar to shake his hand on the way out.

"So hold on," McConnell boomed to the crowd. "This fucking idiot said what? 'Not *tonight*, my man'? Jesus Christ, what else did I miss around here?"

Matty's gut flipped.

Some of the cops, recognizing Billy, quickly looked away, embarrassed and angry, the conversation beneath the music dying down to coughs and mutters. And McConnell, sensing something wrong, picked up from the expressions and the abrupt silence, from the breathless look on Billy's face, from Matty's proprietary hand on his shoulder, that he'd just stepped on his dick big-time. So instead of hailing Matty, he glared at him: The fuck did you just do to me.

Matty felt lousy for both McConnell and Billy, then even worse when Billy said, no need to lower his voice under the music, "It's not his fault. I probably shouldn't have come here to begin with," then led the way out onto Delancey Street.


A few moments later they were standing before the shrine, which tonight looked more scattered than ever; Matty giving it another few days before it disappeared forevermore into the homicide trivia of the city.

"Have you . . . You've had guns pointed at you somewheres along the line, yes?" Billy asked.

"Not as much as you might think," Matty said.

"I did, one time, what was that, twenty years ago? I'm supervising emergency repairs on Avenue C during the blackout? I walk around the corner to a bodega about eleven at night, these two junkies pop out of the shadows, one's got a Saturday-night special, piece of shit probably would've blown off his hand if he pulled the trigger. But I swear to God, someone's pointing any kind of gun at you like that? It is paralyzing. It is *there*. I couldn't take my eyes off it. I couldn't even move to give them my wallet, just told them what pocket it was in, next thing I know I'm alone, my knees are going like jackhammers. So, what Ike, what my son did? Step to a gun like that? Where did he get the guts to do that? Can you imagine that? The courage that took?"

"What did you want to show me, Billy."

"I don't give a damn. Drunk, sober, smart, stupid, staring down a barrel and making a move irregardless?" Billy suddenly twitched, a quick rippling tic. "Fucking hell."

"Billy"—touching his shoulder—"what did you want to show me."

"Do you believe in dreams?"

"I never know how to answer that one."

"Last night?" Billy said, avoiding looking at the tattered newsphoto of his son still taped to the wall of 27 Eldridge. "I dreamt Ike was fighting off lions. I was too scared to help him. I kept finding reasons not to jump in."

"That's just—"

"Guilt. Yeah, I know, but look."

Billy pointed to the building facade and there they were, lions, half a dozen of them ornamenting the upper stories of brickwork in front of the murder spot; pitted, century-old grimestone beasts carved openmawed and snarling.

"I don't understand why that guy won't help you on this."

"Who," Matty asked, feeling for his car keys.

"If he didn't do it, why would he care about immunity?"

There was a dangerous word-for-word repetitiveness in Billy's complaint, Matty thinking, And so it begins.


Half an hour later Matty sat parked with him in front of his building in Riverdale, Billy in no rush to go upstairs.

"So let me ask you something." Matty said. "It's really none of my business, but, your wife . . ."

Billy looked at him.

"Maybe you don't want to deal with her on this for whatever . . . I don't know, you're an adult, she's an adult. But the kid. The girl." Matty shrugged helplessly. "You seem like a decent guy."

Billy's chin disappeared quivering into the arc beneath his mouth. "We talk," he managed to get out. "We talk."

Minette came out of the building a moment later, crossed the pavement barefoot to the car, and reached through the driver's window to lay a brief hand on Matty's arm. "I'm sorry," she whispered.

"Don't be," Matty said.

As Billy got out on the passenger side, she walked around the front to him and he broke down, reaching for her like a child.

Matty watched as she guided her husband back home, then he continued to sit there for a few minutes after they were gone.

On his way back down the West Side Highway, he nearly tore the car apart searching for Sarah Bowen's phone number before admitting to himself that he'd lost it.


Handcuffed to the arm of Lugo's office chair, Albert Bailey winced in ostentatious discomfort as he spoke to someone on a squad-issued cell phone. Daley and Lugo sat facing him in the otherwise deserted room, their fingers laced across their guts and their high-tops ankle-crossed up on their desks.

"How about the boy Timberwolf?" Albert said into the phone. "Timberwolf in Cahan . . . No one's gonna mess with you over there if you're goin' over to do business . . . Just rent it off him or somesuch, I'll pay you back soon's I get clear of this mess, soon's I get clear . . . Bring it to in front of St. Mary's on Pitt and I'll meet you . . . Naw, naw, naw, the police ain't gonna do nothing to you, man . . . Look, I got to get them a hammer or I'm long gone, I swear on my unborn child, man . . . Awright, call me back, call me back. This number right here. Call me back." Then, flipping the phone shut, "He ain't calling me back."

"I hope he does, brother." Lugo yawned into the back of his hand. "For your sake."

Albert started undulating a little, as if to soothe himself.

"Anybody else you can call?" Daley asked, his ankle holster playing peekaboo with the cuff of his jeans as he idly rocked in his flex-backed office chair.

"I would if I could, man, but a gun, I'm not . . . That's never been my thing, guns . . ." Wincing again as he tried to get a new lay of the cuff biting into his wrist.

"No, no, I hear you," Lugo said mildly, "but for real, there are those that subscribe, correct?"

"Yeah, but me, I'm not . . . see, you fellas, you don't know me. All's you saw was a black man in a hooptie holdin' a hundred dollars' worth of brown."

"Don't forget the boxcutter."

"Like, for example, I'm a news buff. You searched my car, I probably had a newspaper in there, right? I could tell you about anything, Tyco, Amron, steroids, bin Laden, Rove . . ."

"Who's Rove?" Daley asked.

"Shit, my girl? She's three months heavy now with my first child. A thirty-five-year-old black man just having his first kid? You *know* I was waiting."

"Well, we're trying to help you here," Lugo said, peering at his watch, "but it's a gun or you might not be there for the coming-out party."

"And then some," Daley added.

Bailey closed his eyes and spoke faster, as if to fend off, to drown out. "See, my girl, she's not, she's not a street girl, has got a college diploma, I mean, I don't know what she saw in me, you know? And like, at first? It was too easy to fool her about this stuff . . . Be high and say I'm just tired. She's innocent, you know? But sometimes being in-nocent, like, if you got a conscience? The innocent ones can be a lot harder to lie to than the wise ones. So like six months ago I went and confessed to her about my addiction? I tell you, man, she up and sur-prised the hell out of me, didn't even blink. Tied me to the bed for two days till I was clean, just like the Wolfman."

"Wow," Daley said.

"But in all fairness to myself? I'm not too bad a guy . . ." Bailey chat-tering, rocking with ache, "Like, out on the street? I'm kind of the neighborhood babysitter. I mean, people know I'm, you know . . . But I don't ever do it in front of anybody, I don't entice and shit . . . I started a, a chess club, a basketball team. In high school? I was a athlete. Man, I never even so much as smoked a cigarette until I was twenty-five. I couldn't stand the smell of them things."

"So what happened?"

"Curiosity," Albert muttered.

"That sucks," Lugo said, eyeing the time on the cable box: 1:15. "Why don't you try your buddy again."

"I do, you know what's gonna happen? He ain't gonna pick up."

"Try," Daley said.

Albert did, and got the voice mail. "Ey, yo . . ." he began halfheartedly, then abruptly jackknifed in his seat, as if attempting to pick something up off the floor, came back up hissing in pain.

"You're starting to come off a little squinchy there, brother . . . You getting the grips?"

"Yeah." His face bunched, then went pop-eyed wide. "I'm feeling it now. This ain't gonna be fun in there."

"We keep wanting to help you out, man." Lugo raised his hands. "But it's a two-way river."

"Yeah, I know, I know, but . . ." Albert's hand fluttered above the cell phone. "Fuck it. It's what I deserve."

The large, near-empty room descended into a brief disappointed silence, which was abruptly disrupted by Geohagan and Scharf escorting their own last-call collar through the door, an overweight Latino kid sporting a Yankees bomber jacket and a long, braided pigtail. They steered him to a desk as far away from Lugo and Daley's play as possible, cuffed him to the chair, and placed Scharf's cell phone on the table before him.

"You know the drill, bro," Geohagan said, "so start dialing."

Matty was at the beach with Minette and his own sons, who were little kids again, when his cell jerked him awake.

"What am I supposed to tell myself," Billy hissed in his ear, "it was his time? He was summoned? It was for his own good? He's better off now? He's romping in some, some, cloud meadow? He was sacrificed to prevent some greater evil from happening?"

"OK, look—" Matty began.

"And my son isn't watching over me. He doesn't live on in my heart. He doesn't *talk* to me. *I* talk to me and what I say to myself—"

"OK, hang on, stop."

"Cherish your memories . . . My memories feel like knives and I would gladly burn them out of—"

"Just *stop*."

"And that guy who's not helping you? A few hours in jail and now he won't go through a *mug* book? The Tombs. *Fuck* the Tombs. My son's got the rest of . . . has *eternity* in the Tombs."

# SIX

# THE DEVIL YOU KNOW

**As Matty was on the phone** with Borough Patrol trying to rejig tours for this evening's canvass, Steven Boulware popped up on the TV again, a clutch of microphones bearding his face.

"At one p.m. tomorrow afternoon at the Eugene Langenshield Center on Suffolk Street there will be a memorial service in honor, in celebration, of Ike Marcus, my friend Ike Marcus, followed by a procession to Twenty-seven Eldridge Street, where he"—Boulware struggled—"where he left us. This will be open to all, I invite you all, to come not to mourn his death . . . but celebrate his life, his spirit, his legacy."

"This Boulware kid's an actor?" Mullins asked.

"Aspiring," Matty said.

"Got the cameras now."

"Matty." Yolonda holding up the phone. "Dargan from Berkowitz."

Matty braced, Detective Dargan, Deputy Inspector Berkowitz's Bad News Bear. "Hey, Jerry."

"Yeah, hey, Matty, look, we just got word, the president's coming into town tonight instead of tomorrow."

"OK." Matty waited for the other shoe.

"So, we're going to need to postpone your recanvass."

"What?" Matty tried to come off stunned. "Why?"

"The word from on high is to pull manpower from all units, including yours. No excusals."

"Are you fucking kidding me? I spent the last two days lining everybody up for this. You couldn't have told me earlier?"

"We just found out ourselves."

"How the fuck can you not know the president's coming in until the *day*."

"Hey," Dargan said calmly, "I have nothing to do with this. I'm just the messenger."

Fucking Berkowitz.

"Is he in? Let me talk to him."

"Not a good idea," Dargan said.

"And you're taking people from *my* squad? It's a seventh-day homicide recanvass. You *can't* take my people."

"No excusals," Dargan said. "Sorry."

"This fucking sucks. Let me talk to him."

"Not a good idea. And Matty? Truly . . . let it be."

As he slammed the phone down, Yolonda snapped off her cell. "They're pulling me and Iacone," she said. "You know something? I don't think I've ever been inside the Waldorf."


At eleven that morning, Berkmann's was once again a white dream, the sun coming in like a brass band through the large windows, bouncing off the artfully mottled mirrors, the eggy glazed tiles, the shimmering racked bistro glasses.

The only customer at this limbo hour, however, was a lone woman at a window deuce getting quietly plastered on Chocolatinis as she leafed through yesterday's *New York Times*.

"Last night there was a small dustup at the bar." Eric Cash's voice rang through the cavernous room as he addressed the assembled waitstaff at one of the back banquettes. "Eric the second, who is no longer with us, lifted someone's change, thinking it was a tip, and the customer, who was drunk, accused him of stealing and threw a punch. Then Cleveland here"—Eric gestured to the dreadlocked bartender—"came to the rescue, leaping over the bar like Zorro and bum-rushing the guy out the door himself, no one hurt and nothing broken."

There was a smattering of applause, Cleveland standing up and bowing at the waist.

"Now, the reason I've invited Cleveland to this meeting is to tell him the following. If you ever try anything like that again, you are gone."

The kid half smiled, not sure if Cash was joking.

"I wouldn't want security making the margaritas, and I certainly don't want you playing amateur hero. You like to read, Cleveland?"

"Sometimes." The kid still processing this, confused and humiliated.

"Then you know heroes are often tragic," Cash said, then dismissed him with a nod towards the bar, waiting for him to return to his post behind the stick before resuming the meeting.

"OK, and lastly," Cash said to the rest, "everybody here . . . when this room is hopping the way it has been recently and the busboys are overextended? You people need to start helping them out, none of this 'It's not my job.' When this place starts to look like some Soviet-style who-gives-a-shit cafeteria, which is exactly what it's been looking like come the peak hours, it damn well *is* your job.

"Everyone at this table is expendable, and this neighborhood is crawling with experienced waiters. So. You take the check but leave the dirty dishes? No. You have ketchup still on the table when the dessert comes out? No.

"The check comes, that table is clean. You want to serve? You have to bus."

Eric Cash flipped over the top sheet of his legal pad. "And that's it on my end. Anybody have anything else they want to bring up? Questions? Suggestions?"

Even in his disembodied state Eric was cognizant enough to sense that no one at the table would risk opening their mouth for fear of saying what they were probably thinking of this prick, this ball-breaking entity who had taken him over. It was if he was watching himself from the sidelines as he turned his own people against him.

"All right then." He raised and dropped his hands on the edge of the table. "I'm still working on the envelopes, they should be ready at about three. Class dismissed."

They all rose in silence, not even daring to make eye contact with each other.

He remained at the table, though, staring straight ahead, the agitation in his features fading into a brooding slackness as he drifted off into tabulating how much he had pocketed from the tip pool so far this week: close to $500; way too much; not nearly enough.

Boulware's studio apartment, in the building next to 27 Eldridge, was a featureless two-year-old efficiency that bore no trace of the building's nineteenth-century exterior; walls, doors, fixtures; everything cheap and new; Matty thinking they must have gutted the whole thing and rebuilt it for the newbies, kids used to dorms.

"This memorial service?" Matty, seated across a coffee table from Boulware, inched forward in the sling chair. "I think it's a great thing you're doing for your friend and we're behind you a hundred percent. Just, it would be good for us to know in advance what you plan on talking about tomorrow."

"Talking about?" Boulware reached for one of the beers standing between them. "About Ike, what else?"

His cell rang. "Sorry," holding up a finger and calling out the name of the person on the other end. "You're coming, right?"

Matty got up and wandered to Boulware's lone window, which looked out on the rear Dumpsters of a Chinese restaurant on Forsyth Street.

The walls were bare save for three framed SUNY Buffalo theater posters—*Mother Courage and Her Children*, *Equus*, and *Lost in Yonkers*—Boulware's name getting either first or second billing on each.

The only other personal touch in here was the dozens of small plastic soldiers and *Star Wars* figures that marched across the back of the convertible sofa and along the kitchen counters or rappelled on shoelaces down the sides of the TV and the refrigerator.

After Dargan's call, Matty had spent the remainder of the morning on the phone, trying to set up his own little backdoor recanvass for tonight in defiance of Berkowitz's postponement; attempted to call in every marker he had in Warrants, Vice, Narcotics, and Borough Patrol and had gotten blown off by people who owed him hugely, which should have told him something, but he was too hot to take the hint.

"I swear to God, if you don't show tomorrow?" Boulware smiled at the response, then, "Peace," hanging up, his face electric with life. "I'm sorry, you were saying." His cell rang again. "Sorry, just . . . Yeah? Hey. I have to call you back . . . I have to call you back . . . I have to call you back . . . Yeah . . . Yeah . . . OK . . . OK." Hanging up. "I'm sorry, it's just this thing tomorrow, it's going to be like, boom."

"That's great, that's good. We just need to know if you're going to be saying anything about the investigation."

"Like what?"

"Like anything."

"I don't understand." And Matty believed him.

"Is there something you *want* me to say?"

"More like, don't say."

"Don't say."

"It's just, it's been difficult, this investigation, but any criticism of us at this point, any negativity to the press . . ."

"Why would I do that?"

"Anything about Eric Cash . . ."

At first the name didn't even register, Matty thinking, Just drop it.

"What about him?"

"We're trying to work with him, but it's a very delicate situation. He kind of needs, feels he needs to lay low for a bit, so maybe you should include him out, if you know what I mean, let him grieve in his own way."

"I'm still not a hundred percent following."

"Don't worry about it."

"OK." Then, "You're coming, right? You and your partner?"

"Most likely."

"This will be a good thing." Boulware nodded. "A very good thing."

• • •

*Lightning frightening*
*Your gut tightning*
*Evidence inamissible*
*Power indivisable*
*Touch me once ill touch you twice*
*Mess with me youll be on ice*

Tristan closed the notebook and headed off to make his delivery for Smoov, this one here his last of three and the easiest, the storefront law office on Hester, just a couple of blocks from the Lemlichs.

The place was long, wooden, and funky like an old-time saloon, and except for a photo of one old white dude with a guitar, the walls were hung with posters of mostly olden-days *morenos* and *borinqueños* with Jiffy Pop dos and dime shades, fists raised in front of microphones or crowds.

Usually he felt tight coming in here, couldn't find his voice, the whole trip barely worth the $25, although since the thing happened, he'd been feeling less jumpy about going into places like this or even the spots uptown. He still didn't feel like talking but . . .

He stepped to the receptionist, a Chinese lady with a tight platinum-dyed crop, who sat up straighter and smiled at the sight of him like he had just made her day, although his guess was that all he did to earn that smile was to be born PR and live in the PJs.

"Che!" Danny shouted from his desk halfway down the loft, waving him over.

Tristan saw that Danny was sitting with a customer, a white guy that looked familiar, but the thing was to deliver the boo, get the money, and go, not take pictures.

"What I'm saying is, I guess I could get a specific order of protection against that particular detective, but—"

"I said I don't want to do that."

Coming up to Danny's desk, Tristan froze with recognition, couldn't even muster the muscles to turn away.

"Then I'm not sure what you want me—"

"Nothing, I don't even want . . . I don't know, I don't know."

"Che!" Danny reared back as if to admire him, then did a naked double take on seeing his clean-shaven chin, the exposed lightning there. He'd been getting that a lot. Keeping his eyes down, Tristan dropped the wrinkled brown bag on the desk.

The other guy was too into his own misery to give him anything more than a distracted glance, but they were as close to each other right now as they were that night.

Danny leaned back farther in his chair to dig the money out of his front jeans pocket, smiled painfully at Tristan, like he didn't know whether to comment about his scars or keep pretending he wasn't staring at them.

"So how you been, brother man?" Danny beamed as he palm-ironed four wrinkled twenties in front of his client, the guy looking like he wanted to jump out of a window with unhappiness.

"OK."

"How goes La Raza?"

"OK." Keeping his eyes on the money.

They were all looking at the money now.

"Jesus Christ, Danny, a twenty's worth twenty wrinkled or pressed," the guy snapped. "Just give it to the kid."

"It's disrespectful." Danny winking at Tristan. "Right . . ."

Tristan knew Danny was just about to call him Che again, then caught himself, that old tag finally out the door.

The other guy looked at him again, and for a second the recognition was in his eyes, Tristan's belly whooping, but just as quickly the light went out, the guy frowning back down at the desk.

On his way out past the receptionist, it was all Tristan could do not to bust out grinning. First that lady detective last night, now this dude. He had always thought of himself as invisible to others but had never thought it before as a superpower.


He was on his way from Boulware's apartment back to the Seventh, crossing Delancey to the west side of Pitt, when he turned to the calling of his name.

There was no one on the street.

"Matty."

They were double-parked on Pitt, Billy and his daughter.

"Hey." Matty stepped to the Toyota Sequoia, the girl in the open curbside window.

Billy leaned across her to make eye contact. "Matty, I don't think you've ever met my daughter."

"No, I haven't." Smiling at her, but blanking on her name, her name, Nina. "Nina, right?"

She nodded, and he offered her his hand. "I'm Matty. Detective Clark."

"Hi." She was strong-looking but small-voiced.

Shaking her long-fingered hand, he took in the bandaging around her biceps, thinking that it was a pretty high spot for a sandwich-cutting accident.

"We just came down," Billy said. "She wanted to meet you."

Nina turned to him, mortified.

"Sorry," he said, "*I* wanted her to meet you."

"Hey, listen." Matty rested his forearm on her open window. "I can't tell you how sorry I am but we're doing everything we can."

She nodded mutely, her eyes quickly pooling.

"Hey, sweetie?" Billy opened his door. "Can I talk . . ." then stepped out into the street. "Just a sec."

Taking Matty by the elbow, Billy led him a few feet away from the car and then just stood there, squinting into the sun coming over the bridge. He was dressed in jeans and a sweat-darkened hoodie like a kid or a Quality of Lifer, but it was one of those days when his face looked puckered and ancient.

Matty waited.

"We played some ball this morning."

"Yeah?"

"I played some as a kid in the Bronx and I wasn't too bad, JV at Evander Childs, but her?" Billy chucked a thumb back to the car. "Oh, man, she's, she's better than I ever was."

"Really." Matty still waiting.

"You know, I would watch the two of them play one-on-one some-times? Ike was something else, but she could give him a run for his money."

"Wow."

"Give him a few scares."

"Yeah?"

A silence came down, Billy's face working.

"I'm trying," he whispered tearily. "I am trying."

"I can see that," Matty said gently, hating to be anybody's father. "I can see that."

"Thank you," Billy said, shaking his hand, then turning back for the car. Matty waved to the sorrow-faced kid, who returned a small glissando of fingers. Then Billy did an about-face, marching back to him.

"Let me just ask, just for my own . . . This Eric Cash . . ."

Fuck.

"Just . . ." Billy reading his mind. "You're him, OK? Now . . . The guy shot your friend, knows you're the only eyewitness. Wouldn't you be worried that that guy might be coming back to tie up loose ends? Wouldn't you be in fear for your life? Wouldn't you get the hell out of Dodge until the cops catch this guy? But this Cash, correct me if I'm wrong, he doesn't do that."

"Billy . . ."

"As far as I know, he still lives where he lives, works where he works, goes about his business like there's nothing, nobody out there to fear. Why is that?"

"Don't do this to yourself," Matty said.

"Can you say to me one hundred percent that he didn't do it?" Squinting up at him.

"That what?"

"Is that the real reason they didn't give him immunity?"

"Look, it's an open homicide. They didn't give him immunity because they don't give anyone immunity. They wouldn't give *you* immunity. Do you understand that?"

"But still, can you say to me, 'Billy, one hundred percent, the guy didn't do it.' "

"Listen—"

"Say that to me. Say, 'Billy, one hundred percent.' "

"I *never* say that."

"OK, then." Bobbing his head. He seemed almost happy.

Over his shoulder, Nina's face was smeared into the heel of her hand as she watched the people passing by on Pitt.

"But this time I will. One hundred percent, he didn't do it."

Flustered, Billy stepped in place like a counting horse.

"I mean, I'm not saying he's the guy, like, pulled the trigger," Billy talking to himself now as much as to Matty. "I'm just . . . I think maybe he's got something to hide."

"Did you hear what I said?" Matty leaned in to him.

"Had a bad day," Billy muttered. "Yeah, true, no kidding, I'll grant him that. He had a very bad day . . ."

"Billy, listen to me."

"But you know who had the worst day of all? My son. My son had the worst possible day you can have."

And with that, Billy returned to the car, Matty watching him go. As nuts as he was, Matty thought, the guy at least had some pep in his step, and why not . . . For today at least, he had found his demon.

Just as Big Dap said, "What the fuck I tell you about that shit?" to Little Dap, who was putting the finishing touches on a laundry-marker dick in the ear of the soldier on the bus-shelter recruiting poster, the corner of Oliver and St. James became awash in the fluttering light atop the Quality of Life taxi; both Daps and everyone else automatically and forbearingly turning their eyes skyward as if posing for a religious painting.

"You tell him to do that?" Lugo asked Big Dap as he stepped from the taxi, Daley, Scharf, and Geohagan exiting after him in a triple slam of car doors.

"What?" Big Dap said, raising his hands. "Nah."

"Vandalize government property?" Lugo began patting him down. "Sabotage the war against terror?"

"Tell *his* ass," Big Dap drawled, roughly jerking his chin towards his brother; Little Dap in for it now.

"Who, Lex Luthor here?" Daley muttered, going into Little Dap's pockets. "This kid ever had an original thought, it would die of loneliness."

Standing off to the side, Tristan watched a play that he'd seen more times than he could count. Ever since Big Dap got away with leg-shooting that cop last year, half the squad cars in the precinct had his mug pasted to the dash; as in, ball-break on sight.

"Holy cow there, Dap," Lugo said, pulling a fat wad of cash from one of Big Dap's knee-high basketball socks. "What's the what on this?"

"I got to buy a crib," Big Dap murmured, looking off.

"An apartment?"

"Naw, a crib. For the baby."

"You got a lot more here than just for that."

"I don't know how much it cost."

"Trust me. I'm a veteran. But so, where'd you get all this?"

"Bank."

"You have a bank account? Which bank?"

"On the, by Grand Street there, it's my mother's bank. I don't know the name of it."

"First Horseshit?" Scharf said.

"Could be."

"We should voucher that," Geohagan said.

"As' my mother, man."

"We will," Lugo said. "In fact, if this is her money, she can come down to the Eighth and claim it."

Big Dap shook his head in sorrowful amusement.

"Come on," Lugo said. "Let's count it together so we both know how much we're talking about."

Dap looked away, drawled, "Motherfuckers prolly take it anyhow."

"Prolly what?" Lugo squinted, his mouth open in concentration.

"Nothin', man."

"Please." Lugo leaning in to get up in his face. "I'm a little hard of hearing."

"Hey, man, do what you gonna do." Dap craning his neck to get some space. "'Cause y'all are like that anyhow."

"Like what?"

"Go on, man, you take it and I'll see you when I see you."

"Excuse me?"

"I'll see you when I'll see you."

"Are you threatening me?"

"What?"

"Did he just threaten me?" Lugo asked Tristan.

Lugo abruptly stepped on Big Dap's foot just hard enough for him to have to swing an arm forward to try to keep his balance; assaulting an officer; then chest-popped him to the ground.

"Hey, shooter." Lugo standing astride him. "You know what this is? This is the song that never ends. I got *no* fucking qualms with you."

Lugo tossed the wad of dough backhand onto Big Dap's chest, then along with the other Quality of Lifers returned to the taxi and peeled out without looking back.

Big Dap ignored the money sliding off his body as he got to his feet and brushed himself off, everyone around him suddenly animated with outrage, Little Dap, in for a beatdown now, the loudest, cursing out the cops as he raced around picking up the strewn dollars.

Tristan stood quietly on the sidelines watching him hop around like a Chinatown chicken.

"Jimmy Crack Corn motherfuckers," Little Dap muttered. "Yo, Dap, you best count this."

"Just pick the shit up." Waving him off.

"Ey, yo," Tristan murmured. "Come here, man."

"You *see* me here?" Little Dap stalk-eyed as he continued to bob for dollars.

Tristan just waved him over again, then waited.

"*What.*"

"I want that whistle back," Tristan murmured, looking off.

"The what? *Hell* no. I told you that's my insurance against you bitching out."

"I want it." Not even looking at him.

"Yeah, huh?" Little Dap started to walk away.

"You can give it to me or I'll fuckin' come get it," Tristan said as if talking to himself.

Little Dap turned back and stared at him.

"All right." Tristan shrugged, then started for home. "I guess I'll see you when I see you, hah?"

Little Dap continued to stare after Tristan until his own brother said, "What the fuck I tell you about doin' that *stupid* shit," then met his turning head with a punch to the temple that had him dancing halfway across the street.

. . .

The chirp of his cell had Matty upright and blinking in the dark, the time on the cable box 3:15.

"Yeah."

"Well, they finally went and did it." Lindsay, his upstate ex, sounded hysterically perky.

"Did what."

"Got themselves arrested."

"What?"

"I just said."

"Who did. The boys?"

"Yes. The boys."

"What happened." His scalp coming alive.

"I just told you."

"What did they get arrested for."

"For?"

"For. Like, what are the charges." He swung to the side of the bed.

"I don't know. It was pot."

"Possession, distribution . . ."

"I don't know. By the way, thanks for having that man-to-man with them when they were down with you, it really paid off."

"Where'd this happen?" Matty got to his feet, promptly banged into the corner of something.

"In town."

"In town. Lake George?"

"Yeah. That's where we live."

"OK. Matty Junior, he has his union attorney, doesn't he?"

"I guess. Isn't that automatic?"

"How about Eddie?"

"How about Eddie what?"

"You're killing me, Lindsay."

"Excuse me?"

He held up his hands in surrender, as if she could see through the phone. "Does Eddie have an attorney."

"I don't know. Wouldn't Matty Junior's guy cover him too?"

"Not at all."

"Well, wouldn't Matty Junior get him one?"

"If he's looking out for him, but . . ."

He felt his way to the balcony, wrestled open the sliding door, the night air racing up his boxers.

"You know what? Just give me the number up there." Then, through gritted teeth, "Thanks so much."


"Lake George Public Safety, Sergeant Towne."

"Hey, how you doing, Sarge. This is Detective Sergeant Matty Clark, NYPD." Then, wincing, "I understand my sons were arrested, Matthew Clark, Edward Clark?"

"You understand right."

"May I talk to the arresting officer?"

"He's out in the field."

"How about his supervisor?"

Towne breathed through his nose, muttered, "Hold on."

Matty assumed that the cops up there were probably talking to the boys right now, and no way would they want him in the mix; if he were in their shoes, and he had been, too many times to count, he wouldn't want himself in the mix either; a kiss-my-ass New York City detective on top of everything else, Matty telling himself: Step lightly or listen to the dial tone.

"This is Sergeant Randolph, how can I help you?"

"Yeah, hey, Sarge, this is Detective Sergeant Matty Clark, NYPD. I understand you're holding my sons?"

"We are."

"Can I ask on what charge?"

"We're still working on that. Basically CP."

"CP . . . CP one? CP five? Ballpark . . ."

There was a long pause, then, "Like I already said, we're working on that."

"I understand," Matty said mildly. "Can you tell me how much weight we're talking about?"

"No, I really can't."

"Do you know if they have representation?"

"No one's called that I know."

"The older one's got a union rep though, correct?"

"I would imagine so." The guy enjoying this.

"Can I speak to them?"

"Well, one's sleeping right now, the other's being fingerprinted, so . . ."

"If it's not too much trouble, can you wake up the sleeping one? I'd really appreciate it."

"How's about I have him call you when he gets up on his own."

Matty stared at the phone in his hand.

"All right, look, I have been doing this for twenty years. I have been on *your* side of this conversation for twenty years. And if I had *your* sons in custody and you were calling *me*?"

"My sons are four and eight," Randolph said.

Breathe.

"Sarge, as a professional courtesy, I'm asking you . . . Don't talk to them without representation. Do the right thing here."

"We always do the right thing."

"No doubt. And, I would truly appreciate, again, as a professional courtesy, speaking to one of my sons. Please."

There was another power pause, then, "You're from New York City?"

"Yes. I'm from New York City."

"Went there about five years ago? Charged me nine dollars for a domestic beer."

"Well, you probably went somewheres near your hotel. Next time you're in town I'd be happy to take you around my neck of the woods, we can knock back all the three-dollar beers you can handle."

Another power pause, then, "Hang on."

Now that he was about to get his wish, Matty felt himself abruptly crashing; he had no real desire to talk to either of his kids.

Still on hold, he glanced down and saw a lone figure dressed in what seemed to be tinfoil, striding north on otherwise deserted Essex Street.

"Hullo?" It was the big one, his voice thick and slightly glottal.

"Hey, it's me. You OK?"

"What do you think?" Like Matty was the idiot.

"What do I think? I think you have a serious problem. I think at the very least you just lost your tin."

"I got woken up to hear this shit?"

"Are you talking to them, Matty? Tell me you're not talking to them."

"I'm not a fool."

"No?"

"What?"

Breathe.

"How much weed they get you with?"

"You're asking me on the phone?"

"You have your attorney?"

"He's coming."

"What about your brother?"

"What about him?"

"What about him?"

"I believe Mom's handling that."

"She thinks you are. Are they talking to him?"

"I don't think so. I don't know."

"Did you whisper in his ear at least? Did you at least tell him to keep his mouth shut?"

"What do you think?"

"What do I *think*? You're a police busted for drugs and you want to know what I *think*?"

"Who are you to talk to me like that. Where do you come off—"

"Matty, Matty, hang on, wait, I'm sorry. I just want you guys to be OK. I just want to be sure you don't make any more stupid—"

"Fuck off."

Over and out.

Matty leaned over the balcony, kept leaning until his feet left the ground, pulled back.

Down on Essex, the tin man was walking back the way he had just come, as if on sentry duty.

He called back his ex-wife.

"Hey. That lady, the court stenographer, she's still living next door to you?"

"What about her?"

"OK. Listen to me. You need to go over there, right now, wake her up and get the name of a lawyer. Eddie's got no representation and I don't trust those fucks for a second."

"It's three-thirty in the morning, Matty. I'm not waking anybody up."

"You woke me up."

"Huh. Now why would I have made that an exception."

"No, I didn't mean, just . . . Please, I don't know anybody up there, otherwise . . . You got to get him someone right away."

"I am not banging on doors now, everybody all of a sudden knows our business."

"Like what, they won't find out otherwise?"

"Forget it."

"Just do it for your son."

"Excuse me?"

"I am not criticizing—"

"Fuck off."

Matty stood there in his boxers, staring glassy at the charcoaled skyline of the financial district until he picked up the flashing lights of the presidential motorcade on its way into the sleeping city via the shutdown Manhattan Bridge; dozens of black SUVs in tight formation, led, bracketed, and followed by NYPD motorcycles and cruisers. Waiting until the entire caravan, silent save for the gargling bikes, had passed beneath his terrace on its way uptown, he finally hauled himself back inside, went to the refrigerator, and opened a beer.

Fucking kids.

**Tristan took the hamsters to P.S. 20,** walked them down the too bright hallway lined with photos of famous graduates from the tore-down building, Jews mostly and mainly from olden-days' movies, and saw them into their classrooms, the smell of white glue making him gag.

Back out on Ridge, he headed for Seward Park, walked into the lobby and up to the security station before remembering that he was carrying, started to back out, then saw that the guards were only doing bookbag inspections and patdowns, which meant that the metal detectors were broken again, which meant you could probably sneak a hand cannon into the building if you knew where to hide it.

The first class was tenth-grade English, which, because he was the oldest student in the room by two years, he hated. But today felt different. Having Little Dap's .22 on him made it feel like today was his birthday, and even though you could say that it wasn't much of a birthday if no one else knew it, for Tristan that was the kick, the secret-identity thing, everybody needing a little secret something in his kit.

As the teacher, Ms. Hatrack, went on about some poem she wrote, he took out his real notebook and knocked out a rhyme.

*Lone ranger*
*Is a stranger*
*Has to be*
*for the danger*

" 'I shall be telling this with a sigh / Somewhere ages and ages hence: / Two roads diverged in a wood, and I— / I took the one less traveled by, / And that has made all the difference.' "

*Cause if people know*
*they blow*
*and out you go*

"Tristan?"

He looked up to see Ms. Hatrack staring at him and pointing to her poem on the blackboard. "What do you think he's talking about?"

"He?"

"The poet. 'Made all the difference.' How so?"

"Difference what."

The teacher took a breath. "He took the road that less people take. What does that mean to you?"

At least three girls around the room were waggling their hands in the air while clutching their opposite shoulders. "Ooo Ooo Ooo . . ."

"What would be the advantage of taking a road less traveled by?"

"No traffic?"

Laughing.

"OK. Fair enough. But then why doesn't everybody take that road?"

"Why?" Tristan clenching his teeth. " 'Cause they stupid." Then, flushing, "I don't know. They get lost?"

"OK, maybe they're afraid of losing their way," Ms. Hatrack said. "How about in our own lives . . ." Looking out on the class but then zeroing in on him again. "Can you ever think of a time when you've taken the road less traveled?"

Everybody looking, their mouths half-open ready to laugh before he even said anything, the stupid bitch not getting it—don't call on me. Don't give them opportunity.

"Tristan? Have you ever—"

"No."


At the end of the class he just left the building and went off to walk the streets. He had no destination, no itinerary, except to hit every one from Pitt to the Bowery, from Houston to Pike, walk down every street, pass every building, go into every store that he'd ever felt bad or afraid or stupid in front of and, with the .22 snug up against his belly, reclaim them all.


The early-to-arrive mourners smoking and drinking coffee on the broad front steps of the Langenshield Center and along news truck–lined Suffolk Street were what Eric expected, mainly in their twenties, mainly white with a sprinkle of everything else; genteel rebels with colored hair, androgynous crops or shaved-headed, high boots, low cleavage, dressed in respectful black, which for some was not that much different from what they would wear on any other day. They were the crest of the wave, young, gifted, privileged, serious for now about making art or launching some kind of maverick free enterprise or just being citizens of the world, and not only reasonably confident in their ability to do so but also in their god-given right to do so. And why not, Eric thought, why not.

The Langenshield had started life as an immigrant dance hall, notorious as the site of a 1910 shoot-out between Jewish and Italian labor racketeers that went on for fifteen minutes and left one fatality, a young seamstress who had been necking in a dark corner with her boyfriend. Since then it had served time as a fraternal lodge, a union hall, a boxing arena, a warehouse, and until recently the largest abandoned building on the Lower East Side.

Now run as a freelance venue, the new owners had left the interior artfully raw: exposed beams, gap-toothed chandeliers, balding velveteen curtains, defunct gaslight armatures protruding from the walls, the walls themselves stripped and peeled here and there to reveal the building's various incarnations, all of it lit from beneath to evoke the atmosphere of a massive archaeological discovery.

. . .

Eric stepped inside with the early arrivers, made a sharp left, and headed up the stairs to the mezzanine, which had been reserved for the media. Picking his way through a jungle of cables and cameras, he made it to the edge of the overhang and looked out over the main floor, as large as a high school auditorium, a sea of folding chairs down there facing both a raised stage and a large, blank portable film screen set up to the side. Four ushers were depositing memorial programs and candles thrust through Dixie cups on every chair. Directly below him, Steven Boulware, wearing a Nehru jacket over a black T-shirt, was talking on his cell as he marched with three others up the center aisle to the rear stairs, to the waiting press, traces of the beating Eric had given him, an amber half-moon spooning his right eye, still visible from the balcony.

As Boulware and the others—a young woman with light green eyes and a tight, expectant mouth and two wary-looking males—levitated into view, they were quickly enveloped in a horseshoe of cameras and thrusting reporters, Boulware looking both sad-eyed and feverishly alert as he waited for calm.

"Can you describe to us what happened that night?"

"Not . . . It all went down so fast. But I will tell you this. Ike . . ." He paused, raised a hand as he collected himself. "No. Let me go at this another way. The mugger? For the fleeting impressionistic second before he fired, I saw the fear in his eyes. And I saw the humanity. As diminished as it might have been, I don't believe he really intended to shoot anybody. He was counting on our fear. He was counting on Ike not being Ike."

"Would you describe Ike Marcus as fearless?"

"No," Boulware said. "He was courageous. He was courageous because he *wasn't* fearless. But he was a lion when it came to standing up for what was right, no matter the consequences."

"Was he lionlike that night?"

"You bet."

"What was he standing up for exactly?" the tall, yarmulke-wearing young reporter who had gone after Eric asked.

"For his friends," Boulware said without hesitation. "And I need to say one more thing about the young man who shot him. He will be caught, have no doubt. But that look in his eye told me that he had sentenced himself the minute he pulled the trigger, and no man has a harsher judge than the face in the mirror."

Eric's fury was equal to his bafflement: why hadn't anybody harassed *this* showboating prick? *He* was the drunk that night, *he* was the one who caused it all; all Eric had done was do the right thing, the smart thing, and now everyone wanted to peel him like a grape.

"And now if I could"—Boulware half-turned to the three people flanking him—"I'd like to introduce you to some of today's . . . I don't want to say eulogizers . . . some of today's . . . celebrants."

Eric marveled at how hungry-eyed Boulware looked, how alive he seemed right now; thinking, I didn't hit him hard enough.


Yolonda and Matty, here to scope out the crowd, sat quietly on the aisle as Billy, Minette, and Nina came into the hall like red-faced royalty and took the chairs directly in front of them. Minette, wearing an anonymously tasteful black dress and a locked-in smile, looked out at the room as if she were worried about everything on earth. Nina, in a dress similar to her mother's, bore an expression of mixed sorrow and defiance as if everyone here had assembled to yell at her. Between them, Billy, clutching his wife's hand, sat like an immobile blur, seeming to materialize and vanish without moving: a radio station on a highway.

Yolonda nudged Matty to make contact but just as he reached for Billy's shoulder, the blank screen set up on the stage abruptly came to life, blooming with a slide show of Ike that jolted his father's spine like a Taser: his son as an infant, at his fifth- or sixth-year birthday party, as a preteen *Clockwork Orange* thug on Halloween, in what looked like a junior high school basketball game setting up a play from the point-guard slot, another of him at the high school level driving to the hoop.

And then the sound track kicked in, Joe Cocker singing "You Are So Beautiful to Me"; Billy responding by shooting to his feet, then just as abruptly sitting back down and careening first into Nina, then Minette, both of them reflexively grabbing a hand to keep him from taking off like an unknotted balloon.

As the dusty chandeliers began to dim, the images sharpened: Ike at a beach party showing off one of those effortless teenage physiques, with this girl, that girl, with Billy, with his mother, with Minette and Nina, getting what appeared to be his first tattoo, the kids in the pews laughing as enthusiastically as they could for that one; Billy now beaming out at them as they gamely tried to embrace the euphemism *celebrate*.

The music shifted to "He's a Rebel," another gut-sock for the guy, but, Matty thought, what song wouldn't be.

The slides appeared to be chronological: Ike in some European city with college-age buddies; at a podium, gesticulating as he read to a crowd similar to this one; shielding his eyes with the back of his hand as he lay on a futon with a long-haired girl, the both of them seemingly just woken up by the camera flash. Again, the crowd whistled their approval.

These pictures seemed easier for Billy to deal with; his son as a man, Matty speculated, probably needing less hovery stuff from him, more just some kind of laid-back supportive admiration or whatever a normal father was supposed to feel for his kid on the other side of adolescence.

The thing about Matty Junior was that he was a bully, and it was so hard to love a bully. But he had always been a not-too-bright, overlarge kid, pressured to play football and basketball because of his size, though utterly without athletic talent, which basically made him an oaf out there. Fairly early on, Matty had gotten into the habit of avoiding all his games. And he was always fighting with Lindsay back then, drinking too much; Matty now remembering one night when the boy came into the living room in his pajamas, couldn't have been older than seven, and Matty, halfway hammered, had blurted, "Jesus, will you look at the size of him," like they had a good shot at winning a blue ribbon at the fair.

And when he was ten, he was sent to the school therapist for some behavior; it was supposed to be in confidence, but every kid in his class knew where he was headed before he even got there, Matty Junior coming home that day laughing hysterically, shouting, "I'm a whack-a-doo! I'm a whack-a-doo! I got sent to the psycho doctor and that's what the kids are calling me!" howling with laughter but not wanting to be touched, Matty anguished but just leaving for work; Lindsay was the one who went into school the next day and gave them hell.

The last slide was of Ike mooning the photographer, and as the accompanying song, Wilson Pickett's "International Playboy," blasted the plaster off the walls, the pews once again broke out in raucous appreciative laughter, and Billy suddenly turned around to Matty as if they'd been talking all along, "These goddamned kids, right?" his voice clotted with gratitude as he squeezed Matty's arm.

The first speaker, a dazed-looking kid Ike's age, stepped to the mike in the expectant silence that followed Boulware's introduction, then just stood there, blinking out at the audience as if there were a flashlight trained on his eyes. Even from the middle of the vast hall Matty could see that his hands were trembling.

"My name is Russell Cafritz?"

"Russell . . ." Billy murmured.

"And, I've known Ike for seven years, since we were freshman roommates at Ohio State." He coughed into his fist and shifted his feet so that his shoes touched each other.

"Go ahead, Russ," one of the audience called out, and he smiled gratefully. "The first . . . Let me tell you what Ike did for me that first week we were living together. I was so homesick, so . . . I cried myself to sleep for longer than I want to admit, until Ike came and sat on my bed one night and told me he felt the same way. He said, 'Here's what I do and maybe you should try it too. Don't call home for a while. You're not alone, you have me, I'm your roommate, just try not calling home so much and don't be embarrassed about how you feel. With any luck we'll both get over it.' And we did. Well, I did at any rate. I think Ike was lying to me. I don't think he was ever homesick a day in his life. But here's the thing . . . I was from Columbus. My parents lived ten blocks from campus. But he never brought that up, and he never told anyone else. He never made me feel more ashamed of myself than

I already was. He was my secret sharer. My secret brother. And he pulled me through."

Minette and Nina sat riveted, but Billy abruptly hunched over, elbows on knees, stared at the floor, and shook his head. Minette palmed his back without looking away from the speaker.

"And in the last year or so, when we reconnected with each other down here and became friends again? It was like dormo redux. Anytime I'd get down about myself, get in a panic about wasting my life, applying for this grant, for that fellowship, working in some stupid restaurant to make ends meet, Ike was always there to pick me up. Say how we were both gonna make it, probably get inducted into the academy together, although I'm not exactly sure what academy he was referring to. He'd say, 'If you fold on me and take the law boards, I will kill you.'"

"Hell, yeah!" someone shouted, and people began laughing, egging each other on.

"He'd say, 'Don't begrudge the gigs that pay the bills, they're going to give you the life experience. Besides, fuck it, man, we have all the time in the world.' . . . All the time in the world." The kid coughing into his fist again to mask his teariness. "Ike made me feel like the world was mine, or if not exactly mine, certainly his, and I had been granted one hell of a backstage pass for it. Ike made me strong. He made me believe in myself, he gave me hope . . . Who on earth will do that for me now? 'Stop calling home for a while.'" Russell's voice finally started to break. "I don't want to call home anymore, Ike . . . I want to call you."

In the vast sniffly rustle that followed the speaker back to his seat, Billy abruptly stood up again, hoarsely whispered to Minette, "I'm sorry, I can't do this." He was halfway up the aisle before she could even open her mouth but then wheeled and came back down, leaning into his daughter this time. "Sweetheart, I'm sorry. I'll see you at home."

Then bolted for good.

"Mom?" Nina's voice floating away from her. "He's not going to hear me talk?"

Minette, suddenly a wet mess, responded by leaning in and touching foreheads.

"*Mom,*" Nina said more sharply, recoiling from the Eskimo tap.

"Just . . ." Minette smiled at her. "Give him a break."

"*Me?* What did *I* do?"

Yolonda leaned forward and touched Minette's shoulder. "Is he OK?"

Minette turned to them while wiping her eyes. "Just needs some room."

"We can probably get someone from the squad to drive him home."

"Just . . ." Smiling tight. "Thanks, thank you."

Yolonda touched Nina's hair, whisper-cooed, "It'll be OK," then leaned back into Matty. "Hope he doesn't step in front of a bus."

Leaning over the balcony between the telephoto cameras, Eric avoided looking at Ike's family, at the two detectives sitting behind them. He gazed instead at the hundreds of mourners, wondering, and how could you not, if it had been he who took that bullet, how many people would have shown up here? Who would even think to put something like this together? And what could they possibly say? It seemed like Ike dead had more of a connection to this world than himself alive.

The second speaker was from the balcony presser, his thin black suit, narrow black tie, and Elvis Costello glasses giving him the appearance of a seventies skatalite.

"Hi, my name is Jeremy Spencer? And I'm an alcoholic."

"Hi, Jeremy!" half the kids in the audience shouted in unison. "We're alcoholics too!" Like the world's biggest in-joke.

"How is that funny," Yolonda side-mouthed. "The kid died drunk."

"The morning after the night that I first met Ike," Jeremy began without notes, "I was just coming off my half of our hangover, sitting there in Kid Dropper's with a soup bowl of coffee, had my first good idea in a week? The minute I put my hands to the keyboard, he snuck up behind me, whispered in my ear, 'Anybody'd write a poem'd suck a dick.'"

People howled, and Jeremy waited for them to quiet down before dipping his head to the mike again.

"No offense to either party."

Another howl, the speaker giving up a half-smile.

"Like Russell said, Ike was always so sure we would make it. To be friends with him was to be a member of an elite club, the future Hall of Famers of America. To be friends with him automatically made you the best unknown writer, actor, singer, accountant, tap dancer, bouncer, social worker, hot-oil wrestler of your generation, and it was just a matter of time before everybody realized it. And, yes, Ike always said, time we had in spades.

"And like Russell too, anytime I felt depressed, started to lose faith in myself, I'd go into whatever bar Ike was working at, he'd take one look at me, slide me a cold one on the house, say, 'Don't even *think* about quitting. You'll regret it for the rest of your life.' . . . He made me feel like we were all blessed with so much talent. Then he'd say, 'But, Jeremy? Talent without drive is a tragedy.'

"He'd say, 'Look at me. Do you think I'd be killing myself doing this shitwork day after day if it wasn't anything more than a means to an end?'

"At which point I would have to say, 'But, Ike, you've only had the job since Monday.'"

Another a big laugh out in the sea, Matty surprising himself by joining in.

He should at least call upstate to find out what was happening in court with the boys, but then was gratefully distracted by a kid from the middle of their row brushing sideways past his knees, trilling, "'Scuse please, 'scuse please," in her eagerness to get to the stage.


"Hi. My name is Fraunces Tavern?"

The crowd laughed and whistled for the dolled-up raven-haired girl onstage in high, fur-seamed Uggs and a low-cut dress the red-orange hue of Fiestaware. "Hi there." Waving to her people. "My perspective on Ike was a little different than everybody else so far? First of all, I'm different. I don't want to be anything? You know, except on Halloween?

"I know Ike because we, how do you say, dated, on and off for about a year, year and a half, not like in-love dating? But Ike? . . . Am I allowed to even *say* this?" she faux-asked Boulware the MC, sitting in the front row. "Ike was like," gazing out, "Ike was like, great in bed."

The cheering was explosive, people jumping up and whoo-hooing.

Minette abruptly turned her head profile to Matty to hide her smile from Nina, who sat there rigid as a stick, Matty smiling in complicity, but he didn't think Minette caught it.

"Ike was like one of those guards in front of Buckingham Palace? You know, totally erect—not, I didn't mean *that*, I'm cleverer than *that*, give me a break, now." She beamed, floating on the laughs.

"I meant he was always ready, you know, clap-on-clap-off ready to, you know . . . I mean, guys being guys, it doesn't sound like that big a deal? But he was always so *present* with me, never, like, you know, close your eyes and go at it. I mean, he had fun, *with* me.

"And for me, it wasn't about, you know," and she cut loose with a chesty yodel, people rolling on the floor. "It was about being with some-one who really, really enjoys you, makes you feel good about yourself. What Ike knew, or just, maybe *intuited* is a better word, was that the secret to being a good lover is that, A, knowing you're not in this alone, and, B, once you get that established? Sometimes you can pleasure the other person most by pleasuring yourself." She paused again, waiting for the first confused laughs to build, then build some more, knowing that people needed to chew on it, then, "That didn't come out right. Oh, c'mon, you know what I'm saying."

The one person not laughing along was Ike's sister, who, cupping her wounded arm, glared at her brother's friends with sheer disgust.

"In my life?" Fraunces Tavern said. "I know, well, I *hope*, that I will be with more, you know, men who I'll maybe have more passion for? But I will count myself very, very lucky if I ever have that much, just, fun with a guy again.

"I miss you, Ikey, and I'll see you in my dreams."

Stepping off to whistles and cheers, red-faced with her coup, she slid past Matty's knees again and collapsed back into her midrow seat, into a flurry of whispers with her friends, her eyes wild in her head.

"You know, if she took better care of her skin?" Yolonda side-mouthed. "She'd be nice-looking."

In the aftermath of Fraunces Tavern's performance piece, the room slid into a coughy silence, everyone waiting a little too long for the next speaker. Checking the program, Matty saw the reason for the delay, then looked to Minette to see how she was going to play it; and when she reluctantly showed the batting order to her daughter, Nina froze, just like Matty thought she would.

*"Now?"* The kid white with horror.

Steven Boulware, rising from his seat on the aisle, looked out over the audience. "Nina Davidson."

"Nina."

"I'm not going up after that!" her voice breaking.

"Do you want another person to go before you?" Minette asked as calmly as she could.

Nina slapped the tears from her cheeks and stared straight ahead.

"Nina Davidson." Boulware raised a finger. "Going once . . ."

To Matty's left, Fraunces Tavern, still flush-faced with victory, alertly and hungrily absorbing every last sigh and coo, every last review, was drawn to the heated whispering in the row ahead of her. And quickly putting together what the drama was all about, what her own unwitting part in it was, she just caved, the sweeping high of a moment ago turning to a painfully transparent self-loathing.

"Nina Davidson, going twice . . ."

"Nina." Minette put her lips to her daughter's ear. "If you don't get up there, you'll regret it the rest of your life."

"Tough shit on me."

Boulware then looked directly at her, smiled with mock reproach. "Oh, Ni-na . . ."

"Mom," she hissed pleadingly, and Minette reluctantly signaled Boulware to back off.

"Well, I guess that leaves me," he said, then headed for the stage.


The notion of sitting there for Boulware's eulogy was intolerable, so Eric trotted down the stairs and out the door, straight into some kind of marching band gathered on the front steps of the Langenshield: a crowd of frizzle-haired kids too young for their beards and handlebar mustaches; sporting Shriner hats, top hats, derbies, jester caps, and burnooses, frogged and beribboned tunics, aviator goggles and Salome veils, with trombones and tubas, slide whistles and sousaphones, cornets and kazoos; too fucking whatever it was, and doing an immediate about-face, he returned to the service, to Boulware, to the exhausting effort of not looking at the cops and Ike's remaining family.

"What to say that hasn't been said," Boulware began. " 'He gave me hope, he made me believe in myself, he made me . . . believe.' 'Where do I go now. Who do I turn to.' " Then, looking out at his audience, "Ah, Jesus, the perils of speaking last."

Nina abruptly stood up and, with her eyes trained on the floor, walked to the short stairs at the side of the stage as calmly as if she were coming up to receive a diploma.

Boulware faltered, not sure what to do. At first he stood his ground, then tentatively backed away from the mike, then offered it to her with a courtly sweep and bow, backstepping afterwards into the shadows like a presenter at the Academy Awards.

Nina stood there, eyes downcast, her multipage speech crushed in her fist.

The silence seemed to go forever, Matty watching Minette's shoulders rise then lock with the breath in her lungs.

The room waited as Nina gathered herself.

"My brother invited me to come down here and hang out with him and see his new place two weeks ago," Nina murmured into the mike. "I said OK . . . But then I really didn't feel like going, so I called him back on the day and said I had a team practice."

Again the room waited for her.

"I'm so sorry . . ." she blurted. Racewalking to the wings, she was back in her seat and staring straight ahead before Boulware could even reclaim the mike.

"Happy?" Wiping her eyes.

Minette just squeezed her daughter's hand, her face, the slice of her face that Matty could see, wet and atremble.

"I have to make a call," he said to Yolonda.

Absorbed in dialing his ex-wife on his way to the front door, Matty almost crashed into Billy, the guy standing with one hand straight-armed against the curved half-wall that separated the rear of the main floor from the vestibule, his head bowed, like he had been listening to the speeches as if they were coming over a staticky tuner.

"Hey," Matty said.

"Hey!" Billy quickly straightening up as if he had been caught at something. "Why didn't you tell me you were going to be here?"

His eyes were flabby with sleeplessness and he looked like he hadn't been near running water all day.

"I didn't know I was supposed to," Matty said.

"That guy ever come in?" Billy said. "What's it, Eric Cash?"

"No."

"No. Why doesn't that surprise me?"

"What did I tell you about that?"

"No, I know."

"You let me worry about that."

"I know. I'm sorry."

"I'm just saying . . ." Matty softened his tone, then jumped as he heard his ex-wife's voice in his hand. He shut off his cell. "You know, I have to say, from everything they've been talking about in there? Your son sounds like a terrific kid."

"Didn't I tell you?" Billy beamed.

"So how are you holding up."

The question seemed to hit Billy like sunshine, provoke in him a rush of euphoria. "Amazingly well actually." And then just as quickly as it came, Matty saw it leave, Billy's features shriveling to the center of his face. "Real good."

"Good," Matty said, staring at the phone in his hand. He wasn't going to call home. He didn't want to know.

"Are you going back in?"

"No," Billy said, then gestured vaguely to the street. "I'm just, you know, waiting on the car." Then, "Could you tell . . ."

"Tell . . ."

"Tell, Nina, tell her what she said . . ."

"Go in and tell her yourself."

"I will," waving Matty on.

• • •

On his way back down the aisle Matty bumped into Mayer Beck, sitting on the aisle in the back row, his skullcap finally in harmony with his surroundings.

"Sad, huh?" Beck said.

"Not now."


"Maybe I should have said, the perils of speaking *next* to last," Boulware started over.

"Jeremy, what was it Ike said to you? 'Anybody'd write a poem would suck a dick'?"

There was a wave of soft laughter in the hall.

"Well, as much as I loved Ike, as much as he was my soul brother, my roomie, my spiritual Siamese twin, I just have got to bust him here. He didn't make that up. He got it from my dad. That's what my dad said to me when I told him I wanted to be an actor: 'Anybody'd write a poem'd suck a dick.' Ike always thought that was a riot, but in my family it was no joke. In my neck of the woods, unless you could play for Joe Pa, throw like Willy Joe, you worked in coal. The first person in the family ever to graduate college goes to his parents and tells them he wants to be an actor? 'Are you mocking us, Steve? Are you spitting in our faces?' It was no joke, Ike . . .

"But I hung in, I hung in.

"Then I gave up.

"Ike came home one day to find me packing. 'Steve, what's up?' I said I was quitting. That I was tired of it. Four years of speech and voice and movement and script analysis and performance technique and improv and Shakespeare and Ibsen and Pinter and Brecht and Chekhov. Four years of workshops and studios and agents and auditions. Four years of rejection. Four years of hearing my dad in my head every time I failed: 'Anybody who'd write a poem . . .' Ike, it's time. I quit.

"And then I braced myself for one of his world-famous pep talks.

"But do you know what he said to me? He said, 'Good. Because you weren't a real actor to begin with.'

"Baiting me, you know? But no. He said a real actor, any kind of real artist, is constitutionally incapable of uttering those two words: I. Quit. 'Real artists don't pack,' he said to me, 'real artists are stuck and all they can do is pray that they get good enough to make it work for them. So, it's good you found out now, Steve. You need any help with your luggage?' "

Boulware took a beat to share a laugh with himself and a few others.

"So pissed off . . .

"Well, I had one last audition the next day. For the second lead in some small movie. The character was supposed to be a drop-dead ladies' man," looking down at himself, waiting for the laughs.

"I go in there, read, the casting director says, 'You're all wrong.'

"Duh.

"I'm halfway out the door, she says, 'Hold on.'

"Then she hands me fresh sides, says, 'But his best friend is a fat guy.'

"My first callback . . .

"I go in the next day, I *am* that fat guy. She says, 'Come back next week and read for the director.'

"My second callback . . ."

He put his hands in his pockets and pondered his shoes for a long beat.

"That's what we were out celebrating that night . . . That's what all the barhopping was about. My *re*-birthday.

"I don't know if I'll get that part or not, but in the end it doesn't make all that much of a difference. Because, Ike?" addressing the ceiling. "I now know this. I *am* an artist. I will not pack, and I will not quit. I'm still here, Ike, and I am staying.

"I would say you'll always be in my memory, buddy, but it's more than that. You will always be at my side."


Eric, unable to believe his own ears, decided he simply misheard the whole thing and so, in the immediate silence that followed Boulware's eulogy, felt nothing.


People were sitting there now in a silence punctuated by scattered gulps and sighs as they pondered a blown-up photo of Ike from his college facebook, Eric Burdon's "Bring It On Home to Me" coming through the speakers. But the slide show was over, the image going nowhere, his never-changing grin up there, the immobility of his languidly curled fingers having none of the life-implying momentum of snaps on a carousel; in fact, it seemed to mock the notion of life after death. No one thought to rise, no one seemed capable until Boulware stood up and, signaling to the back, triggered the surprise entry of that ragtag Sergeant Pepper's Preservation Hall marching band, which began streaming in from all doors, coming down every aisle blasting "St. James Infirmary" like noisy angels of mercy. They made their way down to the front of the room and began to climb the side stairs to the stage from either end, regrouping up there and facing the mourners while still blasting the hell out of that tune, the volume bleaching out the lifelessness on the screen, people so grateful, everybody up, and then like the cherry on top of the sundae, a baby-faced black kid done up like Cab Calloway in a white swallow-tailed tux and white sneakers, his hair straightened and styled with a forelock as big as a horsetail, came slow-whirling down the aisle with an ivory baton in his grip, people screaming out their pleasure, their relief, cameramen scurrying like beetles all over this guy as he slip-slided up the steps to the stage, then down again, up and down those three short steps like the music had him going inside out, until he finally came front and center and arching over backwards began conducting with that elegantly slim stick, the shooters rushing the stage like bobby-soxers now, the mourners outright howling, Ike Marcus going, going, and when that kid started singing, Cab Callowailing like he was at the Cotton Club, gone.

Standing with the rest of the crowd in order not to draw attention to himself, Matty couldn't take his eyes from Minette and Nina, the girl gamely standing and clapping but without any light in her face.

Minette was trying like hell, though, clapping as if she were hit with the spirit, but he could tell she wasn't into it either, was torn between worrying about her kid in here and her husband out there; had already started to make her peace with Ike's death in order to hold her family together, as banged up and scattered and angry as they might be right now.

Because that's what you do, Matty thought, that's what you're supposed to do, you take care of them, you lay down your life for them if
you have to, not spend every night of your aging gerbil on a training-
wheel existence getting wasted and hunting for strange, or waiting on
that sea of malice and mayhem out there to set your chest pocket to
trembling.

"See him?" Yolonda lightly punched Matty's arm. "That kid there?" nodding to an unsmiling and goateed Hispanic teen in baggy jeans and a
hoodie, the only one still seated in his row. "Does he look right to you?"

Matty turned to look, the kid not all that alarming to him but probably worth bracing outside.

"What's wrong?" Yolonda said.

"What do you mean?"

She put a hand to Matty's face, her fingertips coming back wet.

As the band shifted from "St. James Infirmary" to "Midnight in Mos-
cow," Boulware, dragging three of the eulogizers along with him, trotted up onstage and started to dance, a surprisingly elegant minimalist
waggle, a snake-hipped sand shuffle, one hand flat on his belly, the
other up and palm out as if testifying. Fraunces Tavern tried to imitate
him, but still burning from the disaster with Ike's sister, her heart
wasn't in it. Nor were Russell and Jeremy, looking confused and sheepish as they edged as close to the wings as possible.

Calloway Junior produced a second baton from the inside pocket of
his tux and presented it to Boulware, who, after co-conducting for a
minute, turned to the seats, to the cameras, bawled, "Don't forget your
candles!," which was the cue for the band to stream back down both
sides of the stage and up the aisles to daylight, offering people a way out.

As soon as they hit the street, Yolonda was on him.

"Hey, come here for a second?" touching the elbow of the goateed
kid's sweatshirt and casually steering him away from the crowd.

"What for?" as if he didn't already know. He had a gold hoop piercing the outside corner of his left eyebrow that made him rear back to keep that eye open equal to the other and gave him a look of chronically pugnacious surprise.

"What's your name?"

"Hector Maldonado. What's yours."

"Detective," she said. "And the dead guy, how about his name?"

"Why you asking me?"

"I'm just asking."

"*Why* you asking," crossing his arms over his chest.

Yolonda just waited.

"I don't know his got damn name. I'm here doing a homework for media study, and you *know* why you bracing me."

"Yeah? Why am I bracing you?"

"'Cause *you* can't find the dude that did him, and I'm a *plátano* from the PJs. And comin' from a Rican like you? *Fuck* that shit."

"You got your homework on you?" Yolonda asked mildly.

"Got my notes." Maldonado jerked a fistful of loose-leaf paper out of his front pants pocket and held it up for her to read the halfhearted scrawl.

DON'T TAKE THE LAW BOARD CALL HOME BELIEVE
IN ME IKE WORLD WE JUST LIVE IN IT

"Yeah, *Ike* . . . see?"

"What's your name again?"

"I *said*. Hector Maldonado. You should write it down."

"You got a mouth on you, you know that?"

"You got a mouth on you too!"

"How about I take you in right now, we talk about this in the squad room."

"Yeah, you do that! And I'll go right to them news-truck niggers, tell them why you *really* come up on me like this. That would make a mother*fuck* of a media study, huh?"

"Get out of here."

"*Hah.*" Maldonado loped off in triumph, Yolonda shrugging the whole thing off.

• • •

Passing on joining the procession heading to the murder spot six blocks away, Matty lingered on the sidewalk in front of the Langenshield, waiting for Yolonda but fixed on Minette, pacing as she talked to her husband on the cell, one hand clapped over her ear to shut out the din. Nina was at her elbow and took the phone from her mother to talk to Billy too, Matty wondering if he would tell her that he had stayed after all, at least long enough to hear what she had said up there.

Well, whatever Billy was telling her seemed to be doing the trick, Matty studying Minette studying her daughter as the kid's features started to soften.

Yolonda joined the three of them a moment later and looked to Matty, that kid in the hoodie a bust.

"Oh my God, you were so brave up there," Yolonda's voice climbing with tenderness as she enfolded Nina in her arms.

"Thank you," the kid hugging herself.

"Your husband get home?" Yolonda asked Minette.

"Either there or on his way," Minette said. "He just wasn't ready for this."

"You going to the thing?" Yolonda tilted her chin towards the tail of the procession.

"I'll be there." Matty looking at her: Don't break my balls.

"OK then."

All three watched Yolonda walk off, the music growing fainter as the procession, nearly a city block long, hooked a left at the first intersection.

"So," Matty said, "you heading home?"

"In a bit," Minette said. "Give him some room."

"Can I walk around a little?" Nina murmured to her mother.

Minette reflexively looked to Matty for the answer, Matty shrugging, why not.

"Don't go too far, and keep your phone on," Minette said as if Nina had already pulled something, "and don't start screening your calls."

Out on the street the band, led by Boulware and Cab Calloway, seemed to have lost a lot of its magic, the hundred and fifty or so mourners following them as they played "Old Ship of Zion," looking a little embarrassed now, a little shanghaied, the afternoon sky too light for their stubby cupped candles.

Unable to release himself from his outrage at Boulware, Eric paralleled the procession from across the street, riding the herd of crouched cameramen as they shot the show making its way down Suffolk.

But as the band unexpectedly swung into a wild, swirling klezmer tune, Boulware and the black kid began doing slow, graceful synchronized Tevye whirls as smoothly as if they had rehearsed the moves all last night, and the shooters began to cross over and go into an encircling whir-click tarantella of their own, leaving Eric exposed under the yellow and red metal awning of a bodega.


After wandering around the neighborhood all morning, Tristan was now squatting on his haunches beneath the side window of a pizzeria down the street from the Langenshield, his notebook propped open on his burning thighs. He thought he'd have laid down a lot more stuff by now, but that cornball marching band hanging out on the steps of that church up the block had been distracting. And when they started to play as they headed inside, turning the building into a boom box, then came back out *still* playing, there was nothing for him to do but wait until the parade was far enough away that he could hear his own beats again.

But as soon as he got something going, he became aware of a girl, his age about, standing a few feet away looking into the store window next to the pizzeria. Normally he just looked right through white kids, probably pretty much like they just looked right through him, but this one had her arm all bandaged up; either stitches or a tattoo under the wrapping was his guess.

Glancing at what he had written, he imagined he was the girl reading it.

*Droppin jewels front of fools*
*Every word like a school*
*standin high,*
*do or die,*

*you cant never meet my eye,*
*cause you know*
*that Ill blow*
*and your peoples gonna cry.*

When he looked up again, she was gone.

As the procession continued south by southwest, Yolonda slalomed the line, the sidewalks, looking for a wrong face, but it was hopeless, just too many of the neighborhood lifers drawn to the parade, the cameras, the whole shooting match; hopeless.

At each intersection, sawhorse barricades steered them from Suffolk to Stanton to Norfolk to Delancey to Eldridge.

It took about half an hour for everyone to make their way from the Langenshield to 27 Eldridge, where waiting for them in the closed-off block between Delancey and Rivington were a parked sanitation truck, a fire truck, and a life-size straw-stuffed effigy of Ike Marcus lying on a forty-five-degree-angled wooden pallet like a homemade rocket positioned for takeoff. The face was painted papier-mâché.

The musicians and mourners wended their way past the city rigs, the firemen and garbagemen impassively leaning against the cabs, then began to coil around the effigy until they had created a ring of people six candles deep, the mostly ethnic locals, many with small children straddling their necks, making up an irregular seventh ring, the traffic cops just now starting to catch up once the outer blockades were lifted an even more amorphous eighth.

And as they all stood there pondering Ike's likeness, the band continued to mix in klezmer with the jazz and spirituals—"Precious Memories," then "Kadsheynu," "Oh Happy Day," then "Yossel, Yossel"—Boulware and whoever still had it in them singing and dancing, the news shooters getting in between paper Ike and the first ring of his mourners, dropping to the ground like snipers to get up in their faces.

Backstepping to the sidewalk for some air, Yolonda saw Lugo and Daley both smoking, Daley standing ankle-deep in whatever was left of the shrine.

"Wild, huh?" Lugo flicked his butt.

"Oh my God," Yolonda said, "they're so creative, these kids, you know?"

"I couldn't make a puppet if my life depended on it," Daley said.

"So how you guys doing?" Yolonda asked. "You shaking the tree for us?"

"Which one?" Lugo said. "It's fucking Sherwood Forest out there."

An older Hispanic woman carrying groceries as she tried to muscle her way through the crowd and enter 27 Eldridge gave Yolonda and Quality of Life a withering once-over, muttered, "*Now* the cops are here," then slipped into the building.


Seated with Minette on the front steps of the now deserted Langenshield, Matty went through the motions of rattling off a cursory progress report, omitting, of course, the continuing press gag, the scuttled seventh-day recanvass, and the unreturned phone calls.

"So are you getting anywhere or not?" she said.

"Well, there's still a lot of stuff to be done. On a homicide there's always a lot of stuff to be done." Then, sick to death of his own boilerplate mantra, "You know I have to tell you, I was sitting there, you're very good with them, you know?"

"With who."

"Your family. I was sitting—"

"You think?"

With you it would've been different, was what he thought.

"Good with my family." Minette started tearing up. "Yesterday Billy asked me where Ike was. He couldn't remember what we did with the body. *We.* That his mother had him cremated and took the ashes."

"That's . . ." He didn't know how to finish.

"Half the time he can't move a muscle, the other half he's jumping out of his skin. I went out last night, I come back I can hear the music while I'm still three floors down in the elevator. I walk in, he's in the living room blasting some old R 'n' B, covered in sweat, dancing by himself. I'm, 'Billy, what are you doing?' He says, 'I'm watching Ike dance.' " Wiping her eyes. "My daughter, did you see her arm?"

"The sandwich accident."

"The sandwich accident," she muttered, offering no details.

"I'm sorry."

"Do you have kids?"

"Two." Matty sank. "Boys."

"And they're good?"

He said, "Yeah," but Minette read the tell, searched his eyes for what he wasn't saying.

Three bosses, a division captain and two inspectors, fresh from monitoring the street procession, passed by, in full dress to show their solidarity with the family and the mourners. But when Matty half saluted in greeting, they responded with dead-eyed stares, as if this whole dog and pony show out here, as far as they were concerned, had been his idea.

"Is there a problem?" she asked as soon as they passed.

"Uniforms too tight," Matty said, and let it go at that.


The sky above Eldridge Street had morphed from robin's-egg blue to a huskier late-afternoon shade, and Boulware was still drawing most of the attention; dancing like Zorba, like a dervish, like some purple-robed gospel blaster in a storefront church, and good, Eric had to admit, maybe good enough, but who the hell knew these things.

And as they had onstage at the Langenshield, some tried to keep up with him but he was untouchable; Eric not even sure the guy was aware that his Song of Myself was being danced on someone's grave.

It seemed like the music would go on forever, but with the rush hour coming on fast, one of the ranking cops on the scene worked his way up into the front ring, said something to Cab Calloway, and a moment later Boulware was passed a baton, one end wrapped in flaming batten. And as the band played "Prayer for a Broken World," he first ceremoniously raised the light to whatever gods were supposed to be peering down, then lit the effigy; Ike instantly roaring up a fierce yellow-blue, as if finally expressing his outrage at what had befallen him, and despite all the calculated showboating of the afternoon, Eric was left openmouthed, a hand on his heart as this man-boy-golem was enveloped in burly rolls of flame that for a long moment seemed to accentuate the human outline before they finally began to destroy it.

And when the rising waves of heat slowly lifted one stuffed arm in its entirety as if in farewell, Eric found himself paralyzed at the sight of Billy Marcus breaking through from the back of the crowd and running towards his son as if to put out the flames that were killing him, then, like a dog chasing a bumblebee, suddenly reversing himself, nearly knocking over an elderly woman who had just unlocked the front door of her walk-up in order to rush past her into the darkness of the vestibule.

And through it all the locals continued to quietly watch: from the back of the crowd, from windows, from the top of stoops, most with that shy off-balance smile of bemusement, only one woman standing on her fire escape covering her mouth with both hands, eyes wide as if she had just gotten the news.


*Ike was my brother. I wanted to be* him. *I still do.*

That's all she wanted to say. Nina disgusted with herself, cracking up in front of his fruit-loop friends like that, but still, so sorry.

"*Hey, no problem,*" Ike had said to her, "*we'll just hook up next week . . .*"

Fighting off the desire to just lie down on the sidewalk and close her eyes, she wandered into She'll Be Apples, a shop on Ludlow Street so small that there was hardly room in it for the two women working there and herself, the lone customer. Only one pipe-rack stand of clothes for sale, a few hats hanging from pegs high up on the exposed-brick wall, and a scatter of amberish jewelry on a few side tables that to her eyes looked like something she could find in her grandmother's dresser. She was fascinated by the meagerness of the stock, how someone could just toss a few articles around a room so tiny and call it a store. The women were big too, six-footers speaking to each other with an English accent that wasn't exactly an English accent. She began to sift through the clothes on the pipe rack, a seemingly random collection of silk-screened wifebeaters, polyester men's shirts with dagger collars, hippie peasant blouses, and denim micro-skirts, until she came to an itchy-looking red-brown herringbone riding jacket, nothing interesting about it except that it fit, but when, in the absence of mirrors, she half twisted to check the back, she was startled to see a titanic hole cut out from the nape to the tailbone, and spanning both shoulder blades, a perfect circle of nothing, a whimsy of the designer, but the unexpectedness of it shook Nina to the core, almost scared her, and it became the most excitingly beautiful thing she'd ever seen; making this shop, this street, this neighborhood, the most exotic land; and when one of the six-foot-tall women said, "Oh, darlin', it's you," in her English-not-English accent, Nina started to cry.

On Eldridge, as the flames finally died out, just a few wisps of straw doing lazy dips and rolls before settling into the street, the Community Affairs officer finally nodded to his uniforms: Herd 'em out.

But no one seemed willing to leave the scene, the musicians slowly removing their mouthpieces, the mourners hugging and talking, Cab Calloway circulating to hand out his business card.

The firemen started to move into position, sauntering over to the smoldering pyre.

"Folks." The Community Affairs officer dipping into clusters of people now, gently touching shoulders here and there, as if to tell the guests that dinner was being served.

And as the crowd continued to linger, to ignore the cops, the firemen, to ignore the city itself hammering its horns on the choked side streets, the Community Affairs officer resorted to a PA speaker: "People, all due respect. It's time to take this somewheres else."

The firemen allowed some water to pulse through their hose, splash noisily at their feet.

Slipping their work gloves on, the garbagemen began lurching upright from the side of the truck.

But still, hardly anyone left.

As the last of the cameras were being stowed back into the satellite trucks and as the water pressure in the firehouse increased, Boulware, a little wild-eyed now, began to corner his friends and make hasty plans to reconvene at a bar, then announced it out loud, "Going to Cry!" and Eric, watching it all from a stoop, at last felt something akin to compassion for the guy. Over the next few months it would probably be easier for him to get laid around here, he'd take a few more drinks on the house, maybe land a new not-very-good agent, but nothing of consequence would really change and he would spend year after year chasing that flaming straw as it took off into the blue with all his big plans. Basically, what Boulware could look forward to, Eric knew, was a long-term bout of depression and a steadily mounting sense of loss, not for his dead friend here but for this afternoon, the last best day of his life.

"That kid," Minette said, shaking her head.

"Which."

"Ike's friend, the, the master of ceremonies? I mean, Ike wasn't exactly humble himself, but . . ."

They were still on the steps of the Langenshield, waiting for Nina.

"There's this thing we do on a job sometimes," he said, staring at her hands. "When we're interviewing somebody who claims to be a witness but we think was maybe a little more . . . involved than that? It's called an *I* test. You sit them down and take their statement, written, dictated, whatever, and when you're finished, you count up and divide the pronouns. If a girl gets shot and the boyfriend's story consists of sixteen *I*s and *my*s, but only three *her*s and *she*s?—he just flunked."

Minette tracked his gaze to her wedding ring, then slipped that hand beneath her thigh.

"What are you saying, you think he was involved?"

"No, not at all." Matty blushed. "I'm just observing—"

"Let me ask you," she cut him off. "That first day I was down at the hotel trying to find Billy . . ."

"Yeah?"

"Were you ever in that room?"

"Yeah, briefly."

"Was Elena there?"

"I believe so."

"What were they like up there, him and Elena."

"How do you mean?"

She just looked at him.

"They were in pretty bad shape."

She continued to stare at him, but no way would he admit to reading her mind.

Then she seemed to understand that, let it go.

"How can you top that," she said more to herself, Matty about to say something in return when she abruptly turned towards him and leaned forward, Matty thinking, to kiss him, but it was the sight of her daughter, coming up from behind.

"You all right?" Minette's voice peppy with anxiety.

"I used the credit card," the kid said.

"For . . ."

"This." Showing them the small, yellowing campaign button: I LIKE IKE. "It was thirty dollars but the guy gave me another one for free. He said it was a variation on a theme."

Then she showed them the second: bigger and whiter, also saying I LIKE IKE, but with a portrait of Tina Turner beneath.

Tristan was still down the street from the Langenshield when the arm-bandaged girl came back and met up with her mother and a cop. Everybody talked for a minute, the cop went into his jacket to give them both his card, then walked off by himself, the two others walking off together in the opposite direction a minute later.

He half rose from his crouch beneath the pizzeria window to adjust the .22 digging into the small of his back, then dropped into his squat again and took a last look at what he'd written that afternoon, liking it pretty much. He started to get up again, this time to go home, then had a last-minute burst, whispering it to himself as he wrote.

*Sometime I regret,*
*but you can bet*
*im a vet,*
*and I aint*
*buckled yet*

Matty watched Minette and her daughter, deep in conversation, walk north towards Houston. From behind, in their nearly identical slim black dresses, they could pass for sisters, both women tall with long-bow shoulders like competitive swimmers. He stared after them until they were swallowed by the traffic, then turned south and headed back towards the Eighth.

"Hello," into his cell.

"So how'd it go?" Yolonda asked.

"How'd what go."

"You fuck her yet?"

Matty hung up.

A block later he walked by Billy sitting on a stoop so motionlessly that Matty was three tenements past the guy before his presence registered.

"What are you doing here," Matty said.

Billy slowly raised his eyes, then got to his feet. He moved in so close that Matty had to step back.

"Look," he said quietly, his fingertips delicately dancing on Matty's lapels. "How can I help." His mouth started to crumple. "All I want, all I need, is to help."

A squad car came towards them on the narrow side street. A moment later Matty found himself looking into the stony faces of Upshaw and Langolier in the backseat as it almost came to a stop, then, point made, picked up speed.

Matty turned back to Billy, to his searching eyes. "You want to help?"

Waiting until the squad car turned the corner, he went into his wallet for Mayer Beck's card, Damned if I don't . . .

"You call this guy. And here's what I want you to say . . ."


The same thing happened that night: Eric spelled one of the other managers in order to not be alone with his thoughts, then, as soon as the evening crush began, promptly retreated to the cellar. But as he came down the last of the stairs to the beaten-earth floor, he first heard then saw Bree, the Irish-eyed waitress, standing with her back to him dead center in the low-ceilinged room, her head lowered almost chin to chest as if praying. Then, still with her back to him, she sniffed mightily, her shoulders rising with the effort, so, not praying . . .

He didn't want to scare her, but this place was his and he needed it.

He scuffed the stairs, coughed, making her wheel startle-eyed, the coke now clutched in her carefully closed palm.

"Hi," she breathed.

"You sound a little stuffy, you OK?"

"I get this sinusitis."

"You have sinusitis so you come down to a damp cellar?"

"It's a funny kind of sinusitis."

"Oh yeah? Funny how?"

She looked miserable.

"You know, I come all the way down here, it's bad enough I catch one of my staff blowing up, but then she doesn't even offer me a bump?"

"Oh!" she almost shouted, opening her hand and shoving the whole thing towards his face.

The cellar was so low-ceilinged that they nearly had to walk hunched over, all four corners of the woozy room lost to darkness.

"Watch your step." Eric led the way with one of the extension-corded floodlights lying about the floor.

"What do you keep down here, bodies?" Her voice loose and burbly off the blow.

"Mushrooms." He trained the light on the northeast corner of the room, the beam briefly reflecting off the eye of something racing out of there.

"Eeek, a mouse," she said.

"Check it out." Stepping closer to the corner, he high-beamed one of the ancient fireplaces.

"Looks like a barbecue pit."

"It's a hearth. Every corner of the room down here has one, which means people were living down here, huddling around these things. I'm guessing 1880s, '90s."

"For real?" She offered him another line.

"But this one right here"—Eric bowed his head to the coated white paper in her palm, putting his hand beneath hers as if to steady it—"is famous. There's a Jacob Riis photo of a man in a coal cellar seated in front of one of these things, a hunk of bread in his lap, the guy is looking at the camera, and between the beard and the dirt all you can make out are his eyes, guys living one step up from an animal." Eric's jaw was juddering and he tasted the acrid drip down the back of his throat.

"But I'm looking, and I know this photo well, so I'm like, hey, this is just like that Riis picture, and then I see this."

He put the light to a thick, blackened beam inches above their heads.

"Look." He ran his fingers over the writing scratched into the wood, two words, read them out loud for her. "*Gedenken mir.* 'Remember me.' "

"Is that Dutch?"

"Yiddish."

"How do you know Yiddish?"

"I googled it. Anyways, so, just to scratch the itch? I went home and booted up the Riis photos on the Eighty-eight Forsyth House website. And it's got, you can see that this writing here is in the shot, but you can't make out what it says, but it's this. And this is the spot, right here. And now I know what that squiggle, that hand, was trying to tell us. It's like, from that whole, millions coming over, here's this one infinitesimal voice that says, 'I am, I was,' says, 'Remember me,' and it just makes me want to cry."

And then he did, a little.

"Oh." She almost touched his cheek. "Well, don't feel too bad. The guy's in a famous photo, right? So he got *some*thing out of it, you know? I mean, it could've been worse."

"There's that," he conceded, wiping his eyes. "So . . ." Wanting just a tiny bump more, he nodded to the coke. "How's it going?"

"You mean this?" She blushed. "No, no, I'm not, this is just to get me through the double. This is situational."

"No, I meant how's it going up there, the job."

"That? That's situational too."

Eric helped himself to a gum rub to get through the next question. "OK. So. What do you do. Really." Then, "Wait, no. Let me guess. A Riverdancer."

She looked crushed.

"What? No."

"I told you, right? Or were you being sarcastic."

"Oh, Jesus, no. I'm, oh, Christ, what an asshole."

But then she broke character, snorted at his flushed face. "I'm at NYU."

"Oh, thank God." Hands crossed over his heart.

"I *knew* you weren't listening." Helping herself now.

"I had, have, a lot on my mind."

"I heard."

"What did you hear?"

"You were there when it happened?"

"Oh yeah?" Bracing for more shit.

"I saw you at the memorial earlier," she said. "Why weren't you sitting with everybody else?"

"Why?" Eric stalled then, saw Ike's father running towards his flaming son. He jerked as if poked in the ribs.

"It's complicated," he said, then, "You knew him?"

"The guy? No. But the bandleader? In the white tux? Is a friend from school."

"A friend?" He couldn't be balder.

"Yeah." Smiling at him.

"What kind of friend?"

"Who wants to know?"

He just wanted to kiss her. Maybe one more bump, close his eyes . . .

But then Billy Marcus was coming again, coming like a train, and Eric started babbling.

"I had this thought at the service today, like there's one thing, for all their differences, that the audience, and the guys who did the killing, have in common . . . And, it's narcissism. The difference being, and I'm making an assumption here I realize, that the shooters are narcissistic? But their self-centeredness has no real center. They're probably pretty much numb to themselves and everybody else, you know, except for their gut needs and, like, impulse reactions to certain situations. But the, the, others? *Us?* Also narcissistic, but there's a center to our self-centeredness, a little *too* much center and not particularly attractive in most cases but . . ." Pirouetting with tension. "I wish I could tell that to somebody."

"You just did," she said.

"What."

"What." Aping him, Eric laughing; so weird.

And then he just cupped her face in his hands and she let him, she let him.

. . .

"OK," Billy said, slapping his pockets for his statement. "OK."

Mayer Beck, steno pad in hand, waited.

Marcus had called him thirty minutes ago, pulling him out of bed with his girlfriend, who was going back to Ghana in three hours for her sister's wedding. There was a good chance she might not be able to get her student visa renewed, that he'd never see her again, but what could you do.

"OK," Billy said, having found his notes. "The police in this city, from what I understand, are as good as the job gets." He spoke with his eyes closed, from memory. "But they got turned around on this one with some bad but plausible eyewitness testimony, and time was of the essence."

"OK." Beck scribbling.

"This individual, this guy Eric Cash, I understand he's been through an awful ordeal, but my son . . ." Billy paused. Beck looked up.

"It's like, did Eric Cash have a rough day? No doubt. No doubt . . ."

"I hear you," Beck murmured.

"*Do* you now," Billy snapped. Beck could hear the porcelain squeak of his clenched teeth.

"I wasn't being insincere," Beck said calmly.

Behind them, on East Broadway, a van with Ohio plates pulled up, and a heavily tattooed Irish thrash-metal band began carting their equipment into the bar standing next to the old *Jewish Daily Forward* building. Beck knew the band, Potéen, knew the bar; would have offered to talk in there so he could loosen this guy up with a shot of something, but even the jukebox was deafening.

"It's like . . ." Billy closed his eyes again. "Like, OK, Eric, take a moment to smooth your feathers, then . . ."

Beck started writing again, Billy watching him work.

"Then . . ." Mayer prodded carefully.

"I mean, this motherfucking . . ."

Billy abruptly stalked off a few feet and began muttering, his balled fists like bloodless clubs.

At first Beck strained to pick up the specifics of the rant but quickly gave up. He knew what was happening: Matty Clark had sent this guy over as his media beard, no doubt, and now the poor bastard was torn between the carefully worded script he'd been spoon-fed and the explosive bile that kept bubbling to the surface.

Well, he could either help Matty here or he could secure page three.

Fucking his girlfriend for the last time in this life was no longer an option.

"Mr. Marcus," Beck said, "just speak your heart."

As the last rays of day dropped down below the bridges, Matty, standing on his terrace, finally got it up to make the call.

"So how'd it go," he asked, "they split them up?"

"Yeah," his ex said. "I spent all day bouncing from court to court like a pinball."

"And?"

"Eddie was ROR'd to me in Family, Matty Junior's still locked up."

"Charged with?"

"CPM?"

"CPM what degree?"

"First. Man, that judge really ripped him a new one too. Talking about disgracing his badge, betraying public trust, despicable this, reprehensible that."

"Good. Glad to hear it. What's his bail?"

"Fifty thousand."

"*Fifty?*"

"I'm trying to raise the ten percent now, put up the house as security."

"Why are *you* raising it? Where's *his* money, big fucking kingpin."

"I don't imagine you'd consider throwing a little into the pot, would you?"

"You got to be high."

"Just asking."

"Just answering."

"All right then."

Matty was about to hang up, then hung up. Called back right away.

"Hey, it's me."

"What."

"Is the Other One there?"

"In his room."

"Could I talk to him please?"

Matty stood there rehearsing his lines, hearing the footsteps coming to the phone.

"Hullo?"

"Hey, how you doing."

"OK."

"Let me ask, when do you turn sixteen?"

"When's my *birth*day?"

"Just . . . I'm trying to help you here."

"How do you not know my birthday?"

"Eddie, I've been humping for twenty-four hours straight on something," Matty scrambled. "I can't think straight, OK?"

"December twenty-eighth, Jesus."

"And you'll be sixteen then?"

"Yeah, Dad," Eddie honking like a goose. "I'll be sixteen."

"OK. Did you get a visitor today?"

"A what?"

"One of your brother's friends, somebody from the job."

"Cyril came by."

"All right, this Cyril, what did he say. What did he tell you to do."

"I don't know."

"Did he tell you to say that the weed was yours and your brother didn't even know it was in the car? Did he tell you that if the DA knows up front that that's what you'll say in front of a grand jury, there's no way he's going to waste his time trying to prosecute your brother?"

"I don't know."

"Did he tell you that if you *didn't* do that, your brother would lose his tin, maybe go to jail?"

"He *would*."

"And that since you're only fifteen, your slate gets wiped clean in December no matter?"

"It does, so why not?"

"Did he *also* happen to mention that you'll most likely draw three years' probation, mess up once, in you go?"

"So?" A little wavering. "I won't mess up then."

"Meaning what, you won't sell weed or you won't get caught?"

Another heartbeat of hesitation, then, "Won't sell weed. Jesus, what do you think?"

"Eddie, I know what you're doing, and it's sort of noble of you, but I hate the idea of him just walking on this and leaving you with a three-year sword over your head."

"So? So what?" the kid's voice going high-low on the oscilloscope again. "You don't think I can make it?"

"Honestly?" Matty suddenly so tired. "I have no idea if you can or can't."

"Thanks a lot, Dad."

"It says more about me than you. But that's not the point. It's . . . you're being used."

"No, I'm not! I'm keeping my brother out of *jail*. And by the way?" Eddie nearly shouting now. "*Your* birthday is May *sixth*."


It was four hours since they first kissed in the cellar, and even though the restaurant was packed all night long, they kept going back down every half hour, hour or so, for another bump followed by frantic tongues and groping, each time pushing it a little further than the time before. They never spent more than a minute per trip, but Eric always came back up to walk across the crowded room with a hard-on like an Indian club.

On the second trip down she just flat-palmed the bulge in his pants.

Next time it was his turn, taking her nipple in his mouth, one long, slow suck, the thing popping up rubbery and going back in her shirt twice as big as it was when pulled out; looked like a top hat.

The time after that she got a hand down inside the front of his jeans, ice-white fingers stroking his balls.

Time after that, his hand went down hers, down to the curls, her breath in the hollow of his throat.

And each time they came back up the stairs, studiously ignoring each other, the room seemed a little more agitated than before; but he was on tonight, Eric; crisp, speed-reading people like a radar gun; you to the bar, you go home, you right this way, embracing the regulars, giving passing waiters and busboys two-second shoulder squeezes, back rubs, everybody happy? He sure was.

The last time they had gone down there, maybe forty-five minutes ago, she unzipped him, pulled him out, bent over, and put it in her mouth.

And now it was eleven o'clock, the next time down his turn to jack up the stakes, Eric drunk on the possibilities, on hope. He didn't understand anymore why he was being so obstinate about cooperating with the cops. So fearful. Just go in tomorrow first thing and do the right thing. Do it and be done with it. Then write, act, take yoga, take five, whatever, live.

The front door was momentarily clear to the street, Eric seeing the bouncer, Clarence, out there hitting on a tall, redheaded chain-smoker, and then that *Post* reporter Beck curved into the frame, Eric even having a half smile of recognition ready for this foot-dragging vulture.

"Hey, bar or a table," reaching for a Ten Commandment–sized menu.

"Actually, can I talk to you for a minute?" Beck smiled apologetically.

"About?" Eric already sinking.

He heard the words: interview, father, cowardly, unconscionable, unspeakable.

"And I think it would only be fair to give you a chance to tell your side of it before this goes to bed, you know what I mean?"

Eric stood there.

And when he could finally turn to the room, Bree was uncorking a bottle of red at the nearest deuce, looking at him alight with tension, mouthing over the heads of her customers, Shall we?


On tiny, otherwise deserted Mangin Street, Lugo and Daley walked towards the BMW with South Carolina plates parked in the shadows directly beneath the Williamsburg Bridge, each overhead passing vehicle announcing itself with a rattling rumble.

The driver, a black man in a button-down blue shirt, rolled down his window before they got there, regarded Lugo and his flashlight with a sober forbearance, a here-we-go-again tightness around the corners of his mouth. Slowly crossing her arms over her chest, the girl in the passenger seat leaned back and murmured to him, "Didn't I tell you?"

Lugo looked from one occupant to the other, then smiled. "Did I just help somebody win a bet?"

**Eric showed up for work** an hour late the next morning, his eyes as cracked as fried marbles.

Page three:

Did Eric Cash have a rough day? Maybe, but you know who had a really rough day? My son. My son Ike had the day to end all days. You were wronged, Eric, no doubt. So you take a little time to smooth your feathers, then step up. Otherwise it's cowardly, it's unconscionable, it's unspeakable.

He would have gone in to them today. Fired the lawyer and stepped to the plate. Last night that girl, that Irish-eyed girl, the possibility of her, had got him past his own monumental NO, had got him past his terror of that windowless room, had got him past his own desperate and desolate resolve to flee, but it was as if they had been waiting for this, waiting for his heart to reopen, some cosmic cocksucker hiding in the bushes, whispering, Now.

Smash me flat. Again. So, no. Raise me up to slam me down. So, no. No.

People looking at him . . .

Before this morning, the only one besides the cops and his lawyer who knew the full story was Harry Steele. And when he saw today's paper, his boss was sympathetic, although Eric felt that there was something sinister in his commiseration; something on the layaway plan.

He looked across the café to the newspaper dowels; his humilation hanging there like hanks of hair. Shaving the tip pool just wasn't cutting it. He had nine thousand to his name, five thousand of which was the start money on that never-to-be-finished bullshit screenplay, and nothing else, no marketable talent, nothing in his kit but running a dining room and the notion of doing that in upstate New York, or anywhere else . . .

He thought of his parents' house: white chenille bedspreads and floral wallpaper; of Binghamton: fields of slush, gray highways to nowhere.

There was a rumor that Steele was sniffing around Harlem for a new spot. But they had cops uptown too. They read papers uptown too.

The thing to do was make as much money in as short a time as possible and go.

People looking at him.

Fuck you all.

I am gone.


Matty walked into the squad room at noon to see Berkowitz, the deputy inspector, sitting on the visitor's side of his desk, his boiled youthful face staring calmly out the window.

Well, even if Billy had followed the script perfectly yesterday, what the hell did he expect?

"Boss."

"Hey." Berkowitz rose, the John Jay ring on his offered hand catching the light. "Busy?"

"Couple of break-ins around Henry, a shooting at Cahan, Scout troop short a child . . ."

"Khrushchev's due at Idlewild."

"There you go." Matty took his seat behind the desk, waited for Hammertime.

"May I?" Berkowitz gestured for Matty's *Post*, then flipped it to the back sports page: Bosox 6, Yanks 5.

"This new guy, Big Papi, guy has what, five walk-off home runs this year? Huge as he is, can you imagine what a monster he'd be if he played in New York? With the media machine we have?"

And there it was: Matty telling himself to play it smart by playing dumb.

Berkowitz first turned to the photos of the memorial pyre on page 2, then turned to that buck-wild, utterly out-of-control Billy Marcus interview on page 3, folded and flopped it on the blotter, the header facing Matty.

Fucking Mayer.

"What did you not understand about the press gag?"

"Do you see my name anywhere in that?" Matty started working it. "Or with the other, do you think the dead kid's friends came to me for permission on that memorial service? And this fucking reporter Beck has weaseled his way into the father's head since day one. What can I do? I say to the guy, please don't talk to anybody, especially that snake, but you know what? He doesn't work for me. He can do what the hell he wants. And frankly? I wish the poor bastard would stay home and deal with his family, because right now I have got my hands full on this one. I'm like a one-man band on this one. I can't even get anyone on the horn, whoever I reach out to it's 'Oh, Jimmy? He's out in the field right now.' I call so many guys that're all of a sudden out in the field, it's like harvest time. Guys who named their children after me: 'Oh yeah, he just stepped out.' You don't think I get the message?"

"Look." Berkowitz laid a hand on the blotter. "No one wants whoever did this to walk, but there's a right way and a wrong way to go about it here."

"There is?"

Berkowitz gave him a look and Matty got off his horse.

"The fact of the matter is, Mangold, Upshaw, they pick up the paper today, I get called in, 'Is English not Clark's native language?' "

"Boss, I just explained—"

Berkowitz held up a hand. "Perception, reality, whatever. They're not happy, and shit rolls downhill. They're at the peak, I'm like midmountain, and you're in this, this arroyo at the bottom. If I can be any more picturesque than that, let me know."

"In my father's house there are many bosses," Matty said.

"Whatever. Hey, nobody is telling you not to go all out, just do it quietly."

"How can I possibly go all out with what I just told you?"

"Well," sighing, "this too shall pass. Hopefully this week'll bring another headline . . ."

"Why is that a hopeful thing? He was a good kid from decent people, I'm not gonna lay low until some solved triple-header makes 1PP look better in the papers."

"There's this mountain, see?"

"We've been to the mountain."

"Right." Berkowitz crossed his knee, picked a thread from the lapel of his jacket.

The DI sat there fuming, rock and a hard place, Matty knowing enough to keep his mouth shut, at least for the moment.

"You're making your problem my problem, you know that, right?" Berkowitz finally said, Matty almost bowing in acknowledgment. "But, I have to say, you did the right thing at that meeting last week."

"Boss." Matty nearly lunged across the blotter. "You want to help me on this? I need people to go the extra mile. I need people to pick up the phone when I call, I need more than—"

"All right, stop, stop." Berkowitz shifting, bucking, thinking it through. "OK. Here's the deal," lowering his voice. "In order for me to help you here, keep my own head off the block, it's got to play out like this. Anything you need, anything you want, from now on you go through me, only and directly, and I will take care of it."

"Really."

"Really."

"Great." Matty leaned back, then came forward, elbows on the desk again. "For starters? Give me my seventh-day recanvass. Better late than never. But that means I need to be able to get the manpower, I need to be able to reach out to Warrants, Narcotics, Borough Patrol, Anti-Crime . . ."

The DI took out a datebook and a small gold pen from the inside pocket of his jacket, started writing.

"I need targeted narco sweeps and vice sweeps in the Lemlichs and Cahan. I need targeted warrants. I need a Crimestoppers van cruising the Fifth, the Eighth, and the Ninth from the East River to the Bowery and from Fourteenth to Pike." Matty trying to keep his wish list rolling while twisting his head nearly upside down to see if Berkowitz was actually writing any of this down. "I need detectives and patrol from an hour before to an hour after the time of the shooting, that'd be four a.m., passing out flyers on all the key corners down there, doing on-the-spot canvasses . . ."

The more Berkowitz wrote without complaint or question, the queasier Matty became.

"I want detectives on call to go to the Eighth to interview the collars as they come in, and I need all this to happen, when . . . When can I get this . . ."

"Sunday night," Berkowitz said, closing the book like a cigarette case and slipping it back into his jacket. "I'll take care of it."

"Sunday night going into Sunday morning?"

"Going into Monday morning."

"Boss, we're looking for habituals. Who's going to be out there. Who goes barhopping on a Sunday night."

"You want this happening or not. Saturday's too soon, Monday I can't promise, Tuesday's unpredictable to the point of science fiction."

"OK. All right, I'll take . . ." His next worry not even letting him get through the sentence.

"OK?" Berkowitz got to his feet.

"Hang on, wait." Matty putting a hand out. "Just, all due respect . . . Just, let me worry about this going the other way. We're talking Sunday, today's already Friday . . ."

"Did I just not say I'll take care of it?"

"Just . . ." Matty put his hands flat on the desk, lightly closed his eyes. "Can you just indulge me here, let me just paint a worst-case scenario here. OK, tomorrow's Saturday, right? Me being the way I am, I won't be able to help myself but to call you on your day off to get a progress report. If I'm lucky, I'll catch you maybe making breakfast for your kids or coming out of Home Depot with a new sander or whatever, but you'll have your hands full, be distracted, say, 'Yeah, yeah, everything's good to go,' and I won't be in a position to press for details.

"Now, if nonetheless I start calling the promised people Sunday morning and start getting a lot of 'He's out in the field' again? If, and once again I'm talking worst-case scenario here, if it all goes south come D-day? Forget about it. It's Sunday, you're not going to be reachable. Even *I* wouldn't take my call. Boss, make me believe."

"All I can say to you is, barring some massacre over the weekend, I will take care of it."

Berkowitz rose to his feet, draped his London Fog across his arm.

"Boss . . ." But Matty was unable to press for further reassurances, just didn't have the juice, and that was the problem.

"Matty. You're a good guy. I'm trying to keep you from getting hurt."


Alone in the elevator, Tristan whispered new beats to himself, jerking his shoulders and slicing the air with short chops of his downturned hands, then got into being onstage doing it with Irma Nieves in the audience, Crystal Santos maybe, but definitely Irma Nieves—the concert abruptly canceled when the door groaned open on seven and Big Dap got on.

As was expected of him, Tristan backed into the opposite corner of the small car, this being the same elevator in which Big Dap had shot a police with the guy's own gun a year ago.

Dap wouldn't even look his way, but beneath the royal icing, Tristan took the opportunity to give him a good once-over; Big Dap not so big in private, a little taller than him, a lot heavier, but his body was peanut-shaped, pear-shaped, some kind of food-shaped, and he was ugly; stubble-haired with slit eyes under a heavy brow and a sour mouth like a small McDonald's arch.

So what was so big about Big Dap. What was so big was that when the shit went down, he didn't flinch. In a world of fronters he thought with his hands and dealt with the fallout later. But wasn't that what Tristan had done? So we're down to uglier and bigger. And we're down to people knowing about it or not . . .

As the elevator opened on the ground floor, before stepping out into the day, Big Dap slowly turned his head in Tristan's vague direction and sucked his teeth.

"At least mine couldn't get up afterwards," Tristan said a moment later, after he heard the door to the street whack against the mailboxes.

· · ·

As soon as Bree spotted him at the bar, he could tell that she, like everybody else, had read the article.

She crossed to him directly.

"That was true?" Looking at him with those heart-stomping bright eyes.

"It's complicated."

"Complicated?"

It was over between them. Over before it began.

"I don't understand, why wouldn't you help?"

Eric couldn't bring himself to speak.

"I mean, he's dead, you're alive, and you *knew* him?"

"Not that well."

Did he really just say that?

She sounded like the cops now, like the father in the papers, like the official spokesperson for the contempt of this so-called neighborhood.

Cocaine.

He'd have made good money off it the first time if he hadn't then had to host everybody buying it from him at his bar, if he hadn't worried about everybody thinking of him as a great guy.

Keep it tight this time. In and out.

"Can I ask," he sighed, "that stuff you had last night?"

She stared at him. "What?"

What was he thinking?

"Nothing . . ."

"I just don't understand you," she said, giving him a last look, then walking off to the lockers.

He'd been out of the loop for a long time. An ounce these days must go for something like $700 to $900, which could be bagged up into twenties and forties, or straight hundred-dollar grams, times 28 is 2,800 bucks minus the 900 is 1,900 clear in a few days, and that was without even stepping on it.

A discarded copy of the *Post* lay amid the debris of an unbused corner banquette. Eric walked over, slipped it under his arm, and retreated downstairs to the office.

*Otherwise it's cowardly, it's unconscionable, it's unspeakable.*

**342**

And then came the next quote, Eric never having gotten that far in his previous readings.

*And the people of this city are with me.*

He flipped the paper onto the desk.

The people of this city are with nobody.

The people of this city are rubberneckers, he thought, and I'm the car crash.

"That dude look like, what'sit, Ice-T." The voice at Matty's back was young, male, and Latino. He finished taping the new reward poster to the bus shelter outside the Lemlichs, this one featuring Eric Cash's police sketch, the generic lynx-eyed urban predator who looked like anybody but, they had ultimately decided, was better than nobody.

"Twenty-two thousand?" the kid said.

"Yup."

"Huh."

"You hear anything?" Matty purposely keeping his back to him in order not to spook him.

"Me?" the kid snorted. "Nah."

"Twenty-two's a lot of money."

"I mean I heard it was some nigger from Brooklyn, someshit."

"Oh yeah? Where'd you hear that?"

"Just like, in the air, you know what I'm sayin'?"

"But from anybody in particular?"

"I know who told me, but . . ."

"Yeah? Who told you?"

When he got no answer, Matty turned around to at least get a look at the kid before he vanished, but he was too slow.

And then he crossed the street to hit the Lemlich lobbies proper, the posters snug against his ribs, a roll of masking tape around his wrist like a bracelet.

At seven that evening, Eric's girlfriend, Alessandra, live from Manila, came into the restaurant with a man.

After nine months, her unannounced appearance, in the midst of his own furious preoccupations, was so disorienting to him that he had escorted them halfway to their deuce before realizing who she was.

"Jesus," he finally said, hovering over their table.

"Carlos." The guy extended his hand. He had a high black pompadour like an old-time Mexican movie star.

"Why didn't you tell me you were coming back?" Standing there gripping a seatback, he remembered what he had liked about her, those greeny-green eyes in a heart-shaped face, the rest of it never more than what went along with that. She was smart, he guessed, that was something.

They had lived together for two years, a record for him, but right now all he felt was distracted.

"Maybe you should sit down for this, Eric," she said. "Carlos and I—"

"Are in love," he finished for her, surveying the room. "Congratulations."

"Thank you," Carlos said, and offered his hand again.

"So how's it going otherwise?" Eric asked her.

"I'm moving to Manila permanently."

"OK."

"OK?"

"What do you want me to say?" The beginnings of a traffic jam by the door.

"Do you want the apartment?" she asked.

Bree hustled by hefting a tray of entrées.

"Eric?"

"I'm, I don't know, not for long." Then, forcing himself to focus, "Do you two need to stay there tonight?"

"Would that be awkward?"

"Are you fucking *kidding* me?" a female customer screamed from directly outside the front door. "I have my whole *life* in there!"

Clarence the doorman took off after the purse snatcher, seemingly everyone in Berkmann's half rising from their tables to watch the chase, framed by the full-length Norfolk Street picture window. Clarence had the guy by the nape before he could even get past the end of the glass, and the room broke out in applause.

"Eric?" Alessandra waiting.

"What."

"Would that be awkward?"

"What."

"Staying there tonight."

"Extremely."

"That's OK," Carlos said to Alessandra. "We can stay with my aunt in Jersey City."

"Is that OK?" Eric asked.

"Sure," she said haltingly, then, "Are you OK?"

"Am I OK?" He thought about saying something clever, but . . . "Did you read today's paper?"

"About what?" she said.

"This city," Lester Kaufman said, one knee crossed over the other, a cuffed hand dangling languidly from the restraint bar, "people are doing so well, you know? But you can't ask them for shit anymore. It's never been so bad."

Matty grunted in sympathy.

Clarence had told Matty that the first thing this guy had said when he grabbed him after the attempted purse snatch in front of Berkmann's was "Let me go and I'll tell you who shot that white kid."

"I swear, man," Lester said to Matty for the tenth time in the last half hour, "I just said that like in a panic. Like the first thing that came into my head. What's left of my head."

Unfortunately, Matty believed him.

Lester yawned like a lion, revealing a dull steel ball pierced through his tongue.

Iacone, roused from sleep for this, yawned in response.

"But I'll tell you, man, I'm really worried about my girlfriend. I gave her a hundred dollars to get me something, you know, get me well? She said fifteen minutes, then left me standing there three hours. I had no idea where she went, what happened to her. Fifteen minutes . . . I mean I never would have done that if she didn't leave me there like half the night watching everybody coming out of that place for smokes, drunker and drunker, half the damned bags right on the sidewalk." Another titanic yawn, the dirty, dull tongue-pierce winking.

"Sucks," Iacone said. Strapped for a partner, Matty had cajoled him out of the bunk room with the promise of overtime and an easy commute.

"I mean I'm fucked, I know it, but can you just check your computer, see if she's in the system? I'm hoping she just got collared, nothing worse, but . . ."

"What's her name?"

"Anita Castro or Carla Nieves."

Iacone rose and went to the screen on Yolonda's desk.

"Where'd you get a hundred dollars, Lester?" Matty asked.

"Where?" He shivered, then coughed into his fist. "Oh, man, you don't want to make extra work for yourself with questions like that."

"No?"

"Seriously."

Matty let it slide.

"Nothing," Iacone called out.

"You do Brooklyn?" Lester asked.

"No, just Manhattan."

"Can you check Brooklyn? She scores on South Second, South Third. No one scores in Manhattan anymore, Manhattan's dead. You guys took care of that." Lester recrossed his knees, a slice of grimy red long johns peeking out between his pale blue ankle and the cuff of his jeans. "I mean, what the hell happened to her? She was going to take me to the hospital. I have fluid in my lungs."

"That's no problem, we'll get someone to take you soon as we're finished."

"Nothing," Iacone called out. "She got a third name?"

"She's not in the system, huh? Jesus. What do *you* think happened to her?" he asked Matty. "And me here . . . This is a felony too, right?"

"Not necessarily. Depends how you say what you say, you know, vis-à-vis sincerity, remorse."

"I *am* remorseful. I didn't menace, I didn't threaten, I didn't say anything, what's it, terroristic . . ."

"All right, just capture that in your statement. In fact, if you want, we can even write your statement for you. But what can I tell you that you haven't heard a million times before? You help us, we help . . ."

"You think this could go down as a pet lar? I just, I didn't even want, I picked the fucking thing up off the sidewalk. I didn't even think anybody was going to notice. When that big black guy started running after me, I was like, 'Here, take it.' I didn't even get to open the damned thing, I have no idea what was in there. Obviously I'm not a pro at this."

"Now, now, don't get down on yourself," Iacone said from Yolonda's desk.

"You know, I got to say right now we're pretty much eating out of garbage cans, me and Anita, but a few years ago? We had us a store worth like two hundred thousand dollars."

"Oh yeah?" Matty's turn to yawn. "What kind of store?"

"Was like a punk boutique?"

"No kidding."

"Can I have a cigarette? Jesus, I got to get to the emergency room."

"All right." Matty clapped his hands. "Here we go, onetime offer. Fuck the guys who shot that kid, just give us a stickup team, just some names, anybody you know works the hood. They check out, not only do you get a pass here, but we take you to the ER, get you squared away, then we go look for your girl."

"A stickup team?" Lester shrugged, recrossed his legs, looked away. "You know, she used to use Carmen Lopez. That was like her professional name at this one place out in Massapequa. She was a bar dancer, exotic, very good, very popular, had her regulars, guys who liked to see her and she could go to their houses, some of them, borrow thirty, forty dollars, but she's four months pregnant now, so . . ." Resting his brow on the curve of his free hand. "I don't know. Maybe it's time to go upstate. It's getting too hard out here, you know?"

**"I know I just woke you,** but I'm sure you're so dying to find out what happened with the kids in court yesterday, I figured you wouldn't mind."

"Ah shit." Matty palmed his face. The clock read seven. "Sorry." Too tired to work up an excuse. "So how'd it go . . ."

"Well, the Big One's out and back on the job."

"And the Other One?"

"You're gonna love this."

"Love what."

"Let me ask you, how big is your place?"

"Love what, Lindsay."

"And how's the neighborhood?"

"Love what."

"The family court judge? He's got no use for Eddie at all. Especially since he almost cost his older brother his job."

"You got to be kidding me."

"Said if he could, he'd throw Eddie in juvie."

"He can't do that."

"So he said. But he also said that if Eddie violates his probation in any way, shape, or form over the next three years, he is gone for good."

"Jesus. Is this kid going to straighten out?"

"Well, let's put it this way. This wasn't his first encounter with family court."

"You never told me that."

"Why, what would you have done, hop in your car, shoot right up, and give him a good talking-to?"

"I don't know." No. "He's my son too."

"Glad to hear it, because that brings us to the part you're gonna love. Basically, this judge, he just wants Eddie gone, out of the county. The family advocate mentions that his dad's a detective down in New York City, right? So the judge, his eyes light up, and he *strongly* recommends that perhaps it's time for young Eddie to live with his father, get some real parental supervision, since I apparently suck at it."

"What did you say?"

"I agreed."

"Lindsay . . ."

"I believe he needs about a week to off-load whatever dope they didn't find, then he's on the bus to you."

"Hang on, hang on. First off, I don't have any room."

"Eddie says you do."

"He said that?"

"Says you have a convertible sofa."

"Huh."

"He's a bit of fuckhead, but he's got a good heart. You'd probably like him."

"Huh." Then, sitting up, "What grade is he in again?"


As soon as he got off the phone with Lindsay, he started dialing Berkowitz at home to get a progress report on the great Sunday recanvass, but then remembered that it was only a few minutes past seven on a Saturday morning, so cut the call before it could ring through, telling himself to calm the hell down.

It was his day off, so he tried to go back to sleep.

Fat chance.

Everyone had come around the front of 22 Oliver to check out the new poster.

"The fuck is this nigger," Devon said. "Look like Storm."

"Who?"

"Storm, the X-Girl in the *X-Men*, had the weather powers."

"Yeah, that bitch was a*blaze*."

"Who was that"—Fredro snapped his fingers—"Jada . . ."

"Halle Berry, Halle Berry."

"Oh, I'd bone her in a *heart*beat," Little Dap said.

"This dude got a beard, yo. Bone *you* in a heartbeat."

Tristan laughed like everybody else, the hamster in his charge looking up at him in surprise.

X-girl. Bitch.

He wasn't insulted or paranoid or scared, just fascinated, trying to see himself in this drawing, wanting to see himself, but he couldn't any more than he could see himself by looking in a mirror.

"You know who that looks like?" Fredro tapped the poster. "Who's the dude was in the movie, what's that, *The Best Man*, the, the light-skin dude got them lighty eyes?"

"Yeah, yeah, I don't know his name, though."

Crystal Santos, wary and eager, came out of the building into their stares.

"Ey yo, what's that green-eyed nigger was in *The Best Man*, had the guitar."

"Oh, I like him," she said. "Was in *Big Momma's House* too."

"Good for him, what's his name."

"I don't know."

Little Dap spit through the gap in his front teeth. "Still look like a bitch to me."

Tristan cocked his head and waited for Little Dap's eyes, but pretty much like he expected, they never came his way.


At the tail end of the lunch hour, Harry Steele's culture dealer was sitting alone eating shirred eggs, tilting his head sideways each time he lifted a forkful from his plate, then lunging for it halfway to his mouth.

"Can I talk to you?"

The dealer looked around the room for a long moment, then took another lunge at his eggs. "What."

Eric stood facing him across the small table, his hands on the chair-back opposite. "I'm looking to get something, a little something going."

"A little something going. What kind of a little something going." Taking another sideways snap at his fork.

Eric sighed, paradiddled the wood under his fingers.

"Are you talking to me now or not?" The guy had yet to look at him.

Another squeamish sigh, then, "What do you think."

"What do I think? I think I'm not a mind reader, so why don't you just say."

Eric looked off and flicked the side of his nose.

"What?"

"Oh, for Christ's sake, what do you think?"

The culture dealer stopped moving for a beat then resumed eating.

"What's my name."

Eric knew but blanked.

"Right. In the six months that I've been coming in here, you have not so much as once exchanged a single pleasantry with me before, and yet for this you think nothing of making a beeline to my table. Why."

Eric searched the cavernous room for a reasonable-sounding response.

"I just have that, what . . . ferretlike air about me?" Looking at him for the first time.

"I apologize." Every day in every way, Eric sinking, just sinking.

"I come in here because the owner, *your* boss, happens to be a good friend of mine. I come in on my own for a peaceful meal, and his god-damn manager, of all people—"

"I apologize. I'm under a lot of strain right now."

"I read the papers."

"I know, I know I have no . . ." Eric dying to get back to the pulpit, imagining his grip on the seatback splintering the wood. "I'd appreciate you not mentioning this to Harry."

"I'll bet you would," disgustedly flipping his fork on the plate. "These eggs are like ice."

. . .

After everyone left, Tristan pulled the wanted poster off the wall by the mailboxes in his building, and, with the hamster in his charge, the .22 tucked in the small of his back, headed over to Irma Nieves's building, and do what . . .

Show her the poster and ask if she knew this guy? Ask her if it looked like him? Tell her that he knew who . . . that he was . . . No. First say, Oh, I heard everybody was over here now. Huh. Then, Oh . . . you see this? Or . . .

When the elevator came, that fat boy Donald, the one everybody called Gameboy, was in it, the guy's eyes like two BBs in a cave. And just like whenever Tristan saw him, he was carrying his game boxes: today's selection *Tectonic II* and *NFL Smashmouth*.

They knew each other by sight, saw each other almost every day either in school or somewhere in the Lemlichs, but never really spoke.

"You play that?" Tristan said as the car clanked upwards.

"Yeh," Gameboy said, his eyes on the rolled poster. "That's that dude?"

As an experiment, Tristan unfurled it for his perusal, looked him in his tiny eyes.

"Police was mad sweatin' me on that." Gameboy's voice high and wheezy. "But I ain't say shit."

"You know who it is?"

Gameboy pointedly looked at the hamster, then up at the ceiling of the car. "Little pictures got big ears, you know what I'm saying?"

Tristan didn't.

Then as the fat kid stepped out on his floor, "Dude ain't even from around here."

No one answered when he rang Irma Nieves's bell, although when he was back to waiting for the elevator, he could swear he heard laughing from behind her door.


At eight that evening Eric, pondering his dope-buying options and getting nowhere, heard the key in the door, a sound he hadn't heard in nine or however many months.

**352**

"Oh, sorry." Alessandra winced. "I thought you'd be at work."

"Hey, it's your place." Eric shrugged.

She flopped down next to him on the sofa futon.

"Everything OK?"

"Carlos's aunt was giving me the evil eye."

"Oh yeah?"

"Catholic."

"I hear you." Eric staring at the TV as if it were on.

"You're different," she said.

"From him?"

"From you."

"So you need the place tonight?"

"I guess. Start packing stuff up."

"OK." He started to rise, gather a few things.

"You don't have to run out."

"No, I know, I'm just . . ."

"Where are you going to go?"

"I can call some people," then thinking, Like who.

In the brief silence that followed he fantasized about knocking on Bree's group apartment door, he was sure it was a group apartment, her leading him to her room, that mattress on the floor.

Overwhelmed, he sat back down on the futon.

"I didn't mean to kick you out," she said.

"It's fine," avoiding her eyes, then, "So how's your thesis going?"

"Good."

"Great."

She slowly absorbed the lay of the room while gnawing on her thumb joint, a habit Eric had forgotten about and that tugged at him a little now but not enough.

"Have you seen the paper yet?"

"You mean yesterday's?"

"Yeah." Eric bracing.

"I did," she said. "I can't believe you came that close to dying."

"What?"

"You read between the lines, it's kind of like that guy almost got you killed."

Eric's eyes started to sting.

She got up and went to her dirty-book bookshelf, grazed the drunken chorus line of mostly soft spines. "Hello, boys, you miss me?" Then turned back to Eric. "It is so, weird to be back here."

"I can imagine."

"But I didn't mean to kick you out."

Matty had called the deputy inspector four times during the day; in the morning he was told the warrants squad was setting up, but as far as the other units requested, Berkowitz was "still working on it."

At one in the afternoon he was told that lining everybody else up was "just about there."

At four, the phrase used was "iron out some last-minute kinks."

At six he got Berkowitz's answering machine, Matty telling himself at that point that it didn't mean anything other than it was getting to be Saturday night and the guy didn't want to be disturbed.

He had said barring a massacre it was all going to happen, and Berkowitz was about as straight a shooter as you could be for someone in his position, so have another beer.

At eight, though, the TV news led off with the kidnapping of the granddaughter of a politically wired Washington Heights–based minister, and Matty knew that once again, his recanvass was fucked.

It was a funny kind of fucking.

He wasn't even sure they would be sleeping in the same bed, not that there was a second option, and he sat upright on the futon in his street clothes, waiting for the water to stop running in the bathroom to see what would be emerging, and she came out straight-up naked, her body tight and spare and unconflicted, all nipples and hip bones, and Eric just became another person, silently stripping down and then holding her, one hand at her nape and one on her belly, lowering her onto the futon like laying a rare musical instrument into its case. There was nothing hurried but nothing preliminary, just putting himself inside her right away, and moving at the same not slow not rushed pace, hovering but in deep, the concentration like nothing he had ever possessed before. Nothing could make him speed up, nothing could make him stop, and Alessandra started looking at him sideways—Who are you—her body beneath his rigid, sprung against sprung, but she couldn't hold it and started to come, then come some more, and he still wouldn't, couldn't alter what he was doing in response, could go on pumping her all night long, would have if she didn't push up against his chest, needing a break, Eric lifting out of her as barlike as he was going in, still holding her, but having nothing to say, just waiting until she was ready for more, then going back in with the same maddening steadiness, Alessandra starting to go a little wall-eyed trying to look into him, but he was not to be found and soon she didn't even have the strength to ask for another break but just floated away.

At midnight, watching the news updates on the kidnapping while fried to the hat in Waxey's, Matty couldn't remember if his ex-wife had really called him that morning about the kid moving to New York or if he had imagined it, so he stepped into the quieter red-washed back room of Chinaman's Chance and started thumb-stabbing his cell for a verification.

"Hello?"

He didn't know if he had inadvertently called Minette Davidson just now or if she happened to call him at ten after midnight just as he happened to open his phone to call upstate; the question was too complicated to think about at that moment, in any event, so he hung up on everybody and made his way back to the bar.

**Sunday morning Berkowitz** was once again a recorded voice.

And when Matty called a friend from the warrants squad to see how the preliminary sweeps in Lemlich and Cahan had gone, he heard that they didn't.

"Aw, man, all hell broke loose last night with that kidnapped minister's kid. They dragooned us up to the Heights, we hit like fifty doors, going right back out in a few to hit fifty more."

Whomever he called in Vice, Narcotics, Patrol was, big surprise, "out in the field," meaning, presumably, uptown with the kidnapping, and would get back to him as soon as they got in.

At three o'clock Sunday afternoon the girl came back on her own, just walked into her grandparents' house with a story about being abducted by seven men in a blacked-out van and taken to a mansion where she was blindfolded and drugged. She couldn't remember what she did there, what was done to her, or how she got home.

Nonetheless, at five in the evening everybody was still out in the field or had just clocked out after having pulled a double shift and then some, in order to bring that girlie-girl home.

At six he got a call from another buddy in Narcotics, on the q.t., telling him the truth, that they personally were never called up into the

Heights, were in fact in the field all day preparing to hit Lemlich and Cahan for him tonight but were told at the last minute by their lieutenant to stand down, no explanation given.

Matty tried calling Berkowitz continuously after that, got the recorded voice each time, but even if he had managed to get him on the phone, all the guy would do was plead the Higher Powers Act, say his own bosses got wind of it (the rats, they're everywhere in this department) and pulled the plug, and that he tried, he gave it his all.

Matty would never find out who, ultimately, deep-sixed his recanvass again, but it didn't really make a difference.

Screw me twice, shame on me.

And so later that evening, he called in five of his own detectives, all on unauthorized overtime, and did what he could with the manpower he had, which basically boiled down to manning the intersections nearest the murder spot from 3:00 a.m. to 5:00 a.m., bookending by an hour the exact time of the shooting ten days previous; passing out flyers and doing whatever on-the-spot interviewing they could, with Yolanda as the swing man, shuttling back and forth from the corner of Eldridge and Delancey to the Eighth Precinct to interview whomever the overtime-happy Quality of Lifers managed to drag in.

Unsurprisingly, it all came to shit.

So at sunrise, Matty rejigged the game plan.

SEVEN

# WOLF TICKETS

**They sat across from** each other at the Castillo de Pantera, Billy having come back down to the Lower East Side so fast after Matty's call that if he hadn't answered the phone up there in Riverdale himself, Matty would have suspected that the guy had been lurking around the corner all along. The only other customers at this midmorning hour were two young crew-cut women wearing paint-spattered farmer johns, one of them giving her order to the Mayan-looking waitress in halting Spanish.

"Listen." Matty leaned in, dropped his voice. "I've always been honest with you, yes? And, I have to say, right now I see this whole thing going south at warp speed."

"What about Eric Cash?"

"Nothing."

"What if I—"

"No more with him."

"What if—"

"I asked you to say very specific things to that reporter, none of which showed up in the paper. I understand you're emotional—"

"Emotional . . ."

"Yeah. Emotional. But the point was to bring Cash *in*, not bury him."

"Maybe I should talk to him again," Billy said. "Explain—"

"No. Let it be. What we did was a push, any more and we can both get good and bit."

"But what if—"

"I said let it be."

Billy attempted to say one more thing but gave up, subsiding into an alert vacancy, as if that part of his programming had just been removed.

"Look," Matty reaching out and laying a hand on his arm to bring him in. "The powers that be want this case to go away, and I can't let that happen. *We* can't let that happen."

"OK."

"And, at this point the only way left to prevent that, the only way to keep this thing from getting any colder, is to keep it in the public eye, and so here's what I'm thinking . . . The reward at this point is twenty-two thousand, but if we could raise it, say, another twenty? That would justify a fresh presser."

Billy nodded.

Matty waited.

"So, another twenty." Matty cocked his head. "What do you think?"

"Sounds good," Billy said, continuing to look like a facsimile of himself.

The guy wasn't getting it.

"What I'm saying to you is, that in some cases, the family of the victim, if they're in a position, voluntarily kick into the kitty to get some fresh publicity, light a fire under 1PP's ass."

"OK." Blinking at him.

"So. Can you raise . . ."

"*Me?*" Billy jerked back from the table.

The guy didn't have it.

"I have to apologize." Matty flushed. "I thought—"

"No. Hold on." Billy shifting gears, bearing down.

"Look, I feel bad," Matty said. "I don't know why, but I was under the impression—"

"Just hold on."

"I didn't mean to put you up against a wall—"

"I said hold *on*!" A verbal smack that had the urban farmgirls at the other table jumping. "All right, there's an account. His, has about twenty-five thousand."

"OK."

"Accumulated birthday cash, mostly from his mother's side, that I'm, that she doesn't want any part, that, that reverted to me."

"OK."

"It's his birthday money."

"Billy, I can't tell you what to do."

"What do you mean, 'I can't tell you what to do'? You just did."

Matty offered his palms. "I want the best results here."

"Jesus Christ, do I have to take it out today?"

"The sooner the better, but—"

"*Fuck*," Billy barked, jumped up, stalked out of the restaurant, then came charging back in. "It's his *birth*day money!" Spraying the room with gall.


Eric was making a shambles of it today, so shaky he didn't trust himself to pick up a dish. A few of the waiters were giving him the thousand-yard stare, a few customers, one even saying without looking at him on his way out, "What goes around comes around."

But the worst of it was Bree, who continued to take small bites out of his heart every time she walked past him as if he weren't there. The only way Eric could manage to survive the shift was by concentrating on his exit strategy and by reminding himself that in so many ways, he was already gone.

It was easier, these days, back at the apartment; easier as in blanker, purely physical, and nuts; Eric surprising himself and Alessandra the last two nights by fucking as if in her absence he did nothing but study every one of those sex manuals and porno funnies she had left behind. He had never, ever been either that focused or slow to come in his life, making her go off over and over, something he had never been able to do before except when going down on her, his ex-girlfriend waking up Sunday morning, calling her Filipino fiancé in Jersey City to say she needed an extra day, Monday morning, just one more day, *mi amor*, and making Eric do it again the minute she hung up. She took it as a sign of renewed passion between them, but it wasn't her; it was what she had said Saturday night about his being so close to death. It wasn't as if he hadn't known that, but in the week and a half since the murder he hadn't ever had the stillness in him to really reexperience that, be quiet with that, and the shock of seeing her emerging from the bathroom fresh-naked just moments after she had laid that on him really put him right back there in front of 27 Eldridge, the bullet so close he could have stopped it with his palm—Eric fucking all weekend like that, he would hate to tell her, simply to outrace the goddamned thing.

He was coming to the end of his shift, had an hour break before the second half of his double, and could barely stay upright. Punching out, he started to walk the four blocks back to his apartment, remembered that Alessandra was there waiting for him, turned around, went back into Berkmann's, and crashed in one of the subterranean supply rooms.

The store, four blocks from his school, was called BD Wing Funerary, and Tristan had never seen anything like it: nothing but paper replicas of every kind of luxury item imaginable, from Gucci loafers to cell phones to cigarette cartons to a four-foot-tall, three-story private house, every brick and window shade sketched to scale.

"What is this?" Tristan held up a paper tuxedo wrapped in plastic and folded to the size of a pressed shirt.

"Not for you," said the owner, a gray-haired Chinese who had been trailing him from the door on in.

"I ain't stealing nothing. What is it, for kids?"

"For nobody," the guy said, tilting his head to the door.

Across Mulberry Street in Columbus Park, a full-court shirts-and-skins basketball game was being played, every kid Chinese and most probably, like himself, cutting school.

"Ey, yo." Gameboy materialized from the back shadows of the store, from beneath his own brows, a brick of what looked to Tristan like fake Chinese money in one hand, two video boxes in the other.

"He with you?" the old guy said.

"Yeah."

"Tell him buy something or go."

"OK." Gameboy nodded, then tilting his head to Tristan, " 'S up."

"You come here?"

"Yeah."

"What is it?"

"The shit's madhouse, right?"

"You buy something or go," the owner yapped from behind his counter.

"Yeah, yeah." Gameboy waved him off. "I like to get stuff here. I used to keep it like a collection in my house, but then that guy told me it's bad luck, so . . ."

"What is?"

"All this shit's for dead people. You burn it at a Chinese funeral so the dead guy can take it with him to the afterland . . . except this here?" Gameboy passed Tristan the wrapped play money. "These shits are Hell Bank notes. You burn them to bribe the king of hell so that the dead guy don't have to stay there too long."

"In hell?" Tristan eyed the stacked and shelved bogus goods and wanted it all, one of each.

"And you can never give any of this shit for a present to anybody because that's like a curse on them. That's like saying you want that person dead."

"So why do you buy it?"

"Sometimes I like to burn all this myself, like on the roof of my building? And sometimes I just give it to people I want dead."

"How do you know this?"

"I just do." Then, holding up the *Berserker* game box, "You play this?"

"Nah."

"I could like teach it to you in about twenty minutes."

"OK."

"You live in Twenty-two Oliver?"

"Yeah."

"I'm in Thirty-two St. James."

"OK."

"You want to come by sometime?"

"Yeah, OK." No; holding his breath against the fat boy's funk.

"I'm in twelve-D."

"OK."

"Shit's easy."

"Awright."

Gameboy went up to the counter and paid for his money, Tristan following, brushing his fingers along stacks of paper cigarette lighters and Hell Bank credit cards and perforated driving gloves.

Outside on Mulberry, Gameboy peeled off half an inch of money and gave it to Tristan. "This ain't a curse on you or nothing. Just remember to burn them shits. Otherwise the king of hell is gonna come up here and take it from you himself."

"OK." Tristan nodded, then wandered across the street, ostensibly to watch some Chinese full-court, but really to examine more closely the paper Rolex that he had boosted from the store.


Eric had gone down to the basement for a quick nap between shifts and slept for five hours, come to in a panic, raced into the locker room to throw water on his face, brush his teeth, and finger-comb his hair, then charged upstairs still tucking in his shirt.

The first person he saw was the hostess covering for him. "Why didn't anybody wake me?"

"Wake you from where?" walking away without ever looking at him.

The next one was Bree, hefting a tray of drinks.

"You working a double?"

"Yup," throwing him a tight, impersonal smile on her way past.

"Me too," he said to the air.

A few minutes later, heading back to the pulpit after seating a foursome, Eric saw a solo waiting for him there; the guy in his thirties, sporting a striped boatneck shirt and a beret.

"Just one?"

"Are you Eric?"

Bracing for the next shitstorm, Eric just stared at him.

"Paulie Shaw said you might want to talk."

"Paulie?"

The culture dealer; Eric needing a moment to place the name, the conversation.

A vision then came to Eric of the Eighth Precinct detectives entrapping him in a dope buy to squeeze him into cooperating; of more shit in the papers, of killing himself.

"Paulie Shaw?" the possible undercover tried again.

The Picasso shirt was a nice touch.

"I don't know you," Eric said.

"All right, whatever." He shrugged, then nodded to the menu. "Can I get a table?"


An hour later Eric brought over the coffee himself, sat down across from the Halloween Frenchman.

"So, who are you?"

"Morris."

Eric sat there, trying to chess this through.

Bree came over, bused the table without looking at him once.

"Come to my office," Eric said.


"OK. You tell me," agonizing over the least indictable phrasing, "what might I want to talk about . . ."

Morris continued to stroll about the low cellar, eyeing the graffiti on the joists. Then, without taking his eyes from the crude messages overhead, he reached into his jeans and passed over a slim tube of paper like a European sugar packet.

Eric unraveled the twisted ends: four, five lines' worth, a BJ-in-the-bathroom special.

Embarrassed by his shaking hands, he passed it back. "After you."

"I don't do that stuff."

"Me neither."

Sighing, Morris took a Bic pen from the neck of his boatneck shirt and, using the long clip on the cap as a scoop, did half the powder. "I'll be up all night now," passing it back. "Your turn."

The flake brought tears to his eyes; Eric asking the price for an ounce before he was even done blinking away the prisms.

"Twelve hundred," Morris said.

"For an *ounce*?" All caginess lost to the singing in his blood. "What the hell, Maurice, I may not be Superfly, but I'm not Jed Clampett either, man, Jesus Christ, cut a girl some slack." Eric suddenly so slick.

"Well, what were you thinking?"

"Seven hundred."

"Funny."

"Funny?"

Morris spasmed, did a little jig off the coke. "Shiver me timbers, Popeye."

"What?"

"I'll go eleven fifty, but that's it. Guh," tossing his head like a horse.

"Seven fifty."

"Do you see me standing here with a pushcart or something?"

"Eight and that's as I low as I go," Eric said, then, "as high."

"Well, look." Morris patrolled the cellar stiff-armed, silently clapping his hands. "I mean you can bop on over to the Lemlichs, try to score your eight-hundred-dollar ounce there, and either walk away with a bag of Gold Medal or not walk away at all, OK?

"But this right here is signed, sealed, and delivered, no-risk white man's coke for a white man's market. Pricey, but worth it. You can step on it two, three times, it'll still be good to go, or even if you don't want to bother, at twenty a twist, a hundred a gram, you still clear sixteen hundred on the package. It takes money to make money, hoss; if it didn't, every pauper'd be a king."

"Eight fifty."

"Up all night for nothing," Morris muttered, then scrawled a phone number on the back of the empty coke wrapper, passed it back to Eric with another complimentary full twist from his jeans.

"Tell you what. Take this, think on it some more, change your mind, call the number, OK?"

"Eight seventy-five."

"Bye now."

Rejuvenated by the blow and by the knowledge of that second twist in reserve, Eric remained in the cellar after Morris had left. He thought of Ike Marcus, of Bree, of how he could drink all night now and be OK.

And the dig about going to the Lemlichs? Why not? Anybody over there in the PJs who stood to profit off the sale of an ounce, who had their shit together enough to even have an ounce *to* sell, would never be so boneheaded, so shortsighted, as to kill the goose.

Takes money to make money . . .

He was going to the PJs after his shift tonight; no, fuck it, going now, get somebody to cover and go.

He marched back up to the dining room and stepped to the pulpit.

"Listen I have a personal emergency," laying a hand on the hostess who had covered for him earlier, the girl looking down at her arm as if he had just licked it. "I'll be back in a while."

As he made for the door, he crossed paths with Bree, carrying a tray of desserts.

"I didn't mean to come down on you like that," she murmured. "I guess you have your reasons," then moved on before he could respond.

Eric took a breath, rubbed his face, then returned to the reservations pulpit.

Maybe he'd go tomorrow night.


At ten that evening, Matty was at home, gearing up to walk over to 27 Eldridge, hang around the shrine for a while then maybe head over to the No Name to consult with his mixologist, when his cell rang.

"Yeah, hey, this is Minette Davidson. I was wondering, I need to talk to you."

"Yeah, sure."

"I'm downstairs."

"Downstairs?" Then, realizing that she thought he was at the precinct, "Give me two minutes."


She was seated on the bolted rack of molded plastic chairs in the wedge-shaped vestibule where he had first laid eyes on her husband, staring at that same wall of memorial plaques over the reception desk.

"Hey."

She whipped her head to him, looking a little wild beneath the rough corona of her hair, then gestured to the epigraph beneath the bronze profile of patrolman August Schroeder, killed in 1921.

" 'Grief is a country unto itself,' " she read. "No argument there."

"Come on out," he said.

Given the massive bridge supports that dominated the immediate area, at night the view directly outside the precinct was the same at nine in the evening as it was at five in the morning: lifeless, save for the coming and going of police and the overhead rumble of unseen traffic.

They stood next to each other in the desolate silence; Minette, despite a heavy sweater, hugging herself in the still-warm October air.

"So what can I help you with," he finally said.

"Billy spent all day trying to put together twenty thousand dollars for the reward pot, are you aware of that?" Her eyes roaming the shadows without focus.

"Yeah, I am."

"He said it was your idea."

"Look, it was, but—"

"I just want to make sure it was real."

"I mean, there's no guarantee . . ."

"That it came from you."

"It did."

"OK." Nodding, still scanning the heartless view. "That's good enough for me."

"You didn't need to come all the way down here. We could have talked on the phone."

"I'm sorry."

"No, no, I meant as a burden on you."

"Yeah, no, well, I guess I just needed to get out of there for a little, for a few minutes."

"Your place."

"Yeah. It's like a tiger pit now sometimes, so just, you know, for a few minutes."

"Sure," he said, then, "Where's your, where's Nina?"

"At my sister's with her cousins. I just need a little break."

The desk sergeant came outside for a smoke, nodding to Matty, then stepping away to give them privacy, but a moment later a van pulled up, and a moment after that four vice cops were escorting a procession of six Asian women in cuffs to booking, the first in line the tallest, most attractive, and well dressed, the trailing five looking like peasants: squat, with pushed-in faces and dazed expressions.

"Aw, fuck no," the sergeant moaned, "not Oriental Pearls."

"Sorry there, Sarge," the lead cop said.

"Where the hell do I go now?" he bawled, the vice crew cracking up.

"This funny, huh?" the tallest hooker snapped. "I make good money. More than *you*."

"So what? My wife makes more money than me."

"She do half-and-half too?"

"That's what they tell me." Cracking everybody up again.

"You know what?" Matty said, laying a hand on Minette's arm. "Come upstairs."


He steered her through the vacant squad room into the lieutenant's office, pulled the interior blinds, and parked her on a leatherette couch half-piled with case reports.

"Do you want something to drink?" Pulling up a chair.

She shook her head, then hunched over and put her face in her hands, Matty once again giving her a moment, then, "What's going on."

"I didn't bargain for this," she whispered, hiding her eyes.

Matty nodded, thinking, Who does.

"I loved that kid, I swear to God, but Jesus . . ."

"You know what?" Resting a hand lightly on her arm. "You'll do what you have to do."

"How do you know." Hiding now behind the heel of her fist.

He didn't, but what could you say.

"Look, it's only been a week."

"Exactly." Another defeated whisper.

"I tell you what." Matty hunched forward. "You take care of your family, and I'll take care of everything else."

He sounded rock solid, like what he was saying made any kind of sense, but it was more than just a positive-thinking con job; he personally wanted her to be stronger; that's the way she came to him in his visions and he insisted on it now.

"You take care of them. You can do that," he said down low, putting everything he had into coming off both sober and supernaturally prescient, his mouth inches from her lowered head. "I know you can."

She finally raised her eyes to him, to the all-knowing tone of his voice; looked at him with a desperate and helpless attentiveness.

"I know you can."

Looked at him like a rock in a raging sea.

"You just let me worry . . ."

"OK," she said as if drugged, then reached up and, cupping his face in her hands, put her tongue in his mouth, Matty having time only to tentatively rest his fingers on her shoulders before she was already backing away, shocked and done.

For a moment they just sat there, big-eyed with thought, each looking around the room as if having lost a separate item, until Minette got up and without a word headed for the door.

He understood that it was a Fuck God kiss, a onetime protest, he understood and accepted that; and so all he could be right now was relieved to see her go; but when, with one hand already on the door, she turned back to him, breathing like she was confused, like this wasn't what she had expected, took a half step towards him for more, then bore down on herself: No; that was the heart-stomper, Matty slumping as if punched.

She turned again and left, quietly closing the door behind her.

"Jesus," Matty said, wiping his mouth, then wishing he hadn't.

Restless, agitated, trying not to think about the thing that didn't happen, Matty found himself still in the empty office an hour after she left, going through 61s and 494 sheets, perusing that day's mayhem, sorting them into kickbacks to patrol and squad-worthy, felonies obviously but domestics too; always potential starter kits for something more serious; DOAs and Missing Persons for the same reason.

The day had been slow: a few harassment complaints, two weaponless muggings, a few petit larcencies, and an aggravated assault already closed by arrest.

Then a Missing Persons caught his eye, Olga Baker; Matty knowing the kid, a serial runaway, the mother, Rosaria, calling like clockwork once a month, the kid always coming home a day or two later, nothing to worry about, but the last time Rosaria had called in, maybe six weeks ago, he wound up going over there, a well-kept apartment in the Cuthbert Towers, a few steps up from the PJs and slightly off the beaten path. Rosaria, in her late thirties, early forties maybe, short and solid with high-piled black hair, had out of the blue asked him if he had kids, which led to Are you still with their mother, which led to Do you like dancing, which led to his, for some reason he couldn't fathom tonight, getting out of there fast.

He had known cops who had on occasion slept with witnesses, slept with suspected perps, confirmed perps, slept with the wives, sisters, and mothers of victims, and had even slept with the victims themselves if they recovered. You walk into lives abruptly turned inside out by the arbitrary malice of the world, and you, in your suit and tie, your heavy black shoes, your decent haircut, and your air of seriousness, you become the knight, the father, the protector . . . All of which is to say that sometimes it fell right into your lap if you were that kind of individual. Which he was not, was not.

The phone number was on the report.

"Rosaria, how you doing, Detective Clark. Remember? . . . Yeah, that guy. I'm just following up here. Did Olga come home yet?" Doodling. "All right, well, we're out there beating the bushes . . . Just, how are you holding up though, you OK? . . . Oh yeah? . . . If you'd like, I could come by, see if there's any . . . No problem at all . . . Now's good."

Matty went to the bathroom to brush his teeth, tuck himself in, came back out, left the squad room, then came back in, ran Henry Baker through the computer, Rosaria's husband coming up as still in Green Haven, then left for the field.

Rosaria Baker, technically speaking, fell into none of the above categories.


Still cranked, Eric came home, working himself up for another death-propelled slamathon, and walked in on Alessandra in the middle of packing, or unpacking, it was hard to tell until he saw that the bookshelves were half-bare.

"You might want to sit for this," she said.

"What's with all the sitting. Just say."

"It's time for me to go."

"Yeah." Eric tried to look wounded.

"I'm so sorry."

"Yeah, no," he said.

"Maybe I'm making a . . ."

"No, you're not. You're not," he said tenderly, quickly.

"Carlos is picking me up in an hour," she said, looking at the bed.

This was great; this . . . he had to do this more often, Matty necking on the couch like a teenager, his hand inside Rosaria Baker's blouse, hers rubbing him across his thigh like she was rolling out pastry dough, making little noises and smelling like lipstick, like perfume, like hairspray, wearing stockings with garters and snaps, Matty thinking, whatever happened to that, why is that a fetish, that's normal, that's great, everything great, everything a slow-motion heart attack, and then they heard a key in the door and they both started fumbling and scrambling as fifteen-year-old Olga Baker, the missing person, waltzed in; the goddamn case solved.

*King of Hell*
*Know him well*
*I walk right in*
*Don't ring the bell*

Tristan closed his book, regarded the hamsters breathing all around him, the boy with a sleep hard-on like a little periscope every goddamn night now.

He slipped out of bed and stepped out into the hallway. Standing in front of the master bedroom, one hand on the doorknob, he became giddy with fear. He didn't, does not, understand—he *stepped* to him, him and his shortstop-quick hands, took it and then gave it right back to him and saw him back down and call the cops like a little fucking bitch; and still, he felt this; he could kill, was a mankiller, and still, he felt this; like he was going into a lion's den.

He opened the door a crack, then dropped to his belly and crawled inside the bedroom, the smell of openmouthed sleep in here giving him another dizzy rush until he was beneath his ex-stepfather's night table. Reaching up, he eased the top drawer open just enough to slip the Chinese paper Rolex inside, then slid it shut again.

From me to you.

**"I did have,** I *do* have my reasons." Eric was wall-eyed high as he intercepted Bree coming up the stairs from the locker room.

"I'm sorry?" Stepping back from him in a way that told him it didn't
make a difference what he said right now.

"Last night you said to me, 'I guess you had your reasons.' I do."

"OK." She was waiting, not to hear them but to get past him. He
didn't care.

"Could you, look . . . Just come back down with me for a minute,"
nodding to the cellar, then adding, "No funny stuff, I swear."


"Yeah, about that recanvass this weekend," Deputy Inspector Berkowitz
in Matty's ear.

"Boss, I'm not even asking."

"With that bullshit minister's kid . . ."

"I hear you."

"What a waste of time and men."

"Right."

"You know where she got that devil-cult kidnapping story from?"

"The movies?"

"Yeah, but which one?"

"I don't know." Matty tired of the runaround before it even got good and going. *"Rosemary's Baby?"*

*"Eyes Wide Shut."*

"Eyes what?"

"You know, where they have that orgy in the mansion?"

"I didn't see that."

"Everybody's in this mansion, naked and wearing like, owl masks."

"Didn't see it."

"I find it hard to believe that the director who gave us *Spartacus* gave us that crap."

Enough. "Look, I just got a call, the guy has decided to personally toss another twenty thousand into the reward kitty, which puts us at forty-two, so he'd like to have a presser, announce it."

"Whoa, what guy."

"Marcus."

"The father?"

"Of his own money," Matty said.

"A presser *now?"*

"Day after tomorrow, give him time to set up the escrow account."

"Day after tomorrow."

"Yeah."

"Let me get back to you on that."

"Boss, let me just say, he's not asking for permission, he's asking if we would join him for a stronger message."

"What are you, his press secretary now?"

"Are you *kidding* me? You got it ass backwards. I'm doing everything I can to corral this poor bastard, keep him out of everybody's hair. But, hey, if you prefer, I'll give him your number, let you be the point man, maybe this way I could put in some time trying to solve this fucking thing instead of getting my ear bent all day."

"When does he want to do this?"

"Day after tomorrow. At the crime scene. You don't take over, move it to 1PP or the Eighth, it'll be a zoo."

"Let me make some calls."

"Is that a yes?"

"I'll get back to you."

Matty hung up, looked to Billy, sitting hangdog yet eager in the chair opposite.

"So what's happening?" His mouth open like a hinge.

"The usual."

"Nothing?"

"You're a fast learner," Matty said. "All right, here's what I want you to do."


"OK . . . I was scared," Eric began, the cellar air combined with the gram of garbage blow he had test-run purchased in front of Hamilton Fish Park this morning making him sneeze. "Some, some street animals came up on us, shot the guy standing next to me, and me? I just ran. I ran into the building. There was a gun, so you flee. Human nature, OK? But even in hiding, even with the shooter gone, I was so paralyzed that I didn't even think to call 911. I said I did to the cops but I lied. And at first they thought I was lying to cover up something criminal. Like it was inconceivable to them that someone would be so frightened that they would have to lie about something like that simply out of shame. See, but they know how to tease apart lies, those people. They may not know what's behind the lie, they may think they do, but at first it doesn't make a difference to them, they just go after the lie, pick at it, pick at it, just watching me fall to pieces before their eyes, like rooting it on. And, I felt like my life was in danger all over again. And all I wanted was out. I just wanted out of that room.

"And right up to the end, they wouldn't grant me my cowardice, it just was too inconceivable. I mean, I guess they pretended they did, towards the end this one cop ripped into me for it in kind of this last-ditch ploy to make me lose it and confess to salvage my, my manhood or something, but you could tell he still thought I was playing them about it."

Bree stood there looking at him like there were other people in the cellar and he was monopolizing all her time, Eric thinking, How can people turn on you so fast?

"But worse than the humiliator?" Eric coked on. "Was the other one, the comforter—"

"It sounds awful," she said before he could get to the point, the measuredness of her tone just tearing him up. It was as if their lightning-fast sex tussles down here a few nights ago had been nothing more than a dream.

"And there's other stuff, stuff that's hard to find words for at the present time, so . . ." He trailed off.

"Jesus." She winced, her gaze darting right and left like the tail of a cat clock.

"Anyways," waving vaguely to the stairs behind her; prisoner released.

He waited until she disappeared above the line of the low ceiling before doing the last of the gram.

How could people change up on you so fast?

An hour after leaving Matty's office, Billy stood with Mayer Beck again, this time in front of 27 Eldridge, both of them staring at the trace remains of the shrine: nothing there now but some hangdog balloons down to the size of basting bulbs, the increasingly shredded newsphoto of Willie Bosket flapping against the building, and the last rays of sun sparkle coming off a few fragments of colored botanica glass that had been swept to the wall.

"So." Beck turned to him, easing a steno pad from his back pocket. "What's up?"

Eric waited for the anticrime taxi to roll off from in front of the Lemlich Houses, then walked past the small miniplaza directly across the street: four shabby shops—a pizzeria, a corner store, a Chinese takeout, and a Laundromat—all inset farther back from the curb than the buildings on either side of them, the few extra square yards of pavement a natural arena-lounge for the young men toddling in place there now, most sporting sideways baseball caps and billowing white T's down past their knees.

It would be nothing to walk by them later tonight into the pizzeria; it was the coming out with the slice and just standing there like a yuppie piñata that would be the sticky part.

"I told him," Billy said, worrying the fabric of his trousers as he faced Matty across the desk. "Thursday, one o'clock."

"And he knows the deal," Matty said, "that 1PP's not on board."

"Yeah. He gets it. Totally."

"And you didn't go off?"

"Off?"

"On a rant."

"No. I, no."

"OK. Good." Matty patted Billy's hand on the blotter. "You did good."

Billy bobbed his head in acknowledgment, continued to sit there.

"I'll call you." Matty made a show of doing something else. "As soon as something jells."

"Can I just stay here for a while?" Billy winced. "Not to get in your way."

"I think you should go home, rest up for—"

"Right now?" Billy's voice started to rise. "All I need to do is *look* at my bed and I start having nightmares from across the room."

Matty hesitated. "All right. Yeah, sure. Relax here, then."

After a few moments of head-down paperwork at the desk, Billy sitting there lost in thought, Matty caught Mullins's eye and hand-signaled, Call me. "You want something, Billy? A soda? Coffee?"

"I'm good," he said, then, leaning forward, "I had this dream last night?"

Matty's cell rang. "Clark."

"What do you want?" Mullins asked.

"Are you serious?" Matty shot to his feet and began scribbling down some bogus address. "I'll be right there." Then, to Billy, "Something just came up."

"On this?"

"On something else. We could be gone for a few hours. Let me get you a ride home."

Once his slice was gone, he had no idea what to do with his hands, where to rest his eyes.

At ten in the evening, the foot traffic between that four-shop mini-plaza and the Lemlich Houses directly across Madison Street was never-ending, but the group of tent-wearing young men more or less stayed clustered up near the stores.

The more they seemed to be ignoring him, the more powerfully he felt watched.

There was no way he'd approach them; or was he supposed to . . .

After a few excruciating minutes, one of the T-shirts walked away, ambling back across Madison into the Lemlichs, Eric thinking maybe he should take off too; back to Berkmann's, no way would this end well.

Then one of the other kids, without ever looking at him, began to slowly waddle-walk in his direction, his oversize T and mannered side-to-side gait making him look like a hard-core penguin.

"What you need, Officer," the kid said, still looking off.

A gold medallion, one of three around his neck, announced his name: David.

"I look like a cop?" Eric asking for real.

"Not supposed to."

"I'm no cop."

"OK."

Eric started to walk away.

"Hey, Officer?" the kid called out, and when Eric turned around, the whole crew finally came to life, laughing and low-fiving each other.


"He ain't police." Big Dap waved off his brother from his perch on the ramp rail in front of 32 St. James.

"I don't know about that," Little Dap said. He had crossed over from the miniplaza because he didn't know if that guy from the shooting had come back here to look for him.

"I *know* you don't know," Dap smirked, then nodded to Hammerhead, one of the older guys always hanging with him: Step to it.

As Hammerhead broke into a lazy jog back across Madison, Little Dap started to take off too, heading upstairs until this thing was over, but . . .

"Oh, yo. Get back here, little man. Gotta be in it to win it."

"Naw, see . . ." But his brother just waved him quiet.

"I'm in it," Tristan said, but as usual, nobody heard him.

Humiliated but thinking, Better a live asshole, Eric continued down Madison towards Montgomery, then froze as he heard feet coming up fast behind him. "Whoa, whoa," felt a hand on his elbow.

The guy pulling his coat was older than the others: mid-twenties, with a soul patch under his lip and so bulge-eyed that his gaze appeared wraparound.

"Them hoppers don't know shit. What you need."

"Nothing."

"How much nothing."

"An ounce." Didn't mean to say it . . .

"A what?" his gibbous eyes glistening with surprise. A half block behind them that younger crew waddled in place as they watched the exchange from their two squares of pavement. Eric thinking, Just go, started to walk away again.

"Ho ho ho, hold it, hold it," the guy half-laughing, taking Eric's wrist. "That's just a lot of product on a spur-of-the-minute walk-up. But that's OK, can be done. Y'all just come with me," lightly tugging him towards the Lemlichs.

"No offense"—Eric went into a slight water-ski crouch to stand his ground—"but I'm not going over there."

"Hey. Let me tell you something about me because I realize no way you can know." He was still holding Eric's hand, Eric too embarrassed to ask for it back. "I am a fully endowed undergraduate student at the Borough of Manhattan Community College, something like six classes shy of accredidation, so . . ."

"What's your major?"

"My what?" Then, "Science."

"I'm not going over there." Eric finally getting his hand back.

"All right, fine, strip out here then."

"Strip for what, a wire?"

"Yes sir."

"Look, I don't even have any money on me." Turning out his pockets.

"That's OK. I don't have no product. We're just conversing here, maybe go to the next level if the shit's copacetic."

They compromised on the bathroom of the pizzeria, the two of them walking through the dining area, then past the Bangladeshis kneading dough at the back-room prep table.

The bathroom was bigger than it had to be but tearingly pungent from the scented urinal cakes.

The guy squatted on his hams as he carelessly patted Eric down, then took two steps back.

"Awright, boss, drop them skivvies."

"The fuck," Eric just saying it to say it, then dropping his jeans and looking off, holding down his boxers.

"Awright, awright." The guy backed up farther. "I don't need to see any more than I do."

Not that Eric had that much experience in this, but there was something disturbingly insincere about the whole routine.

"Say again what you want?"

"I said already."

"What." The guy grinned, his wraparound eyes pulsing. "Y'all want to check me for a wire?" Standing with his arms wide.

"I said to you already."

"You did. You did." Then, "Ounce a G."

"No."

"Then we're done."

"OK." Relieved, Eric reached for the bathroom doorknob.

"Ho ho ho." The guy pinched the back of Eric's shirt. "What did you think it would be?"

"I was told seven."

"*Seven?*" Laughing. "Who the fuck down here, in *this* neighborhood, said seven."

"OK, I heard wrong." Reaching for the door again.

"I'll go nine."

"I'm sorry," Eric said, "what's your name?"

"You hear me ask yours?"

"OK, whatever. It's like, I'm going to say seven fifty, you're gonna say eight fifty, I'm gonna say eight, you're gonna say eight twenty-five, so OK, eight twenty-five."

"Eight fifty."

"Bye."

"Awright, awright, eight twenty-five. Damn."

"OK, then." Eric feeling trapped by his win. "How soon can you get it?"

"How soon can you?"

"Me? The money?"

"Yuh-huh."

"Half an hour?" Just wanting to get it over with, whatever this would turn out to be.

"Hang on." The guy raising his eyes to the ceiling, doing the time math. "Make it forty-five."

"OK, forty-five."

"All right, I'll see you back here then."

"Not here." Eric thinking, thinking. "I'll meet you somewheres inland."

"In what? What the fuck is *inland*."

"Somewheres near Orchard, Ludlow, Rivington."

"Oh. You mean *white* land." Laughing. "Just say that. Where at?"

"Where at?" Eric stalling. "There's a taco place on Stanton and Suffolk, you know it?"

"I know Stanton and Suffolk."

"There's a taco place."

"Does it say taco on the sign?"

"I assume so."

"Then we're good."

"Forty-five minutes?"

"Forty-five."

Eric faltered, then reached for the bathroom door again.

"Ey, yo." The guy turning him around at the last moment. "I can tell y'all nervous and shit?" Pulling a five-pointed badge out of his pocket and grabbing Eric's wrist. "Y'all had every right to be."

Eric stood rooted, half-smiling in shock.

"*Bawwww,*" the guy howling as he reared back and clapped his hands. "I'm sorry, I'm sorry." Showing the badge again, a thin tin saying SUPER SECRET AGENT. "I'm sorry, bad joke, bad joke."

"Yeah." Eric's forehead creamed with sweat.

• • •

The worst part of his being arrested those many years ago up in Binghamton was the day-after-day waiting for it; so when that fucking idiot in the pizzeria flashed the badge in his face, Eric had been flooded with relief. Now, as he walked home from the Lemlichs, he tried to recapture that sensation, as if whatever was to happen had happened already, the piper paid in full.

This would not end well; he was pretty sure of that, but he felt powerless to stop it.

Over the last two weeks it had felt to him as if he'd slowly been devolving into one of his own Lower East Side ghosts; and ghosts, he believed, were nothing more than mindless reenactors, in possession of only the faintest sense of déjà vu.

And so he floated into the vestibule of his walk-up, floated up the five flights of cockeyed stairs and into his denuded apartment like he had only the dimmest memory of ever being under this roof before.

But when he pulled his accumulated tip-pool skimmings out of a hiking boot in the closet and began to count out $900, $75 going into a separate pocket as an emergency reserve for the inevitable last-minute hustle, something in him shifted; it was as if the blunt value of the bills flicking between his hands lent more substance to him too; substance and confidence, and for the first time all evening he had a glimmer of himself not as some witless shade following a preordained script but as an individual who was in the process of taking control, of turning things around for himself.

With his jeans front-loaded with cash, he poured himself a vodka bracer, then just stared at it. Dumped it down the drain.

Not tonight, my man.

Feeling lighter and sharper than he had for days, he locked the apartment behind him, tripped down the stairs, got as far as the mailboxes; he could see Stanton Street through the glass of the lobby door, then felt the wind go out of him in a whoof.

At first he thought he'd stepped into the path of something moving at warp speed, maybe a bullet, maybe *the* bullet; getting shot, he heard, sometimes felt like that, a massive hammerblow; but when he looked up from the grimy tiled floor into the Lemlich faces, he knew it was nothing more than a punch to his unbraced gut.

One of them, wearing a bandanna up to his eyes, immediately stooped over and started going through his pockets, looking for the buy money, the kid's billowing T covering Eric's head and giving him an intimate view of a taut gut and flat chest.

Then one of the others hissed, "Hold it, hold it," and he felt himself being dragged by the ankles along the tiles around to the wedge of space beneath and behind the stairs, out of sight from the street, another punch to close his eyes, his brain a tuning fork, then a scrabbling through his pockets, one of them saying, "Seventy-five? He say eight hundred something," then another punch, Eric hearing more than feeling something crack beneath his eye, then, "Ho ho ho, here it is right here," the rest of his roll liberated, then another face close to his, no mask, chewing-gum breath, "We know where you *live*," then a final punch, his right eye ballooning in its socket, then the door opening to the street, letting in a slice of oblivious female laughter from up the block, then silence as the door closed again, Eric thinking, This'll do.


After fretting all day about sucking Billy Marcus into something for which the guy was completely unprepared, as night came down, Matty also found himself thinking about Minette Davidson again, and so almost as an act of penance he wound up heading over to the No Name to subject himself to his mixologist, practicing saying her name all the way, Dora, Dora, Dora, feeling slightly less of a hound for remembering it this time.

But when he made it through the heavy black curtains into the room, she wasn't there.

Her replacement behind the bar was just as compellingly moody and distant, though, long and lean with plum-colored eyes and slick black bangs; and she served up his pilsner with a tight smile that made him want to chat.

"I was looking for Dora."

"My English . . ." Squinting at him.

He waved it off, just conversating here; but she turned to the male mixologist, speaking to him in what Matty thought was Russian.

"She's sorry," the young guy said, "her English . . ."

"Forget it." Matty shrugged.

"You said you are looking for your daughter?"

Tristan sat on the roof of his building looking out on the East River, its muscular flow gleaming beneath the light-strung bridges going across to mostly dark Brooklyn. What did that cop say the night him and Little Dap ran up here? A billion-dollar view on top of ten-cent people. Something like that. He scanned the top-floor windows of the nearest Lemlich high-rise, maybe fifty yards away, saw the lives in there like little mouse plays, mostly everybody watching TV or talking on the phone.

*At night*
*All this light*
*And Im still*
*out of sight*
*movin like a ninja*

He stopped, unable to come up with anything that rhymed with *ninja*, then switched the words around:

*Like a ninja Im movin*

It wasn't coming.

He closed the notebook and walked to the opposite side of the roof to the spot where Little Dap had him hanging upside down that first night, upside down and looking at the sidewalk fifteen stories below.

Tried writing here.

*Just a drop*
*That could stop*
*The pain*
*The brain*
*The insane flame*

He draped himself over the edge, trying to get as close to the position that Little Dap had alley-ooped him into that night. With the low guardrail cutting into his hips, with more of his body over the side of the roof than not, he let his feet leave the gravel and tried to balance himself. He could do it for a few seconds, but then he started tipping forward and had to clutch the grillwork under his belly to catch himself, a bad thrill.

Little Dap. Little Bitch.

Dizzy but upright he walked back to the other side of the roof, took the .22 out from the back of his jeans, scanned all the living room windows in the building closest to him, all the mouse plays, then turning his head away, squeezed off two rounds before trotting back down the stairs.

**Matty sat at his desk,** elbows on the blotter, today's *New York Post* before him and Berkowitz in his ear.

"Where the fuck does this guy get off—"

"Boss, I gave you the heads-up yesterday."

"No way he's doing this at the crime scene. He'll never get the clearance."

"Clearance? What are we going to do, lock him up? Look, he's not a bad guy, he's just, he's flailing here."

"Flailing."

"That being said, I can't actually see it being a bad thing, you know? Because unless someone picks up a phone, says a name, right now we're nowhere."

The DI muffled his receiver to talk to someone on his end, Matty closing his eyes as he waited.

"Yeah, so . . ." Berkowitz got back on the line.

"So what about it?" Matty said. "Do the presser, get that tipline ringing. I'll take a bum lead over no lead at this point."

Silence.

"The guy had to fly to Miami this morning to see his son's grandparents, but he's on his way back first thing tomorrow for this."

"We need a letter of intent from the bank."

"I believe that's already been faxed to you," Matty wincing as he said it.

"You're pretty on top of this, aren't you."

"Honestly? It's not my call, but I am desperate for something to go here, otherwise . . ."

"He wants this when?"

"Tomorrow."

"I don't know, we have to see what else is jumping off around here. I know there's a big immigration sting going down in Ridgewood tonight, DCPI's definitely gonna want to run with that tomorrow. Maybe Friday'd be better."

"Friday?"

"Call me tomorrow."

Matty hung up and looked to Billy across the desk.

"Why am I flying to Miami?"

"Makes you sound like a guy with a timetable."

"But I'm not really going."

"No."

"Friday . . ." Billy absently tapping the side of his head. "You know what I was thinking? Maybe I should sign up with Victims' Services."

"Definitely." Matty nodded. "Get some help."

"Well, no, I meant like, volunteer, you know, give help *to* others."

Matty stared at his blotter.

"I don't know," Billy said. "Maybe not."


Little Dap, who, from what Tristan heard, was not only scared out his ass last night, but wearing a mask like Jesse James the whole time, was nonetheless the one telling the story.

"Guy's like, 'Whup, whoa, hey, what's, 'scuse me, fellas?' you know, we're like dragging him around the stairs, start going through his pockets like seventy dollars in there, Hammerhead said like eight hundred, so Devon's *bam bam bam*, pounding on him, 'You cheatin' ass motherfucker!' then I'm in the other pocket like, 'Uhh, it's right here,' Devon's like, 'I don't *give* a fuck! He shoulda said it's the other pocket!' *Bap, bap, bap.*"

Everybody was laughing, ho-shitting in the postschool afternoon.

They were all hanging in front of 32 St. James, perched on or leaning into the paint-chipped three-rung railings that ran along the wide steps that led to the lobby door.

As always, Tristan had one of the hamsters with him, those long fingers of his extending like suspenders down the front of the boy's shirt.

He took a few steps away from the others and picked a spot where, if he called for someone, he would have to leave his perch and go to him.

"Dev, yo"—Little Dap snapped his wrist across his body—"the boy's wound *tight*."

"Ey, yo." Tristan nodded to Little Dap, who ignored him. "Yo." Staring at him until he reluctantly slid off the rail and trundled over.

"The fuck you want?"

"Give me a dollar." Looking away from him as he spoke.

"A what?"

"I need to get him a Nesquik." Rippling his fingers on the hamster's shirt.

"So?" Little Dap shrugged. "Get him a motherfuckin' Nesquik."

"Give me a dollar."

"Is you *deaf*?" Walking away.

Waiting until Little Dap had hopped back up onto his perch, Tristan said it again and no louder than when he was standing right next to him. "Give me a dollar."

Little Dap looked at him.

"Give me a dollar." Staring at him until he came back down.

Clucking his tongue, Little Dap stomped back to Tristan and slipped him a bill. "Just to hear you quiet," then stomped back to his aluminum perch, Tristan watching him go.


They were knocking on doors again, this time in the Walds, looking for the grandmother of a kid traffic-stopped last night in North Carolina heading for the city with four shopping bags full of handguns in the front seat, including three .22s; no one home; then drove to the Cuban place off Ridge for some coffee.

As Yolonda went to the bathroom, Matty stepped back outside and encountered a crime scene across the street in the Mangin Towers so fresh that people were just now coming out from wherever they were hiding when the shots went off. Without going back in for Yolanda, he ditched his coffee and hustled over just as the ambulance pulled up, the medics inside sitting tight until the first patrol car swung in directly in front of them, the body waiting patiently on the pavement.

The first few moments were a riot of people running both to the scene and away from it, of uniforms corralling and expelling and securing, no one paying them any attention, the sound track a cacophony of crying and screaming and sharp, angry male barking, both civilian and municipal; Matty content to just stand there while it sorted itself out.

And then he spotted the girl standing in the shadows of the building breezeway, quietly crying. Hands in his pockets, he got within conversation range, then looked away from her.

"White man in a suit," she muttered.

Matty tilted his chin towards Yolanda, just now crossing the street.

"You want to talk to her instead?"

"Her?" The girl pulled a face. "I hate that bitch." Then tilted her chin to Jimmy Iacone, just rising from a sedan. "The fat guy."

"You know Katz's?" Matty asked without looking at her.

"My cousin used to cut meat there," she said, "till that bitch locked him up."

"All right, just start walking to Katz's, the fat guy'll be right behind you."


Ike had to be reburied. He was laid out on the futon in Eric's flat, which now had a high footboard attached, which was good because it blocked his view of the body.

Then the two guys Eric had been waiting for finally showed up with the half ki of coke that he ordered. They laid it out on the drainboard by the sink. The only problem was that he had gotten mugged and so now he had to go to the Diners Club building to get the cash to pay for it, which meant leaving these guys alone in here with Ike's body, but he had no choice. He wanted that coke for the road trip he planned to take directly after the funeral. He was going to go straight north, possibly past Canada, and was really jacked about it; in fact it would be his reward; that and the coke, for putting up with this whole reinterment, reburial thing, which was Ike's sister's idea.

As he walked out of the flat, leaving the two drug dealers, the body, and the coke behind, he was surprised to see that his building had come back to life with the tenants of a hundred years ago, everybody walking, running, trudging up and down the stairs carrying all sorts of shit—suit patterns, buckets of water, chamber pots—the entire building reeking of sweat and heavy cooking and excrement. But that was OK too because if anybody happened to go into his flat while he was out and see the half ki just lying there, unless they were Hudson Dusters they wouldn't even know what it was, so . . .

But halfway to the Diners Club building in Times Square, he recalled something funny about all those reanimated tenants: yes, they were dressed for the turn of the century in battered derbies and tattered waistcoats and multilayered dresses, but they had long, curved nails on their left pinkies like all the pimps and hustlers and every kind of mack pappy player back in the seventies, the sole purpose of which was to more easily scoop coke from a baggie . . . so that couldn't be good. There was nothing to do but race back to Stanton Street and make sure the phony greenhorns weren't hitting on his stash.

And sure enough, when he busted back into his parlor, a dozen of them were bending over and snorting away. But hang on, the coke was still on the drainboard; they were behind that obscuring footboard bending over Ike's body, noisily dipping and snorting and please, God, can you wake me up, but when he does, Eric is in a hospital bed, the right side of his face is on fire, and it's worse.

Eight hours later, a few minutes past midnight, Matty was on the roof of the precinct smoking a cigarette and looking at Brooklyn.

The crying girl from the Mangin Towers had given it all up to Iacone over two franks and a Cel-Ray. The shooter's name was Spook; the victim, who pulled through in surgery, Ghost; the jokes to come off those two tags unbearably predictable. The beef, if anybody cared, was over some other girl named Sharon who didn't like either of them and was going into the army next week anyhow.

She'd given it all up to Iacone right down to the location of Spook's bedroom in his grandmother's apartment in the Gouverneurs; but instead of immediately heading over there with the kid most likely in hiding somewhere else right then, after some minor agonizing Matty had made the decision to sit tight.

Experience had shown him that when it came to self-preservation, the overwhelming majority of knuckleheads out there were terminal amnesiacs; hopefully, if they gave Spook enough downtime, he would come home on his own, and so they had held off; were still holding off.

Matty checked the time; one more cigarette, then do it.

His cell rang.

"Oh." Minette.

"Hey," Matty said calmly, as if he'd been expecting the call.

"I'm sorry, I thought . . ."

"This is Matty Clark."

"I know. Sorry."

"Everything OK?"

"What? Yeah, well, yeah."

"What."

"Billy checked in to a hotel. That Howard Johnson's down by you."

"Jesus Christ."

"He says he needs to be near the precinct. That you're working together."

"You know what? People go home every day. It's called commuting."

"Look. If that's what he needs to do . . . But let me just ask. That *is* what he's doing, right? Helping you?"

"Believe it or not?" Matty watching from above as Quality of Life made a car stop just off the Williamsburg. "At this point, yeah, he is."

"OK. That's good. I guess."

"He'll come home."

"I know." Her voice a husky hush.

"So you're OK?"

"Yeah."

"You'd tell me if you weren't . . ."

"I would."

For a few seconds the silence hung between them like a weighted curtain.

Then Yolonda stepped up behind him. "Are we gonna capture this mutt or what?"

The whole thing went down as easy as delivering the mail: Matty book-ended by Yolonda and Iacone, ringing the bell, Spook himself coming to the door barefoot and with a sandwich in his hand. A two-shot der-ringer lay on the kitchen table behind him, clearly visible from where they were all standing.

Matty said, "Let's not get your grandmother all upset. Just come out in the hall," and he did.

And that, was fucking that.

A textbook arrest perfectly played from crime to cuffs. *This* was how to get the job done. *This* was how it was supposed to go down; Matty wishing, as he head-steered the silent, pliant Spook into the backseat of his car, that he had never even heard the name Marcus; Ike, Billy, Minette, any of them; imagining what a bowl of cherries his life would be if the goddamned kid had only gone and got himself killed last week three blocks south in the Fifth.

**On Thursday Matty started calling** Berkowitz at nine, leaving message after message, each one a little testier than the last, Billy sitting in the chair opposite working a rubber band like a spinning wheel around the fingers of one hand. A whole day before the most optimistic go time for a presser, he was already dressed in a sports jacket and tie. At eleven, still not having gotten a callback and with Billy alternately staring at him and taking endless trips to the bathroom, Matty told him to go home or wherever he was staying these days, and he'd contact him as soon he got through.

When Eric opened his eyes, two detectives were at his bedside, a black woman in a pantsuit and a Chinese guy in a three-piece.

"How you doing?" the woman said, offering him a blur of names as the other one stepped off to take a quick call. "Do you want to tell us what happened?"

"Not really."

"Not really?" as if he were giving her shit.

The other detective snapped off his cell. "Sorry."

"He doesn't want to tell us what happened," she said.

"Oh yeah?"

"It was my own fault," Eric said.

"All right." She shrugged. "It was your own fault. Just tell us who else was involved."

"Nobody." Flinching as he said it. He should have said, *They came at me from behind*.

"Well, if this 'nobody' comes back, they might just want to finish what they started," the Chinese detective said. He had a surprisingly heavy accent for someone who had made it out of uniform, Eric thought, but what did he know.

"Look, we can't make you tell us."

"That's right."

The female detective shrugged, not really giving a shit but pissed at the stonewall.

The other one's cell went off again and he stepped away to take it.

"Ow," Eric said, then went back beneath whatever drug they had put him on.

Berkowitz didn't return Matty's call until one in the afternoon.

"What's up?"

The blitheness of the question told Matty everything he needed to know about the nonstatus of the presser.

"Well, he's here."

"Who is?"

Matty stared at the receiver in his hand. "Marcus, he took the red-eye in from Miami."

"Yeah? How's he doing?"

"He'll be better after tomorrow's presser."

"Tomorrow?" Berkowitz said as if it were news to him.

It was as if the two of them were in a play, neither allowed to acknowledge that they were simply reciting lines.

"OK," Berkowitz said. "What's the reward up to now?"

"Forty-two thousand dollars," Matty said slowly.

"All right, you know what? I need to get back to you. I just have to talk to a few people."

• • •

An hour later Billy came back into the squad room.

"What's happening?"

"I'm waiting on a callback," Matty said. "Still waiting."

"Jesus Christ." Billy flopped into the chair sidesaddle to the desk.

"This is four-star foot-dragging, four-star buck-passing."

"I don't know how you put up with it." Billy closed his eyes, his breath too sweet.

"Have you been drinking?"

"Yeah, but I'm OK."

"Yeah?"

"Yes."

Matty stared at him assessingly for a moment. "You know what?" Snatching up his desk phone. "Fuck it."

"Yeah, hey, boss." Matty angled the receiver so that Billy could listen in.

"I was just going to call you," Berkowitz said.

"You know I have to say"—Matty eyed Billy—"this guy Marcus is getting good and pissed."

"Yeah? What's his problem?"

"His problem? He caught a predawn flight to do this and here it is two days later and he's still sitting on his hands waiting to hear if we're on board or not."

"Well, I just got off the horn with Upshaw about that. Turns out there's a problem with the reward money."

"Oh yeah?" Matty scribbled a gouge into his steno pad. "And what would that be?"

"His end of it? The twenty? He didn't set up the escrow account properly. According to the letter of intent it's in his name, which means he controls the payout. We don't work that way."

"What the fuck?" Billy lunged forward drunkenly, Matty glaring him into silence.

"The letter of intent, huh?" Matty said, a finger to his lips.

"At first Upshaw was going to put it through, but then he got nervous, called Mangold, the chief says no press conference. Says, 'I thought I made myself clear on this one. Let it die.'"

"Let it *die*?" Billy hissed to himself, Matty thinking, Coffee.

"I'm being as candid with you as I can," Berkowitz said.

"Yeah? Then let me be candid too. The bank letter, the escrow account, it's all in good faith and you and everybody else in that building knows it."

"That's not the point."

"Look, boss, the guy flew all this way and he wants his presser with us. He wants it done."

"Well, he'll have to deal with it."

Matty looked at Billy like he wanted to punch him.

"You know what? I'm gonna have him call you directly because I didn't sign up for this, and if he goes and embarrasses the job, I don't want everybody pointing the finger at me."

"Fine, have him call me."

"*Me?*" Billy suddenly looking terrified, then completely checking out, going into an Ike-drift like slipping under the covers.


Matty took Billy back to the Castillo de Pantera, set him up at a corner table, and plied him with coffee.

"Here's what I need you to do. One. Sober the fuck up. Then I need for you to call this guy, Deputy Inspector Berkowitz, and tell him you want this to happen. You raised the money and now you want that tipline ringing off the hook. You bring up all those reporters' cards you have and you tell him how all these vampires ever really want to hear you talk about is how the police have fucked this up from the door on in, but how you've never bit on that. You've never talked bad, but, Deputy Inspector Berkowitz, I wind up doing this presser solo, and I swear to Christ, all bets are off and I am going after you, your boss, the chief of D's, and the PC, but *your* name is going to come out of my mouth first, Deputy Inspector Berkowitz, Deputy Inspector Berkowitz, just keep saying his name like that, and say it first."

"You want me to call him?"

Matty leaned into the table. "Are you hearing anything I'm saying?"

"Yes."

"I am putting my balls in a sling for you right now. Do you get that?"

"Yes."

"This is not part of my job, fucking with these people. Do you understand that?"

"Then why are you doing it?" The question popping out of Billy's mouth like a frog.

Matty hesitated just a hair before saying, "For your son."

Hesitated just long enough for Billy, even in his frightened and boozy daze, to pick up on the hollowness of the declaration.

But Matty picked up on it too; hustling the dead kid's father like that . . .

"You know what?" Matty said more softly. "All due respect to your son and hopefully this'll work in his favor, but it's just that they have been fucking with me on this since day one, and I am so very, very tired of it. I just want to do my job."

"I can see that," Billy said evenly, and once again his refusal to be judgmental reinforced Matty's wanting to go the extra mile.

"Look," Matty said, "do you want to just blow this whole thing off?"

"No." Billy gulping down coffee.

"Do you want me to go over everything again?"

"No."

"Nothing?"

"No."

"All right, brother." Matty dialed Berkowitz for him, then slapped the cell phone into the guy's hand like a gun. "Show me what you got."

But when Berkowitz came on the line, Billy was so frightened that the first thing out of his mouth was a complete hash.

"Mr. Berkowitz, I would really like you to join me at this press conference. If I'm up there by myself, I have no idea what to say," then closing his eyes in self-disgust.

"Well, look, Mr. Marcus," Berkowitz said, his voice coming through to Matty tinny but clear, "first off let me say how sorry I am for your loss."

Billy seemed grateful for the smooth and sober voice coming back at him. "Thank you."

He should have better prepared him for this; did the guy really think Berkowitz would have come at him like some animal?

"I have two sons myself and I can't even begin to imagine what you're going through right now."

"Thank you," Billy said softly, looking at Matty.

"And from what everybody tells me, Ivan was a great kid."

"Ivan?"

"A real comer."

"Ivan?"

Matty either imagined or actually heard the rustle of papers on Berkowitz's end.

"Mr. Marcus, is there a number that I can call you back?"

"Not really." Billy suddenly dead sober.

"Then maybe we should talk face-to-face."

"Maybe we should," Billy said coldly, Matty finally feeling calm enough to go outside and have a cigarette.


Billy came out a few minutes later.

"Where at?" Matty asked.

"Green Pastures on East Houston?"

"When."

"Hour and a half."

"Hour and a half?" Matty startled. "All right, shit, OK . . . First I need for you to go back to wherever you're staying and get every reporter's card you have."

"He called him Ivan," Billy said.

Matty lit another cigarette off the last one. "Don't forget it."


They sat in Matty's sedan a half block west of Green Pastures, a vegan deli founded by white pioneers in the mid-seventies, situated at the ass end of East Houston, the dying sun tinting their chests and chins orange.

Billy seemed to be having a hard time breathing, as if the righteous fury in him had been smothered by a mortal stage fright.

"Billy." Matty grabbed his biceps. "Listen to me. Are you listening to me? You look like you're going to have a heart attack, but fuck it. *Be* pissed. You have every right, you hear me?"

"No. I know. I just don't want to fail him, you know?"

Matty hesitated, fail who, then, "You won't."

Billy nodded briskly, then reached for the door.

Matty grabbed his arm again. "One more time. Chief of Manhattan detectives?"

"Upshaw."

"Chief of D's?"

"Mangold."

"Commissioner?"

"Patterson."

"Go."

But then grabbed him again, Billy looking ready to puke.

"And where am I?"

"What do you mean?"

"Berkowitz asks you, 'Where's Detective Clark right now.' You say . . ."

"How the hell should I know?"

"Beautiful. Go."

Billy bolted for the door, Matty holding him one last time. "You got those reporters' cards?"

"Fuck," Billy said. "I forgot."

Billy left the car and headed towards the deli looking as if he were about to pull his first stickup, Matty feeling like a backstage mother, praying the poor bastard wouldn't fall to pieces in there and blow the play.

Look at him; Matty watching helplessly as Billy walked right past the deli, then kept going all the way until he ran out of sidewalk at the FDR roundabout.

A moment later, after he had corrected his course and doubled back, Berkowitz pulled up in front of the deli in his personal car, no driver, and Matty slid down in his seat. The DI stepped out, intercepted Billy with a handshake, walked him around to the passenger side, and opened the door for him as if Marcus were his date, Matty thinking, Christ, I have to tail a DI, but once inside the car, they stayed put and began to talk.

• • •

"As I said to you on the phone, Mr. Marcus," Berkowitz palmed the Pepcid foils lying in the cup caddy between them, "I can't tell you how sorry I am for your tragedy."

"Thank you," Billy said. Too nervous to look at the deputy inspector directly, he was staring at a girls' soccer team walking across the highway overpass to the riverside park at the far end of the Drive.

"Look, I think it's great that you have this commitment and interest . . . and I just want to reassure you that we're doing everything we can to bring this to a close so you can grieve for your son properly."

"Properly?" Billy getting a little head of steam off that. "Like I'm sitting here with you right now in order to fend off the grieving process?"

Berkowitz quickly put his hands up. "I wouldn't presume to know that."

"Because personally?" Billy finally turned to him. "I think I'm grieving great."

"All I'm trying to say, Mr. Marcus"—Berkowitz put a hand to his arm—"is that I understand your eagerness for a press conference, but I've been working these cases for thirty years, and when it comes to the media, it's all about timing."

"Timing."

"For example, OK? If we had done it today like you originally wanted? Page twelve. At best. Are you reading the papers? They found an infant in a dumpster last night behind Jacobi hospital up in the Bronx. Not to sound callous about these things? But it would've shoved us into the car ads."

"OK." Billy shrugged. "How about tomorrow?"

"Depends what happens tonight," Berkowitz said patiently, "I don't have a crystal ball."

"So, what are you talking about, laying in the cut? You've got nothing, and cool gets cold gets frozen. I want a news conference."

"You're not hearing what I'm saying."

"I'm hearing every word." Billy seemed exhilarated by his newfound lucidity.

"We're on the same side here."

"You know what?" Dry laughing. "The very fact that you think it's necessary to reassure me of that tells me we're not."

Berkowitz took a moment, studying the traffic building behind them on the northbound FDR.

"Look." He put his hands together in an attitude of entreaty. "You seem like a hands-on guy. I respect that. I'd be the same way if I didn't know better, but I do. And what you're asking for isn't going to happen. We'll do this conference when we can get maximum bang for the buck. When thirty years' experience says, 'Now.' "

"No." Billy brushed lint from his pants legs. "That's when you'll do *your* conference. I'll have mine when I want to. You don't want to be part of it? Fine. But I swear, I have been praising you people every step of the way, and, well, that's going to end right here, right now, so when they ask me, and they will, where the hell are the cops? I'm answering as honestly as I can. I'm going to say I had a sit-down with a Deputy Inspector Berkowitz, who I have to assume spoke to me on behalf of Manhattan Chief of Detectives Upshaw on behalf of Chief of Detectives Mangold, on behalf of Police Commissioner Patterson, and according to this Deputy Inspector Berkowitz, the official attitude towards disseminating news of this increased reward here, the official position—"

"All right, all right." Berkowitz briefly lowered his head as if taking a quick nap, then came up shrugging. "I get it."


From his slouched roost across the street Matty saw the whole thing unfold in pantomine.

You had to give it to him, Matty thought, the DI was a pro; played his hand, got trumped, switched teams, moved on.

A moment later they both got out and shook hands, Billy then walking off, Matty suddenly knotty about his making a beeline back to his car under the DI's gaze, feeling like a jerk as he put a hand to the side of his face and averted his eyes, Billy heading right back to the fucking car, Matty dying until Billy abruptly took the last possible turn before reaching for the door, down Attorney, and with enough presence of mind that he never once looked directly at Matty or the car, Matty wondering if there was any kind of payback in the choreography of that very close call.

. . .

A few minutes later, Berkowitz reached him on his cell.

"Yeah, so listen, we're gonna do it. I need to make a few calls, set things up, today's shot, let's say tomorrow afternoon, one o'clock?"

"I greatly appreciate this," Matty said as he trolled Attorney looking for Billy. "As you could probably tell, that guy means business."

"Yeah, I sensed that."

"Anyways, thank you."

"He almost walked right back to your car, didn't he?" Berkowitz said mildly.

Matty froze.

"Just make sure the paperwork's all in."

"Thanks, boss."

"Fuck it," Berkowitz said, "I would've done the same."


When he finally found Billy at the corner of Attorney and Rivington, the blind bearish tilt of his stride made it painfully apparent how much this showdown with Berkowitz had taken out of him, and so Matty held off on calling out his name, just rolled parallel to give him some time to deal.

From working the press to raising the cash to facing down the brass, Billy had come through like a champ, but Matty knew that the victory was a setup; that what Billy was to discover now, if he hadn't already, was that even though the best of all possible outcomes had been achieved here, there would be no relief for him from that grinding sense of anticipation he'd carried in his gut for the last few days, that no matter what came down the line, what measures of justice were ultimately portioned out, what memorials or scholarship funds established, whatever new children would come into his life, he would always carry in himself that grueling sensation of waiting: for a tranquil heart, for his son to stop messing around and reappear, for his own death.

Matty trailed him until Billy made it to the corner of Broome, then finally tapped his horn, Billy turning to the noise but not seeing the car, five feet away.

"Billy."

At the sound of his name he stepped to the passenger door, leaned into the open window.

"Whatever you said to him, brother, you did good."

"Yeah?" Billy looked right through him.

"Seriously." Matty leaned across and carefully pushed open the door. "You did great."

When Matty got home, a message on the answering machine from his ex told him that the Other One was coming down to him in just another day or so and that she'd ring him back as to the exact time and bus line tomorrow. Lindsay called the house only when she didn't want to talk to him, otherwise she called his cell. He understood why this news was reaching him like this: she didn't want to afford him the opportunity to back out.

He stood in his living room staring at his couch as if it were a puzzle, then pulled it out into a bed. Opened up, it took over the entire room, took over the apartment.

On the other hand, what did he really need? The kitchen for making coffee, the terrace for drinking it, and the bedroom. He didn't even watch the TV.

At eleven that evening, Gerard "Mush" Mashburn, three weeks out of Rikers, sat cuffed in the back of the Quality of Life taxi, Geohagan riding next to him, Daley and Lugo up front.

When Daley slipped on the baseball glove wedged between the dashboard and the window and absently started pounding its pocket, Mush piped up, "You got to put some tung oil in that thing."

"Put what?" Daley twisted around.

"Oh, fuck me." Lugo grinned through the rearview. "We got *Field of Dreams* back there."

"Knew a shortstop in high school used bacon grease," Mush said. "Now *that* was a glove with some flex to it."

"You a ballplayer, Mush?" Geohagan asked.

"Was. Left field, right, first base, you name it I played it. Junior year? Made all-county honorable mention."

"No kidding. What county?"

"Chemung, in upstate? And we had us some ballplayers 'round there."

"So how'd you go from that to this." Daley mimed shooting up.

Mush looked out the window, shrugging, Why ask why.

"You want to come play for Quality of Life?" Lugo asked. "We're light some big bats this year."

"Yeah, that would be good. Make a team out of your collars," Mush said. "You put your snatch-and-grabbers around the horn, you know, good hands, quick on they feet, strong-arm boys in the outfield, and, yeah, a killer behind the plate, get the batters all distracted and shit."

The cops beamed at each other, chucking thumbs at the joker in the backseat.

Seeing this, Mush warmed to his audience, just a trace of anxiety in the unconscious and repetitive flick of his tongue.

"Just make sure none a your sideline coaches are sustance abusers, you know, base runners tryin' to read all that scratchin' and noddin', don't know whether to shit, piss, or wind they watch."

The cops were straight-out howling now, bucking in their seats with glee.

"Now the pitcher, he could be problematical. Give me a minute here . . ."

"Nah nah nah, I got that one," Lugo said, seeking Mush's eyes through the rearview again. "You know who'd be perfect? Anybody you call tonight could bring us a gun."

**The briefing for the presser** was set up in the captain's office at the Eighth, twenty or so reporters crammed into the room an hour before showtime to get the ground rules.

The police commissioner had wanted no part of this dog and so passed it down to the chief of detectives, who passed it down to the Manhattan chief of d's, who fobbed it off on Deputy Inspector Berkowitz, who, to Matty's surprise, said he'd do it, claiming that this one had gotten under his skin and he had a personal interest in a successful closed-by-arrest.

Neither Billy nor Minette had shown up yet.

"OK, basically," Berkowitz speaking from his perch on the corner of the captain's desk, "we're going to review the details of the homicide, announce an increase in the reward, and have Ike Marcus's father read a statement." He looked out at the cramped room, ignoring the already raised hands.

"Given that it's an ongoing investigation, we're not going to speak to the progress we've made or give out any details about the investigation itself. Mayer."

"Are you going to talk at all about the catch-and-release of Eric Cash?" Beck asked.

"No, don't go there with that. We're not doing this to get hammered. We're trying to get results."

"But basically, you have no leads, right?"

Berkowitz stared at Beck. "See the above."

As the hands continued to rise, Matty quietly left the room and called Billy's cell from the hallway. It went to the recording, Billy's greeting voice, taped in the pre-apocalyptic days, jarringly buoyant.

Then he called the Howard Johnson's, Billy apparently still there but the line to his room either off the hook or busy.

Which left Minette's cell, but when he called, Nina picked up, her "Hello" tentative and frightened.

"Hey, Nina, this is Matty Clark, is your dad there?"

In the background he could hear Minette: *"Billy . . ."*

"My dad?"

"Are you, you're at the hotel?"

"Yes."

"Billy, get *up*."

"Look." Matty started to pace. "Should I come over there?"

"Should what?" the kid sounding as if she were speaking to him from a foxhole under heavy fire.

"Should—" Matty cut himself off; asking the kid of all people. "Can you put your mom on the line?"

"Mom . . ." Nina's voice fainter as she turned to the room. "It's Matty the cop."

Matty the cop.

"Yeah, hey," Minette speaking in a rush. "We're coming, we're coming."

"Do you want me to—"

"No, we're OK."

"You can make it—"

"I *said* yes."

"—on time?"

"Yes. If I can get off the goddamn phone now," then hung up.

Eric woke up to the sound of a newscaster on NY1 coming from the TV suspended above the bed of his new neighbor, an enormous man of indeterminate age and race, his hands, wrist to knuckles, dope-swollen to the size of catcher's mitts, the fingers lost in the lower ballooning like pigs in a blanket.

On Eric's bedside table there was a wicker basket from Berkmann's, from Harry Steele, holding an assortment of Carr's biscuits, some milky Burrata cheese wrapped in cloth, an Asian pear, and a bottle of Sancerre but no corkscrew. The note read, *Anything I can do. H.S.*

He couldn't find the remote for the TV above his own bed, so as he waited to be discharged, he watched his neighbor's.


A pulpit had been set up on Pitt Street, directly outside the precinct, feeder cables for the various mikes and cameras trailing back into the building like the tendrils of a jellyfish.

Matty stood there now with DI Berkowitz, a full inspector from DCPI, and a raised easel displaying Eric Cash's generic-predator sketch.

It was one-twenty, and still, Billy was nowhere in sight, Matty back to dialing everyone's cell number.

Berkowitz made a small show of scowling at his watch, then reared back in reproachful scrutiny. "Is this guy for real?"

The shooters and reporters, all neck-wedged cell phones and drooping cigarettes, were getting deeply restless, a crop of empty coffee cups sprouting on the roofs and hoods of the patrol cars and unmarked sedans slant-parked at the curb.

"Unbelievable," Berkowitz muttered. "You guys cook this headfuck up together or was it just you?"

Matty didn't think he was supposed to answer.

A handcuffed perp being hustled into the house behind the pulpit tripped over the cables at the door and fell flat on his face. When hoisted upright by the cop who'd collared him, he had a scraped cheek.

"Y'all got that on film," he bawled to the press. "Y'all material witnesses!"

The arresting officer stooped to the curb, retrieved the guy's hat, and popped it back on his head before hauling him inside.

"The hell with this guy," Berkowitz said, then leaned into the beard of mikes on the pulpit.

"Unfortunately, William Marcus, the father of Isaac Marcus, has been called away on urgent family business, but we spoke to him earlier and his family in conjunction with the New York City Police Department . . ."

And then Matty spotted them, the Davidson-Marcus clan, on the far side of Pitt and Delancey, as they emerged from the shadows beneath the Williamsburg Bridge, wild-eyed and unstrung like some multiheaded creature out of the desert.

Billy stood before the microphones, squinting at the white carnation of crumpled paper in his hands, his mouth working but the words unhatched.

"In conjunction with . . ." Billy looked out at the assembled press, coughed, shifted gears. "Every life . . . ," then stopped to cough again.

Minette leaned into Matty, whispered, *"That room . . ."*

"My son . . ." Billy coughing and coughing like to die from it.

Finally one of the reporters stepped up and handed him a bottle of water, Billy taking the time to unscrew it to compose himself.

"My son, Ike, loved this city." He finally bore down, glaring at his notes. "Specifically, he loved the Lower East Side, both his ancestral"—without looking up, he gracefully extended his hand in a sweeping arc as if to suggest a kingdom—"and adopted home . . . In the full embrace of that love . . . he was gunned down in cold blood without profit by opportunistic and low-consciousness thugs. By opportun— By gutless . . ."

Berkowitz, long-faced, his hands crossed over his belt, tilted forward to catch Matty's eye.

Matty reached out and touched Billy's arm; the guy startled by the contact, but he got the message.

"My son, Ike, loved New York . . ."

From the basketball courts across the street by the live-poultry market, the teenage girls playing there abruptly filled the air with their profane and oblivious shouts, Billy closing his eyes, his face storming up red.

"My son, Ike, loved New York," warbling with rage now, "and this city chewed him up . . . This city has blood on its muzzle. This city . . ." Billy swallowed, then dropped his notes like litter.

"What does it take to survive here. Who survives. The, the already half-dead? The unconscious?"

Berkowitz gave Matty another look.

"Do you survive because of what is *in* you? Or because of what *isn't* . . ."

Matty began to reach out to him again, but Minette whispered, "Let him."

"Is, is *heart* a handicap? Is innocence? Is *joy*? My son . . ." Billy's mouth writhing. "I made so many mistakes . . . Please," looking out at the assembled, "who did this . . ."

"Raw stuff," Berkowitz murmured to Matty a moment after Billy stepped off into his wife's embrace, "but he forgot to mention the money."

Fully dressed, Eric sat on the side of his hospital bed still staring at his neighbor's TV long after the live feed of the presser had ended.

A nurse's aide came in, pushing an empty wheelchair.

"You look sad to be leaving here," she said.

"What?"

"What is it." Kicking back the foot pedals for him. "Our fine cuisine?"

"Not tonight, my man," his neighbor drawled then changed the channel.

Within an hour of the presser being shown live on NY1, Matty and the rest of the squad were trapped behind piles of pink slips brought up in a constant stream from the Wheel downstairs, the detectives quickly filing them into Pursue and Not Entertained piles, the one's worth investigating running at about 10 percent of the lot, the other 90 percent the usual crackpots, chronic dime-droppers, and, his favorite, the grudge settlers, who offered up cheating boyfriends, ex-boyfriends, alimony skippers, do-nothing landlords, and deadbeat tenants; who offered up perps of the wrong race, wrong class, wrong age, and wrong neighborhood; shooters who lived on Sutton Place, on Central Park West, in Chappaqua, in Texas, in Alaska for now, but that's just where he's stationed; and as always, the Lords of Transportation calling in by the dozens: the guy was just at my token booth, on my train, on my bus, in my cab, in my dollar van, in my dreams; all of these invariably dropped into the Not Entertained pile; but how could you call it Not Entertained when it included an old lady in Brooklyn Heights giving up her son who lived in Hawaii but could have flown in for this, he does it all the time; when it included a collect call from Rikers, an inmate there giving up the judge who sentenced him and wanting to know if he could get that $42K in cash because he doesn't have a checking account; when it included a female cop in Staten Island calling in to drop a dime on her boyfriend, also a cop, who had just knocked up another female cop.

But then there was that other 10 percent, the Pursue pile, the unavoidables; the third-party verbals, people calling in to say a guy in Fort Lee, in Newark, in Bushwick, in Harlem, in Hempstead told me, or I overheard him say that he did it, or knew who did it, yeah, the dude has a gun, but I don't know guns; or better yet, the caller nails the right caliber; but even with those calls, no one ever knew anybody's real name: Cranky, Stinkum, Half-Dead, House, as in big as a . . .

The best, of course, were the guys they already knew from the neighborhood calling to drop the name of another guy from the neighborhood whom they also knew; a guy with the right kind of history, a guy who had friends with the right kind of histories; so-and-so from Lemlich who runs with so-and-so from Riis and so-and-so from Lewis Street, everybody having the proper pedigree for this . . . But so far they weren't getting anything that good.

"Yeah, this is Detective Clark from the Eighth Squad, who am I speaking to?"

"Who wants to know?"

Matty stared at the receiver. "Detective . . ."

"Oh, oh yeah, this is me who called about the reward?"

"What do you got." Matty already mentally hanging up the phone.

"There's this boy Lanny, I had heard him bragging about doing that other boy ever since the news was on today."

"Yeah? Does Lanny have a gun?"

"Yeah, uh-huh."

"Do you know the caliber."

"I think it's like a .22."

Matty woke up a little. "How do you know him?"

"He was in Otisville with my brother. He just got out."

"Who did."

"Lanny. My brother's still in."

"Really. What was he in for?"

"Lanny or my brother?"

"Lanny."

"A armed robbery on a boy in Brooklyn."

Matty looked to Yolonda; maybe something here.

"You know where he is right now?"

"In the bathroom."

"When you say 'just got out,' how long ago?"

"This morning."

Matty flipped his pen.

"So you comin' over now?"

Matty took down the address. Might as well. Guys like that always knew other guys.

"I got three people calling in on some dude Pogo from Avenue D," Mullins said from behind his pile of pink.

"Pogo from D?" Yolonda answered from behind hers. "I know him. He's a drug dealer. He's not gonna go robbin' anybody."

"Fuck it," Matty said, "bring him in too."

"Ho *shit*, then there's *this* chinny-chin nigger!"

Everybody perched on the rails turned to Tristan, just coming out of the building, and started laughing.

It was Big Bird back in town from that special school and holding court.

"Where's your thing at, man?" Big Bird waggling his hot-dog-sized fingers under his own goatee.

"What you looking at." Tristan murmured, addressing nobody. "You see me every day."

"What did he say?"

"He say something?"

"Least now we know why you grew that motherfucker to begin with," Bird said, wincing.

"But you don't know why I shaved it," Tristan couldn't help replying, although as usual, no one heard him.

Big Bird Hastings, all-city at Seward Park last year, was supposed to be in a fifth-year prep school outside Baltimore for high-prospect, low-reading-level ballers; a place with tutors, where you had to wear a tie and talk about discipline and promptness all the time, but something happened up there and not only was Bird back after just a month but had enlisted in the army too.

"That's cool though, bra," Bird said. "You ain't afraid to show who you are. Most niggers 'round here got a scar like that, never leave the house. So you a *heart*ful nigger, man." Big Bird tapped Tristan's chest with a slow overhand left. "Y'all got *heart*."

It was everything Tristan could do not to bust out in a grin.

"Why don't y'all come with us tonight," Bird still talking to him in front of everybody. "Met this girl at the recruiting center yesterday up in the Bronx? She got a whole bunch a female friends signing up too, ast me if I knew some boys 'round the way to party with, you know, like the last kick-up before all that ten-hut shit starts . . . You up for that?"

"Yeah." Tristan giving it a little smile.

The girls sounded good, but Big Bird calling him "heartful" like that rang in his head like a church bell.

"Bird, you all got room in that for everybody?" Little Dap raised a hand to Bird's Mercury Mountaineer with its Maryland plates sitting at the curb, then shot a look of undercover hate Tristan's way. Little Dap, Little Bitch.

"For *Scar* here?" Bird said, putting a hand on Tristan's shoulder. "Oh, *hell* yeah." Then started to walk to his ride.

"We gonna jump off 'round ten, awright?" Bird called back to the rails, got into his Maryland Mountaineer, then peeled out, Tristan watching until he disappeared around corner.

Scar.


"This Steak Lips," Matty asked, the heel of his palm starting to leave a permanent red half-moon on his forehead, "he's got a gun?"

He was speaking to the third of three people who had called in about some guy Steak Lips up in White Plains, each giving roughly the same story.

"Yeah."

"What kind?"

"I don't know. A gun."

"Where's Steak Lips live."

"With his aunt."

"Who lives where."

"She moved."

"In White Plains, though?"

"Could be."

"All right, let me do some legwork here, I'll get back to you."

Matty was about to punch Steak Lips into the city database, hoping they had one in the system, otherwise they were dealing with a home-grown Steak Lips, which meant driving up to White Plains and hooking up with the local PD, getting their Steak Lips picture in order to make an array for the three callers, so that everybody was on the same page as to exactly which Steak Lips they were talking about; Matty about to do this when Eric Cash walked into the room and all bets were off.

He walked directly to Matty's desk. "What do you need me to do."

"Where's your lawyer?" Matty asked calmly.

"Forget about my lawyer."

"What happened to you?"

The guy's face was a mess.

"Just, please," Cash said, "what do you need me to do."

•  •  •

The first step was to show him their Want Cards, their most likelies, the guy eagerly looking at all twenty-five faces as if looking for love, but it was a no go, which surprised no one.

"OK, look," Matty said, perched on the edge of the lieutenant's desk. "What we need to do now is have you take us through the night again."

"I did that."

"OK, but the difference this time?" Yolonda slid closer to him. "And it embarrasses me to admit it, but this time we're listening with different ears."


For two hours they made Eric review every moment of the night: every bar, every encounter, every conversation with other parties, and when it came to the encounter to end all encounters, their demands became excruciatingly minute; angles of approach to 27 Eldridge, their own, the shooters'; the quality of light, who stood where, who stood in front of whom; any shred of recalled features, postures, hairstyles, wardrobe; any shred of remembered speech, their own, the shooters', in what sequence. He said this, then Ike said that, then he said this? Because the first time you told us . . . Any inconsistency in Eric's tale pointed out as gently as possible, backed with another reminder that he was a sacred witness now, not a suspect; then let's go back to the lighting, at what angle did it fall and on whom, and the gun; forgive us but just one more time, how did you know it was a .22? Then flight patterns, where did they run, did they go together or split up, were they running or walking, any third parties, any vehicles, any other people on the street . . . Two hours and nothing more than he had given them the first time; all three of them at the end of it looking like wet wash.

"All right." Matty stretched. "I think what I'd like to do is go over that sketch you gave us."

"I have to tell you," Eric said, gently massaging his fractured cheekbone, "it's more that I can recognize him than create him."

"Nonetheless," Matty said, then, "You want to get something to eat first?"

"Let's just do it," Eric said, dropping his head into the cradle of his crossed arms.

Yolonda moved in to knead his shoulders. "Oh my God," she said, "it's like you have golf balls under there."

As the sketch artist, carrying a portrait barely different from the one he came in with two hours earlier, closed the lieutenant's office door behind him, Matty looked to Yolonda with impassive disappointment, then uncharacteristically put his own consoling hand on the bleary, fuck-faced witness. "All right, Eric, we appreciate your coming in. I know we didn't exactly make it easy for you."

"That's it?"

"That's a lot," Yolonda said. "We can pick this up tomorrow."

"Maybe we should go back to the scene," Eric said, "I'm OK to do it. Maybe it'll shake something loose."

"You telling us how to do our job?" Yolonda asked mildly.

"No no no." Eric reached out for her. "I'm just suggesting."

"Eric," Matty said. "She's kidding you."

"She what?"

"I'm erasing the tension," Yolonda said. "You want to go? Let's go."

It took twenty minutes to locate the car key, which was not on the board like it was supposed to be, then another twenty to locate the car, which was not parked where it was supposed to be. On foot, 27 Eldridge was ten minutes from the precinct, but with rare exception, no one ever walked anywhere.

As Yolonda reached for the driver's door, Eric sidled up to her, spoke urgently into her ear. "Can I go alone with you? Just for the ride."

"Why?"

"Or walk with you, either way."

"Just, why?"

"I need to tell you something." His eyes were as red as if he'd been at a fire.

In order not to embarrass Cash at being overheard, Matty started walking off as if that had been his intention from the jump. "I'll meet you over there," waving them on.

Eric started in before Yolonda could even put the key in the ignition. "I need for you to know I'm not like what you think I am."

"I think you were in a tough spot," she said, backing out.

"I was a bug."

"What do you mean, a bug." Yolonda taking the long cut to give him the time.

"You turned me into a bug that day."

"Well, Matty was going for the gold there, when he unloaded on you like that, but you have to understand . . . ," waving to a squad car.

"No." Eric's voice started to waver. "You did. With that one question."

Yolonda turned to him.

"You asked me why, why, after talking to you all day about what happened, hours and hours of review and recap and going over it, going over it, I never once asked how Ike was doing, or just even whether he was dead or alive."

"Wow."

She pulled up three blocks from the scene and threw it into park. This could be a long one.

"And I hadn't. I hadn't because I was so scared of the two of you in that room, I was so busy trying to survive, it slipped my mind. Can you imagine that? Becoming like that? What kind of human being just mentally blots out another life like that? Abandons the most basic . . . All it took was a few hours with you two and I turned into a bug. But *I* turned, you see what I'm saying? You couldn't have done it without me. You just brought it to the surface. I mean, what the shooter started, you finished, but it was *in* me, you see? Do you understand that?"

"Huh."

"And so when you finally put the cuffs on? That was nothing. That was peanuts. Three hours, three years, at that point it felt right."

"Yeah," Yolonda said, "sorry."

"But I'm so much better than that."

"OK."

"I'm so much better than anything I've ever done."

"I hear you."

"I need you to know that."

"Absolutely."

"*I* need to know that."

"Don't be so hard on yourself, you know?"

Eric wept into his hands.

"You're a good guy, OK?" pulling back out into traffic.


Matty was waiting for them in front of 27, nothing left of the shrine now but Willie Bosket glaring at them through the tattered, wind-wafted newsprint, looking as if he were peering out from behind his own image.

As they came out of the car, Matty looked to Yolonda, What was that about?

Yolonda shrugged.


"He didn't mean to do it," Eric said within a minute of standing at the scene.

"Who."

"The guy with the gun."

Matty and Yolonda looked at each other, Eric off in his vision.

"The guy with the .22. Ike moved to him and he just squeezed one off. Then he leaned in like"—Eric lunged forward, closed his eyes— "'Oh!' or 'Oh shit!' The other guy without the gun grabbed his partner, said, 'Go!' and they were gone."

"Gone which way."

"Downtown."

"Eric, I'm not trying to trip you up here, but you originally told us east."

"No. Downtown."

So, Lemlich.

"The guy with the .22 said, 'Oh.' The other one said, 'Go,' and they went."

"Anything else they said?"

"No. I don't . . . No."

"The shooter, he leans forward after the shot, his face is in the streetlight?"

"Maybe, I don't . . ."

"Close your eyes and see it."

"A wolf. I know that's what I said before but . . ."

"Hair?"

"A goatee. I said that from the first too. Pretty sure a goatee."

"Hairstyle?"

"Short, shortish."

"Straight, curly, Afro . . ."

"Not Afro, maybe curly, I'm not . . ."

"Eyes?"

"I don't . . . I wasn't going to look at him like that. Meet his eyes . . ."

"Sometimes you do, not meaning to."

"No."

"Scars?"

"I don't . . ."

"How old."

"Late teens? Early twenties? I'm sorry, the gun, it takes all your attention."

"Sure."

"Wait. He might have had a scar."

"What do you mean, 'might'?"

"There was this whitish shine under the goatee."

"Whitish shine . . ."

"I don't know. Like a bald streak in the beard? I don't know, maybe. It could have just been the lighting, the streetlight, I don't know."

"A bald streak?" Yolonda looked to Matty, who scribbled it down.

"Am I . . . Is this helping?"

"Oh yeah," Yolonda said, Matty nodding in agreement, Eric crushed by the absence of electricity, by the politeness.

After twenty more minutes of frustrating *Maybes* and *I'm not sures*, the door to the adjoining building opened and Steven Boulware came outside, looking down at them from the top of the stoop, a knapsack slung over one shoulder.

"Hey." Smiling as he made it down the crumbling stone stairs. "How's it going?"

"Still working it," Yolonda said.

"Yeah." Boulware frowned at the sidewalk, hands on hips. "It's, I can't even . . . It's like a nightmare, a living nightmare."

"Anything ever kick loose?" Yolonda asked. "Anything you can help us with?"

"I wish. I'd almost make shit up if it would help."

"Going on a hike?" Matty nodded to the backpack.

"Oh no, no," giving it another reflective moment. "An audition. This TV thing, it'll probably be for naught, but . . ."

"For *naught*?" Eric blurted.

Boulware cocked his head and squinted at Eric as if he were mildly puzzling, Matty and Yolonda looking from one to the other to see what would shake out.

"But"—Boulware shrugged the knapsack higher up on his shoulder—"you can't win it unless you're in it, you know? So . . ."

He shook hands with the cops and walked off towards Delancey, Eric staring after him, then up at the sky, up at the gods.

"You know what?" Matty said. "I think we should call it a day."

"That's it?"

"Would you be willing to come in tomorrow, look at some more photo arrays?" Matty asked.

"What's wrong with now?"

"The thing with right now?" Yolonda chimed in. "People tend to get fried pretty quick if you load up the day on them. Especially with mug shots."

"We're talking hundreds of faces here," Matty said. "You glaze over pretty quick. Next thing you know the bad guy went right past your eye."

"Yeah, we need you fresh for that."

"I'm as fresh as fuck," Eric squawked. "Let's do it now."


Stopped at a light on their way back to the Eighth, they saw Boulware, a cab waiting for him at the curb as he comforted a crying young woman on the corner of Delancey and Essex, his fingers caressing the small of her back.

Yolonda turned to Eric and touched his arm. "I want to write this book when I retire," she said, " 'When Good Things Happen to Bad People,' " then reared back to get in his eyes. "Know what I mean?"

"Thank you," Eric said, barely able to get the words out.

*Scar*
*The face*
*No one can place*
*The man the plan*
*The gun in the hand*
*No one can understan*
*But its better that way*
*Stay out and play*
*All night all day*

Tristan heard the big chair out in the living room dragged into position, heard the Yankee theme music come on, which meant roughly seven-thirty, which meant his ex-stepfather would be passed out by nine-fifteen, nine-thirty at the latest. Perfect.

*Scar scar*
*Get in the car*
*It's just a short ride*
*But I'll take you far*

Two and a half hours to go.

They could tell right off the photo manager was going to be a bust, Eric looking too hard, sitting there hunched over, mouth agape, wanting to ID the shooter or his partner so badly that he was taking forever with each six-man array, studying each face as if his salvation were to be found in this one's half-dead eyes, that one's freshly busted lip.

At the current rate of scrutiny, Matty calculated that it would take him over eleven hours to work his way through the lot.

At the forty-five-minute mark, one of the faces made him nearly jump out of his seat: Milton Barnes, a twenty-one-year-old walleyed strong-armer from Lemlich.

"What." Yolonda blowing up the image.

"No," Eric saying it faster than any *no* previous.

"Are you sure?"

Matty came to the desk. "Hammerhead."

"No. He just looked like, never mind." Eric ran a fluttering finger across his brow.

"You never did tell us who gave you that beatdown."

"Just, no . . ." Eric tilted his chin to the photo manager. "Keep going."

Matty wandered back to his desk, made a note to bring in Hammerhead Barnes for a lineup, although it would be hard to find five other look-alikes with oblique peepers like that.

"You want to rest your eyes for a little?" Yolonda offered.

Eric wouldn't even look away from the screen to answer her. "Not really."

Over the next hour Yolonda would periodically stare at Matty until he finally gave her the go-ahead to insert the Moment of Truth array. Ten minutes later it was over, the screen of the monitor dark, Yolonda turning Eric's chair to face her.

"Eric, that's it for today."

"Why?"

"You're fried."

"No."

"We appreciate your dedication, but you're done. We can pick up where we left off tomorrow."

"I don't understand, you hound me for weeks to come in, and when I finally do, you what, send me home?"

"Let me show you something." Yolonda punched in an array on the monitor, then leaned back with her hand over her mouth to study him, the gesture accentuating the size of her eyes.

When the six faces that composed the Moment of Truth popped up, Eric looked at the screen, then reared back in confusion.

"Is this supposed to be a joke?"

On the monitor were photos cropped to look like mug shots, of

Jay-Z, John Leguizamo, Antonio Banderas, Huey Newton, Jermaine Jackson, and Marc Anthony.

"What is this?"

"This is an array you looked at five minutes ago and didn't say shit."

"What? No."

"Yes."

"That's the most racist thing I've ever seen," he said desperately.

"Well, no," she said mildly. "We have a white one too."

"Eric, go home," Matty said. "We'll pick it up again tomorrow."


"Can I tell you something?" Matty sat on the edge of Yolonda's desk ten minutes after Eric had left. "I think that guy was telling us the truth from day one more than he knew. I think he didn't see shit. And I'll tell you something else. If we're ever lucky enough to collar this guy? No way is Cash getting anywhere near that lineup. He'll fuck it up for us with a wrong ID." Matty tapped the blank photo manager with a knuckle. "I'm serious, Yoli, he's useless."


At nine forty-five, because of a goddamn middle-of-the-game rain delay in Boston, instead of its being the bottom of the ninth or thereabouts, it was only the top of the sixth. But sixth or ninth, enough time had gone by in front of the tube that his ex-stepfather should still have been passed out; and as Tristan snuck a peek from around the edge of the bedroom door, he saw that his eyes were closed; but something about him, the smoothness of his lids, the lack of any of the usual sleep noises, made Tristan feel like he was pretending, was waiting for Tristan to try to cross the danger zone between the chair and the TV to the front door, *had* been waiting for a moment like this ever since Tristan had beat his ass over a week ago, and this new tactic spooked him so bad that once again, despite his shots-traded victory, he couldn't get it up to make his move and so waited in his bedroom until the snores came in the eighth; but by the time he made it downstairs at ten-thirty, Big Bird had already taken off with everybody to that party in the Bronx and the streets were dead.

Matty was on the phone with a third-person verbal from the Pursue pile, an older black man who owned a candy store outside the Red Hook houses in Brooklyn claiming that he overheard a girl this morning commenting on the reward money and how badly she was tempted for her kids' sake, but how it wasn't worth it if you believed in what goes around comes around.

"You know her?"

"I know her voice," the man said.

"Can you describe her?"

"It was low, what I'd call caramel-toned, with a Puerto Rican inflection, talking to a African-American girl had braces that made slishing salivary sounds."

Matty closed his eyes, took a three-second nap.

"How about what she look like?"

"The Puerto Rican sounded on the petite side, the black girl overweight."

"Sounded?"

"I'm blind, son."

Tristan went back upstairs, crossed between the chair and the TV, Joe Torre on the postgame show looking like an undertaker, went into the bedroom, and without waking any of the little kids got the .22 from under the mattress. He came back out into the living room, stood behind the chair, and aimed the gun at the back of his snoring, slumping dome.

He didn't even know if there were any bullets left, and he couldn't quite get it up to find out, just stood there experimenting with the trigger pressure and glassily watching the TV, the muzzle almost kissing his ex-stepfather's scalp.

Derek Jeter came on, then an ad for *Survivor: Komodo Island*, then one for the new smaller Hummers, then the eleven o'clock news.

Hypnotized by the TV, he lost track of time so he didn't know how long the wife had been standing there, but there she was, on the far side of the dining table, just watching him with the gun to the back of her husband's head. They stared at each other in silence, the woman expressionless, Tristan unable to lower the gun, and then she just walked back to her bedroom without saying a word, quietly closing the door behind her. It was the most scared Tristan had been since that night; worse even, he could barely move, then his ex-stepfather cut loose with an abrupt and loud snort, and startled, Tristan squeezed the trigger. The gun clicked on an empty chamber.

Still thinking about the wife's deadpan face, Tristan went back to his bedroom and, just as she had, quietly closed the door behind him.

The full-up Mercury Mountaineer with Maryland plates abruptly pulled to one side of Clinton, blocking the narrow street and making Lugo slam on his brakes. The driver then leaned across his passenger to roll down the curbside window and hit on three girls sitting on a stoop.

Lugo tapped the horn. "C'mon, let's go there, Humpy."

Without taking his eyes from the girls, the driver just gave them a raised finger via the rearview and continued making his play.

"Oh no he di'ent," Lugo said to Daley to Scharf to Geohagan, then mounted the misery light onto the roof of the taxi.

Having found three sticky buds of Purp underneath Little Dap's seat, Lugo and Daley were by the Xerox machine, photocopying the contents of his wallet as the kid looked on from the minuscule holding cell.

"Hey, the last police told me anything under a dime bag is a walk-away."

"Did he now," Daley said.

"And that's a police sayin' it."

"What's this?" Lugo held up a much creased never-endorsed check.

"What." Little Dap squinted through the bars.

"This."

"Hah?"

"Who the fuck do you know in Traverse City, Michigan?"

"In where? Oh. Yeah. This dude gave me that. This guy I met."

"What dude. What's his name. And don't bullshit me, it's right on the check." Lugo hiding it now as if they were playing liar's poker.

"Aw, man. Fuck I remember."

"OK . . . How about this," Daley chimed in. "What's Traverse City famous for, huh? This dude's your buddy, he'd've told you this. As a Traversian, he'd be very proud of this."

"Hell I know. What."

"It's the cherry-picking capital of America, Fucknuts, and I don't think you know this guy at all except to jux him. We're calling up there first thing tomorrow, but you'll be right here coolin' your jets when we do. And if this is what I think it is? We're talking interstate indictability."

"Ouch," Lugo said.

"What?"

"Crossing state lines in the commission of a crime."

"I didn't cross no state lines."

"Your vic did."

"I ain't tell him to come." Little Dap blinking like a ship in the fog.

"So he *was* your vic, huh?"

"What? No. I ain't *say* that."

"Hey, you jux someone from out of state? That's a guideline felony."

"A what?"

"Classical guideline felony."

"Plus this whole area is historically landmarked," Lugo reminding Daley, "which makes it . . ."

"Pre-indicted."

"As in federal."

"And federal crime . . ."

"Means federal time."

"The fuck! It's just a check, man, I ain't even cashed it!"

"They'll just take him away from us, the feds."

"I hate those pricks, everybody's bin Laden to them. Won't even listen to us."

"I don't feel too good," Little Dap slurred.

"You're kidding me."

"Where am I?" Lolling his head, then resting it on the bars.

"About two inches from a supermax."

"How about I get you a gun?"

"Hey, that's our line."

"You niggers always asking a gun."

"We're all ears."

"Shit . . . What if I give you the shooter of that white boy?"

"All ears, brother."

"But 'fore I tell you jack, you all got to get me some immunity. You know, like, first one talking gets the deal? You know how you do."

"All ears."


Lugo woke Matty up an hour later.

"And after all that, he says to us, 'I want immunity.' "

"And you said . . ."

"We'll see what we can do, but for now start taking plenty of C, B complex."

"Good." Matty got up, rubbed his face.

He wasn't all that excited, but still . . .

"So, anyways, that's what the kid is saying, but who's to say."

"All right, I'll be there in a few minutes." Then, reaching for his shirt, "So what is he, hard, soft?"

"Butter."

**After six hours** of going over it, then going over it some more, Arvin "Little Dap" William's story still held water. He didn't know Tristan's last name, but he knew where he lived, and by the time Yolonda came in the next morning, Matty had already gotten all the vitals from the Housing Wheel.

An hour later, with Iacone and Mullins standing out of sight halfway down the hall, Matty murmured to Yolonda as he knocked on the door, "You sure you don't want to have another little one-on-one pep talk with him?"

"I'd like to drag this fucking kid out by his hair," she said through her teeth.

Matty knocked again, and a woman wearing yellow Playtex cleaning gloves peered through the width of the top chain, then opened up when she saw the badge.

"We'd like to speak to Tristan," Yolonda said. "He's not in trouble or anything."

"Tristan?" her face crinkling with anxiety as she reflexively looked towards a bedroom. "You should wait for my husband."

"We'll be quick," Yolonda said.

Leaving Iacone in the living room, Matty, Yolonda, and Mullins walked past two small kids quietly watching TV to the bedroom, Matty sliding the woman off to the side before opening the door.

Tristan sat on the foot of the bed hunched over his spiral notebook, his Beatbook, alternately squinting at his ex-stepfather's House Rules and dropping rhymes.

*Rules by fools to be observed by tools*
*Don't dicker with my liquor*
*Drugs are quicker make you sicker*
*Blood runs thicker*
*in the street*
*where we the elite*
*defeat*
*any kind of heat*
*you want to bring*
*aint no thing,*
*Im a player a slayer*
*so be understandful*
*of the handful*
*that I am*

Shadows darkened the page, Tristan looking up to see the three detectives standing over him.

*And if you say obey?*

"Get up, please?"
"Hold on." Tristan still head-down, scribbling as he gestured for them to wait.

*You better pray*
*Cause its a brand new day*

Then hands on his biceps lifted him like a child, the notebook hitting the floor.

It was midday and Eric was trying to remember how to get out of bed. At this point in time no one seemed to care whether he was human garbage or not, and it was just killing him.

The indifferent choir in his head consisted, among others, of Ike Marcus's father, those two detectives, and Bree.

Strangely, Ike Marcus himself was not among them; most likely because he had died oblivious to what Eric was about to do or not do for him, although they would play catch-up somewhere soon enough.

There was no office for assistance here, no grievance committee, no redemption center.

And then he saw Harry Steele's gift basket.

Eric sat at the granite kitchen island under the parti-colored wash of the stained-glass Star of David.

"I hear you fired Danny Fein," Steele said.

"Didn't need him anymore." Eric looked off, his kneecaps pumping under the table. After half a lifetime in Steele's service, it still made him nervous to be alone with him outside of a restaurant.

"OK."

Eric sipped his cold coffee, then stared at the dregs like they were legible.

"What," Steele said.

"What?"

Steele breathed through his nose, his restless gaze all over the room, critiquing, redesigning. "Anything else?"

With his eyes beading wetly at the corners, Eric took the plunge.

"I'm a thief."

"You're a thief."

The quiet came down again, accentuated by the ticking of an unseen clock.

"I shave points off the tip pool, once or twice a week, comes to about ten thousand a year going back about five years. Maybe a little more. I fuck everybody. Waiters, the bar, busboys, runners. And you. Ten thousand about. Every year."

"You're serious," Steele said.

Eric didn't respond.

"Ten."

"Yes."

"I actually figured you for about twenty."

"What? No."

"Why are you telling me this?"

"Why?"

"You're supposed to keep your mouth shut."

"What?"

"Everybody steals from me. They just don't piss me off by telling me about it." Then, "Ten," shaking his head.

"Yes."

"Compared to everyone else around here? The bar? The kitchen?"

This wasn't going the way Eric envisioned.

"What's your problem exactly?" Steele asked.

"My problem?"

"What, your conscience is bothering you? And so you want me to do what. Fire you, sue you, press charges, what . . ."

"I want to pay you back," Eric said by reflex.

"Not me. You're talking the tip pool. You have to track down all those busboys over the years, all those three-weeks-and-see-ya wait-resses from God knows where."

Eric sank into a hopeless silence.

"You know why you're telling me? Because you feel bad about your-self, about Ike Marcus, and you want somebody to punish you or for-give you or who the hell knows." Steele shook his head in marvel. "Ten thousand. My kid's babysitter probably steals more. My *kids* steal more. Jesus, do you have any idea what *I* take out of there?"

"No."

"Well, that's a bit of good news."

Eric looked down at his fingers, twisted between his legs.

"You're a good guy, Eric, I've always known that."

"Thank you," Eric whispered.

"And you're my guy." Steele leaned forward. "As I am yours, yeah?"

Eric balked a tic, then, "Yeah," then just let go in a gush of grati-tude, "Yes."

"You come to my home for some kind of exoneration or, or validation, and I can't even begin to give you enough . . . *Years* together, you and I. You're like family. You *are* family."

"Yeah."

Steele got up, Eric following his lead, but Steele gestured for him to sit and brought a fresh press of coffee to the table.

"That being said"—he poured—"you must be pretty tired of this neighborhood."

"Yeah."

"Raked over the coals like that."

Eric couldn't answer.

"Well, then here's some good news for you . . . I'm opening a new place."

"I heard something about that," Eric's voice quickening. "Harlem? I could go for that."

"That's still just a rumor, but I'll tell you what's for real."

"OK."

"Atlantic City."

"Where?"

"I've been in meetings with the Stiener Rialto, they're developing a new concourse off the casino floor."

"Where?"

"You know how in Vegas they've got the Pyramids, Eiffel Tower, and whatnot? . . . Well, these guys want to create a Little New York arcade, historical, three sections, Punky East Village, Nasty Times Square, and Spirit of the Ghetto Lower East Side."

"Atlantic City?"

"You know, tenements, pushcarts, no synagogues of course, but an egg-cream joint, and for the high rollers, a Berkmann's."

Then, seeing the vapor-locked look on Eric's face, "I mean, you and I know ten years ago Berkmann's was a crack squat, but it looks like it's been there forever, and what's the difference? This whole neighborhood, I mean, it's all what the realtors want it to be anyhow, right?"

"Atlantic City?"

"Besides, it's over. It was over the minute people knew to come here."

"Yeah, no."

"All these kids down here, they walk around starring in the movie of their lives, they have no idea."

"No."

" 'Not tonight, my man' . . . I mean, where did he think he was?"

"No. Yeah."

"If you think about it, A.C.? The artificiality down there will be the truest part of the whole setup."

"Sure." Eric's screen a blank.

"Anyways, I'd like you there."

"OK."

"I need someone I can trust."

"OK."

"Someone who keeps it to ten thousand."

"OK."

"Yeah?" Steele poured him some more coffee.

"Yeah."

"It'll be a new start for you."

"Yeah." Sinking, then grasping, "Can I ask you one favor for this?" Steele waited.

"Let me offer someone a decent job down there. At least offer it."

"Offer to who, that waitress? Whatsit, Bree?"

Eric sat back.

"C'mon, Eric, the kid's a kid, let her live the dream a little."

"OK."

"And, no more trying to sell coke in my place."

"No."

"All right then." Steele rose, made the sign of the cross, *"Ego te absolvo,"* then disappeared behind a door.

Eric sat there, wondering what just happened.


Yolonda asked Matty if she could do the shooter solo; kids like this one were her meat and potatoes, and the last thing she needed in there when she started asking her touchy-feely questions was some big, bucket-headed Irishman inhibiting the flow. And he knew from experience that when it came to perps like Tristan Acevedo, it was sheer self-destruction not to give Yolonda her way.

**434**

Nonetheless, the kid seemed unbreakable; as in, broken so many times there was nothing left to break; coming off as if he were sitting in the back row of a meaningless class, barely interested in his own lying answers as to where he had been that night, as to how he came upon the gun found under his mattress; indifferent to the point of boredom to all the contradictions pointed out to him in his narrative; indifferent to his own fate. None of which was a deal breaker in itself, since they did have the gun and Little Dap's testimony, but they couldn't take a chance on this kid being stony now, then turning into a motormouth at the trial, revealing that Ike Marcus had brutalized his little sister or something, the DA winding up looking like a horse's ass.

After an hour Yolonda came out of the interview room at the end of their first go-round to get the kid a snack and give herself a breather.

"You're putting him to sleep," Matty said.

"Kid's retard tough," she said, blowing a strand of hair off her face. "I hate that shit. Kids don't care if they live or die. It's sad, you know? Fuck it. I'll get him."

Twenty minutes later, armed with a soda and a Ring Ding, she went back inside.


"Tristan, you grew up around here?"

"Yeah." Staring at his treats. "Some."

"Your mother had problems?"

"I don't know."

"You lived with her?"

"A little."

"How old were you when you moved out?"

"Which moved out."

"The first moved out."

"First grade."

"And why was that?"

"What."

"Why did you have to go?"

"I don't know."

"Was she sick?"

"Yeah."

"Drug sick?"

He shrugged.

"You were so little."

Another shrug.

"You moved in with your grandmother?"

"Some."

"Then where?"

"My mother again some. Her boyfriend. I don't know."

"What else was it like for you as a kid?"

"Hah?"

"What kind of childhood did you have?"

"I just told you."

"Tell me more."

"I don't know no more."

"You don't know what kind of childhood you had?"

"I don't know. What kind a childhood *you* has?" his voice a queru-
lous murmur.

"Mine?" Yolonda leaned back. "Bad. I was in foster homes because
my mother was too high to take care of me and my father was in jail for
dealing heroin. We used to stand on line for hours every week to get
these big government blocks of cheese, then we'd take 'em home, cut
'em up into smaller blocks, and sell them to the bodegas. It sucked."

It was all bullshit except for the cheese, but she got him listening.

She reached out but didn't touch his left cheek, the scar running
from there into the left corner of his mouth, then out the right corner,
and continuing in a downward jag to the right side of his jawbone.

"What's that from?"

"I chewed into a cord."

"A cord. What kind of cord?"

"'Lectrical."

"You what? You're lucky you didn't kill yourself."

Another shrug.

"Why?"

"I wanted to put my house on fire."

"Why?"

"It's a secret."

Yolonda had thought so. She had been in too many rooms with too many kids like Tristan not to be able to recognize that eerie stare of his, both averted and burning.

"How old were you?"

"I don't know. Five. Six."

"Aw, Jesus," sounding like she was about to cry. "And who did it to you?"

"I just told you, I did it myself."

"That's not what I'm talking about, Tristan."

"Nobody did nothing to me."

Yolanda stared at him, her chin resting on the knuckles of her fist.

"Did what," he said.

"Was it that asshole guy you live with?"

"No." Then, "I ain't telling you." Then, "But not him."

"OK."

"And I never did it to them."

"The little ones."

"Yeah." Looking off again. "And I could've if I wanted to."

"That's because you know right from wrong."

Another shrug.

"You do." Touching his arm. "And for what you been through? You're strong. Stronger than anybody knows."

She could feel his tendons begin to unknot beneath her fingers.

"If we ever get to be friends, me and you?" She waited until he looked at her. "I got some secrets that'll make your hair fall out."

"Like what."

"My father was in jail, but not for drugs."

"Then for what."

"You look at me and you answer your own question."

He didn't look at her, couldn't look at her, she knew, if he expected to see his own experience mirrored there.

Just as well, since she wasn't crazy about this kind of lying.

She squeezed his hand in communion.

"So, Tristan, this *blanco* on Eldridge, did you know him from before?"

"Before what."

"That night. That incident."

"No."

"What did he do to you?"

"Nothing."

"Nothing?" Then, leaning in, whispering, "I'm trying to help you."

He stared at her hand.

"He must've done something."

"Scared me."

"Scared you how."

"He started to like, step to me, and I flexed. Bap."

"Bap. Meaning you shot him?"

"I don't know. I guess."

"Just say it to me. Say what you did. You'll feel better."

"I shot him."

"OK." Yolonda nodded, patting his hand. "Good."

Tristan exhaled like something punctured, his body slowly sinking in on itself.

"I miss my grandmother," he said after a while.

# EIGHT

# 17 PLUS 25 IS 32

**Back at Chinaman's** Chance, they sat facing each other in the otherwise shut-down club, the smell of Clorox wafting in from the front room.

"I don't want to know his name." Billy's voice quivering.

"I understand," Matty said, thinking, Then move to Greenland.

"I don't want his name in my head."

"No."

"I'm not going to ask to see him," Billy said.

"That wouldn't be a good idea."

"He said he did it?"

"Yeah." Matty sipped his third drink. Lit a cigarette. "Plus we have his partner and the gun."

"Why?" Billy scowled as if looking into the sun.

"Why'd he do it?" Matty expelled a shred of tobacco from the tip of his tongue. "Sounds like a robbery gone bad. Sounds like what we figured from the jump."

Billy did an abrupt half-turn to hide an anarchic gout of tears, then turned back. "Is he sorry?"

"Yeah," Matty lied, "he is."

They sat in silence for a moment listening to the Chi-Lites coming in from the front-room jukebox, the half-a-homeless-guy mopping the floor out there entertaining himself.

"So what'll happen to him." Billy asked.

"He's seventeen, so he'll be charged as a juvenile, but he'll get the big-boy treatment. The DA'll go for hard time, felony murder in the commission of a robbery, twenty-five years automatic."

"Huh," Billy breathed.

"Here's the deal." Matty leaned forward. "The DA keeps a score-card, OK? Now, this is a projects kid, nobody's stepping up for him, no family, nobody. So, the guy knows he'll be going up against some Legal Aid lawyer, and it's pretty much a slam dunk.

"Now, this lawyer, he'll bring up the kid's age, the fact that he's got no record, et cetera, et cetera, but the DA knows a winning hand when he sees one, so he'll stand pat on the twenty-five. Problem is, he'll have to go to trial to get that, which no DA ever wants to do, so then he'll come to you, as father of the victim, say something like 'We could stick it to him for the full quarter, but to spare you having to relive the whole thing in court, I'll let his lawyer plea out for twenty and you can just get on with your life.'"

"Huh."

"But what the DA *won't* tell you is that once he's inside, twenty, with good behavior, becomes more like fifteen."

"Fifteen?" Billy slowly raising his eyes. "How old is he again?"

"Seventeen," Matty said. "Which puts him back on the street at thirty-two."

Billy churned in his chair as if his back were killing him.

"I'm sorry, I'm just trying to give you the true picture."

"I don't want to know his name." Billy grinding in his seat.

"I understand," Matty said patiently, pouring himself another few inches from the bottle he had liberated from behind the darkened bar.

"In or out, he'll be in my life forever."

Matty's cell rang.

"Excuse me," half turning away.

"Got a pen?" It was his ex.

"Yup." Making no move to find one.

"Adirondack Trailways 4432, arriving Port Authority, four-fifteen to-morrow."

"A.m. or p.m.?"

"Guess."

"All right, whatever," glancing at Billy. Then, "Hey, Lindsay, wait." Matty lowered his voice, his head. "What's he like to eat?"

"To *eat*? Whatever. He's a kid, not a tropical fish."

Not a tropical fish; Matty hanging up in a rage; Lindsay always with that mouth, that superior attitude. He drained his fourth and glared at Billy.

"Let me ask . . . Are you still down here?"

"Kind of." Billy looked away.

"Kind of?"

"I just need to . . ."

"Because I want to tell you something," Matty said. "You got a nice family, you know?"

"Thank you."

Matty faltered, then . . . "So don't make this into a multiple."

"Don't what?" Billy said.

Matty held off for another moment; then, Fuckit, leaned forward again in the rattan chair, elbows on knees. "Here's what happens." He waited for Billy's eyes. "Any way you cut it, it's gonna be rough for you and yours for a long time to come, OK? But I swear to God, if you continue to bail on them like this, pretty soon everybody in your house is gonna start doing some variation of the same, and it's gonna be *bad*." Matty drew a breath. "Who finished the vodka, there was a whole bottle here yesterday, where's my sleeping pills, there was a whole bottle here yesterday, this is Officer Jones, I have your son here, your daughter here, your wife, your husband, lucky no one was killed but they failed the Breathalyzer, refused the Breathalyzer, this is Assistant Principal Smith, your son was fighting again, your daughter was stoned again, drunk again, found a gun in his locker, a bag of dope in her locker, this is Happy Valley Rehab, this is family court, this is the Eighth Precinct, the ER, the morgue, could have been an accident, could have been something else, that's what the autopsy's for, but just so you know, we found her in back of a club, in a motel room, a bus station, a dumpster, wrapped around a tree, a telephone pole . . .

"That poor Marcus family, they lost the one boy last year, now this."

**443**

Billy gawked at him, held out a hand like a stop sign, but Matty couldn't stop.

"Are you *hearing* me? Everybody starts closing doors on each other, and I promise you, I will stake my pension on it, someone else is not gonna make it."

"No, you don't understand."

"I mean, Jesus, if I had a wife—"

"I know, I know."

"—and kid like that. The sister, the girl."

"Nina," Billy said as if ashamed.

"Did you ever find out what's under those bandages? Or would you rather not know."

His knees running like pistons, Billy drained his third glass as if he were late for something but made no move to rise.

Matty's cell rang again.

"Now what."

"Excuse me?" Yolonda said.

"Sorry, I thought . . ."

"We got a body in the Cahans."

"In the Cahans?"

"I just said that." Then, "You sound like you're chewing glass."

"Like what?"

"Are you too shitfaced for this?"

"No, I'm good."

"Yeah?"

"I'll be right there. Where in the Cahans?"

"I'll pick you up," she said.

"I'm on Clinton and Delancey."

"Which means you're in Chinaman's. What the fuck, it's not even dark yet."

"Clinton and Delancey."

Matty hung up then struggled to his feet.

"Where are you going?" Billy asked.

"Christ, I'm blind off my ass."

"Can I help?"

"You're done with helping." Matty widened his eyes to get air around the sockets. "Go home."

"I just need to go back—"

"To where, the hotel? Why. What's there."

Billy stared at him.

"Billy"—Matty laid a hand on his knee—"your son's not down here anymore. Go home."

In the darkened room Billy's eyes seemed to glow then dim, as he sank into what Matty hoped was acceptance, although he continued to sit there as Matty weaved his way through the empty tables then out the side door to his next customer.


By the time they made it to the Cahans there was already a shrine going, a cardboard humble, two open grocery cartons laid on their sides to make a shelter for the half-dozen botanica candles placed inside. A few cellophane-stapled bunches of flowers lay on the sidewalk. Iacone and a new kid, Margolies, a white shield fresh from Anti-Crime, were already interviewing potential witnesses.

The heart-shot body starfished on the pavement in front of a projects bench was a Cahan kid, Ray-Ray Rivera, wearing an oversize white T and shin-length shorts, his belly a sizable mound even beneath his tentlike shirt.

There were two separate clusters of weeping people standing at opposite ends of the crime-scene tape; one, a group of teenage girls, the other made up of old people, again women mostly, surrounding a short, stocky white-haired man in a guayabera whose reddened face was clenched with grief.

There were no boys or men even close in age to the victim.

Crime Scenes hadn't shown up yet.

"His friends suck," Iacone said.

"Where are they?"

"Exactly."

"But they were here?"

"Apparently. Well, find 'em. Where the hell they gonna go?"

"How about them," Yolonda nodding to the girls. "You talk to them?"

"I thought I'd leave that to you."

"Any cameras?" Matty asked, squinting at the small strip of stores across the street.

"None working," Iacono said.

Yolonda studied the group of seniors, keyed in on the weeping man in the middle. "Oh shit, I know that guy. He's got the candy store around the corner, been running *bolita* in there since I was little. What's, why's he here?"

"It's his grandson."

"You're kidding me, his grandson? His son got shot too. Oh my God, Matty, you remember five years ago on Sherrif Street? Angel Minoso? Jesus. This guy's been running numbers for forty years around here without a scratch. His *grand*son now?"

"Does he know anything?" Matty asked.

"I don't think so," Iacono said, "they came and got him when it happened."

Yolonda stepped toward the body. "Those girls there?" addressing the new guy, "get them corralled and down to the house."

"I talked to a few already," he said.

"Yeah?" slipping on her gloves. "And?"

"Nobody saw nothing. They heard something about a black guy from Brooklyn. But apparently nobody knew him."

"No? Then how did they know he was from Brooklyn?"

"That's what I said."

"Yeah? And?"

He looked at her then back at the girls, two of whom were already wandering off.

"Down to the house."

She watched him approach the girls with his arms out as if to scoop up strays.

"Who is that again?" she asked Matty.

"Something Margolies." Matty shrugged. "We should check the notes in those boxes there too."

"Well, not in front of people," Yolonda said.

"I didn't mean right now," Matty snapped, slightly insulted, then went off, thinking about the difference between Raymond Rivera's shrine and the one for Ike Marcus.

He'd go to his grave swearing that he cared equally about his victims, that if there was anything that got him more pumped over one than the other it wasn't race or class but innocence. He cared equally, well, maybe some more equally than others, but even if he was selling himself a bunch of wolf tickets with that one, Yolonda here was the great leveler, because this was where she came from, where she felt the need to shine, and where she found it easiest to locate that shred of genuine pity that made her so effective in the box.

Looking up, he saw a kid in a marshmallow T and stubbled haircut similar to the vic, peeking from around the corner of a Chinese restaurant across the street to see what was happening. Matty pointed a finger at him, Stay right there, but the kid took off anyhow. Matty started out after him then stopped. Like Iacono said, where's he going to go.

When he turned back to Yolonda, she was inside the yellow, dropped to one knee alongside the body, staring at it vaguely perplexed, as though she could revive him if she could only remember how.

"You want to hear something?" she said. "I knew this kid too. Not like to say hello to, but he lived in my grandmother's building. I used to see him in the elevator."

"Oh yeah? Good kid?"

"I think he dealt a little weed, but he wasn't bad."

Still on one knee, she scanned the greasy-bricked Cahans like a tracker, a hand over her mouth.

"So his friends suck, huh?" she said drily. "We'll see about that."

And then she looked up at Matty with that look.

My turn.

# NINE

# SHE'LL BE APPLES

**The ground floor** of the Stiener Rialto hotel in Atlantic City had no end to it. It took five minutes for him to get from the front doors to the cordoned-off construction site, the indoor New York theme park going up on the perimeter of the casino floor. Separated only by a spattered sheet of plastic from a red and gold acre of slots, it seemed to him, big surprise, that the constant shriek of band saws and groan of cement mixers did nothing to shake the concentration of the players sitting there moon-eyed, clutching milk-shake cups filled with silver.

The Berkmann's sign was up already, but the restaurant, half the size of the original, was still a work in progress, all hammer bang and power whine.

Twenty feet away, trompe l'oeil tenement scrims were being hoisted into place and nail-gunned into their wooden braces; some windows adorned with cats or aspidistras, others with fat-armed Molly Goldbergs, their elbows propped on pillows.

Around the bend from Yidville was the hotel's Times Square Land, all neon girlie-show signs, kung-fu-movie marquees, and a functioning Automat.

And around the bend from that was Punktown, one long poster-plastered, graffitied mock-up of St. Marks Place circa 1977, tattoo parlors, vinyl-record shops, and a rock club/restaurant, BCBG's.

As far as Eric was concerned, Harry Steele was attempting to ship him off to hell.

Then he saw a face he thought he knew, Sarah Bowen, she of the seven dwarfs, arguing with a guy in an expensive suit and a hard hat outside a nearly completed reconstruction of the Gem Spa on St. Mark's Place and Second Avenue.

Eric waited until they walked away from each other before going up to her.

At first she couldn't place him either; it was the surroundings, at least that's what she told him and what he chose to believe.

She had just landed the job of hostess at BCBG's.

"That asshole wants me to wear safety pins through everything as part of my getup, can you believe that? The last time I wore a safety pin I was in a diaper."

"Me, I think I'm supposed to be wearing a derby and arm garters."

They took it out on the boardwalk, where the gulls ate cigarette butts, twenty-four-hour gamblers staggered around like sunstruck vampires, and the sand resembled kitty litter.

"I figure it this way," she said. "I'll be making more here, saving more here, two maybe three years from now I'll finally have enough to go back to Ottawa and open that massage parlor."

"There you go." Eric felt himself relaxing.

"So when are you moving down?" offering him a cigarette.

"I don't know if I am."

She gave him a long speculative look, then returned her gaze to the waves. "You better."

"Yeah?"

She shrugged, continued to look out at the water.

"Do you remember me and you one time about a year, year and a half ago?" he asked.

"I'm lucky if I remember my name from back then," grazing her chin with a long nail.

"Thanks. Thank you."

"But, yeah, I do." Then, "It wasn't a very good year for me. Do you ever have years like that?"

"No." Eric finally took one of her cigarettes. "I've been blessed."

"So I hear," she said, smiling in sympathy as she lit him up, her hands cupping his against the breeze. "You know, just because you earn here doesn't mean you have to live here. Me and a few other refugees rented a house three towns over, big old Victorian, backs up on a preserve. There's a bedroom available. You want it?"

"Refugees from what. The city?"

"From some city or other. New York, Philadelphia, or wherever. We're all pretty much in the same boat, down here hosting or managing something, no drifters, killers in the rain, or whatever . . . So, I'm thinking, if this Filthy McNasty's, CBGB, BCGB thing doesn't work out, maybe we can all get a sitcom out of it or a reality show or something."

"You were with Ike that night?" Eric catching himself by surprise with his own question.

"Yeah," she said carefully.

"What was that like."

"Excuse me?"

"Who died with me. Who was I with."

"Honestly?" she said. "I didn't even know his name until the cops came and talked to me."

Eric waited.

"I don't know . . . I was stoned, but . . . He was pretty enthusiastic, you know? Like a big puppy. But very sweet. And very flattering."

"Huh," wanting more.

"So, that bedroom, do you want it?"

Eric looked out on the water. How the hell could a major ocean, one of the biggest we have, he thought, look like it needed a garbage pickup; look like a flooded back alley off East Broadway.

"Going once . . ."

"Flattering," Eric said. "What did you mean when you said he was very flattering."

"Ike? Like, like he couldn't believe he was actually making it with me. Like it was the luckiest night of his life."

"Oh." Eric exhaled.

"Going twice . . ."

"Hold it. Jesus, just . . ."

"Going . . ."

"OK, OK." He took a last drag then flicked his butt into the sand beneath the boardwalk. "I'm in."


He hated Port Authority; fifteen years ago, when he was a uniform assigned to Midtown North, its gliding predator/prey vibration had always made him feel like he was underwater.

But before that, for the three semesters that he lasted in college, he was in and out of this place a dozen times a year, back and forth between his home in the Bronx and SUNY Cortland upstate.

Getting off the bus back then meant holiday, meant reunion, meant family; the younger Matty too full of his own sensations to see the place as it was; to see himself in it through the eyes of the carnivores around him.

And as he sat here now, waiting for the bus to arrive from Lake George, he wondered if the Other One would experience this place in that same way, coming in here, that surge in the chest triggered by the hydraulic hiss of bus doors released, that wide-open readiness for whatever was to happen next.

As the kid's bus, originating in Montreal, rolled into its bay, Matty stood with a few others directly inside the receiving doors, his eyes on the silhouettes of the disembarking passengers backlit by the subterranean garage lighting.

No Eddie.

His first thought was that the kid hopped off somewhere in between Lake George and New York, a little escape artist, scam artist. Drug boy.

He didn't have the kid's cell number so he called his ex and got a recording. "Where is he, Lindsay? I'm standing here like an asshole at an empty bus. Call me."

In a ballooning rage he began to pace the floor, saw a girl roughly Eddie's age, doughy, not too bright-looking, but with the vacant wariness of the runaway in her eyes, then saw, or imagined he saw, the hunters, quiet, alert, solo, moving cautiously, patiently, and he decided that something had happened to his son.

"Lindsay, it's me again. Call me. Please."

She rang back twenty minutes later.

"Where is he?"

"You were waiting for the four-fifteen? He missed that bus."

"Where is he, do you know where he is?"

"Yeah, he got on the next one. Should be getting into New York in about three hours."

"And you couldn't bother to call and tell me this?"

"He said he would."

"Well, he fucking didn't and I'm standing here like a maniac."

"He said he'd call. What can I tell you?"

Matty seething, I don't need this, I don't want this.

"What is wrong with this kid?"

"I don't know, Matty, maybe his phone's dead, maybe he spaced out, I don't live in his head."

"Give me his number." Taking it down on his steno pad in the same hurried chicken scratch of a million vital stats for a hundred thousand crimes on ten thousand nights. "What time's his bus get in?"

"Seven-thirty about," Lindsay said, then, "Enjoy," signing off in that gallingly unnecessary singsong.

Matty sat on a bench next to the runaway girl, possible runaway girl, thought about saying something to her, decided against it. From across the hall a middle-aged man began to approach, giving Matty a long, wary look all the way, Matty feigning obliviousness but primed. Before this character reached the bench, however, the girl rose to greet him, throwing her arms around his neck, the guy saying into her hair, "Mom's on pins and needles," then raising his head to give Matty one last good eyeballing.

Embarrassed, Matty briefly looked away, then turned back to watch them as they negotiated the crowd, as they evaporated into sunlight.

He remembered Minette telling him the other day how hard it had been for Billy to leave his first wife and son for her and her daughter; as for himself, however, the toughest thing about splitting from Lindsay and the kids was how nauseatingly easy it had been.

He stared at the phone in his hands, then started to dial the Other One's cell, ready to rip this kid a new one, lay down the law, but wound up killing the call before it could ring through.

Seven-thirty: three hours from now. He decided to sit there and wait, do it face-to-face.

# ACKNOWLEDGMENTS

Irma Rivera, Kenny Roe, Keith McNally, Dean Jankolowitz, Josh Goodman
Bob Perl, Arthur Miller and the POMC, Steven Long and the staff of the Lower East Side Tenement Museum, Henry Chang, Geoff Grey
Rafiyq Abdellah, Randy Price, the Seventh Precinct
Judy Hudson, Annie and Gen Hudson-Price, just for being around
My editor, Lorin Stein
And John McCormack—my good friend and tutor